EMPIRE OF BONES

Liz Williams is the d_____ ____ a Gothic novelist, and currently lives in Brighton. She received a Ph.D. in philosophy of science from Cambridge, and her career since has ranged from reading tarot cards on the Palace Pier to teaching in Central Asia. She has had short fiction published in *Asimov's Interzone, The Third Alternative,* and *Visionary Tongue,* among other publications.

Empire of Bones is her second novel; her third, *The Poison Master,* is also published by Pan Macmillan.

LIZ WILLIAMS

EMPIRE
OF
BONES

TOR

First published in the United States by Bantam Books,
a division of Random House Inc. 2002

First published in Great Britain 2003 by Tor
an imprint of Pan Macmillan Ltd
Pan Macmillan, 20 New Wharf Road, London N1 9RR
Basingstoke and Oxford
Associated companies throughout the world
www.panmacmillan.com
www.toruk.com

ISBN 0 330 41323 6

1 3 5 7 9 8 6 4 2

A CIP catalogue record for this book is available from
the British Library.

Typeset by SetSystems Ltd, Saffron Walden, Essex
Printed and bound in Great Britain by
Mackays of Chatham plc, Chatham, Kent

. . . Especially to Ashok and Bithika Banker and family, for welcoming us to Mumbai and being so generous with both time and information (and for getting us to Varanasi)

. . . as ever, to Anne Groell and Shawna McCarthy for all their hard work, encouragement and help

. . . to everyone in the Montpellier Writing Group and Neville Barnes

. . . to David Pringle, for accepting the original story for *Interzone*

. . . to my parents and to Charles.

. . . to everyone at the Shanti Guesthouse in Varanasi

. . . and lastly to Sappho the cat, whose continual interruptions have saved me from RSI.

Open your eyes again and look at Shiva up there on the altar. Look closely. In his upper right hand ... he holds the drum that calls the world into existence, and in his upper left hand he carries the destroying fire. Life and death, order and disintegration, impartially. But now look at Shiva's other pair of hands ... It signifies: 'Don't be afraid; it's All Right.' But how can anyone in his senses fail to be afraid? How can anyone pretend that evil and suffering are all right, when it's so obvious that they're all wrong?

FROM ALDOUS HUXLEY'S *ISLAND* (1962)

PROLOGUE

KHAIKURRIYË, RASASATRAN SYSTEM

'They're all starting to die,' IrEthiverris whispered, wringing long, jointed hands.

'Who's dying? What are you talking about?' Sirrubennin EsMoyshekhal asked, wearily. Why did emergencies always seem to happen in the middle of the night? He frowned at the wavering image of his friend, gleaming behind a veil of communication mesh. IrEthiverris' fingers wove together in agitation. His mouth moved but no words came forth. Sirru raised his voice, hoping he wouldn't wake the whole house.

'Verris, I can barely hear you. I think your transmission is breaking up. Now *who* is dying?'

'All of them!' IrEthiverris cried. His quills prickled up from his scalp, rattling like spine-leaves in a breeze. He looked wildly about him; Sirru wondered what his friend might be seeing, there on distant Arakrahali. There was a shimmer of alien sunlight behind IrEthiverris' image. 'The natives!'

'Well, there are bound to be a few problems at first, aren't there?' Sirru said, his heart sinking. 'Not every planet is easy to colonize – it's usual for there to be *some* resistance, until people realize that we've got their best interests at heart. Things will settle down. Are the locals rioting, or what?'

'No! I think it's the communications network. It's killing them.'

'I don't understand. You've got a *khaith* administrator, haven't you? Isn't she any help?'

The transmission wobbled, sending tremors through IrEthiverris' already shaky image. Fragments of words came through.

'... *khaith* administrator is doing her utmost to ... none of my messages even reaching Rasasatra – using an illegal channel ... Can you please find out what's going *on*?'

'I'll do my best,' Sirru said. 'Listen, I'll need some way of contacting you. Can you—' But IrEthiverris' image crackled, and was gone. Sirru gave the communication matrix a shake, then turned it off and on again, but even that did not work. IrEthiverris' transmission had been swallowed by the immensity between the worlds.

Sirru walked out onto the balcony and stood staring out across the city of Khaikurriyë. The vast multiple curves of the caste-domes stretched as far as the horizon, gleaming in the soft red moonlight. Rising behind them were the peaks of the mountain-parks. The air was summer-warm and fragrant with pollen, but clouds were massing over the coast. There was a snap of lightning as the weather systems harnessed the monsoon; there would be rain before morning. Sirru was suddenly glad that he was here at home and

2

not on some primitive alien world, surrounded by unforeseen horrors. His quills rose and shivered, despite the warmth of the night.

But what could be going so badly wrong on Arakrahali? Worlds were colonized all the time by the various castes under whose aegis they fell. That was the whole purpose of írRas society, the drive which impelled them as a people. From ancient times they had seeded worlds; kept a distant but kindly eye upon them as they evolved, then stepped in when the time was right to shape the inhabitants to proper specifications and bring them into the fold of the írRas' huge biological empire. Granted, Sirru thought, this was not always a simple matter. Colonies occasionally had to be terminated if their populations had degenerated past a certain point, but that was part of the natural order, just as gardens needed to be pruned and weeded before the plants within them could reach fruition. Did not the oldest texts describe the galaxy itself as just another garden? And were not the írRas the only intelligent form of life in all that sea of stars? As such, they surely had a responsibility to generate new phenotypes, and to bring all people beneath their benevolent rule.

Moreover, Arakrahali had seemed such a quiet little world; with an industrious population who had bypassed the excesses indulged in by some cultures. The planet had not had a war for generations and the system of land ownership entailed that no one was starving. Arakrahali, IrEthiverris had confidently declared at the beginning of his colonial appointment, would be like a stroll in the park.

Yet now it was all going wrong. Sirru shivered. Verris had been a friend all his life – they'd practically come out of the same tank together – and Sirru knew how competent and conscientious the man was. He'd never seen Ir-Ethiverris panicking. In the morning, he would try and find out what was going on. Nothing could be done about it now, but Sirru was too worried to sleep. He made his way down into the gardens, pushing his way through the dense and fragrant growth of pillar-vine and *inchin*, until he reached the irrigation pools. There he sat, in the quiet summer darkness, waiting for the storm to break.

THE CONJUROR'S DAUGHTER

VARANASI, INDIA, 2030

I used to be a goddess. Not that that's much use to me right now, Jaya thought, as she stood angrily in the hospital corridor. Catching a glimpse of herself in a laminated display cabinet, she had to stifle a smile at the notion of deity. They'd issued her with a shapeless nylon gown; she looked small and bent and old, somehow out of place in this gleaming new ward. She gripped the edge of the cabinet to steady herself.

'Mrs Nihalani,' Erica Fraser said, with barely concealed impatience. 'This is the fourth time this week! Whatever are we going to do with you?'

'I want to leave.' Jaya tried to sound calm, but her gnarled hand shook as it clasped the edges of the cabinet. She could feel her body trembling. 'I'm not a prisoner here.' That was true enough; this was nothing like jail in Delhi, nothing like Tihar.

'Well, I'm afraid you can't. You're in no condition to go wandering off. And where would you go? When we found you, you were living on a waste dump. You're crippled with rheumatoid arthritis. Mrs Nihalani, we're only trying to help.'

'I know that,' Jaya said, through clenched teeth, 'And I'm grateful, but—' It was a lie. She knew she should have felt a little more thankful, but Fraser was so patronizing. Every day, Jaya was reminded in one way or another how fortunate she had been that the UN medical team had chanced across her crumpled body and brought her here to this shining new hospital wing. She was safe now, the doctor told her. Here, she would be cared for, perhaps even healed. Inside a little bubble of the West, sealed off from the unspeakable chaos of her country, which Jaya called Bharat, and the doctor called India. She was very lucky, Fraser told her each morning. It was starting to sound like a threat.

'And what about other people?' Fraser demanded now. 'This part of the world's seen a dozen new diseases in the last ten years alone, and I'm damned if I'm going to release another one into an overpopulated area.'

There was nothing she could say to that, Jaya thought. How could she tell the doctor that she knew her illness wasn't contagious, presented no threat to anyone but herself? *And how do you know that?* Fraser would ask. Jaya would have to reply: *Why, because the voice in my head tells me so.* But if she said that, any chance she'd have of getting out of here would be gone. She felt her hands clench into fists, the joints stiffened and painful.

'I don't understand why you want to leave,' Fraser said plaintively. Jaya could almost hear the unspoken thought: why are these people so *ungrateful*? 'You told me that you've spent the last few years scavenging for medical waste on the dumps, ever since you were widowed. What kind of a life is that?'

The life of a jackal, hunting the edge of sickness, where life wears thin. The voice echoed in her head, a little wonderingly, as though the notion was new to it. For the thousandth time, Jaya asked the voice: *What are you?* But there was no reply.

'Mrs Nihalani!' Fraser said, sharply. 'You're looking very tired. I think we'd better get you back to bed, hadn't we?' She took Jaya firmly by the arm. For a crazy moment, Jaya wondered what the reaction would be if she turned to the doctor and told her: 'Sorry, can't stay. I've got a voice in my head and a revolution to run.'

Well, that would really put the cat among the pigeons, in Fraser's favourite phrase. The truth was one luxury Jaya couldn't afford. How could she tell the doctor who she really was? There had been a time, after all, when a photo of her face adorned every wall from Mumbai to Calcutta. It was a miracle that she hadn't been recognized already; she supposed she had the unwelcome transformations of the illness to thank for that. If Fraser realized that she was harbouring a terrorist, Jaya's life would be over. The government wouldn't imprison her this time. They would send the butcher-prince after her. She would rather the sickness took her.

But then she felt her knees beginning to tremble, a reaction that always happened if she stood still for too long. Scowling with frustration, she let the doctor lead her back to bed.

7

'Tranquillizers,' Fraser said, holding out the little capsules. The look on her face brooked no argument. 'I think we've had quite enough excitement for one day, don't you?'

She stood over Jaya, watching like a hawk. Jaya mumbled her thanks, and reached shakily towards the water jug. The doctor's gaze flickered for an instant, and that was all the time Jaya needed to palm the pills and slip them under the pillow. She swallowed, and Fraser looked pleased.

'There. Now, no more nonsense. I'll be back later, to run a few more tests. You have a nice sleep.'

Jaya's hand curled around the tranquillizers, and she closed her eyes with relief at the small victory. She had almost ten pills now, carefully collected in a fold of the mattress. The doctor might think that Westerners knew it all, but Fraser was no match for a conjuror's daughter. She looked down at her withered hand. The knuckles had swollen, but at least it kept the old ring on her finger: a band of cheap bronze, with a garnet set crookedly in it – the last and only legacy of her mother. Her hands were those of an old woman, a grandmother. When she looked at them, it was hard to believe she was only twenty-eight years old.

Jaya lay back on the pillows and closed her eyes. She would wait until she felt a little stronger, and then she'd make another bid for freedom. Until then, there was nothing she could do but lie still, and remember.

*

ing the knife, her father pretended to sever the tongue. Jaya made a convincing grunt of anguish and the crowd flinched. Jaya rolled her eyes in mute horror.

'Now. Lie down.' Jaya's father covered her with a grimy cloth, blew into the fire so that the smoke swirled upwards, and swept the blade of the long knife across her throat. She saw the blade come up, red and dripping. The crowd gave a great gasp, but Jaya lay still. Once, the smoke had made her eyes water; she had long since learned to keep them closed. She held her breath. The thick goat's blood seeped in a pool beneath her neck. She could feel the punctured bladder nestling softly against her ear. Her father was speaking, covering her deftly with the cloth, and she knew that he was drawing the attention of the crowd, the conjuror's sleight of hand and slip of voice that makes everyone believe that nothing has happened at all. A few seconds: enough for Jaya to worm her hand up to her throat and wipe away all trace of the blood from her neck. The cloth was snatched away; she sprang up, smiling.

'I'm alive!' she cried. The crowd, pleased to be so deceived, burst into applause.

After the show, Jaya's father sat and smiled beatifically, staring into the hot pale sky as if his gaze was fixed on heaven. He did not ask for money, but soon the bag that Jaya held was full of notes. Jaya closed the bag and her father took her by the wrist and hauled her up from the ground. The villagers were reluctantly dispersing.

'Well?' Jaya's father said sharply, into her ear. 'That showed them, eh?' There was always this same sour triumph after a successful performance. 'Your dad might be just a poor untouchable, but he can still fool his betters, isn't that so?' His face twisted and Jaya held her breath, waiting for the familiar litany. 'Untouchable, indeed! I had a good job, once – I worked in a laboratory. I was paid decent wages, and then they brought in this caste restoration programme – *The old ways are the best ways*, they said. *The country needs stability*, they said. *We all have to knuckle down.* Who has to? Us, that's who, the lowest of all, nothing but cheap labour and now even less than that . . .'

It was a familiar complaint, and the slightest thing would set it off. Jaya just nodded dutifully and followed her father as he limped through the village, his head held high with the pride he could barely afford.

Later, beneath the shadows of the neem trees, which lay beyond the village, her father said, 'Show me again.' He watched closely as Jaya held her small hands out before her, ghostly in the light of the fire. A coin tumbled from her fingers.

'Again.'

She palmed the coin, twisting her hands over and over to show that there was nothing concealed, the coin resting between the backs of her fingers.

'No, that's no good. I can see the edge.'

Jaya looked up and said with guilty defiance, 'I can't do it. My hands are too small.'

'It doesn't matter whether your hands are small or not. These tricks are best learnt while you're young; I've told you a thousand times. If you were a boy—' He broke off. His hand cuffed the side of her head, not lightly. 'Watch what I do.' The coin glittered in the firelight as his skilful hand turned. 'Now, again.'

She thought she would never learn, Jaya remembered now. Once, these tricks would have been the province of the conjuror's son alone, but Jaya had no brothers. Her mother had died, leaving only a cheap garnet ring and the memory of sandalwood, faint and fragrant as the smoke from the funeral pyres. Her mother, so her father said, had not liked tricks and conjuring, for all that she'd married a *gilli-gilli* man. But within a year or two, Jaya had picked up all the tricks that had made her father's name as a magician, a man to whom gods listened.

Memory unscrolled like a film: now, from the prison of the hospital bed, Jaya watched herself travelling the dusty roads of Uttar Pradesh. She saw her father sitting back on his heels in the dirt as his magical child conjured ash and money and medals and rings to fool the villagers of rural Bharat. She saw the avid gaze of the crowds as she was killed and resurrected, over and over again. She saw the seeds of her life beginning to green and grow.

The summers wore on and the rains still came, but each year was drier than the last. By the time she was ten, Jaya had made a name for herself in the district. People seemed to trust her, though she didn't understand why that should be. Even then Jaya knew that her life was a lie. Tricks and conjuring and illusion, it was like eating air. Every time she performed a faked miracle in a god's name, she expected heaven to strike her down. But it never happened, and at last she came to wonder whether the gods were even there.

Yet she was always troubled by the sense that there was something more, something beyond the lies and the tricks. In the stillness of the long burning nights, she lay awake, listening, and it sometimes seemed to her that she could hear a voice, speaking soft and distant beyond the edges of the world. It was faint and blurred with static, like a radio tuned to the wrong station, but she did not think it was a dream. Maybe it was just that she wanted too much to believe. The voice fell silent, for months at a time, and Jaya would give up hope all over again, but then she'd hear it once more. It was the only secret she had.

Lying restlessly in the hospital bed, she blinked, conjuring the memories back. She was thirteen years old. The monsoon season was beginning, and Jaya ran out into the welcome rain, spinning in the dust until the fat drops churned it into mud. She span until she was dizzy and her sari was soaked, then she bolted for the shelter of the trees. She crouched in the long grass, revelling in the feeling of being unseen. Then she realized that something was watching her after all. There was a locust climbing a stem of grass. The grass bent beneath the locust's stout green body and Jaya held her breath, waiting for it to reach the tip of the stem and leap away. And as she stopped breathing, so time stopped, too. The day seemed to slow and slide. Darkness engulfed Jaya's sight and then there was a brightness at the edge of the world, like the sun rising. The locust turned to her, gazing through golden eyes, and said without words, /I have been waiting for you./

Jaya felt her mouth fall foolishly open. The locust said impatiently, /When the Tekhein designate speaks, you hear, do you not?/

'I don't understand,' Jaya whispered, and the locust gathered itself up and sprang away out of sight. She sat in the grass for a long time, listening. She could hear something humming, just at the edge of sound, and she couldn't get it out of her head. Slowly, she rose and made her way back to the hut.

She wondered whether she had imagined the whole thing, but she had become too used to telling what was real from what was not: the legacy of the conjuror's child. Her throat was dry with the thought that there might be something beyond the tricks after all, but then with a bitter pang of disappointment she learned what she then believed to be the truth.

The magical locust, and the voice that she heard, were nothing more than the result of sickness. That night, she woke in a fever, and the next few days passed in a blur of heat and pain. Her father's worried face swam above her, begging her to get well; promising her that if she did he'd give up the tricks and listen to the gods. Even in the depths of the fever Jaya didn't believe him. She heard a woman's calm voice saying in poorly articulated Hindi, 'I'm giving her a dose of antibiotics; we'll see if that brings the fever down.'

'But what's wrong with her?'

'I don't know. I'm sorry. We're seeing a lot of new diseases; some people say it's due to the crops they're growing now, the genetic modifications . . . No one knows for sure.'

And later, her father's uneasy, shifty voice: 'I don't know where I'll find the money to pay, you see.'

'The mission will pay, don't worry. That's why we're here.'

Eventually, Jaya woke and found that the fever had gone. Light-headed, she stumbled through the door of the hut into the compound. Chickens were scratching in the dry earth and a small child, one of the neighbour's babies, stared at her with an unblinking gaze. Then suddenly the child's eyes were as yellow as the sun and Jaya screamed, but no sound came. The baby's gaze was abruptly soft and dark. Shaking, Jaya leaned against the wall of the hut. Her joints burned and ached, and when she reached for her plait of hair she was horrified to find that it had gone. Tears welled up in her eyes. Then her father was there, with the nurse from the mission.

'Where's my hair?' Jaya shouted, and saw the nurse stifle a smile.

'Don't worry, sweetheart, it isn't gone forever. It'll grow back. We had to cut it, you see; it was full of lice. You wouldn't want that, now, would you?'

In a little voice like a child's, Jaya heard herself say, 'No.'

'Well, then. Now, do you feel better?'

'A bit. My hands hurt.'

The nurse took Jaya's hand in her own pale fingers and turned it over, as though she was going to read Jaya's palm.

'How does it hurt?'

'It burns.'

'Your knuckles are swollen. You poor little thing! I'm going to leave some medicine with your dad; we'll see if that works. We'll soon have you feeling better, won't we?'

Jaya was silent. The nurse was very kind, but she was talking to Jaya as though she was a baby, not an almost-grown woman with a role to play in the world. Her father nudged her. 'Thank you,' Jaya said, after a pause, and the nurse smiled.

'You're a good girl. You'll soon be well again.'

But this, too, turned out to be a lie.

'Could we just go over this again, for the benefit of these people?' Doctor Fraser said. It was the day after Jaya's latest escape attempt. She'd had it figured out. This time, she'd use the tranquillizers to drug the duty nurse and slide out down the back stairs. But just before six a medical team had shown up from England, arriving on an early flight. Now, the team were clustered around the bed: two men and one woman. All of them were staring at Jaya as

17

though she was nothing more than an interesting problem to be solved. Fraser continued, 'Let's just run through your symptoms, shall we?'

Jaya sighed. 'At first, my joints would get stiff, like arthritis, and they'd burn in the monsoon season. I used to feel shaky and hot. But it came and went, and it didn't really get that bad until a few years ago.'

Dr Fraser reached for her laptop and began to download data. She made a great effort to explain to Jaya what she thought was wrong, in between discussing the case with her colleagues in English. She used clear, simple words and drew little pictures on the screen with a light-pen. Jaya bit back a sharp remark. A cigarette might have helped her mood, but she knew it was illegal in the West and she hadn't dared ask the doctor if she could smoke. She had a feeling that the answer would be an outraged *No*. Only Westerners could refuse you something on the grounds of your health when you were on the verge of death.

On the little laptop, Jaya could see the spirals of her own DNA uncoiling, strands highlighted crimson and green, bright as jewels against the dawn-background of the screen. There was a part of the pattern that the program seemed unable to represent properly: it shifted and changed, twisting around the core in unstable formation. It was, Jaya was given to understand, a mutation, lodged deep in her genetic makeup, and it was this that was probably the reason for her long illness.

Someone said in English, 'Doctor Fraser, is your view

18

that whatever this woman is suffering from is in some way related to the Selenge retrovirus?'

The speaker was a middle-aged man, with fair, thin hair and a high-arched nose. His face was red from sunburn. Jaya became very still. Fraser glanced at her, and she schooled her face to show nothing.

'It's okay,' Fraser said, off-handedly. 'She doesn't speak English,' and Jaya thanked whatever gods there might be that she had lied to the doctor about *that*, too. 'Well, to be honest with you, I'm not sure. We still know so little about Selenge. She has some of the hallmarks of the disease, but it's as though it's in a chronic form, rather than the short-term, fatal variety.'

'And she's an untouchable?' He reached out, and without even looking Jaya in the face, turned over her wrist to display the scarred circle of skin. 'Yes. I can see where she's had her caste mark removed.'

Fraser looked uncomfortable. 'Well, she is *dalit*, as they prefer to be called – that or Scheduled Caste – but—'

'And the retrovirus is principally confined to that particular caste,' the male doctor persisted.

'Yes, that's true. But Selenge is a relatively new disease, and as I'm sure you're aware, we're not really sure what the ramifications of it might be. It seems to be related to a virulent form of lupus, but it doesn't respond to treatment.' Fraser added, 'This might be a related set of symptoms, or it might not.' She was trying to be conciliatory, but Jaya could hear the edge of anger beneath her voice and smiled to herself.

The doctors began a long discussion. Jaya wished they'd go away. She could even smell them: they stank of milk and meat and disinfectant. She turned her head away and closed her eyes, forcing their loud voices out of her mind. Drifting back into the past, she did not even notice when at last they left.

Her father was unusually gentle with Jaya during the days of her convalescence. He brought her food, anything she fancied, and he told her stories about his childhood in far-away Mumbai: the long struggle to get out of the slums, only to be plunged back into poverty with a shift of political mood. His kindness made Jaya nervous. She could feel a kind of tense impatience underneath it, as though he couldn't wait for her to get back to work. She knew he only wanted the best for her, and yet . . . The countryside was full of miracle workers: people playing on the need and greed of the villages, and the Rationalist Society following hot on their heels, showing how the wonders and miracles were done.

'Rationalists,' Jaya's father said with a snort. 'They're right, of course. It's nothing but tricks, but that's not the point. People want to believe, Jaya. That's what the movies are all about, after all. There's a *shrine* to Amitabh Shektar down the road – he's not a bloody god, he's an actor. I knew his brother-in-law back in Mumbai. But they've seen him as Shiva in the films and that's what they want to believe in, don't they? City folk say they're stupid, but they're not, it's just that they need *something*. Don't you agree?' He was pleading with her, asking her to sanction a lifetime of fraud. 'These people, the Rationalists, they don't understand what our lives are like. If you live a life of drudgery, you need magic. You need to believe in something beyond yourself.'

He talked on, trying to persuade Jaya and himself that it was a public service they were performing. Jaya huddled on the slats of the *charpoy*, not listening. *There has to be something better than this,* she thought. *There has to be something more than cheap tricks.* She wished she could believe in gods, but perhaps they were all just actors, too.

Heat spilled over the sill of the window and dust danced in the heavy air. The compound smelled of fried cumin and the astringency of the cow piss that the women swilled over the floors to keep the insects away. She could hear a bird in the trees beyond the village: a long, repetitive call like a drop of water falling into a pool. And gradually, slowly, she heard the voice again.

It began to tell her about the sun, and how it absorbed the light of the sun into itself. The voice told her many things, all at the same time. It started to relay information: telling her that Assam and Kashmir would soon be at war, that the government of Bharat was planning a treaty with the Novy Soviet. And as it spoke, Jaya began to echo what it said, beneath her breath, over and over until she realized that her father had fallen silent and was staring at her.

'What?' she stammered, and the day span around her. 'What did I say?'

Her father was looking at her with an unfamiliar expression: wariness, calculation, a hint of fear. 'How do you know all this?'

She said, 'I – I don't know. Something's speaking to me.'

'You're making it up, aren't you? You're lying to me!'

She flinched at the whip of anger in his voice, protesting, 'No! I'm not making it up. How could I? I don't know about these things. Something's *talking* to me,' she repeated, desperate to make him believe that what she was saying was the truth. At the time, she did not realize it was a mistake.

It took a while for Jaya's reputation as an oracle to grow. But the villagers of Uttar Pradesh remembered the little girl who could so wonderfully produce objects out of thin air, who for a short time satisfied them that the gods were real, and over the next few months a steady stream of people came to visit her. When she realized what she'd done, she tried to convince her father that it was nothing more than the usual lies after all. But perhaps he wanted to believe in something other than himself, too, for he wouldn't listen. He started to talk, to anyone and everyone, telling them that his daughter spoke with the voice of the gods. More visitors came, and Jaya began to learn the extent of her powers. The voice, it seemed, was telling the truth. Things that Jaya predicted came to pass, and word spread. It both elated and scared her. Having believed in nothing for so long, she couldn't quite bring herself to succumb to her own growing legend. Her talent was impressive, but the visitors didn't want to hear about grand events on the world scale. They wanted to hear about their own futures, their own lives, and about these things Jaya knew nothing.

'Just tell them anything,' her father raged, frustrated.

'But I don't know!'

'Then make something up. You've had enough practice.'

She refused at first, but after a while she came to see that her father was right – in a way. People needed so much to believe that any vague hint would satisfy them. It would be easy to despise them, to become a cynic like her father, but even though it kept the money coming in, Jaya couldn't help feeling guilty.

The nurse at the mission came to visit, and she seemed concerned as much by the pain in Jaya's joints, which had still not gone away, as by the voice that Jaya said she heard. The nurse did some tests, but they didn't show anything, and soon after this Jaya's father took her away. They had a new place, he explained, granted by a bene-factor. At first, this was no more than a larger, white-washed hut from which goats had hastily been evicted, but the money kept coming in and soon they moved to a small house. Jaya had never known so much luxury. She had *chappal*s on her feet now, and a new dress. She wore wealth in her ears and on her fingers, alongside the old garnet ring, which now fitted closely onto her finger. Then

Westerners started coming, to see this new guru for themselves. They brought dollars with them, and everything changed.

By Jaya's fifteenth year, the ashram extended over several acres and the visitors were flooding in from America and Europe. Jaya's father hired a tutor – a good one, educated at Oxford, who crammed her full of knowledge like someone stuffing a fig. She learned mathematics, history, geography, English, a host of things, and she drank in the knowledge as though it were water after a long thirst. After all, her father said, what was the use of being a prophet if you didn't know what you were talking about? Education, that was the thing.

Articles were written about the young oracle, whom some people were claiming was not an ordinary *dalit* girl after all, but an avatar of Sarasvati, goddess of wisdom. But Jaya knew that it was the same old thing: illusion and lies, with the disturbing, discordant voice of the truth running beneath it like water under mud. Sometimes she thought she might simply be mad, lying awake in the soft darkness with that remote murmur of information travelling through her mind; sometimes she believed it was just the sickness.

The pain still hadn't gone away. It twisted her body, sometimes so badly that it bent her forwards like a little old woman. There was a thick white streak in her dark hair. Sometimes she wondered whether it was a punishment for the throat-cutting trick, for cheating the gods of what was rightfully theirs, the power over life and death.

Maybe threefold Shiva was watching – the creator, the destroyer, and the balance in between – reaching down with his trident to cut her life away, piece by piece. If this was what it was like to be a goddess, Jaya thought, then she'd rather just be a girl.

And then something happened to change her mind.

The woman and her small son had come all the way from Mumbai; they were untouchables. They had saved money from rag-picking, the mother told Jaya, and eventually they had enough for the bus fare. It had taken three days to reach Varanasi. The mother was widowed, and she wanted Jaya to tell the little boy's future for him in exchange for a bag of rupees. It was all the money they had, she said anxiously, but she wanted Jaya to have it. Jaya looked at the woman, saw the holes in her nose and ears, and knew that she had sold her rings to pay for the offering. Her sari was worn, and stained with mud and dust from the journey. Jaya was about to tell the widow to keep the money when her father reached over her shoulder and whisked the bag away before she had time to protest.

'Well, what are you waiting for?' he snapped. 'This lady's come halfway across the country to hear her fortune.'

The widow's face was full of hope. Jaya, feeling like the world's biggest fraud, put a benedictory hand on the little boy's head. And instantly, she knew that something was very wrong. The voice was a murmur in her mind, telling of sickness, of death. As the child gazed up at her, Jaya could see the first faint silvery striations of Selenge beneath the skin of his throat. Her father had seen it, too; she glimpsed the warning in his eyes.

'Can I speak to you privately?' she said to the widow.

'Jaya—'

'The gods have a message for this woman, father,' Jaya told him, sounding as pompous as possible. 'No one else must hear it.'

Standing, she swept the widow and the little boy into the sanctum that stood behind the main room, and as gently as she could, she told the woman that the child was sick. She did not say that she had seen his death. Selenge took its victims hard; the muscles wasted away, the victims failing fast. The widow's face buckled with shock. She plucked at Jaya's sleeve.

'Are you sure?'

'It's possible I might be wrong,' Jaya said, clumsily. 'But you can see it for yourself.'

And then she realized that the widow already knew. Like the conjuror's audience, she was blotting out the truth, seeing only what she wanted to see: hoping to be deceived, praying for a last-minute miracle. Jaya expected tears and recriminations, but after a long moment the widow said quietly, 'Do you believe in karma? Do you believe this is somehow my fault, and the fault of the child?'

Jaya thought for a moment. One of her earliest memories was of her father, shouting that fate was unkind, railing about what he must have done in a past life to be made so wretched now. But then the voice had come and

26

brought them riches; was that destiny, too? Was it some virtue inherent in her soul that made her superior and blessed whereas this woman was about to lose the thing most precious to her? And was it the destiny of the *dalits* as a caste, that had seen them fall from grace beneath the whim of Hindu fundamentalism and the curse of a modern plague, reversing the beneficial consequences of half a century of progress? Jaya decided, once and for all, that karma had nothing to do with it.

'No,' she said. 'I don't believe in karma. I don't think any of it – your position, your caste, the boy's illness – is your fault. You're not responsible for this.' Anger rang in her ears. 'But the system is.'

She told the widow they could stay at the ashram as long as they wanted, free of charge. Her father protested, but Jaya wouldn't listen. And the widow was only the beginning. Disregarding her father's pleas, she began to house more and more people at the ashram, and put money into adding more buildings. She read Gandhi, and Marx. She read about the green revolution of the twentieth century. And she started to have ideas.

'Think what we could do,' she urged her father as they sat in the flower-filled hall of the ashram. 'Look at the others. Shrimati Avati. Rama Krishna. Those Mumbaikars running Rajneesh's old outfit. They publish *books*. People buy them in London, even. New York. And they're no more than showmen, like we were. If I start speaking out against the caste system ... Just think what we could accomplish.'

At that point the first visitors of the day came in. Jaya and her father hastily composed themselves into smiling serenity before anyone noticed anything, and the consultation of the oracle began. But throughout the day a thought kept returning to her, fuelled by what she later realized to be adolescent idealism. *I know I'm not a goddess, but maybe the gods are real and put me here . . . Maybe I can make a difference.*

She stood in front of the mirror, gazing at her own grave face: thin, with the bones too-prominent and her eyes like wells beneath the arched brows. She wondered, as she always did, whether she resembled her mother. A not-quite Dravidian face: sharp northern bones and dark southern skin. Her face looked fierce.

She found that it was frighteningly easy to become Joan of Arc, or Phoolan Devi. When she spoke out, questioning the injustices of the restored caste system, questioning the ancient hierarchies on which Bharat was based, it was as though her words were a flame racing through the dry grass, setting everything on fire. She wasn't saying anything new; the system had been questioned many times before, and changed, and changed back again. But now it was as though everyone was waiting for a new figurehead. A stream of people queued at the gates of the ashram: ardent young men; angry dispossessed widows; civil servants who had lost their positions to the upper castes in the last stages of restoration; Western idealists. Before Jaya knew it, she had an army.

When she first saw that some of the visitors were

carrying guns, Jaya went into her room and slammed the door. Her heart was beating fast, pounding against her ribs, and there was an acid dryness in her throat. *This is where it starts*, she thought. *This is where we go to war.* Doubts welled up, and she couldn't afford the luxury of reflecting on them. The voice echoed in her head in time to the beat of her heart. There was a sharp knock on the door.

'Jaya?' It was her father.

'Go away,' Jaya shouted.

'Open the door. You have to come out. They're waiting for you.' He was trying not to sound impatient, but she could hear the threat in his voice.

You started this. Don't weaken now. Taking a deep breath, Jaya stepped onto the terrace that overlooked the courtyard, and the crowd fell silent. She didn't know what to say. Buying time, she raised her hand as if in benediction. The garnet winked in the sunlight and she thought again of her mother, who had despised tricks. The day seemed to grow darker. It was as though everyone was holding their breath.

'Jaya Devi!' A young man shouted from the crowd: *Victory Goddess*. Jaya froze, seeing a fierce bearded face and a clenched fist swung up in mimicry of her own. The young man was easily a head taller than the rest of the crowd. 'We're ready to march for you! We're ready to fight!'

Ready to die. Jaya let her hand fall. She didn't need to say anything, in the end. They did all the talking for her.

She spent the rest of the afternoon in her room, trying not to think. Towards evening, when the light lay heavy and golden across the fields, she slipped through the door and down the hall. The *sannyasin* who guarded her door was nodding in the coolness of the hallway. Jaya's joints glowed with a faint pain, but she needed to run.

She took the back way through the compound, into the fly-humming cattle sheds. A black buffalo lifted its mild head and stared. Behind it was a gap in the wall. Half running, half stumbling, Jaya found the path that led down towards the river. The Ganges ran slow and old between its banks, glistening like oil in the heat. Jaya crouched in the cool mud by the river's edge and plunged her hands into the water to wash her dusty face. She wished she didn't have to go back. The voice was silent now, but she could still feel it inside her. She wondered for the thousandth time what it really was: sickness, a god, a demon, nothing. Dragonflies skimmed the surface of the river.

A voice said, 'Miss?'

Jaya jumped. Climbing awkwardly to her feet, she turned to see a young man watching from the top of the bank. His mouth fell open in dismay as he recognized her.

'Jaya Devi?'

'Don't call me that,' Jaya snapped.

'I'm sorry, I didn't mean any disrespect, I—'

'Just Jaya,' she said, suddenly tired of everything. 'Nothing special. What's your name?'

He stammered, 'It's – well, it's Kamal. Kamal Rakh.

My brother's the one who shouted out this afternoon. The big guy?'

He had a round, worried face beneath its beard. Jaya stared at him: at the neat turban, at his faded T-shirt and the old M16 slung across one shoulder.

'I suppose I should go back, shouldn't I?' she said, and he nodded with relief. He helped her up the bank.

'That's a pretty ring,' he said, shyly. Her mother's garnet gleamed wetly on her finger and Jaya found herself smiling.

'It's a magic ring,' she told him, very solemn. 'It'll stop me from getting killed.'

'Really?' He smiled back and she saw with a leap of the heart that he didn't believe her. It was so good not to be treated with deference that she laughed.

'No. It's just a bit of cheap glass. No magic.'

'What about your prophecies, though? They're not just cheap glass, are they?'

'I don't know,' Jaya said, honestly. 'What do you think?'

He shrugged. 'Prescience? Precognition? Probably not magic, though – and I don't think you're a goddess. I did an engineering degree, before they started discriminating against Sikhs, too. But what you say comes true, and that's what matters, isn't it?'

'I don't know if I'm doing the right thing,' Jaya said. 'What if I've started a war?'

'Then it's long overdue, Jaya. We can't go on like this. You're the catalyst, but we've been waiting for you. Don't worry. You can only do your best. You can only tell the truth, as far as you can.' He glanced at her. 'Do you believe in karma?'

The widow's voice echoed in her head. 'No. I think you make your own destiny.'

'I think you're right. Well,' Kamal added, 'we'll make it together, then.'

Jaya couldn't think of anything to say. They reached the ashram in silence.

That night, Jaya woke with a start. Her heart was beating loudly enough to wake the world, thundering against the walls. Then in the next moment she realized that it wasn't her heart at all; it was the sound of a helicopter. A single sharp cry came from the courtyard, followed by the rattle of gunfire. Jaya snatched her clothes from the chair and ran out into the compound. The helicopter soared up, splintering the lamplight, and the wind from its rotor-arm sent her hair flying across her face. A woman was lying face-down in the courtyard, not moving. Intermittent gunfire barked from the gates.

Jaya ran, keeping close to the wall and crying, 'Dad! Dad, where are you?'

A bullet whined past her and shattered against the plaster. Jaya ducked beneath a doorway and found herself in the main hall. It was empty, eerily silent. 'Dad?'

Someone stepped out from behind one of the plaster columns: a tall man, in uniform. As he came forward into the light, with the gun at the ready, Jaya saw a handsome, melancholy face, noted the elegant curve of nose and cheek.

A northerner; probably of the *kshatriya* caste, a warrior. And an aristocrat.

'Well,' the man said, in a soft, cultured voice. 'So you're the cause of all the fuss.' Casually, he raised the gun and fired. Jaya found herself flat on the floor, with her scream echoing down the hall. It was a moment before she realized that she hadn't been hit. The man fired again, sending a bullet ricocheting away from the stone floor, a few feet from her head. It deafened her. She stared numbly up at him as he prowled down the aisle to stand over her. His eyes were a pale, startling blue. He was fumbling with his belt and she thought *Oh, god, no.* Her fear must have been plain in her face because his eyes widened with distasteful surprise.

'You?' he said. His face froze with disdain. 'A *dalit*? Do you know who I am?' He unfastened the new ammunition clip from the belt and slid it up into the gun.

'Well, goodbye,' he told her and the muzzle of the gun fell within an inch of her eyes. There was a loud, sharp crack. She thought for a second that the gun had gone off, but it was only the bang of the door against the wall. She heard her father's voice, shouting, and then the deafening blast of the gun. The hall caved in, disintegrating in a shower of plaster, flower petals and fire. Jaya's assailant was sent sprawling across her, and his weight knocked the breath from her body. He swore, struggling, and then collapsed. Someone was dragging her out and up, pulling her across her father's body to the door.

'No! My dad's hurt!'

33

'He's dead.' The hand around her wrist was like the paw of a bear; she recognized the big man from the afternoon's rally. Kamal was waiting in what remained of the hallway, looking more worried than ever. It almost made her laugh. Between them, they half carried her to the shattered wall of the compound, where an ATV was waiting. The driver was slumped over the wheel with a red wet hole in his head; Kamal hauled him out.

'Get in. Quickly!'

She looked back as the ATV bounced down the track. The compound was blazing. Sparks sailed up into the night sky like souls flung from the wheel. Kamal said urgently, 'Keep your head down. Satyajit, where are the others?'

The big man mumbled a reply. Jaya whispered, 'Who was he? That man?'

Kamal crammed his turban more firmly onto his head and twisted in the seat to look at her, saying, 'His name is Amir Anand. He's a colonel in the provincial militia, but his family are aristocrats. People call him the butcher-prince. Among other things. Don't worry. We'll get you out of here.' He turned back to the wheel and they sped down the road.

Someone was saying in a high thin voice, 'Oh, God. Oh, God, it's over. It's over.' With a distant sense of amazement, Jaya realized that the voice was hers. Kamal's hand left the steering wheel and fumbled for her own.

'But Jaya . . .' he said. His fingers tightened around hers and she looked down to see her mother's ring between their interlocked fingers. 'Jaya, it's just begun.'

THE *RAKSASA*

VARANASI

Jaya struggled up from the pillows and reached for her water jug, angry with herself for once more falling into the doze of memory. *I can't afford the past. It's the future that matters; I've got to get out of here.* Her mouth was still filled with the memory of ash and death. Kamal had been right. It was only the beginning. After that came the years of fighting and love and rebellion and sickness; the life that led her here to yet another role, this time as case study. From oracle to goddess, from terrorist to fugitive, from jackal to patient.

My people have many names, thought Jaya, *and all of them mean the same thing:* dom, dalit, harijan. *Untouchable. We deal in death and darkness: we handle corpses, tan hides, trade in shit. We have been farmers, whores, terrorists and Presidents, and now, because of a quirk of political fate, we are right back where we started, the lowest of the low.*

But of all the peoples of Bharat, Jaya knew, it was her caste who lived closest to reality, for the nearer a person is to death, the better that person may understand life. *Someone has to take the blame, and surely we are the*

35

*heroes of India, for we see what others cannot see, touch
what others may not touch. As a woman, and* dalit *and
dying, I am the lowest of all – closer to animal than
human, closer to death than life, and that's what has
made me privileged, in the end. Because I have so little to
lose.*

/*Yes, you told me,*/ someone said, with distant amusement. /*You are a jackal.*/

Startled, Jaya looked up and stared.

There was a being sitting on the end of the bed: golden
eyed and many limbed. It had all the unreality of a dream.
It shimmered as though seen through heat, and with the
numbness that sometimes comes in dreams, Jaya reached
out and touched one of its four hands. Her own fingers
passed straight through the being's parchment skin, and so
she knew that it wasn't real.

Strangely, it was then that she began to tremble. The
being was both like and unlike a god. There were four
stumpy arms, ending in almost fingerless hands. It had no
hair, there was a ridge beneath its robe where its breast
ought to be, and its face was a series of smooth soft curves,
like a plump locust. Its eyes were round and golden, and it
had a small, splayed nose. Its mouth was curled like a lotus
bud, and when it spoke the mouth did not move.

/*I am a goddess,*/ it told Jaya, with patronizing kindness, and fright flooded through her. She realized that
she'd been holding her breath, but though the being's
words echoed inside her mind, it wasn't the voice that

she'd heard since childhood. She did what she had done so many times before, and converted fear to anger.

'What a coincidence,' Jaya snapped. 'So was I.'

The goddess didn't seem to know what to make of this, for her petalled lips curled and twisted. Jaya added with temerity, 'There are over thirty thousand gods in this country. They're as common as beetles. Which one are you?'

/It is interesting to see what the Tekhein desqusai have become,/ the goddess said, ignoring Jaya's words. She sounded indifferent and remote, as befitted a deity. /What do you call yourself?/

'Jayachanda Nihalani.'

The goddess repeated it; at least, Jaya thought she did. The sounds didn't really resemble the words she'd just spoken. /Interesting. You are neither one thing nor another. You are invisible due to your caste and your gender, yet here you are under constant observation. You are human, yet you describe yourself as an animal, a "jackal". You are young but your sickness gives you the appearance of an old person. You intersect with many margins: life, death, illness, health. Your identity is fluid. This is encouraging./

'Who are you? What are you? And why is it "encouraging"?' The being might claim to be a goddess, but she was talking about Jaya as the doctors did, as though she was not a real person at all. Not someone afraid and in pain, but just another interesting phenomenon. Jaya felt a tight knot of anger and fear.

/*Why, I am a* raksasa,/ the being said, and was abruptly gone. And Jaya couldn't feel anything anymore; she was like a reed with the pith sucked out.

She blamed the *raksasa*, in the seconds before she passed out.

Later, the nurse came to wake her and she was brought food on a tray. It was only dhal and rice, but it smelled horrible and Jaya could not eat it. The inside of her mouth tasted of metal. The nurse took the tray away and Jaya looked up to see that the *raksasa* had come back. The thought floated into her tired mind: raksasa *does not mean "goddess". It means "demon".* Jaya struggled to sit up to look at the creature, but she could barely move. Her joints were burning, and the flesh of her hands seemed too fluid, as though the skin was nothing more than a bag of blood.

/*You are ill,*/ the *raksasa* said, as though this was some moral failing of which she disapproved. /*Can your people not cure you?*/

'They are trying. But they don't even know what's the matter with me. They think it's probably genetic, or that it's a variation on a disease my caste has been suffering from.'

The *raksasa's* face seemed sharper than before, the bones arching underneath the papery skin. Within her gilded eyes, Jaya could see the filaments of crimson veins. She felt something flex and stir inside her mind, and felt

38

also suddenly sick. She groped for the jug by the bed and spat into it.

/A pity,/ the *raksasa* mused. /Perhaps the fragility of the Tekhein gene strand should have been taken into consideration when the regeneratives were first released./

'What? I'm sorry. I don't understand.'

/That does not matter. Now that you are activated, we will see if you can be made into a more integrated component. It is to be hoped that fracture will not occur,/ the *raksasa* said inside Jaya's head, then spoke her name. /Listen./

Jaya could hear others. They whispered inside her head; she could see through their eyes.

'What/who?' someone thought, and looked up sharply. Jaya felt the sun on a face.

'I'm Jaya,' she said – but the distinction no longer made sense; they were becoming fluid, and there were more of them, waking.

/This will be real,/ the *raksasa* said, briskly. /I am showing it to you so that you may recognize it when it happens. Now, I must consider the best manner in which to process your integration./

Jaya blinked. The *raksasa* was abruptly gone. She could hear other sounds out in the hallway: anxious, startled voices. Doctor Fraser, and someone else – a male voice, speaking in Hindi. Jaya listened idly, and then froze. The voice was a cultured one, and horribly familiar. Jaya's throat grew cold and dry. Holding the tube that attached her arm to the drip, Jaya got out of bed and walked as quietly as she could to the door.

Dr Fraser was standing in the hallway, talking to someone: a tall man in a military uniform. Memories swam through Jaya's mind: a room filled with fire, her father's body motionless against a white plaster wall speckled with blood. A man was standing over her, lowering an automatic rifle. Then it was years later, with moonlight over a river, and her husband Kamal down in the cold rushing water where she couldn't reach him. She had not seen the man who now stood in the hallway for over three years, not since the night when he murdered Kamal and made Jaya even more of a fugitive than she already was. *His name is Amir Anand. He's a colonel in the provincial militia, but his family are aristocrats. People call him the butcher-prince. Among other things.*

There was a sudden sting in Jaya's hand. She had pulled out the drip with the clench of her fist. A thin smear of blood glazed her skin and the air felt cold, as if the blood was beginning to freeze. Jaya gazed down at it, stupidly, then instinct took over. Slipping off the hospital gown, she reached for the blouse and sari in which she had been admitted. They were cleaner than they'd been for some considerable time. It seemed to take hours to dress and her hands were shaking. She tried to blame the sickness, but she knew it was simply fear. She put her eye to the door again. Erica Fraser was saying in bad Hindi, 'Are you sure?'

'She's calling herself Nihalani?'

'I told you. I—' Dr Fraser seemed uncertain whether she was doing the right thing by telling him the truth. As well she might, Jaya thought.

'An assumed name,' Anand said with disdain. 'In the hills they called her Jaya Devi, after the Bandit Queen of the last century. Jaya means "victory". Ironic, really.' His head half turned. Jaya caught the glitter of a golden tooth as he smiled at the doctor. His face was fleshier now, the elegant bones beginning to be blurred, but the pale blue eyes were as cold as ever. 'You've been tricked, I'm afraid. She's wanted for trafficking in black market medicine, arms dealing, offences against the State ... She's a criminal, a terrorist. You'll be well rid of her.'

But Jaya had heard enough. Jaya Devi might have died that day in the Himalayan foothills, but Jaya Nihalani suddenly found that she had every intention of living on. She snatched the accumulated tranquillizers from the mattress, then quietly opened the door. No one else was in sight, apart from the duty nurse at her desk. Jaya could see the back of the nurse's head bent over a screen. She slipped past, scavenger senses alert to danger, moving barefoot and silently even though the pain was screaming through her joints.

The nurse did not look up and Jaya slid through the doors and away down the corridor. As soon as she could, she found the stairwell and stumbled into the depths of the hospital. She knew from her familiarity with the boneyards at the back of the building that somewhere there was a door that led out into the yards. Pausing for a moment, she smelled the air, catching faint traces of antiseptic, chemicals, and death. Her joints blazed with arthritic pain.

Another door and then the basements, filled with the humming of the hospital incinerators. She wondered how long it would be before they found out that she was gone. Not long, she suspected, but the thought was still exhilarating. She had stopped being observed, the object of enquiry and expectation. She had taken control of her life once more. The smell of machine oil was overpowering. She slipped between the incinerators and there was the door before her. It was bolted, but she tugged hard and the bolt slid back. The door opened onto evening, and Jaya hobbled through.

The boneyard was silent. The familiar rows of bins were locked against scavengers; easy enough to open if you had the codes, but tonight she resisted the temptation of scavenging for any valuables that might be lingering amid the rubbish. Instead she headed between the bins for the sewer hatch. Gritting her teeth against the pain, she dropped through into the warm stinking darkness below, and tugged the hatch closed above her.

Dim light filtered down through the cracks, and as she made her halting way along the reeking edges of the sewer she saw that there was another *dalit* jackal waiting, a boy of no more than nine or ten. Jaya knew him. His name was Halil, and when he was not raiding the hospital waste bins, he caught rats to feed his family. His face was carved with the silvery striations of Selenge, and already one hand

42

had become crabbed into a claw. She wondered with a pang how much longer he had left to live. Usually, Selenge gave its sufferers only a few months of miserable life once the striations had broken out, wasting away muscle and eroding flesh until the cramps and contractions that signalled the end.

Halil broke into a great smile when he saw her. 'Jaya! They told me you were dead.'

'They lied.' She smiled down at him in return, and reached out to touch his face. 'How are you, Halil?'

He shrugged. 'The same. Did they cure you?'

'No, they didn't.'

'Where are you going now?'

'To the river,' she told him, and as soon as the words were out of her mouth she realized it was true. It was where the sewers led, after all. 'I'm going to the river. Halil, I'd ask you to come with me, but it might be dangerous. There are people after me.'

He accepted this with a nod. 'Good luck,' he said. A filthy hand clasped her own, and reluctantly she left him there in the dim light and stinking air and headed on her way.

When at last Jaya surfaced, Varanasi was lost beneath a haze of heat, and the iron roofs of Jalna Street were baking in the dying day. She could feel the warmth beating up from the road. The air smelled of cooking and smoke, familiar and pleasant after the antiseptic smell of the hospital. She headed into the maze of streets that made up the oldest part of Varanasi: Goudalia. Anand's men would be lucky to find her here; the place was like a warren. Goudalia had no electricity, only a few private generators, and in twenty minutes or so, darkness would fall.

Families and friends were gathering in the tiny shops, settling down on cushioned floors and lighting candles for the evening. Jaya hurried past vendors of curds, rows of tin buckets, silks and charms and garlands. Schoolchildren roared by, balanced on the handlebars of their brothers' motorbikes, and she even saw a Western boy: one of the few backpackers who remained undeterred by the threat of disease. She knew that they would see only an old woman in a tattered, stained sari; just another of the thousands of widows who still came to Varanasi to die by the river. The illness that had so aged and debilitated her was also her weapon, her cloak of invisibility.

The narrow strips of sky above her head turned the colour of cinnamon in the polluted haze. Night was coming fast and the Ganges drew her like a magnet. She hastened down a narrow lane towards the woodyards at the edge of the river: Malikarnika, the Burning Ghat. An ironmonger, a shrine to elephant-headed Ganesh – Jaya smiled at this, for he was the God of Overcoming Impossible Obstacles – then a hole-in-the-wall cybercafé and out between the high stacks of timber.

Jaya drew aside into the fragrant sandalwood shadows to let a funeral procession go past: the corpse on its bier neatly wrapped in tinselled cloth, the shaven-headed mourners following. Faces peered from the shadows, and in the firelight she saw the silvery markings of Selenge.

She was among her own kind here: the *dalit* workers who tended the fires. Ever since Selenge had fallen upon her caste like a bolt from Hell, the numbers of those who congregated around the ghats had increased. She could see them in the upper storeys of the ruins above the river, hovering like ghosts.

Jaya slipped through the timber yard, around the side of one of the great ruined palaces that still graced the river front, and down onto the ghat. Behind her, a corpse on its pyre sparked and smouldered into the evening air.

It was marginally cooler by the water, although the stones breathed heat into the evening air. She found a place in the shadows beneath the bulk of the ghat. It was good to sit down. From here she could see the whole curve of the river, golden in the last of the sun: a great sheet of light. At the edge of the ghat a group of women stepped, one by one, into the purifying waters of the Ganges, and after a while Jaya joined them when she could no longer bear the stink of the sewer. But she kept well out of their way, staying downstream. She ducked beneath the gleaming water. When she rose, there was a soldier standing on the ghat, looking around.

Jaya froze. It wasn't Anand; it was a younger man, in a crisp khaki uniform. An automatic hung from his shoulder holster. Four years ago, she'd had weapons of her own, and a good eye, but now she'd barely be able to pull the trigger. She swallowed fury, took a deep breath, and sank beneath the water. When at last she dared to raise her head, her lungs bursting, the soldier was gone.

She stayed in the river for another twenty minutes, until she was reasonably sure that the soldier wasn't coming back. Then, cautiously, she climbed back up onto the warm stone of the ghat. The evening *puja* had begun; each woman lighting the tiny candle in its nest of marigold petals and setting the papier mâché bowl so that it bobbed on the water for a moment before being taken by the lazy current.

Shrinking back into the concealing shadows, Jaya watched each little light drift down the river, and her thoughts followed. Without understanding how this might be, she knew more than she did yesterday: a day older, five times more wise. Fragments of information swam up from her unconscious mind: long skeins of encoding, jigsaw images. They came from nowhere and vanished into nothing. Information without context was also without meaning. Jaya sat with her back to the warm stone and waited for it to make sense.

Slowly, fragments began to cohere, though not in words. It was more than a dream. It was like the old days of oracle, and rather than shutting it out, as she had become used to doing, Jaya simply listened. The war in Sri Lanka was escalating: a JNLR guerrilla faction had broken away. American gunships had surrounded Taiwan in a protective cordon and the US was threatening further action against the Chinese government, the last engagement in thirty years of chilly and intermittent conflict.

The scraps of data were as clear and perfect as pearls, embedded in the oyster casing of her neocortex. She watched them pass with a sudden guilty sense of exhilaration, like a child who wakes in the night when everyone else is asleep. She opened her eyes and sat up. The sun was gone; the women in their ochre saris dipped and swayed along the edge of the water. Someone was suddenly sitting beside her.

Jaya turned to see a pallid, plump face and golden eyes. The *raksasa*'s lotus mouth curled open in what might have been a smile. Graciously, she inclined her head. Jaya blinked, and the *raksasa* was gone.

Night fell. Jaya considered moving up into the ruins, already filled with widows and the homeless, but she knew that the men up there would demand money or sex. So she drew closer into the cremation ground, creeping into the darkness behind the woodpiles. Even if the soldiers came back, the priests would not allow them here; some places were still sacred. And the people who tended the pyres were themselves untouchables, with no love of the military. She was as safe here as anywhere else.

The skeins of data continued to unravel through her mind, running like mercury. Now, it was beginning to weave together. It seemed to relate to the satellite communications systems woven above the continent: information from the military colonies, troop movements, weather reports. And then she heard a note through the mesh of information; something utterly strange, like the voice of a god, and wholly familiar. It lasted no more than a split second, and then was gone.

It was the voice that she had heard from childhood, but

now it was much clearer and closer. It brought her upright, backed panting against the woodpile. She listened for it with all the concentration that she could muster but she did not hear it again.

At last she slid into real sleep, waking only when the dawn began to come up over the river. The ghat came back to life; holy men splashing noisily about in the shallows. She could hear voices raised in prayer and a bell tolling out; the funeral ceremonies were beginning again. Restlessly, she left the ghat and the smouldering pyres and wandered back into the maze of Goudalia. The pain was still there but it felt muted, as though someone had turned down the volume of a radio.

Life began early in Varanasi, in the cool of the day, and the lanes were filled with people. Jaya passed a boy on a bike with a basket full of watermelons, an office worker in a suit and high heels, a group of ancient women in ochre saris. Their faces were silvered with Selenge and their hands were clawed. They huddled together as if for protection. The office worker gave them a wide berth, and the boy on the bike veered away as he saw them and made a sign against evil. The old women drew back into a filthy alley and hastened away.

Jaya followed them into the shadows, and it seemed to her that she saw the blood-coloured word of plague written on the doors and death in the air. Jaya's caste passed reviled or unseen, but now she was invisible even to herself. She did not know what she had become. She flattened herself against the wall to let one of the sacred cattle go by, and saw with a shock that it looked at her with golden eyes.

Towards noon, Jaya found herself crouched against the wall of the Temple of Durga. The stone was red like desiccated flesh. Within, the great bell tolled. Although she knew where she was, the town was becoming increasingly insubstantial, as though she was watching a film. She was no longer concerned about the soldiers, about Anand, and somewhere deep within she felt dimly surprised that this should be so.

The sweat and heat on her skin seemed separate from herself; she had become no more than a shell, a carrier for another consciousness. It seemed to Jaya now that she was travelling further and further beyond the net of satellite communications, far from Earth to the edge of the system. She opened her eyes and saw with a start that the *raksasa*'s insubstantial form was once more sitting by her side, watching her. She could hear the voice more clearly now, calling to her in opaque symbols across the void. And now, after all these years, the voice told her at last what it was: not a god, or a vision produced by sickness, but a ship.

'What are you?' Jaya whispered, fighting panic, but the *raksasa* only smiled her curled smile. 'Where have you come from?'

/Watch./ the *raksasa* said blandly. /Integration has commenced./

—and Jaya looked through the *raksasa*'s eyes as the ship slowly turned, out beyond the warmth of the sun, and began to move into the boundaries of the solar system:

ice frosting its ancient sides, its organic systems resurrected into life, viral nexi filamenting within its cores. And she listened to it singing as she summoned it in, singing of what she did not yet understand: the progenitor of plagues, made by our makers, sailing down to Earth.

RASASATRA

KHAIKURRIYË, RASASATRAN SYSTEM

The immense expanse of the city was rosy with sunset light, causing the arches of the caste-domes to glow, as if lit from within. The ribbed walls of Rasasatra's huge living buildings flexed and stirred as the light faded, releasing pollen into the evening air. The crimson sun was balanced on the horizon like an eye, highlighting distant pylons, and a red wind was blowing up from the desert parks of the Zher, stirring a singing vine into agitated life and rattling the quills at the back of Sirru's head.

The walls of the little domed house, however, remained as closed as a disapproving mouth. Sirru leaned forward and whispered impatiently to the house, 'But I've already explained it to you half a dozen times. I have an appointment with your mistress. At least let me send her a *message.*'

He had tried any number of verbal modes, none of which had been successful. It seemed that the house was not open to persuasion. Despite the protection of the nanoscale that filmed Sirru's skin beneath his robe, the house seemed to sense both his insecurities and his hopes, which were already becoming more than a little forlorn.

His quills drooped. The palm of his hand still tingled with the message that Anarres had pressed into it the previous night at the Making celebration: her locative and a time, elegantly inscribed in pheromonal signature across his tingling skin. It was only the third time they had been out together, but Sirru was already incapable of thinking about anyone else.

Even though he was nothing more than a civil servant, Anarres seemed genuinely interested in him, and her invitation to visit had appeared sincere. Now, however, he couldn't help having doubts. *What if Anarres didn't really want me to come? Maybe she's got bored with me. Maybe she was just being kind . . .* In terms of caste, after all, Anarres was out of Sirru's league. Wasn't she an *apsara*, a highly-regarded courtesan-interpreter, whereas he was merely a minor functionary?

But that lowly status could soon change, Sirru reminded himself. He reached into the folded pocket of his robe and took out the sliver that contained the message, reassuring himself once more that it was real.

We have an urgent matter to discuss with you. Kindly present yourself before us, Third-day, Fifth-Hour-First-Morning. That was tomorrow. The message was signed: *EsRavesh.*

Clearly, the message had come from a *khaith*; he would have been able to determine that even without the locative and the signature. The *khaithoi* might have been only a couple of castes above his own, but they gave themselves enough airs and graces to suit the most elevated echelons

52

of society. It was typical of the constant jockeying for position among the castes.

Sirru wished he could place EsRavesh. The name had a nagging familiarity, and yet he was sure that he had never met this particular *khaith* before. He had no idea why he had been summoned. Perhaps the family was being offered a raise in status, and in that case, his relationship with Anarres could only be strengthened. It was a comforting dream, especially after the terrible events of the past year, but Sirru couldn't bring himself to believe in it.

He looked back at the stubbornly closed house and sighed. Doubtless he was just being naïve in entertaining these vain hopes. The walls were prickling with distaste, but he refused to be so easily defeated. *Time to try more unorthodox methods.* He reached beneath the wide, loose collar of his robe and touched the nanoscale implant. He felt the sudden cool flush of the nanoscale over his skin as its modulation changed to the specifications that Sirru's friend in the emergency services had previously programmed in. He'd always thought that the specs would come in handy, ever since the friend had offered to trade him the codes. You took power where you could get it, these days.

The house sensors glowed in the growing dusk. Sirru stood on the entry platform, as nonchalantly as he could manage, and let his clothes lie for him. He tried to suppress the rush of satisfaction as a small slit appeared in the wall. The house had believed the lie: *Emergency! Permit access immediately!* The wall manifolded back to let him in and

Sirru stepped quickly through before the house realized that it had been tricked.

Inside, the place was as beautiful as he had expected. Mesh webbing outlined ceiling and wall, and the floor was covered with soft black matting. The house was filled with its symbiotic flowers, which rustled and whispered as he passed. Sirru walked quickly through and found Anarres sitting out on a little terrace, surrounded by night lilies. The flowers were slowly opening as the sun sank. Anarres glanced up as Sirru stepped out onto the balcony, her leafgreen eyes alight.

'Sirru! I thought you weren't coming.'

'I'm sorry I'm late,' Sirru said. 'I had a few problems with your house.'

Anarres face was dismayed. 'Wouldn't it let you in? Oh, I'm sorry. It's been like that for *weeks*. I keep changing the parameters, but they never seem to stick. How did you get in?'

'I lied.'

'So embarrassing . . .' Anarres murmured, flustered. But Sirru had already forgotten his problems with the house and was gazing at her in admiration. Either she had just been entertaining another visitor, or (a more flattering explanation) had taken pains solely for him. Her long rustling quills were bound in a glistening web of wire, and a subtly expensive aura of pheromones surrounded her like a mantle. Thus enhanced, she seemed to glow. Every gesture she made was filled with meaning: limitlessly seductive. He swallowed.

'I'm so glad you've come.' Anarres said, undulating up to him. 'You see, I've been having a few – well, not *problems*, exactly, but a bit of a difference of opinion with someone. It's upset me.' She placed her hand intimately on the inside of his elbow, beneath the loose sleeve of the robe.

Sirru's breath stopped short in his throat. Anarres was not as tall as he, and was also more sinuous than was usual among her caste, suggesting some expensive modifications. Silver wire bound her elbow spurs and the prominent vertebrae of her spine, revealed under the mesh of her garment. She was darker than Sirru, her skin dappled with the colours of storm cloud and rain. She reached up and touched the tip of a jade green tongue to the implant below his collarbone. The scale vanished; Sirru's skin was suddenly cool beneath the robe.

'Now you'll know what I'm thinking,' he told her, embarrassed.

She leaned her head against his shoulder.

'But I want to share things with you.'

'You'll think I'm an infant,' he said. 'An infant who can't control its own thoughts ... And compared to your *khaithoi* affiliates, it's probably true.'

Anarres shivered in his arms. 'But that's exactly my problem. You see, I've been doing some work for a *khaith* – a person called EsRavesh. And he's somehow got the idea that I'm his exclusive *apsara*, that I shouldn't be sleeping with anyone else. But of course that's simply unreasonable. After all, it's my job as a courtesan-interpreter. Anyway,

EsRavesh has no right to tell me what to do in my private life, has he?' She glanced up, and Sirru realized that without the scale, she had felt his sudden alarm.

'Sirru? What's wrong?'

'Nothing,' Sirru said, firmly. 'I'm just worried about you, that's all.' Gently, he released her and went to stand at the edge of the balcony.

EsRavesh: the *khaith* whom he had been summoned to see on the following morning. It could not be coincidence. Was that why the name was so familiar? Sirru tried to stifle his dismay. Had Anarres mentioned EsRavesh before? No, he was certain she had not. But was he being brought before the *khaithoi* for his involvement with Anarres? It seemed unlikely – higher castes rarely concerned themselves with the sexual entanglements of their social inferiors. But if, as Anarres had said, EsRavesh was being unreasonable . . .

He hoped this wasn't going to turn into some horrible political complication. What with poor IrEthiverris and the disaster on Arakrahali, the past months had been bad enough already.

'Sirru, you don't know what it's like, dealing with the *khaithoi*,' Anarres said behind him. 'It's like being surrounded by mirrors. You never have any privacy. They can feel everything you think. They won't let me wear scale, of course; it's as though I'm raw, all the time. When I'm interpreting for them, they just reach out and take my thoughts.'

Now that Sirru's own scale had been deactivated, he

could feel the frustration emanating from Anarres like steam. He wondered what her suppressant prescriptions might be. Her honesty was startling.

'I'm sorry,' Anarres said abruptly. 'It really isn't fair to ask you to listen to all my problems. But you're so easy to talk to . . .'

'I'd been wondering what you see in me.'

Anarres looked a little startled. 'You're kind. And you listen to what I'm saying instead of looking at me as though I was some kind of ornament. Anyway, all the people I ever seem to meet are politicians, and it's nice to spend time with someone uncomplicated for a change.'

Sirru was not sure whether to regard this as a compliment or not, but Anarres' mood was changing. She was broadcasting /attraction/affection/regard/ and a promise beyond all these that made him gasp. He felt her tongue slide across the sensitive skin of his throat, trailing excitement in its wake. His quills prickled, rising slightly from his scalp. He managed to say in a reasonably normal voice, 'Actually, my own status may be undergoing a revision. I have an appointment with the *khaithoi* tomorrow.' He did not mention the name of EsRavesh. 'I've been given to understand it's important, but who can feel?'

'You're representing your caste? Or just your clade?'

Sirru smiled. It was a compliment for her to think that he might be representing the millions of people and sub-species who comprised his caste, but he knew she was just saying it to flatter him.

'The latter. Usually my family wheedles me into representing them, but this time the *khaithoi* asked for me personally.'

The leafgreen eyes blinked up into his own. 'Be careful when you go to see them,' Anarres said, emanating anxiety.

'I intend to be,' Sirru replied, and kissed her.

She responded with enthusiasm, then drew back. 'Sirru – do you know whether you'll be engaging in sexual mode with the *khaithoi*?'

'I don't know. I don't think so.' He frowned. 'We've communicated in the usual combinations up until now: I speak with words and modes; they're just patronizing. I suppose if they had anything very complex or lengthy to discuss, they'll convey it sexually. Hope not, though.' Sirru sighed. It was not an enticing thought. He had secrets that could prove dangerous if he let them slip at the wrong moment.

'I only asked because, if so, you and I don't have to sleep together tonight. If you'd like to conserve your energy, that is,' Anarres murmured.

'Thank you for being so thoughtful, but that really won't be necessary,' Sirru said hastily, and kissed her again.

At dawn, the wind veered round to the north, bringing the scent of snow and rock resin from the distant mountains. The singing vine, evidently reminded of winter, shivered with a disconsolate chord. At the sudden song, Sirru woke, blinked golden eyes and yawned with a snap of teeth. Anarres lay beside him, coiled in the hollow of his arms, and Sirru watched her for a moment as she slept, moved by her fragility. In sleep, Anarres' mouth was slightly open and he could see the tip of her jade tongue, just touching her lower lip.

Sirru smiled, remembering the night, and shifted against her. He held her close for a moment, twisting so that his throat was pressed against her own, and the soft skin at the inside of his elbow rested against the lower part of her breast ridges. He sent her a message: a complex combination of desire, gratitude, and anticipation.

He pressed against her for a moment longer, wishing he could stay, then rose fluidly from the sleeping mat and slid into his robe. Rainwater had collected in the curled leaves of the singing vine. Sirru paused to drink, then walked through the walls of the house and out into the morning. He was irritated to see that the house had no reluctance in letting him out.

It was early, but there were already a few people about. Sirru passed an elderly *shekei* on its way back to its own quarter. He looked hastily away but not before catching a rank whiff of hierarchical disapproval. *Shekei* weren't so far above his own level, only about four grades, but in the hundreds of middle ranking castes – such as the *khaithoi* and his own – nuances of social position were important, and people would seize on the slightest thing in order to prove themselves superior.

That was not an encouraging thought. The connection

between Anarres and EsRavesh was gnawing at him. *Face facts,* Sirru told himself. *If this khaith has become enamoured of Anarres, then it's hardly likely to bode well for you, is it?*

He stepped impatiently out onto the platform above the airwell. Khaikurriyë stretched below, fading into the morning haze at the horizon's edge. He could see the pale pylons of the Fourth Quarter rising up against the mountains in the park and this reminded him of the nightmare of the previous year. IrEthiverris had lived in Fourth Quarter, before being packed off to Arakrahali. A person at the edge of the platform gave Sirru an angry glance; he had transmitted his unease, a measure of his nervousness this morning.

Embarrassed by his own impoliteness, Sirru activated the scale. Despite the risk he was running in having illegally engineered clothes, he was sure that he would be glad of the scale's modifications before the day was out. Sirru did not trust the *khaithoi* in any circumstances, and since he had learned of Anarres' connection with EsRavesh, his trust was at an all-time low. Rumours of alterators ran through his mind: pheromonal boosters, illegal manipulations. He wished he was still asleep in Anarres' arms.

Sirru stepped off the edge of the platform and plunged into the airwell. As he slowly descended, his anticipation increased, mixed with a growing sense of unease. Soon, he reached the Marginals.

The domes towered above him, looking like a tumbled

collection of gigantic, ribbed seeds which, in a sense, they were. The Marginals extended as far as the eastern horizon; he could see their oval spires rising faint and shadowy against the growing sunlight. The air was thick with pollen, which swarmed in golden skeins through the warm morning and filled Sirru's head with a pungent mixture of spices. Somewhere in the midst of this vast construction lay the Core: the oldest thing in the universe, a place central to the life of all írRas and, to Sirru, literally unimaginable. He could only think about it in very vague terms, as one might glimpse stars from the corner of one's eye. The Marginals, the nearest expression of the life of the Core, were impressive enough.

Sunlight shimmered from the walls, releasing a scented waft. Taking a deep breath, Sirru placed his palm on the entry mechanism of the Marginals' quarantine dome. Hoping that the scale's undetectors would hold, he walked slowly through the decontamination system before reaching the far end of the dome. The *khaithoi* liked to see themselves as superior to Sirru's own caste because of where they lived, but they were one of the lowest castes of the Marginals, really, confined to its farthest edges.

This was fortunate, because it meant that Sirru did not have to go very deep into the Marginals. A more extensive decontamination would have revealed the scale in moments.

After a brief pause, the wall opened and Sirru stepped through into a long narrow chamber, lined with antique metal panels. A group of *khaithoi* were waiting for him.

Their eyes glistened in the dim, filtered light; their quadruple arms were folded around their stout waists. Their petalled mouths fluttered in and out, tasting the air, listening for what he might inadvertently say. Sirru inclined his head and sent a carefully compiled greeting of *place/status/ affirmation*. A rustle ran along the lines of the *khaithoi*, but when he cautiously explored the air there was nothing but a wall of blankness. They were blocking him.

Sirru fought down a sudden, unfamiliar sense of panic; it was though the *khaithoi* were no longer real, merely plump shells of flesh. He knew they were doing this to unsettle him. A thin glaze of sweat filmed the inside of the scale, which minutely rearranged itself and prevented Sirru from revealing his disquiet. Sirru waited. A head turned: the *khaith* who was nearest to him. Sirru was granted a portion of the *khaith's* locative: IrHirrin EsRavesh. So this was the person who had summoned him. This was his rival. Gritting his teeth, he provided the relevant fragment of his locative in turn.

'Sirrubennin EsMoyshekhal/genestrand seventy billion nine/'

'We already know where you come from,' EsRavesh said, with a subtextual trace of disdain. 'Speak when you are invited to, and not before.' His complex mouth curled and folded in an expression that Sirru found difficult to interpret. EsRavesh was using the Present Remote Plural, laced with expressives so smooth and bland that they ran off Sirru's skin like rain. And beneath that, a hint of

62

something much spikier. The scale shot a warning across Sirru's skin. Wisely, he did not reply.

'You're *desqusai*, aren't you?' the *khaith* said, frowning, as if the lower castes were so similar that it was beyond his ability to tell them apart. Since his status was perfectly obvious, Sirru evinced no more than a flicker of affirmation. The petals of the *khaith*'s mouth folded abruptly inwards, leaving a small pinhead hole. 'Then you will no doubt be overjoyed to learn your caste is about to be honoured,' EsRavesh said. 'Come with me.'

The *khaith* spoke slowly, using clear, precise verbals to disambiguate the complexities of his pheromonal speech. All the *khaithoi* spoke like this, as though the castes below them were idiot children, incapable of understanding the refinements of the hierarchical languages that lay above. The fact that this was largely true did not help Sirru's mood. Honoured? What was the *khaith* talking about? He tried to focus on what EsRavesh was saying.

'It seems that another of your caste's seed colonies has become active. The one you call Eir Sithë Tekhei,' EsRavesh told him. 'Observe.' He touched an implant in the wall. A small glowing globe emanated from it and hovered before Sirru's face. Gradually, the glow faded and a world appeared: small, blue, marbled with cloud, beneath which continents swam in ochre and grey. Ice dappled each pole; a tiny moon orbited slowly. Sirru frowned. He'd seen a representation of this world before, among the ranks of *desqusai* planets that had not yet reached fruition.

'It's activated?' he echoed.

'Indeed. A depth ship has been broadcasting for generations, but to no effect. Now, however, it seems that a Receiver, a female, has finally grown to fruition and come on-line. The Receiver, after an apparently shaky start, has entered into reliable communication with the depth ship. The ship has a *raksasa*, of course – an administrator. She is a caste/clade member of mine. She is requesting a suitable mediator between herself and the colony's inhabitants. That mediator,' EsRavesh said with a buttery trace of satisfaction, 'will be you.'

'Me?'

'You,' EsRavesh repeated, with a trace of sharpness. 'Perhaps I do not make myself sufficiently clear. Eir Sithë Tekhei is a *desqusai* world, the home of a sub-species of your own caste. Your caste has therefore been selected as being responsible for this particular colony – an appointment that reflects your ancestors' role in forming the colony itself. Your job will be to go to Tekhei and solve whatever problems have accrued in its evolution. I understand that there are a number of difficulties.'

'What sort of difficulties?' Sirru asked. The scale clamped down on his stirrings of unease.

EsRavesh said wearily, '*Desqusai*, hmmm.' *Always a problem*, his words implied. *But what can you expect of the lower orders?* 'The Receiver herself is extremely fragile; I understand that there has been some kind of malfunctioning in her genetic programming. The depth ship's *raksasa* is even now working on a way to modify her so that she can operate more effectively. It also seems that the colony has not adapted well to the regeneratives that were aligned to it. Genetic patterns designed to form the basis of communication have become distorted across millennia, and have either atrophied or become structurally damaging.'

Unbidden, the voice of Sirru's lost friend IrEthiverris echoed in his head. *It's the communications network: it's killing them!* He shivered. The disaster on Arakrahali was the last thing he wanted to think about now. EsRavesh continued, 'Political structures are rudimentary, as is to be expected in such a society. The world is suffering from a population explosion; its environment has been rendered unstable by injudicious economic decisions. The colony must be brought under the aegis of the írRas. It must be *pruned*, before it goes entirely to seed. If such pruning proves unsuccessful, the colony will have to be terminated.'

'Terminated?' Sirru's quills rattled.

Hissing in exasperation, the *khaith* stepped forwards. 'I realize that it's a difficult notion to entertain. But you do understand?'

'Yes,' said Sirru, wincing. He added, 'My caste would be most unhappy if that were to happen.'

'The decision is not in the hands of the *desqusai*,' EsRavesh snapped. 'It is the Core's. You know as well as I do that the Core cannot allow unviable colonies to spread like poison-briar throughout the galaxy. Unruly populations must be controlled, governed, their savage impulses contained within the proper boundaries. I'm sure you agree. Or,' a trace of sarcasm tinged the air, 'have you become a Natural, arguing for some nonsensical notion of social chaos?' He did not wait for Sirru's murmured refutation. 'As I had said, your task will be to set things to rights.'

'I am honoured. But I am also surprised that a minor person such as myself should have been selected for such a task,' Sirru said, trying not to sound as though he was protesting.

'The project is not a difficult one, compared to others. This is a little, primitive world, hardly a matter of great complexity. You,' EsRavesh said with a withering glance, 'have been deemed appropriate. Nevertheless,' the *khaith* added, and his golden gaze became beady, 'I do not need to remind you that the last attempt to bring a *desqusai* colony into the fold ended in termination. No one wants such a debacle to happen again. I believe you knew IrEthiverris EsTessekh?'

'Yes,' said Sirru, bleakly.

'A friend of yours, I understand. A pity. He seemed to be a reasonably capable administrator, at least at first. And Arakrahali was a minor colony, too. It is still unclear what went so tragically wrong . . . I understand you have been investigating the incident?'

'Yes,' Sirru said, suddenly wary. He thought he had taken care to be discreet. 'As you so rightly say, Ir-Ethiverris was a friend of mine, and obviously I was concerned to discover the reasons for the tragedy.'

'Reasons?' EsRavesh asked. 'What reasons do you need? IrEthiverris administered his colony with increasing ineptitude. His *khaith* colleague reported a series of misjudgements; she was most concerned about the deteriorating relationship between the locals and IrEthiverris himself. I need hardly remind you that the situation seems to have created a most disastrous plague and, shortly after that, IrEthiverris disappeared. Tragic, yes, but not something that needs further investigation. We are looking into the case ourselves.'

Then why are there so many things about Arakrahali that don't add up? Sirru thought mutinously, but said nothing. The thought was painful; as it occurred to him, his epistemic suppressants clamped down. The whole Arakrahali affair had been difficult to think about; he needed a lower suppressant level, but that wasn't possible. He bowed his head. 'Doubtless you are correct.'

'*Desqusai* are so *emotional*,' EsRavesh mused, as if to the empty air. 'There has even been talk within the Core that the *desqusai* castes are degenerating, their colonies proving unsuitable for sustained development. It would be a pity, if that were so. Your caste remains a valued part of this society.' He did not sound as though he believed it. 'I'm sure your future success with Tekhei will help redeem *desqusai* standing in the senses of the higher castes.' The expressives that EsRavesh was sending to Sirru were bland, as smooth as sweet oil, but even through Sirru's epistemic suppressants and the soothing scale, the warning was clear: *Sort out your new colony*

*and don't mess it up, otherwise it will the worse for both
you and it.*

Sirru was to be sent from Rasasatra, then, summarily
dispatched across a span of stars. This talk of ancestral
connections between his own caste and the new colony was
true enough, but there were many people of more proven
experience than Sirru. Why not send them? There were
two reasons, one of which was Anarres.

Women like Anarres made their own sexual choices,
but those choices were supposed to reinforce the values
of hierarchy. So was he being sent halfway across the
galaxy to a primitive and marginal planet as a result
of EsRavesh's snobbish jealousy? Sirru closed his eyes
for a brief, bitter moment. But when EsRavesh had
summoned him, he realized, he hadn't even slept with
Anarres.

That led to the other possibility, which was even worse.
EsRavesh knew about his enquiries into the Arakrahali
tragedy. What if he'd stumbled across something important and the *khaith* was getting him out of the way? And if
so, what could that important information possibly be?
The band of headache tightened around his skull.

'Are you all right?' EsRavesh asked with mocking
solicitousness.

'Perfectly, thank you,' Sirru said icily. Thinking fast,
he considered his options, then sent a shower of instructions to the scale, which obediently broadcasted the lie:
/*Unworthiness/ respect for superiors/overwhelming sense
of gratitude./* Either the scale's lie was successful or the

68

khaith's arrogance was such that Sirru's message was accepted with barely a flutter of doubt.

'We understand you are honoured,' EsRavesh allowed graciously.

Sirru had one question. 'When do I leave?'

'As soon as possible. There is a raft leaving tonight for an orbital; translation will take place from there.'

Life has to change, Sirru thought angrily, *but why now?* Useless to speculate on the laws of the world; he was well aware that he had no choice.

'I have affairs to put in order,' he told the *khaithoi*, and then permitted himself to ask the question which he was privately dreading. 'How long am I to be absent?' The scale sent: /*hope for an honourably lengthy appointment*/ concealing Sirru's true feelings.

'Translation, of course, will take no more than the usual instant,' EsRavesh said, and the petalled mouth unfolded in a fleshy smile. 'But mediation will take – well, as long as it takes for us to decide whether or not the project has been successful.'

'I see.' Sirru lied once more: /*relief/surrender to superior's wishes*/

The *khaith* rose from his mat and came to stand before Sirru. EsRavesh was a head or so shorter than Sirru, and stout where Sirru was lean. Folds of pale, mottled flesh rippled beneath the *khaith*'s robes. Sirru stared down at him, giving nothing away. He could feel the *khaith*'s efforts to influence him. Beneath the scale, his skin flushed dark with sudden unwanted arousal.

Sirru found this gratuitous sexual harassment irritating. He could feel the quills at the back of his neck beginning to rise, but a mistake now could cost him and the rest of this caste dearly; it wasn't worth the momentary satisfaction of a response. The scale kicked in, clamping his system into calmness. The tip of a dark brown tongue fluttered briefly between the *khaith*'s petalled lips and then EsRavesh turned away.

'Go back to your temenos and your clade. Explain the dignity that has been conferred upon them. Present yourself at the landing ledge – ' and here he pressed his palm briefly and with distaste against Sirru's, conferring coordinates and time ' – for translation.' The rest of the *khaithoi* stirred briefly. A ripple of communication, too advanced for Sirru to comprehend, passed between them, and EsRavesh turned his back in dismissal.

Once out of the chamber, Sirru paused and leaned against the wall. Beneath the scale, his skin crawled with agitation. It was difficult to believe this was happening. Suddenly, he wanted nothing more than to leave the Marginals. He switched off the hot scale and in a swirl of robes strode through the labyrinth and out into the day. First to the temenos, and then to see Anarres, if her damned house would let him back in.

The problem is status. Status and caste. His life, and all their lives, were governed by it. Quite apart from any *khaithoi* scheming, it was the main reason why his clade had to take what they could get and why he would be compelled to leave mat and home and new girlfriend and traipse across the galaxy to sort out somebody's long-dormant planet.

At that point his epistemic suppressants kicked in, causing a sharp neural twinge, and Sirru winced. *Tekhei's only got one moon and a couple of seas*, he thought in exasperation. *It isn't even pretty*. It seemed such a dull little world.

But then again, so had Arakrahali.

THE TEMPLE OF DURGA

1.
VARANASI

The Temple of Durga – the goddess known as the Terrible One – red as old blood, rose above the noisy streets of Varanasi. Its tiers crawled with monkeys, which chattered and shrieked at anyone who came too close. The temple had been closed for several years now, deemed structurally unsafe after one of the province's infrequent earth tremors, and even though the faithful still drifted past its walls, it was still completely closed to non-believers. However, a non-believer was a difficult thing to be these days, now that a goddess had come to the world.

At the heart of the temple, in an echoing chamber that blew dry with dust and shadows, Jaya Nihalani was sitting on a wheelchair throne. Behind her, she could feel the presence of the goddess, concealed behind a door in a small, glittering shrine. The shrine was like a cave, Jaya thought, gleaming with mica and crystal. Only when you looked closely could you see that the glitter was tinsel and beaten metal.

Whenever she was filled with doubts, which was often, Jaya closed her eyes and reached back to the presence of the goddess: Durga the Vengeful, who tramples demons

72

beneath her feet and of whom Kali is only an aspect. Yet Durga was also the Protector, whom young married women used to invoke in the earliest days of their marriage, to guard their homes and families. What frightened Jaya was that despite all that had happened, despite the failure of her revolution, she still seemed to occupy Durga's dual position: to protect, and – Goddess forbid – perhaps to revenge. Everything now depended on Ir Yth.

Jaya had spent the last few days interpreting the demands, blandishments and suggestions of the *raksasa*, whose full name was revealed as Ir Yth írRas EsTekhei.

/*Perhaps I am Durga,*/ the *raksasa* whispered sweetly into Jaya's mind. /*Maybe I am She who is come again to the world.*/

Despite the astonishment that still possessed her whenever she looked at Ir Yth, Jaya felt that there was very little truth in this. Ir Yth, despite her bizarre four-armed appearance, reminded Jaya of her father – the man who had taught his child, above all else, to smell out a lie. Ir Yth was no goddess, any more than Jaya herself. Nor was she really a demon, though on that score Jaya was still keeping an open mind. As far as she knew, Ir Yth was the projected image of an alien, the sole crewmember of the vast and living ship which had been waiting so patiently beyond the edges of the solar system and which now orbited the world. And the ship was also the originator of that voice which Jaya had heard since childhood. Her connection was with the ship, not with the *raksasa*.

But Jaya said nothing, for if it pleased the *raksasa* to be regarded as a deity, then it was as well to go along with the lie until Jaya found out precisely what Ir Yth was capable of. She swallowed the implied insult that she was nothing more than some local primitive who would be confused and awed by clumsy lies. It was as annoying as hell, but it might be useful for Ir Yth to underestimate her. Amir Anand had consistently underestimated her, in the early days of her attempted revolution. She'd use it now, as she had used it then.

From what little Ir Yth had said on the matter, it was clear that she knew nothing of Durga; even the self-granted title of *raksasa* was wrong, being the male form of the word. Clearly, Ir Yth had armed herself with a few cultural stereotypes and, like every conqueror, was arrogant enough to think these would be enough. But it might even be that the *raksasa* realized this, and did not care.

Certainly, Ir Yth had been quick with promises. Initially, she had vowed to give Jaya worshippers of her own, having failed to grasp that this was the last thing Jaya wanted. Giving the matter some thought, Jaya had decided to take matters into her own hands and present the *raksasa* with a fait accompli. Stealthily, Jaya had gathered together the remnants of the core cabal of her revolutionary army. These numbered no more than five people, and as far as she knew, the government was not yet aware of their presence in the Temple of Durga. The Bharati government did know, however, precisely who and what their new envoy to the stars was and had been, and they were far from happy.

Jaya, former oracle, former terrorist, was now the Receiver, the chosen one, and one of the *raksasa*'s first public actions had been to communicate this fact to Bharat's media networks.

For those who had been expecting the alien ship to land on the White House lawn, Jaya's appointment was baffling, and Jaya herself was no less bewildered than everyone else. She had become addicted to the news reports, trying to make sense of her new position. Her former lieutenant, Shiv Sakai, monitored the Web daily from what had once been the temple administrator's little office in the forecourt. Peeling calendars with smiling deities filled the walls; a kettle hissed unendingly on the stove as Shiv fuelled himself and everyone else with tiny cups of strong sweet *chai*. Flexible optics hid his eyes. He sat hunched in his seat as data unscrolled onto his visual cortex.

Shiv Sakai, a software engineer before caste restoration turned him into a revolutionary, had become used to watching history happen. He reported to Jaya on the hour:

/The alien presence has still made only a single broadcast, stating that the contact on Earth is to be Jayachanda Nihalani, formerly known as Jaya Devi by her devoted followers, and whom the Indian government has formerly described as a terrorist ... /The government of Bharat claims that reports that an alien is in the country are false and misleading/ ... The current location of the purported alien is not known ... / ... Nihalani is believed to be in hiding in a secret location in Uttar Pradesh, having recently received hospital treatment for a mutagenic* *disease contracted, some sources say, from her activities in black market medicine . . . / Attempts to contact the ship have so far failed; a joint NASA/EU probe is to be sent within days/ . . . It is not known what the aliens want nor why they are here, if indeed there is any truth to the persistent rumours of an alien presence on Earth . . . /the Indian government has refused both American and UN requests to send troops into Uttar Pradesh . . . /The United Nations have issued a further statement saying that there is no truth to any of the current rumours./*

Shiv Sakai read out each fresh contradiction with relish, his thin body twisted in his chair and his fingers splayed over the keypad of the monitor like spiders. Since the failure of Jaya's revolution, her loyal army had been scattered to the four corners of the subcontinent, but now she had brought her commanders together again, and Jaya couldn't help feeling a little vindicated, despite her distrust of the *raksasa*. The huge figure of her old friend Satyajit Rakh now stood just inside the temple gate, glaring at anyone who might be permitted through. Rumour had it that he took his rifle to bed with him. Jaya knew that rumour was right. Rakh was the brother of her dead husband Kamal, and Rakh would follow her anywhere.

The *raksasa* had promised that when an administrator arrived from the homeworld of Rasasatra, Jaya would be taken to the ship and cured of her unnatural ageing, though not of the capacity to hear the voice of the ship.

'And suppose I don't want to go?' Jaya had asked, nettled. Ir Yth reminded her of Doctor Fraser; with the

76

same assumption that she'd be unquestioningly grateful for the munificence placed before her. Goddess knew, she'd like something better than the body of a ninety-year-old, but what kind of price might she have to pay?

/Of course you will want to go,/ the raksasa had said, startled. /Why would you not?/

'Well, I'd like to know what sort of cure it is, before I agree to anything. Is it likely to be painful, for instance? Are you sure you know what you're doing?'

/Our medical knowledge is far beyond that of your people,/ Ir Yth replied, loftily.

'That doesn't answer either question.'

/No,/ the raksasa said, with a glare. /There will be no pain. And yes, I am quite sure./

Grudgingly, she went on to describe the process to Jaya. It seemed there were trifling genetic modifications which could be made, filtering out the deleterious side effects of Jaya's particular DNA, but the mediator must authorize these.

'Why must these be authorized?' Jaya asked, curious to know more of Ir Yth's relationship with others of her kind. 'Does the mediator outrank you?'

/He does not,/ the raksasa replied, somewhat stiffly. /He is of a lower caste than myself. But his caste have an ancestral connection with Earth, and the planet falls under their guidance. I am here to assist; final authority for all decisions rests with the mediator./

'And what if the mediator and myself disagree?'

/I will be there to smooth things over,/ Ir Yth said.

/*And you'll have power, too. You'll be able to do whatever you want. As long as you do what we say.*/

Jaya said nothing. *The British, the Americans, aliens, whatever.* They all made promises. They all lied. Better to wait and see. She was not so worried about a cure for her own illness, whatever it was, but she could not help thinking of the boy in the sewers and the widows who thronged the ghats, and all the others like them. For a treatment for Selenge, Jaya was prepared to do whatever Ir Yth wanted. But it would be on her own terms, not those of the *raksasa*.

Ir Yth, like any deity self-professed or otherwise, was definitely not to be trusted. In the presence of the *raksasa*, Jaya (mindful of the virtues of being underestimated) did her best to be humble and polite, causing Ir Yth to assume an air of plump satisfaction. It wasn't easy. Jaya had been used to arguing each and every decision, ever since the day at the start of the revolution when she had discovered that, oracle though she might be, Satyajit Rakh intended to treat her as a figurehead and not a leader. The row had simmered for a week, with a worried Kamal caught in the middle. Then both Satyajit and Kamal had been caught behind enemy lines, and Jaya had been the one to rescue them. After that, there was no more talk of figureheads, however frail and ill Jaya had become.

/*You must not be afraid of me,*/ Ir Yth would say, with condescending kindness. /*Remember, I am your friend.*/

'I will try not to be afraid,' Jaya would reply, meekly

bending her head to conceal her gritted teeth. She wondered how long she could keep this up.

When she was alone, Jaya let the mock humility drop and paced up and down like a caged tiger, regardless of the pain in her joints. But aloneness was an increasingly difficult state to attain these days; the ranks of those who wanted an audience were swelling by the hour. Jaya found that the situation possessed a certain dark and obscure humour. Far from being invisible or shunned as befitted her untouchable status, all eyes were now upon her.

She intended to make the most of the irony. She had a meeting that morning, with Bharat's Minister of the Interior, Vikram Singh.

Minister Singh was visibly nervous, Jaya was pleased to see. The guards let him into the temple and he was obliged to walk down the long, hot path, flanked by muttering monkeys, to the chamber to where Jaya sat silent and watchful.

'Good morning,' Singh said, after a moment. He blinked as his eyes adjusted to the shadows. Jaya stared up at him, seeing a small, wiry man with skin that looked as dry as a lizard's. He had been associated with the government for over forty years. It did not look as though it had been good for his health.

'Good morning,' Jaya echoed.

'Well,' the Minister murmured. 'This is most unprecedented.'

'It is, yes,' Jaya said, although she was not sure what he was referring to.

'It is an honour.' Singh spoke flatly, disbelievingly.

'What is?' Jaya reached for a cigarette. She had wrestled with her conscience over this – so disrespectful, in a temple – but unfortunately addiction had won over deference. Every time she lit up, she had to stifle a twinge of guilt. Maybe Durga would understand.

'That our nation should be chosen, out of all the world, to represent the planet Earth.'

Jaya, gratefully inhaling smoke, replied, 'Why should we be so surprised that these aliens have chosen this city, out of all the world, in which to make their first appearance?' Her voice dropped a seductive octave or so, the legacy of her days as an oracle. Now that she had so unnaturally aged, her voice was one of the last weapons she had left. 'It is said that Varanasi is the oldest inhabited city in the world, conjured by Lord Shiva himself. Isn't it told that it was above the skies of Varanasi that a pillar of fire, *jyotirlinga*, first manifested thousands of years ago? And isn't this supposed to be the greatest of the *tirthas*, the crossing places, where gods may meet us and we may meet gods? The cremation ground where the universe itself will come to burn?'

She was unable to stifle a pang of unease at that thought: the notion of everything in existence spiralling back to the long hot shores of the Ganges, to go up in Agni's fire. She swallowed hard, and added, 'After all, maybe they've been here before . . .'

Singh was circling her, stalking around the back of the

wheelchair. Jaya felt the hair rise at the back of her neck and forced herself not to turn.

'*Shrimati* Nihalani. Receiver. What do they *want*?' He sounded almost plaintive, and for the first time Jaya could regard him with something akin to sympathy.

'Do you know, Minister, I've been asking myself that very question. And not only myself, either. I have pestered Ir Yth as much as I dare, and every time I get a different story.'

'Trade? Invasion? Reciprocity?' The Minister was guessing aloud.

Jaya said, 'Trust me, Minister Singh, I intend to find out.' She smiled, but she was by no means as certain as she pretended. 'Besides,' she added, 'Bharat suffers from an inferiority complex these days. I imagine that similar questions were asked when the first European colonists arrived. Curious, how amenable we are to potential conquerors. I blame the caste system, myself.'

Clearly, this analogy had struck the Minister before. A sour unease crossed his face and he sighed.

'Yes. The caste system. Your appointment has been . . . not entirely appreciated . . . in certain quarters.'

'Given that the last fifty years have seen certain members of the upper classes immolating themselves at the possibility of my caste entering even the civil service, I can hardly say I'm surprised. Let alone the more – *colourful* – details of my background. Minister, you know as well as I do that my caste have been woefully short-changed. At the turn of the century, we could do any work we pleased, at least in theory. From shit shovellers to software engineers, in less than a hundred years. And then the government managed to get itself ousted by a bunch of right-wing self-professed fundamentalists who were only interested in lining their own pockets at the expense of the lower orders. Bharat's a rich country, but as soon as that wealth looked as though it was about to start trickling down – well, we couldn't have that, could we?' She was starting to sound like her father, Jaya thought.

'History will state that they stabilized the nation,' Singh said.

'Oh, come on. You don't really believe that, do you? I've heard rumours of your lifestyle, Minister, in spite of your religious affiliations.' Jaya bit back details of those rumours; she should try not to antagonize him too much. She added, 'And then there's the Selenge virus, of course, which hasn't helped. Yes, given all that, I should think the Brahmins are dabbing petrol behind their ears even as we speak.'

Singh said hastily, 'I am not among them. I have always been on record as progressive, despite the problems with which your caste has been associated, and—'

'I know that, Minister. I want an assurance from you.'

Rising from the wheelchair, Jaya came to stand before the Minister. Vikram Singh was not tall, but she still had to look up at him.

After a pause, the Minister said warily, 'What?'

'Your hired hyena, Amir Anand, has been after me.

The man they call the butcher-prince. He pursued me into the hospital; if I hadn't overheard him and fled, I imagine I'd be dead by now. It's the third time that Anand has come close to killing me. It's not a feud I ever invited. Call him off.'

Singh said dryly, 'Amir Anand has simply been doing his job. If you had not entertained ideas above your station—' He coughed, and added, 'Anyway, the past is the past. I'm ordering troops to surround the temple, but they are for your own protection and that of your people. I see you have imported some additions to the wanted list.'

'How do you know that?' Jaya asked before she could think better of it, then cursed herself for her naivety. The intelligence services would have all the technology at their disposal trained on the Temple; she had been a fool to think she could smuggle anyone in unnoticed. She would never have been so stupid a few years ago. Was it the illness, or was she simply losing her touch?

The Minister was watching her narrowly. He said, 'I've spoken to the anti-terrorist squad. A temporary pardon is in place for you and your men. We are protecting the temple from intruders. As you'll have noticed.'

Jaya nodded. She could hardly have failed to do so. The large square beyond the temple held a crowd of hundreds, and many more thronged in permanent encampments in the streets beyond.

'I'm grateful.'

Singh's gaze travelled past her shoulder and the lizard

eyes widened fractionally. Turning, Jaya saw that Ir Yth had appeared at the far end of the chamber. The *raksasa* floated a foot or so above the ground, lending her much-needed height.

'It's for your protection,' Singh echoed.

'I can be sure of that, can I?' There were few circumstances in which she would trust any politician, and this was not one of them.

Singh said swiftly, 'Whatever our – differences – might have been in previous years, we are still both of Bharat.' He did not need to add: *And still human.*

'Well, I'm glad you remember that. I was under the impression that the bulk of your political career has been spent in doing deals with the West. Or the East, come to that – with industrialists like Naran Tokai.'

'Naran Tokai has invested heavily in Uttar Pradesh, even more so than his American counterparts. And his association with our nation goes back almost thirty years. I myself have known him for much of that time. Are you suggesting that we do without the pharmaceutical industry? Oh, I was forgetting – you relied upon the black market medicine trade to fund your revolution, didn't you? But Western investment is not the issue here. That, I court. What I don't want—' and here he leaned forwards, confidingly. The *raksasa* had faded from view but Singh kept one eye on the place where she had stood. 'What I don't want is for this situation, this *opportunity*, to be hijacked by the West. By the Americans. The US is still a superpower; it feels it has a right to be considered first by any – visitors. It may be that it is right to do so. I have already had talks with the US Ambassador, and I have been trying to downplay the situation. I have alluded to rumour, conjecture, scaremongering. The Ambassador is an intelligent man. I do not think I can distract him for long, and the American media are already here in force.'

Jaya met his eyes. For once, they were in perfect understanding. 'Agreed.'

'These beings have chosen to make contact *here*. I regard that as significant.'

'Believe me, Minister, so do I.'

'Find out what they want, and what advantages this may bring, before they realize that they might be better off talking to the Pentagon. In exchange, I'll see to it that you receive an official and permanent pardon for your past . . . errors in judgement. In the meantime, I've told the butcher— I've instructed Anand that you are not to be touched.'

'Thank you. But I want assurances for the rest of my people, as well.'

'Your people? You mean your cadre – Satyajit Rakh, Sakai and the others? I think I can arrange that.'

'No. Not just for them.' Jaya took a deep breath. It was an outrageous demand and Singh wouldn't consider it for a moment, but when you bargained, you went for the best deal first. 'The *dalit*. I want the caste restoration programme rescinded. Equal opportunities for untouchables, for all castes.'

Singh grimaced. 'That might be difficult to pass.'

As expected, he wouldn't consider it, but at least he hadn't rejected it out of hand. That suggested he was reluctant to offend her. He went on, 'It's rather unpalatably Marxist, and there's a lot of opposition in these uncertain times to any notion of change.'

'So I've noticed. Given that this country has one of the highest wealth differentials in the world, combined with manifold success in developing new technologies, I am rather unpalatably Marxist, too. However, Minister Singh, I have a hunch that the world is about to change forever. This is no time for either of us to hang onto antiquated hierarchical systems.'

'I'll do my best. As, no doubt, will you.' The look in his eyes lay halfway between threat and grim amusement.

Jaya had to give him some credit, but she did so reluctantly. She did not say: *Three years ago, you would have put a bullet in the back of my head. And your colleagues sent Anand after me, that hound out of hell, to murder first my own father and then the only man I ever loved. So I don't think I owe too much to you and your conniving government.*

When Singh had left, Jaya hobbled across to the stairs that led up to the temple's gallery. The wheelchair had been a thoughtful gift from Varanasi General Hospital – it had even come accompanied with a garland of flowers – but Jaya preferred to walk whenever she could; it reminded her of what was real and what was not. The pain acted as a useful antidote to Ir Yth's smooth blandishments. Jaya got the impression that Ir Yth was failing to get her points across. There was a distinct air of frustration about some of the *raksasa*'s pronouncements, and sometimes she seemed to be waiting for answers to questions that had not, to Jaya's knowledge, been asked. Their discourse had a gap, and both Receiver and *raksasa* were floundering about inside it. Ir Yth also seemed to be postponing real decisions until the arrival of the mediator . . .

Opening the door, Jaya hauled herself up the twisting stone staircase to the gallery that ran along all four sides of the temple. Looking across the temple, she could see an immense concrete pool, normally filled with water but now drained to accommodate troops, journalists, and a slew of bystanders. Beyond the temple courtyard, the street was also crammed with people.

Even for Bharat, it was mayhem. Opposite the temple, onlookers hung out of the upper storey of the Krishna laundry which must, Jaya reflected, be making a fortune in viewing fees. All traffic had been stopped, with the exception of the bike rickshaws, who had latched onto the presence of foreign journalists on expense accounts with the avidity of vultures. Jaya grinned. Not even the most hard-bitten hack stood a chance against the average Varanasi businessman. Everyone in this town had the confidence bestowed by three thousand years of practice in fleecing the faithful.

Up here, she could hear the cries of vendors, flogging charms and garlands and plastic UFOs and God knew what else. Maybe she could persuade Ir Yth to take a break from impersonating deities and go souvenir shopping.

87

As she took a careful step down onto the gallery the monkeys, who had been chattering and yelping and throwing orange rinds at the men below, fell suddenly silent and watched her with bright, anxious eyes. At the end of the gallery, Ir Yth turned to greet her. The *raksasa* was indistinct; she seemed to fade in and out of view. Jaya thought that this must have something to do with the orbit of the ship, where the *raksasa*'s real body was located. Jaya made her way along the roof to where Ir Yth was standing.

What are those people doing? the *raksasa* asked.

Jaya looked over the edge of the roof at the crowd gathered below. Soldiers lined the outskirts of the temple, giving credence to rumour. Every media network on the planet seemed to have sent a representative and Jaya had already imposed a caste system of her own upon them: the local networks at the front, CNN at the back. She was mindful of Singh's concerns – keep the Americans out of this, for as long as possible. Added to these were pilgrims of a multiplicity of religious persuasions; scientists; tourists; lunatics. It reminded Jaya uneasily of the old days at the ashram. She was doomed to be the centre of attention.

One of these days, she told herself, *I'm going to become a normal person, neither invisible nor the focus of everyone's gaze.* But the only person who had ever seen her as ordinary – as a girl who liked parakeets and hibiscus flowers and green tea, who got sick and scared that she couldn't cope – had been Kamal. And Kamal was dead. For the thousandth time, Jaya thrust the memory away.

/*I asked you a question,*/ the *raksasa* said.

'Which people in particular do you mean?' Jaya replied.

A permanent small group of Brahmin students were waving placards, protesting Jaya's appointment. Yesterday there had been a riot in Delhi and there were likely to be more. The *raksasa* pointed a rudimentary finger at the students.

'Oh, those. They're objecting to me.'

The *raksasa*'s mouth pursed and curled in a gesture that possibly indicated surprise. /*Please explain.*/

Jaya sighed. 'I've told you that I am of a certain caste, that there are hierarchies in this society.'

The *raksasa* gave a careful movement of her head, a gesture she had learned from Jaya.

/*Yes. Hierarchies are something that I understand very well.*/

'I have told you that there are certain things I am allowed to do, and others that I am *not* allowed to do.'

/*What is permitted to you?*/ Ir Yth asked.

Jaya swallowed an old shame. She had avoided the particulars of her position up until now. She said, carefully, 'To handle corpses, excrement, leather, earth. It used to be different; there was a period back last century when almost all work was open to us. We were organized – a self-empowerment movement called the Dalit Panthers emerged, based on an earlier struggle in another country. Then the government changed.' She thought back to her conversation with the Minister. 'It started closing off our privileges. There was protest – a lot of people objected to the government's attempts to restore the caste system, but then years ago now a great many of my caste became ill, with a virus they call Selenge. It mainly affected us, no one knew why, but it led to my caste being persecuted.' She held out her scarred wrist. 'We were branded again as untouchables, as disease carriers, even if we weren't even suffering from the illness. If it were left to some of my fellow citizens, I would be probably one of the last people on Earth to be chosen as any kind of representative.'

/It is not a question of choice,/ the raksasa said, irritably. /That is what you are. Caste must be accordingly revised. Please instruct your hierarchical regulators of this fact./

'I'll point it out to them,' Jaya replied, smiling. Ir Yth made it all sound so simple.

/People have been coming here all day. What do they want?/

'They want to know why you're here. What your plans are.'

Ir Yth looked at Jaya as though she had made some casual remark about the weather, and did not reply.

'Ir Yth . . .' Jaya sighed.

/I must leave now. I have things to do. We will discuss this later,/ Ir Yth said, and was abruptly gone.

2.
KHOKANDRA PALACE, JHAIPUR
PROVINCE, INDIA

The man making his way through the marble corridors of
the palace did not need the cane which appeared to guide
his steps, for he was perfectly able to see. Smell was the
only sense that Naran Tokai did not possess. He swung the
ivory cane from side to side as he walked; nanofilters
embedded within its intricate whorls picked up the odours
in the air. It was pleasant to be back in the perfumed air of
the palace; the odour of the funeral pyres as he had driven
through the villages had been initially overwhelming,
penetrating even the air-conditioned atmosphere of the
limousine. The aftermath of another outbreak of Selenge,
no doubt. Tokai had merely switched off the cane and
watched the smoke drift by.

Amir Anand was here, an hour early, and the old man's
lips pursed in disapproval. The butcher-prince was getting
above himself. Perhaps it was a mistake to meet him here
. . . But Tokai dismissed that thought. He wanted to show
Anand who was the master of Khokandra Palace; a firm
demonstration that although this might once had been
Anand's ancestral home, those days were long gone. The
gilt and marble halls of Khokhandra belonged to Tokai
now, and the place had been relegated to no more than a
summer house in the hills, a charming cottage for week-
ends away whenever Tokai visited India. He already

possessed palaces in Delhi and Kerala, and something more rural seemed in order.

Naran Tokai smiled to himself as he walked. The palace was still run-down, and Tokai planned to have it redecorated as soon as possible; import a little Japanese taste and refinement to replace all that ostentatious opulence. Perhaps he'd have the gardens done as well, and bring in some of the re-gendered geishas that currently decorated his mansions in Kyoto or Singapore. His smile widened. He did not think Anand would like that at *all*.

He could smell the butcher-prince already. The vestigial traces of sweat and food and urine, masked beneath deodorant and an aftershave that Tokai found offensively pungent, were channelled through the sensory units of the cane. It was far more effective than his own senses; Tokai reflected once more that the laboratory accident which had deprived him of his sense of smell had really been a blessing in disguise. As he approached the chamber, the odours grew stronger. He paused in the doorway, the cane extended before him. From within, Anand said, '*Shri* Tokai?'

The voice was respectful and cultured, but Tokai could detect something beneath it, like the human smell underneath the artificial ones. He tapped his way into the room and Amir Anand rose too quickly to greet him, bowing low over the old man's hand. It must hurt, Tokai reflected. The princeling forced to sell off the family silver to a Japanese industrialist, to someone in trade. Politely, Tokai said, 'Sit down, please. Would you like water, perhaps tea?'

'A glass of tea, thank you.'

Tokai rang the bell for the servant and stepped unsteadily to the edge of the couch, then lowered himself.

'It is so hot,' he sighed. 'Really, one can't venture outside before evening. My late wife used to say that she longed for the rain when the weather became like this ... Such a horrible climate.' He rambled on, covertly observing Anand's irritation with pleasure. The pale blue eyes were expressionless, but something moved within their depths as Tokai's calculated insults continued. *Must remind Anand that being the son of a maharaja amounts to very little, these days. Especially if one's managed to disgrace oneself by failing to prevent the escape of a political prisoner like Jaya Nihalani.* Anand was an aristocrat, after all, and one with fanatical ideas about caste purity, but what were such upstarts compared to the Japanese?

'Well, one must abide by one's sense of duty, don't you agree, Amir? I'd much rather be back in Kyoto, but there are all these contracts, and the natives don't really know what they're doing. They require guidance, isn't that so? Of men like ourselves. *Civilized* men.'

Warily, Anand agreed. Tokai continued to complain about his workers, spinning fine lines between concepts of caste and race to confuse Anand. The latter, not a stupid man, was clearly unsure as to whether he was being insulted or not. At length, Tokai gave up the game and said, 'Now. This most interesting question of these supposed aliens. Who would have thought it? They say there

93

is a vast ship orbiting the world, and an alien itself is not a hundred miles away in Varanasi.'

Immediately, Anand made a gesture of negation. 'Nonsense. Nothing more than rumours and tricks.'

'Are you quite sure about that?'

'What else could it be?'

Tokai was not particularly interested in Anand's opinions, but he was intrigued to note that Anand did not like the idea of aliens at all. The prince's discomfort, relayed into pheromonal outlay, was being transmitted along the cane with some force. Perhaps it had something to do with Anand's outraged hierarchical certainties. Whatever the case, Tokai thought, it might prove useful.

To Amir Anand he said, 'Oh, but I think it is more than tricks and rumours. My old friend Vikram Singh, Minister of the Interior, has seen the alien with his own eyes. In the Temple of Durga, in Varanasi. It resembles a god, he tells me. It has four arms ... and who do you think was with it?' The question was entirely rhetorical. Unless Anand had spent the previous week in a darkened room with his head in a box, he could hardly have failed to take note of the multiple – and confusing – news announcements that had nonetheless managed to focus on one important fact.

Anand scowled, as if in preparation for hearing the name.

'Jayachanda Nihalani.' Tokai rolled the syllables on his tongue with some relish, as though they were a Cuban cigar. 'The little caste revolutionary. And not long after your failure to capture her at the hospital. What a pity, Anand. History, I've often thought, depends on so little – a chance meeting, a missed opportunity. If you'd taken Nihalani into custody as planned, who knows who'd be in receipt of otherworldly favours now?' He smiled. Anand gave him a wary glance, evidently sensing where the conversation was heading. 'Tell me again what happened at the hospital. There is a very big gap between being a fugitive lying sick in a bed one moment, and becoming the favoured representative of an alien people in the next. I would like to know what happened, in the day or so that Nihalani went missing.'

He listened carefully as Anand began to speak. The man was brutal, but brittle, and there were still alarming areas of weakness which would have to be corrected. Anand recounted his last confrontation with Jaya Nihalani with as much measured objectivity as he could muster, but Tokai could sense the rage beneath the words. It was hardly surprising. The whole Nihalani affair had been a chronicle of ineptitude: first a bloodbath at the ashram all those years ago, leaving Nihalani free to rally the masses and instigate a caste-based revolt; then redemption when Anand finally captured her a full ten years later, only to lose her again in a prison breakout . . .

The government of Bharat was fortunate that Tokai had offered his services in solving the problem, and even more fortunate that he specialized in ingenious solutions. The thought of the Selenge virus drifted into his mind, and Tokai smiled to himself: *that* had been an inspired solution, for example, in response to a much earlier crisis. Not without its drawbacks, of course – no biological weapon was perfect – but really Selenge had exceeded expectations.

Tokai said, lightly, 'So you would have no objections to – retrieving – Nihalani? Privately, this time, and without the hindrances placed in your way by unsympathetic government departments? A chance to redeem yourself?'

There was an electric pause, then Anand said, 'You mean I'd be working for you?'

After a very long time, during which he could smell the growing odour of Anand's sweat, Tokai answered, 'That's right. You'd be working for me. The thought bothers you, perhaps?'

'No, no, of course not,' Anand said hastily. 'Why should it?'

'No reason. Ironically, Nihalani is under the protection of the security forces at the moment, but I'll have a word with Vikram Singh. I'm sure I can convince him where his best interests lie. We're *very* old friends. After all,' Tokai smiled benevolently, 'it really is for the best, Anand. A treasured alien visitor in the hands of a terrorist? No, no, no. We'll be doing everyone a favour if we secure Nihalani and invite the alien to make full use of our resources. And if the being proves hostile, then I'm sure all concerned will agree that it is better off under my control than Nihalani's. And the powers of the Japanese axis would much rather involve India than the West.'

Of course they would, Tokai thought, watching Anand

narrowly. Heavy investment on the part of the Japanese axis entailed a degree of control over the subcontinent, whereas influencing America and the European Union would be an entirely different story. 'In recompense, I might be prepared to restore some of your fortunes to you.' He glanced around the shabbily ornate room, leaving no doubt as to his meaning. 'You'll want to marry that charming actress of yours, no doubt, and this really would be a delightful place to raise a family ... Go back to Varanasi, Anand. Find out what you can and get back to me. And then we will consider our options.'

He watched as the tall figure made its way through the overgrown gardens, pushing aside the roses. The butcher-prince left a drift of petals in his wake, red as spilled blood. Tokai watched until he was out of sight, then crossed to the phone and called Tokyo.

3.
RASASATRAN SYSTEM

Sirru was still ruffled by the time he reached the sprawl of black domed buildings that was the Moyshekhali temenos. It seemed that the temenos already had some idea of what had happened. Everyone was in the central chamber, all talking at once, and the house itself could be heard beneath the hubbub, trying ineffectually to calm its inhabitants down.

Sirru stepped through into a morass of /protest/doubt/

fulfilment/speculation./ Bad as Naturals, he thought. He clapped his hands around his throat and said plaintively, 'Quiet! *Please!* I can't feel myself think.'

'A new colony? Is it possible?' – this from Issari, his clade sister, always careful with epistemological niceties.

'Yes. More than possible; fact. We have a new *desqusai* colony, a planet named Tekhei. I am to go there, to manage it.'

'Tekhei has become active, then?'

'Apparently so.'

'This can only be a good thing,' Issari exulted, but a wave of doubt rustled around the chamber.

'More problems, you mean.'

'The *desqusai* are always the poor relations. Tekhei is worthless, surely. There's nothing there – a handful of minerals, a couple of seas . . .'

'Its people are *desqusai*,' Issari bristled. 'They are kin. We have an obligation to them, as to all our colonies. This is the way it has always been done.'

'We need to consolidate here in the inner systems, not out on the shores of the galaxy! And besides, look what happened to Sirru's poor friend. What about Arakrahali?'

That was the last thing Sirru wanted to discuss. 'We can debate the matter all we like,' he said, before the argument could get under way. 'But the *khaithoi* have decided that I go, and that is that. We'll just have to make the best of the matter and see how we can turn it to our advantage.'

'Why should the *khaithoi* be the ones who decide?' a

98

small, young voice cried from the back. The thought twinged painfully inside Sirru's neural cortex; his epistemic suppressants clamped down.

'Don't hurt us with heresy,' Issari snapped. 'Have you been missing your suppressants? Do you want the Prescriptors to pay you a visit and cost us a fortune?'

Sirru wondered, fleetingly, whether Tekhei might actually turn out to be more restful than home. The clade grumbled, but more as a matter of course than from any deep sense of violation. Tekhei was a *desqusai* world, after all, and project development was what the EsMoyshekhali had been designed to do. The family saw his new role as an honour; Sirru did not want to talk about Anarres, and he certainly did not want to mention the possibility that he was being dispatched to Tekhei to get him out of the way.

Once more, his thoughts returned to the tragedy of the Arakrahali colony. What had really happened? He leaned his head against the warm, pulsing wall of the temenos and closed his eyes. The irony was that he had learned very little about Arakrahali, despite all his investigations. On the face of it, EsRavesh had been entirely right: IrEthiverris had fouled things up. The denizens of Arakrahali had succumbed to a virulent and fatal disease, apparently spread through the new communications network. Most of IrEthiverris's own records had been lost, but his *khaith* administrator's dispatches had survived. Sirru had read them through a dozen times, and he still couldn't decide why they felt so wrong. The *khaith* had written clear,

99

succinct accounts, and her increasing frustration with IrEthiverris' mismanagement was palpable. Yet there was something that just didn't ring true about those reports . . .

It occurred to him then that perhaps the *khaith* had lied outright – but that thought hurt Sirru so much that he gasped. His head rang like a bell, and his neural distress triggered a surge of implanted suppressants. Then his serotonin levels balanced out, and he relaxed. It was nearly time for his next implant, but he wouldn't have time to see to that before he left. There would be facilities on the Tekhei depth ship; he'd just have to do it when he got there.

Patiently, Sirru sorted out the logistics of his absence and delegated tasks to various members of the clade. After some thought, he left the encoded documents relating to his Arakrahali investigation with his clade-sister Issari, with instructions that they were only to be opened if anything went wrong.

'You must have more confidence, Sirru,' Issari admonished him. 'What could possibly go wrong?'

'That's what IrEthiverris said. And look what happened to him. Keep the encoding in a safe place, and don't let anyone else near it.' He patted Issari on the shoulder. 'I'm relying on you.'

'I'll keep it safe,' she promised.

By the time Sirru had finished his preparations, the afternoon was already well advanced. He hurried up through the city, heading for the heights and Anarres.

It seemed that the *apsara*'s house had been reinstructed

for his presence, for it admitted him with only a ripple of protest. Anarres was once more sitting out on the balcony, overlooking the expanse of Khaikurriyë. Reinforced by the previous night's activities, her effect on Sirru was immediate and distracting.

'Anarres . . .' he whispered, trying to retain control of himself. 'Please . . . Not now.' The *apsara*'s arms were already around his neck; he nuzzled her throat. 'Listen to me. I'm leaving. I—'

But she murmured in his ear, 'I know. Word travels fast from the Core. Sirru'ei. I don't want you to go. Or I want to go with you.'

'I couldn't afford to take you, even if they let me,' Sirru said, mentally cursing the *khaithoi*. 'It's EsRavesh, isn't it?' He could smell the sour odour of her sudden distaste.

'EsRavesh has peculiar desires. And I told you – he wants exclusivity, to prove how powerful he is. I'm not going to give him that.' She undulated against Sirru until he was close to losing control.

'*Anarres*. Listen to me for a minute,' he managed to say. 'The posting will allow me to enhance my locative. I'll buy up my status once I get back from Tekhei. I'll help you dissolve your affiliations.' If EsRavesh didn't manage to sabotage his life first, he thought. He couldn't help adding, on every level: *I really like you* – and could have bitten his tongue. It sounded so juvenile.

'I like you too,' Anarres whispered. Then her hand slid beneath his robe, down to the ridges at the base of his

101

stomach and Sirru abandoned all attempts at rational analysis.

When he left her, Rasasatra's crimson sun was already sinking below the edge of the city and the air was filled with incense, pollen and dust. The red wind was blowing, bringing the scent of the distant desert with it. Sirru tried not to look back. He caught a transport barge at the EsKhattuyë dock and sat staring into solidifying air as the barge glided down through the ribbed seed-walls of the city, descending through the locks until they reached the quay for the landing ledge. From here, Sirru took a second barge to the ledge, then waited for the raft to float down like a hot coal.

He stepped on board. The raft checked the verification that he had been given by EsRavesh, and allowed Sirru to strap himself in. He was not the only passenger. The raft was full of outworkers returning to the depth ships: *khai-thoi* and *hessira*, folding their manifold limbs awkwardly into their mesh; *rhakin* disdainful of anyone who wasn't of their own caste. Sirru glanced around and saw that he was the only *desqusai* on board. The thought of being solitary, of leaving the temenos, was suddenly a frightening one, and he pushed it aside. He thought that he would rather not see his world fall away, so he closed his eyes, but just as the raft was about to break atmosphere he relented. Gazing through the transparent vane, he could see the whole of the city of Khaikurriyë, a continent wide, spreading below him. Lights spanned the world, defining the city, and the line of the coast showed him where the temenos lay. The protection of the scale prevented him from spreading dismay and loss throughout the raft, but he watched until Rasasatra fell behind, a dark sphere against the oceans of night.

Once Rasasatra had slipped away, however, the movement of the raft sent Sirru mercifully to sleep. He rocked in the mesh, listening to the raft murmuring to itself. The sound reminded him of the vine singing outside Anarres' window and he smiled, before he remembered that it was likely to be a very long time before he heard that particular song again. He should be preparing himself for translation, marshalling his emotional firewalls and trying to puzzle out exactly why he was being sent to Tekhei, but all he could think about was Anarres.

This had to happen now, Sirru thought, silently cursing his fate. His attraction to Anarres couldn't be just any old sexual arrangement, either; some inter-clade status-swapping or interpretative transaction. This was love.

Sirru sighed, trying to be philosophical.

He was also not especially happy about the prospect of whatever was waiting for him at the other end of the translation plate. Who could have thought that a little colony like Tekhei would ever amount to anything? It reminded him of one of those plants that languished at the end of the terrace, sulking in its pot, growing maybe a claw's length every year and then suddenly, just as you were about to lose patience and throw the thing into the recycler, putting forth some poky little blossom. Enough to give you hope that the thing might actually do some growing after all.

With a rising sense of disquiet, Sirru remembered IrEthiverris' first communication from the colony of Arakrahali . . .

. . . *all the locals are peculiarly charmless. Tiny little people with domed heads. Not one of them evinces even the slightest interest in their own project, they all say they're happy as they are. And the food is dreadful* . . . Then IrEthiverris had added, heretically, *If the Core wants these projects to be managed properly, they should have placed them under decent supervision from the start* . . .

But you'd never get that "decent supervision", Sirru thought, because the *khaithoi* never wanted to get their hands dirty. Or whatever they'd replaced hands with these days. He remembered with distaste EsRavesh's stubby digits pressed against his own, no more than buttons attached to a pad of flesh. Everyone knew perfectly well that the *khaithoi* had subsidiaries to do everything for them these days, so why bother with proper fingers? Pure affection. His head twinged. The suppressants must be wearing low. High time he got another implant.

He glanced through the vane. Stars shimmered and passed as the raft departed the Rasasatran system and steered itself towards the local depth ship, humming all the while. There was a brief, liquid shudder as the raft docked and the mesh dispersed. Wheezing with the sudden change of air, Sirru stepped through the airlock of the shuddering raft and into the labyrinthine bowels of the depth ship. Neurochemical drifts, keyed into his personal DNA, directed him to the translation chambers and he glided through the silent cells until he reached his destination.

The *hessirei* translator was waiting for him. It sat on its mat with its six attenuated arms undulating around it, as though caught in a wind that Sirru could not feel. It was making a series of complex adjustments to the equipment. Its eyes were like two hot coals, glowing in the smooth darkness of its face. As Sirru watched, it reached out with a prehensile foot and tapped the translation mesh, sending a jangling coil of chemicals out into the air. The air became stuffy and hot, thick with synthetic alkaloids. Sirru sat down opposite the *hessirei* and took a deep, slow breath.

/Verification./

Sirru delivered this and the *hessirei* affirmed him.

/Remove your robe. If you are wearing scale, please deactivate fully. Lie down./

Sirru did as he was instructed. He felt the mesh close around him; cool, slightly sticky, not unpleasant. His throat was dry with anticipation. In a few moments, he would lose consciousness. A billion fragments of data would be channelled through a quantum relay to the depth ship Eir Sithë, which currently orbited Tekhei.

The depth ship, Sirru thought, trying to take his mind off what was about to happen to him, must be very patient. It had been waiting for an administrator to come ever since a day several million years before, when the project engineers had returned home from their initiation of First Stage. Eir Sithë had been stationed outside the Tekhei system ever since, occasionally grazing off sunlight and whatever nutrients might come its way, using its light-veil to hide its presence from whoever might have the technology to glimpse it, but mostly sleeping.

Sirru's last thought, before his Second Body was reconstructed inside the translation chamber on Eir Sithë, was whether the ship would be pleased to see him.

4.
MUMBAI

One of the rebels, braver or more foolish than the rest, leaped onto the battlements of the ancient fort and brandished his weapon. The army commander, a brutal man in an eyepatch and a black uniform, gave the signal to close in, then took careful aim. A red fountain blossomed on the front of the revolutionary's shirt and he fell, twisting as he went. Across the compound, the rebel princess cursed. She checked the time bomb strapped to her wrist: *Thirty seconds*. One hand fumbled with the strap of the bomb as she sped across the compound, dodging a hail of bullets as she raced towards the enemy commander. Glossy dark hair spilled down her back as she ran. Her beautiful face was barely distorted with the effort, and as one man, the rebel troops behind her burst into a song which praised her valour. She was close enough to her enemy now to detach the bomb and fling it in his mocking face . . .

'Cut!'

The singing stopped, abruptly. The rebel princess skidded to a halt in the dust, ripped off the bomb and hurled it petulantly at her feet.

'What? What was wrong with that? You tell me!'

'Sorry, Kharishma; sorry, darlings. The light's still not right.'

'For fuck's sake.' Kharishma Kharim turned on her heel and strode from the set, ignoring her producer's protests. 'We've been here for nearly eight fucking hours. If your crew can't do their jobs properly, you'd better get someone who can. I shouldn't have to put up with this sort of incompetence.' She felt like adding, 'Without me, this picture would be nothing,' but that was already obvious and she had her dignity to think of.

Inside the trailer, she crossed to the mirror that hung above her dressing table and gazed anxiously at her own reflection. The vast, kohl-rimmed eyes, that could so convincingly brim with tears, made her look as mysterious as ever. And her fall of dark hair still reached her waist, still shone. Kharishma had once come across the term 'mahogany tresses' in an English romance, and she supposed that it might have been a bit corny, but it still seemed accurate, somehow. The heavy nanofilament makeup had transformed her skin into a mask and Kharishma checked its perfection with obsessive concentration, occasionally glancing at the photographs of herself that were pasted around the mirror, like a shrine. From the corner of her eye, reflected in the mirror, she could still see the crumpled up copy of *Screen* in the corner of the trailer, where she had hurled it that morning, missing the waste bin.

Word comes in from Mumbai that Kharishma Kharim – now taking a starring role as celebrated freedom fighter Jaya Nihalani in the new movie *Warrior Tigress* – celebrated her 29th birthday at the exclusive Ambar restaurant last week. We'd offer congratulations, but rumour has it that lovely Kharishma's now been 29 three times in a row. What's the secret, sweetie? Maybe screen goddesses really are like the real thing: they just don't get any older . . .

Bitch! Kharishma thought, not for the first time that morning. *What do I care what some dried-up old hag of a hack thinks?* But at the back of the thought, there was an edge of panic. After all, no one's looks lasted forever, and it was beginning to look as though Kharishma's ingénue days were long behind her. Still, if she had just one triumph in a character part, that might be enough to get her firmly established in the canon of deified screen idols. And Jaya Nihalani was certainly a plum role, now that the government had decided that its formerly most wanted terrorist had better be rehabilitated as quickly as possible.

And if the parts still continued to dry up – and if envious people who'd never got any further than the production staff continued to spread that idiotic rumour that Kharishma was 'difficult' – well, she'd just take her talents into other areas. After all, the state of Tamil Nadu had had superstar Ramachandran as their chief minister for years, and look what happened when he died. People had cut their own arms off in mourning. And look at his wife and mistress. Both had been *revered,* and neither of them could have held a candle to Kharishma Kharim. It had been the same thing in Karnataka five years ago. So why shouldn't she capitalize on her talents and go into politics? After all, she ought to be running something. India needed her.

When Kharishma had finished adjusting her makeup, her gaze strayed past the piles of movie magazines down to the fuzzy photograph of Jaya Nihalani that sat on her dressing table. Jaya wore a bandanna around her hair, and her haggard face was lined with pain and despair. It must have been taken shortly after her surrender. Her shoulders were unnaturally rigid and her jaw was lifted, as though her arms were pinned behind her back. She was surrounded by guards, who towered over her tiny frame. Kharishma spent a long, blank moment staring at the now-familiar photograph and then she looked back at the mirror with a brief grimace of satisfaction. *At least I look better than her.*

The door of the trailer swung open. Pale blue eyes met her own in the mirror. Hastily, in a reflex action, Kharishma turned the photo face-down. Jaya Nihalani's picture wasn't something that Amir Anand liked to see. He had even forbidden Kharishma to take the role, but she'd got her own way in the end. She usually did.

'Amir! I didn't think you were coming.' With a smile of welcome, she hopped across the trailer and threw herself into her lover's arms. Amir's arms tightened about her and he rested his cheek against her hair. He murmured, 'I've been sent back here. To do something that I think will make you very happy.'

Kharishma twisted around to look into his face, thinking, as she always did, how handsome he was. It really was a true romance, like a fairy story.

'What?'

'To find Jaya Nihalani. And to kill her. But this time, without anything to stand in my way. No capture, no taking her back to prison. Just death. It'll have to look like an accident, of course.'

Rising from his lap, Kharishma went to the window of the trailer and lifted the net curtain aside, peering out at the glaring day. She bit her lip, thinking back to the photograph that sat on the dressing table. And that turned her thoughts back to her latest obsession: power.

She remembered her mother sitting before her and telling her that their family should have been the ones destined to rule. Not the Ghandis, not the Parbutans, but the Kharims. She had heard the story countless times: how her mother's kin were cheated out of their rightful heritage by her great-grandfather's scheming brother. How, if it hadn't been for the sudden loss of their wealth, her grandfather would have been elected President of Bharat, and how it had surely been this shock that had killed him. Kharishma could have been the inheritor of a mantle of dynastic power; instead, she was up there on the movie screen, and something about this had never seemed quite right. She was made for wider audiences and greater adulation than she'd ever receive from Bollywood. She glanced wistfully at Amir Anand, another disinherited princeling.

Don't worry, my darling, Kharishma thought, *one day we'll both regain what's rightfully ours*. Deep in her heart, Kharishma had never quite managed to dislodge a fundamental belief in the precepts of her religion: *Good against evil, justice against injustice*. Kharishma knew, too, how the minds of her audience worked. When the *Ramayana* had been filmed, many years ago now, people in the villages had erected shrines to the actors who played the gods, insisting on the belief that some element of divinity remained with them.

Jaya had been popular among the country folk. Once they saw Kharishma on the screen in this new role, and once Jaya was out of the way, then Jaya's legend would become Kharishma's own.

She did not hear Anand move, but suddenly he was behind her and his arms were around her ribs. He squeezed just a little too tight, hurting her breasts, and for a moment she found herself fighting for breath. She knew he adored her, but sometimes his devotion frightened her, just a little. He murmured into her ear, 'You know I'd do anything for you, Kharishma,' and released her so abruptly that the air flooding into her lungs made her dizzy, turning the bright scene outside into a negative image of itself, like a shadow that crosses the sun.

5.
VARANASI

It was as though Jaya stood outside her body, watching once more as the events of her life unravelled. She saw the fortress vanishing in the smoke from the shells; the troops moving in. Then Amir Anand standing tall in the front of a jeep, his pale gaze searching for her. She saw Kamal's round face, looking surprised as the first bullet hit and he spun, falling from the rocky ledge down into the cold waters of the Yamuna. Even in death he looked worried.

The horror of the moment was still cold inside her, like a lump of ice that would never melt. Jaya watched herself start up from the hiding place, mouth open to cry Kamal's name, then Rakh pulled her down out of sight. She watched herself fire and reload, fire and reload; mouth in a tight numb line, no time even to mourn. Now, she wondered how she could have done such a thing, how she could have been so cold as to just keep on going. Her heart felt as tight and hard as a clenched fist. Her hands were clammy with the memory.

That morning, Kamal had been alive; he had even brought her *chai* in an old metal army cup balanced on a battered tray, as though she were a princess being brought breakfast in bed. And the next day, he was dead. Simply not there any more. The transition still made her dizzy, as though she couldn't grasp how it had happened.

If these aliens have the power to do anything – anything at all – then maybe I'd forget all the noble causes and the struggle and everything, and just go back and live in a hut with a little garden, just Kamal and me in the middle of nowhere. In the mountains, maybe, with the hawks and the silence. Kamal had never wanted to be a revolutionary, but he had hated the unfairness of things, and she was the same, even though she sometimes wondered whether that was really true.

It never was about power, or glory, or sacrifice, she told herself. *It was just about trying to secure a reasonable life for everyone. Giving them something to believe in.* But Kamal had died anyway.

She saw herself helping carry Kamal to his resting place at the lake on the glacier's edge, and then the tattered remnants of her army creeping up into the barren heights to lick their wounds. And as silent and bodiless as a ghost, Jaya watched herself walk back down, to pick her way between the dead and surrender to Anand's troops, in return for the lives of the captured . . .

She woke with a start. Her heart was pounding erratically against her ribs. The darkness swam with lights, as though a fire blazed above her head. It took her a moment to realize that her eyes were filled with tears, and that the illusory flames were Ir Yth's golden gaze.

/People are here,/ the *raksasa* said with manifest disapproval.

'What people?' Jaya's head felt muzzy with the sadness of her dream. 'Do you mean my men?'

/It is difficult to tell you apart,/ Ir Yth said, pursing her petalled lips. /But I am certain. These are not your assistants. I believe they are carrying some kind of weapon./

Now Jaya was fully awake. She scrambled to her feet, hissing, 'Where are they?'

/In the courtyard. They came over the wall. There are four of them, perhaps more. Why did your assistants not intercept them?/

'I don't know, Ir Yth. Show me.'

With a sound like a sniff, Ir Yth's incorporeal form drifted towards the door. Jaya followed, sidling along the wall until they reached the balustrade that overlooked the courtyard. At first she could see nothing, then the faintest glimmer of movement drew her attention. Someone was standing over by the gate. She could see into the gatehouse, and there was no sign of Rakh. Jaya swallowed a cold lump in her throat.

The person at the gate glided forward. Jaya's hand slid towards the gun at her hip, and then she was picked up and carried backwards. A hand like a paw was rammed against her mouth. She struggled and kicked out, as hard as she could. Rakh's voice whispered, 'Sorry. But there are too many of them. We can't risk a firefight.'

'Who are they?'

Imperceptibly, Rakh shook his head. 'I don't know. Anand's men, at a guess.'

'I thought we were supposed to be under governmental protection!' *So much for that*, Jaya thought. She'd never believed it in the first place.

'Best that we leave,' Rakh murmured and Jaya suppressed a rueful grin. He'd certainly changed; years ago, his brother had been the cautious one.

'Agreed.' The temple was no more than a convenient shell; all their advantages now lay on the ship orbiting hundreds of miles above their heads. It gave Jaya a curious sense of security.

'What's the best way out?' she whispered.

'I'd say the cellars – there's a concealed door beneath the stairs – but they're already in the hallway. We'll have to go over the wall.'

Jaya nodded. 'All right. Let's get going.' Rakh's hand gripped her arm, helping her up the steps that led to the gallery. As they reached the balustrade, Jaya peered cautiously around the side of a column. She could hear voices below: a susurrus of sound amplified by the echoing halls of the temple. Directly beneath her, the shrine of the goddess Durga glittered on its metal plinth. Jaya found herself murmuring a prayer: for fierceness, for safe flight. Fleetingly, she wished she had a tiger to ride, like the goddess.

Rakh pulled her on.

/*Where are you going?*/ Ir Yth asked petulantly, gliding behind.

Hastily, Jaya whispered, 'I think these people mean us harm. We're leaving.'

/*But where to?*/ the *raksasa* demanded.

'Anywhere but here.'

/*I do not wish to accompany you. This is a great inconvenience! I have duties in my solid form; I can spare little attention at this moment.*/

'Well, don't come, then,' Jaya snapped under her breath. It felt good to stop kowtowing to this condescending creature. 'It's all very well for you. You're not even really here, so I don't see why it's so inconvenient. I'm in contact with the ship, aren't I? And I can't stand here arguing.' Urgency nagged her like a kite tugging a string.

/*It is true that if you go wandering off, the ship will locate you,*/ the *raksasa* admitted grudgingly.

'Then what the hell's the problem?' The only difficulty, Jaya was sure, was that this did not fit in with Ir Yth's plans and the *raksasa* therefore resented the loss of control. 'I suggest you return to your solid form on the ship,' she added. 'We'll make our own way out. And if the ship can do anything to help us, I suggest it does so.' Turning her back on Ir Yth, she followed a fidgeting Rakh to the doors that led out onto the courtyard balustrade. She glanced back once. The *raksasa* had gone.

Outside in the murmuring shadows, Shiv Sakai was waiting with a rope and a harness. 'The others are down already. Put this on. Rakhi and I will lower you.'

Jaya slid her arms into the harness and froze. There were voices in the courtyard below: soldiers were fanning

116

out into the courtyard. She recognized the khaki uniforms, and it came as no surprise. *Anand's men*. Along the balustrade, no more than a few yards away, one of the yellow monkeys gave a demonic shriek and leaped onto the stone coping. Gunfire stitched the balustrade. Jaya threw herself flat as a ricocheting bullet whined overhead.

From below she heard someone shout, 'What the fuck do you think you're *doing*?' It was Amir Anand. Again, no surprises there. But there was a raw edge of panic in Anand's voice that she did not recall ever hearing before. Beside her, Rakh hissed, '*Go*.' He hoisted her up to the narrow slit of a window, so that she was suddenly perched high above the street. She could see movement in the shadows, the glint of a gun at the end of the road where a soldier stood. The street was still cordoned off. Was Anand acting on his own initiative, then? Jaya swore under her breath.

'Ready?' – but then Rakh spun around. There was an electric flurry of noise from the temple courtyard: a burst of gunfire, Anand crying out, the sound of running footsteps. Jaya glanced back from her perch on the window sill to see the robed figure of Ir Yth gliding soundlessly across the courtyard. There was the hiss of a dart gun. Anand's men sprinted forwards with a net and cast it over the gliding figure. The net passed through Ir Yth's ghostly form and fell harmlessly to the ground.

Jaya felt Rakh's hands around her waist, passing her through the window. She spun above the street, like a parcel in a spider's web. Then the rope was lowering and

within a few seconds she was in the hands of Sokash and
Ajit, being helped down onto the street. Minutes later,
Shiv and Rakh joined her.

Abandoning the rope, they melted around the sides of
the temple to the place where the army cordon was least
guarded. From behind, there were shouts. Jaya glanced
back to see a familiar stout figure sailing past the main
gate as lightly as a leaf on the wind. Soldiers' feet pounded
over the dusty earth, but Jaya and her men slid between
the tailgates of the vehicles and into the maze of streets
that surrounded the temple. Ten minutes later, they were
out onto the ghats by the gleam of the river.

'Now where?' Jaya asked, panting against the warm
wall of the ghat. The night seemed to close around her like
a glove. Shiv Sakai's teeth glimmered in the soft darkness.

'I was thinking we'd borrow a boat.'

'Good idea.' Jaya rubbed gritty eyes. 'But they'll probably be looking for that. Here's what we'll do. Rakh comes
with me, up into Goudalia. Shiv, you and the others cross
the river, and—'

/That will not be necessary,/ the *raksasa's* voice said
inside Jaya's mind. Jaya looked up to see Ir Yth floating
several feet above the surface of the Ganges. /I have
distracted your pursuers./

'Thank you,' Jaya breathed.

The *raksasa* made a dismissive gesture with a lower
arm. /It was a simple matter. But it is clear to me that we
cannot continue with this sort of distraction. We must put
you where you will be safe./

'That might be tricky.'

/Not at all. You will come here to the ship. I am dispatching a raft,/ the *raksasa* said. She seemed to be looking down at something that Jaya could not see. Reaching out a hand, she turned an invisible dial, ran fingers across the air. A hard, tight bolt of fright twisted Jaya's stomach. The thought of actually visiting the ship, the originator of the voice, both exhilarated and terrified her.

She turned her face away so that Ir Yth could not see her expression, determined not to let the *raksasa* know how scared she was. There was a sudden flurry of wings from the towers of the ruin behind her, and a flock of crows and parakeets whirled up into the darkness. High above Varanasi, something glittered, like light reflecting from a window in the distance.

'What's that?' Jaya whispered, but she already knew.

/It is the raft./

They watched in a tense silence as the raft drifted down. It did not seem to have any definable shape. Four immense vanes shifted and coiled, and within them something was twisting. As it floated down, Jaya saw that the vanes were transparent, but they glittered in the light and filaments ran across them, red as blood. Jaya instinctively ducked, but as the raft settled above the river it suddenly retracted its vanes and sank, light as air, to the edge of the ghat. It was perhaps the size of a large car. She heard someone gasp.

'I'm going up in *that*?' Jaya asked, alarmed.

/Unless you propose to fly,/ the *raksasa* said, with the

119

first flicker of anything approaching humour that Jaya had yet to see.

'What about my men? It's not large enough for all of us, and there's no way I'm leaving them behind.'

/You will have to,/ the raksasa said, impatiently. /You are the Receiver; no other is designated./

'Then I'm not going. I won't let them face Anand alone. I—'

'Jaya,' Rakh said, from behind. He touched her arm. 'Go. Go to where you'll be safe. We've been looking after ourselves for long enough.'

But will I be safe? Jaya thought, with deep unease. What if all of this is no more than another lie? But then why go to all this trouble? If Ir Yth had wanted her for some dark purpose, why not simply take her?

'Rakhi's right,' Shiv Sakai added. 'You're our best chance, Jaya.'

/Touch it,/ the raksasa said.

Jaya put out her twisted fingers and tentatively rested them on the glistening side of the raft. It felt warm and soft, like flesh in the sun. It pulsed beneath her palm.

'It's as though it's alive,' Jaya said uncertainly.

/It is between,/ Ir Yth informed her, with maddening smugness.

'How do I get in?'

/Touch it./

With a doubtful glance, Jaya stroked the side of the raft and a slit opened up. It looked disconcertingly animate.

'Am I doing this right?' She ran a finger along the slit.

Something about this felt very wrong, but the slit widened, and with a noise like a seed pod the raft opened up. Inside was a complex wet webbing. It smelled like an overripe melon.

/Settle yourself within./

'Wait a minute,' Jaya said.

/There is no more time. They are looking for you, the ones from the temple – the ship tells me this. You have no choice,/ Ir Yth said, and there was something like a hot clutch inside Jaya's mind. Her vision swam momentarily red. She felt herself tottering forwards to step over the lip of the raft.

She heard Shiv cry, 'Jeete rahon, Jaya!' in traditional farewell. Keep living. It seemed all too appropriate. Still moved by a force that she could not repel, she sat down, wondering if this was going to be the last thing she ever did. She glanced frantically up at Rakh's dismayed face, but then the webbing folded itself around her. Jaya tried very hard not to think of spiders. Grimly, she shut her eyes. The webbing seeped over her mouth, forcing it apart. Surrender did not come easily. There was a bitter taste in her mouth, like ash or aloes, and then a numbness. It was putting her to sleep. Panic finally overtook her. She started to struggle. It was, of course, much too late. The raft sealed with a sound like someone splitting a watermelon and Jaya fell into the depths of night.

6.
DEPTH SHIP, ORBIT: EARTH

When Jaya woke, she was somewhere dim and empty and quiet. She blinked, feeling an unaccustomed euphoria spreading through her. She rolled over, unimpeded, and sat up. She felt strange – light and mobile – and only when she looked down at her hands did she realize what had happened. Her hands were young again, the skin dark and smooth, with a slightly unnatural texture like plastic. The garnet of her mother's ring gleamed in the faint light.

Jaya stared down at her healed self, incredulous and strangely dismayed. Then relief flooded through her, so suddenly that tears sprang to her eyes. *Cured.* Ir Yth had told her that she would be healed, but the *raksasa* was so slippery she hadn't dared believe it. And if they could cure her with such apparent ease, then surely they could cure other sufferers, of diseases such as cancer. Or Selenge.

She reached up wonderingly and touched her face. No lines, no wrinkles; just skin stretched over angular bones. She could see something pale out of the corner of her eye and when she touched it she saw that it was her own hair. It had changed, falling in a long white skein down her back. The texture was as fine as silk, but it seemed that whoever had cured her had mistaken its paleness for her natural colour. She was barefoot, and wearing the same camouflage trousers and vest that she had worn in the temple. She was dying for a cigarette. Maybe they could cure that, too.

The thought of being inadvertently forced to give up smoking was an alarming one. The floor was as smooth as her own new skin. She reached out to run her hand along it and the floor rumpled and arched beneath her touch. She snatched her hand away. *Not alive; between.* She was on an alien ship, high above the Earth. Her brain couldn't take it in; it was surely nothing but a dream . . .

Abruptly, Jaya stood up, stretching with the pleasure of painlessness. But it was more than just the absence of pain. She reached down, legs straight, palms flat on the floor. Then she sat back down and slipped a foot onto either thigh. Full lotus; effortless. She arched back, her arms flat behind her head and her knees resting on the floor, and laughed for pure pleasure.

Ir Yth hadn't just cured her. The *raksasa* seemed to have turned her into a yoga master as well. A whole new body. She had never believed it would be possible to feel like this, and if Ir Yth had drifted in at that moment, Jaya would have hugged her. *Let's hope it lasts.*

At that thought, she sat swiftly up again. Memory flooded back, accompanied by urgency. What about Rakh and her men? Had they melted away to safety while she floated up into the heavens like Sita in Rama's chariot? She had to find out.

'Ir Yth?' Jaya asked, experimentally, but there was no reply. The room curved above her; pale and dappled like the skin of a sacred cow. It smelt of nothing. Then the wall opened and the *raksasa* was there. Jaya scrambled to her feet. This time, the *raksasa* was solid. Now that she was no longer merely a simulation, Jaya could see that Ir Yth's skin had more texture. It looked glistening and hard. The petalled interior of her mouth was wet. Jaya could smell her, too: a mustiness like decayed spice, overlaid by a complexity of unfamiliar odours.

/*You are pleased? The modifications are acceptable?*/ Ir Yth asked. The scent of spice deepened.

'Thank you. Yes, yes they are. Thank you very much,' Jaya said, sincerely. She wanted to ask about the wider implications of the cure, and about her men, but Ir Yth continued, /*The mediator has contacted me. He was most concerned with the risk to your safety.*/

'That was very kind. When am I to meet the mediator?'

/*Soon. Do you require food? It is here.*/ The *raksasa* caressed the wall and something like a spout appeared. Jaya watched warily as a viscous drop of something dewy appeared at the end.

/*Nutrients.*/

The tempting vision of a glass of tea swam before Jaya's inner eye. *Samosas. Brinjal pickle, chapatis. Goddess, I'm hungry.* But the viscous drop smelled strong and strange, dispelling appetite.

'I don't want any food at the moment. But thank you. Listen, Ir Yth, is there a way of communicating with my men? With the one called Rakh?'

/Rakh is not a Receiver,/ Ir Yth said, severely. /You are safe. That is all that matters./

'It is not all that matters! There was danger. I have to know what happened to them, whether they are safe, too.'

/Why? Can they not look after themselves?/

'They're my *friends*. I'm worried about them.' She ran a distracted hand through her new hair.

/I will ask the ship if a search might be made. Perhaps you might speak to the ship, too. And now I will show you your world,/ Ir Yth said, with the air of one about to bestow a great favour. Jaya sighed with frustration. She was truly grateful for the cure. If only the *raksasa* were not so condescending . . . But Westerners were the same, always expecting you to exclaim over marvels that were to them mundane.

She followed Ir Yth through the wall and into a maze of cell-like chambers, trying to note where they were going. There were no corridors, and no windows until the *raksasa* paused and fluted a command. Then a whole expanse of mottled skin peeled away and there was Earth, disorientingly vast, looking as it did in all the photographs Jaya had ever seen. There seemed to be nothing between herself and space; she stepped back with a gasp. Ir Yth was watching her expectantly. Evidently some further response was called for.

'Wonderful,' Jaya said, feeling completely inadequate. She noticed that the *raksasa*'s attention had been distracted. Ir Yth was staring beyond her shoulder. Jaya turned. Someone had entered the chamber.

The person was tall, and wore a long, pale robe. After a moment of confusion, Jaya identified him as male. He was glancing absently at the planet below, and at first sight he appeared far more human than Ir Yth. Only two arms, for a start. His face was cast into shadow; the angles of bone and brow were initially familiar. Then the light shifted and changed and Jaya saw that the newcomer had a pointed face that was the same dappled colour as the ship's skin. He had molten eyes with a vertical pupil, and a shock of what initially appeared to be hair, which Jaya then realized were hundreds of thin quills held back with a band. A narrow mouth, more or less human, lay beneath a bladed nose not unlike a beak. The quills lifted slightly and rattled.

The newcomer said something to Ir Yth, and as he did so, Jaya was washed with a wave of conflicting emotions: /surprise/enquiry/concern/ and several more that she couldn't even identify, but which sent shivers of contradictory impulses across her skin. Why couldn't she sense Ir Yth like this? Before she knew what she was doing, Jaya wrapped her arms around herself. This, she realized, must be the mediator.

Ir Yth inclined her head in what could almost have been a bow. The mediator stared at her, and Jaya thought he looked puzzled. But it was hard to read the alien features; very probably she was wrong.

/The mediator will communicate his wishes through me,/ the raksasa said. /I have explained to you that he is of a lower caste than myself; he does not have my speech capacities. Until you develop a mutually satisfactory *means of communication, I will interpret your responses to him./*

'Please tell the mediator I am honoured to meet him,' Jaya answered, feeling unsure of herself. Ir Yth seemed perfectly capable of mediating, so why had this person been brought in? She called on her jackal senses, looking for clues. But though she was adept at assessing a possible enemy, this unhuman person eluded her. A sense of welcome rippled through her as the *raksasa* translated. They seemed to communicate through mood, through emotion, and Jaya wondered just what she might be conveying to the mediator. An unhelpful mix of fear, distrust and fascination could be surging towards him even as the thought occurred to her.

She had not noticed this phenomenon with the *raksasa*, but then, until now she and Ir Yth had never been physically present together in the same place. Just how far did Ir Yth's 'speech capacities' extend? She seemed able to place statements in Jaya's mind, but not to read the complexities of Jaya's own thoughts. If they communicated through mood, Jaya wondered whether her own speech might be too primitive and confused for Ir Yth to grasp correctly. If that was so, then she might be able to use it to her own advantage.

She did not want to dwell on this idea in the *raksasa*'s presence, just in case. A possible answer came: *meditate.* Jaya took a deep breath, reached inside, imagined prana gliding up her spine. Her heart rate slowed, obedient as a yogi's. She thought: *If only I'd had this body, back in the revolution. Imagine not being weak, not getting sick all the time.* And she had a moment of pure and irrational regret, that Kamal would never be able to see her new hair.

/*The mediator said that he is delighted to see you well,*/ Ir Yth conveyed.

'Please thank him very much for curing me.'

She was lapped in a bath of positive feelings; feedback took a hold. Suddenly Jaya liked the mediator very much. She wanted to know more about him, become his friend. *Hang on. What's happening to me?* She wondered whether the mediator was deliberately influencing her in some way and risked a glance. The golden eyes were round and mild, with nothing of the predator in them.

'Please forgive me,' she said, truthfully. 'I know nothing of your customs. I do not know what is considered polite and what is not. I do not wish to offend you.'

The mediator spoke. Subtle, many-layered feelings slid over Jaya. Ir Yth replied, /*The mediator understands. Allowances must be made, on your part as well as his. He wishes you well. You are both* desqusai, *after all.*/

'We're both what? I'm sorry, I don't understand.' The sense of the word as it came to Jaya's mind was: *category/ caste/level/position/obligation.*

/*Desqusai,*/ the *raksasa* said, with a touch of impatience. /*You are the same.*/

Jaya looked at the quills, the yellow gaze, the pale, hard skin. 'I don't think we're the *same,* somehow.'

/*I suppose I cannot expect you to understand even elementary concepts of resemblance,*/ Ir Yth said, with

128

evident frustration. /*You share the same originator gene-strand, which is what makes you both* desqusai./ She glanced at Jaya's blank face and gave an exasperated hiss. /*Oh, never mind.*/

After a long pause, Jaya asked, 'What is his name?'

/*We do not have random names, as you do. The closest term that you have is: 'address'. We call it a locative. The mediator's current full locative is Sirrubennin Es-Moyshekhal írRas SeTekhei.*/

The expression on Jaya's face must have been obvious even to the *raksasa*, for Ir Yth hastily added, /*I have explained your methods of identification and the use of the contracted diminutive. He says you can call him Sirru.*/

'Then perhaps he could call me Jaya,' Jaya said. Sirru was staring at her with an expression she could not interpret. Curiosity? Concern? The smooth angles of his face gave nothing away. He said, testing it, 'Jaya.' Aloud, just as she did. He had a soft, sibilant voice.

Ir Yth interrupted. /*He says: if you do not have a locative, perhaps you could indicate where you are from?*/

Jaya pointed to the no-space between herself and the world.

'Can he see? There is Bharat.'

Sirru ducked to follow the line of her pointing finger, and murmured, 'Bhara'th.' Then, carefully, 'EsAyachantha IrNihalani IrBhara'th.' The words slurred and shifted in the soft alien voice; it was a moment before she recognized her own name.

'Do you think,' she asked Ir Yth, 'that I might try to

129

learn your language?' Somehow, she did not much like the thought of doing all the talking through Ir Yth.

The *raksasa*'s mouth convoluted in an expression that Jaya had come to recognize as disapproval. /*You could not. We do not communicate like you. Something is amiss with the basic speech structure of your people; you have only verbal tones. It would be impossible.*/ Here Ir Yth glanced warily at the mediator, but Sirru gave no impression of having understood or, indeed, heard.

'So why can I hear your voice in my head, but not his?'

/*We have innumerable means of communication – verbal, pheromonal, transmitted, to name but three examples. I feel that this is why you so frequently fail to understand what I am trying to tell you. I can do this because, as I have endeavoured to explain, my caste is more adept at higher levels of communication than Sirru's and your own, and I might add that I have to do quite a lot of work before you even appear to hear me. You, in turn, are not capable of communicating properly with Sirru, since, as I have just told you, something is wrong with your speech structures.*/

'I thought you said Sirru and I were the same,' Jaya countered.

/*The same, yes, but you occupy different levels of category. All desqusai are primitive, particularly those from the colonies.*/

Ir Yth appeared dangerously close to annoyance. Jaya thought with sudden suspicion: *Is it just that you're tired of trying to make yourself understood to an obtuse primitive, or is it that you don't want us to communicate without you? You say that Sirru is the mediator and yet the only one who seems to be doing any mediation is you. What are you hiding, Ir Yth EsTekhei?*

Sirru turned and said something to Ir Yth, but the *raksasa* did not translate. Jaya saw the mediator's golden eyes narrow briefly, and wondered whether this meant the same thing as it would in a human. Did Sirru distrust Ir Yth? And if so, why? Jaya was adrift in a sea of speculation, but suddenly her new, improved body felt too weary to remain standing.

'Ir Yth—' she started to say, but it was Sirru who stepped forward and caught her before she fell.

Jaya was taken to a small chamber and encouraged to lie down in a net. It encased her like a hammock. Filaments ran along her skin and she could feel a prickling sensation along her left calf as something slipped beneath the skin. Soon everything was light and pleasant, cocooned against an unimaginable reality. She looked up and saw that Sirru was standing by the side of the net.

'Jaya.' Then something else: a slurring, lisping, clicking that she could not even differentiate into words. Perhaps there were no words there. She felt Sirru's cool hand touching her wrist. She realized for the first time that the *raksasa* had never laid even a rudimentary finger on her. Ir Yth's manifestation on Earth had done so, but since Jaya arrived on the ship, the *raksasa* had kept her distance.

Consideration? Unlikely, given the character of Ir Yth. If they communicated through emotions, perhaps Ir Yth had something to hide . . .

But Sirru was touching her now, and she did not know whether the reassurance she felt was a result of the drugs or of his hand on her wrist. She gazed up at him trustingly, despite herself, and his expression did not change as he looked gravely down at her, and sent her into sleep.

7.
KHOKANDRA PALACE, UTTAR PRADESH

Naran Tokai brushed the sensory cane against the fallen petals of the roses, experiencing sweetness. He took a few halting steps across to the stone seat, flanked by ornamental lions, and sank back against sun-warm marble. Turning, he placed the computer scroll on the seat and activated the screen. Memory fluid seeped out across the stone, settling into its familiar pyramidal configuration. Tokai stroked a forefinger across the base of the screen, summoning the Web. He watched as the Han Seng closing index rolled down the screen: shares in Tokai Pharmaceuticals were rising. Tokai permitted himself a small smile of self congratulation, then checked his personal mail.

The Indian headquarters of Tokai Pharmaceuticals were based in Delhi, but there had been factories across the subcontinent for some years now, manufacturing a wide range of medical products. Turnover from the Indian division was now running at some $400 million per annum, a fraction of the wider profits. With methodical patience, Tokai ran through the more minor aspects of the operation before returning to the R & D divisions. He summoned up the hierarchies until he reached the file marked 'Hive'. Taking the little sliver of the pen, he inscribed the character for 'Creation', and his personal password: a thumbprint of his own pheromonal signature, to deter hackers. A sequence of results rolled up. Tokai took his phone from the pocket of his austere jacket and dialled.

'Sir?'

'I see we have finally had a happy result.' *Finally*, Tokai thought with distaste, *was the right word*. After yet another debacle involving Jaya Nihalani and Anand, and the apparent disappearance of the alien, he needed some good fortune for a change. Anand's failure was still sour in his mouth, although there was, he supposed, some balm in the fact that the government of Bharat did not seem to know where the alien was either. Nor did anyone else.

'The results came through this morning. Of course, we're all thrilled.' Doctor Jamahl's whispery little voice was high with excitement.

'So you should be, my dear. Do you have a release date for me?'

'July 31st.'

'I see. Not soon enough. I've been speaking to my old friend Minister Singh this morning. I understand there's unrest in the south of the province; he's looking for results. I took the liberty of reassuring him that we'd have something helpful for him very soon.'

'We still need further tests . . .' the doctor fluttered. 'I don't think—'

'Bring the release date forward. Let's keep our customers happy. After all, they do make your life and mine very much easier, don't they? And Minister Singh assures me that as long as there isn't too much collateral damage, he'll be entirely satisfied. Please keep me informed.'

Before the doctor could protest, Tokai hung up. He sat among the roses, their odour seeping into his brain with narcotic insidiousness. What was that Western expression? Something about killing two birds with one stone . . . Jaya Nihalani might have escaped the first round of Selenge, but perhaps she'd succumb to this new, improved variety. That, Tokai thought, would be a very satisfying implementation of resources.

8.

DEPTH SHIP, ORBIT: EARTH

It's like the hospital all over again, Jaya thought, pacing restlessly up and down the small chamber. She had not seen either of the aliens for the past day, and the ship's voice inside her head had fallen silent. Was it all a trick, then? She turned, striking her fist against the wall.

'Ir Yth! Are you there? Can you hear me?' There was

134

no reply. 'I won't be caged like this!' She was growing used to her new body: to the novelty of lithe movement and a prowl instead of a limp, and she wanted out of this small enclosed space. Then the wall peeled back and Ir Yth bustled through.

/You are making a noise!/

'Why am I being shut up like this?'

/We do not wish you to damage yourself./

'How would that happen? You cured me, didn't you?' Jaya put out a hand and touched the *raksasa* lightly on one of her chitinous arms. 'Ir Yth, it isn't that I'm not grateful. But I don't like being cooped up. If there are areas of the ship that are dangerous, then tell me so, and I'll avoid them. I don't want to damage myself any more than you do.'

Ir Yth seemed to bristle. /You are most obstreperous!/

'What are you – my *ayah*?'

The *raksasa* stared at her blankly. /It is for your own good. I do not intend—/

But at that point, Sirru stepped enquiringly through the opening in the wall.

'Sirru,' Jaya said, warmly. Stepping past the *raksasa*, she smiled up at the alien administrator. She pointed to the wall, and did her best to look questioning. Sirru said something mildly to Ir Yth, who responded with a cross chittering sound and a glare of annoyance. Jaya did not wait to see what the result of their debate might be. She headed quickly for the hole in the wall, and out into the ship.

Sirru followed. He made no attempt to interfere with her exploration, only seemed curious to know what she was doing. It could not really be called exploring, though, for however hard Jaya tried, she was unable to keep track of her wanderings. The ship changed constantly, its fluid interior shifting and altering. Somehow, she seemed to know where her own little cell was located, as though she had gained some sixth sense: the labyrinth leading Ariadne. The ship also smelled strange, emitting odours as though each cell was coded, but her sense of smell – though sharper than it had been before – still wasn't good enough for her to be able to find her way.

After a while, the murmur in her head returned. The ship began to guide her, steering her through the maze of passages with a sequence of strong, strange impressions – a mixture of hallucination and déjà vu. She tried to speak to the ship, to ask about Rakh and the others, but the ship merely sang to itself inside her mind: a contented refrain. They had been apart and now they were together. She was where she belonged and nothing else was of importance.

No matter how hard she tried, Jaya was unable to convince it to contact the world below, to find out what had become of her men, and the worry was starting to eat away at her like a sore. Sirru trailed behind her, smiling benevolently and saying nothing that she could discern. Eventually, she found herself back at the cell again. The ship was concerned, and wanted her to rest. Reluctantly, she settled herself against the wall, within the cradle of the sleeping mesh. When she awoke, the wall remained open.

A day after her arrival on the ship, Jaya's menstrual cycle began again. It had been absent for years, and she greeted its troublesome appearance with annoyance and relief. Despite her condescending stance, the *raksasa* seemed to know relatively little about human biology, a fact which Jaya stored carefully away. Ir Yth, after much explanation on Jaya's part, supplied water to wash with.

It did not take long for her to realize that her courses could also be useful. On her next foray into the ship, she marked the walls that she passed with a thin smear of blood, starting with the wall of her own cell and moving out from there. She planned to make an inventory of the ship, to trace its central point of function, but when she got back to her cell, she found to her frustration that the blood had gone, as though the wall had absorbed it. She smacked the wall in fury, but her hand simply glanced off its smooth, warm surface and the air around her became soothing and bland. This only annoyed Jaya more.

She came across nothing that resembled instrument panels or flight mechanisms, though on the second day she found an area the size of an aircraft hangar, filled with tanks which were themselves made out of some kind of organic material. These contained the translucent nutrient, and something that looked like a mass of spiny black seeds. Jaya investigated the tanks, but she couldn't make any sense of the contents.

Food was not proving to be a problem. She took in nutrients from the wall, but although she was used to the often unsavoury quality of life in Varanasi, she could not bring herself to put her mouth to the nutrient drip. She was not entirely sure why; perhaps because the ship had a disturbing likeness to flesh. Instead, she held her hand beneath the drip as though it were a tap and licked the sweet/salt nutrient from her palm. Her reproductive functions might be working again, but her digestive system had closed down; she did not become hungry, and generated no waste. Although this was an advantage where hygiene was concerned, it was a further annoyance. She could have used her shit to mark the walls; the ship might have rejected that. Plus, it made her feel unreal, smooth and sealed like a plastic doll.

The situation still seemed like a dream. Ir Yth and Sirru seemed to be keeping to themselves. She was unable to locate them, and the ship would not tell her where they might be. It was too peaceful, for someone who had spent their life surrounded by millions of other souls: the crowded, desperate, sick and dying. It did not take long for Jaya to feel anxious and bored, but whenever the edge of stress appeared she was suddenly filled with peace, prana rising up her spine and bringing a lightness in its wake. This was so far from her usual edgy mood that she quickly realized it was the ship that was doing this; solicitous, attentive, it was taking care of her every emotion.

'Ship! Don't *do* that. I can take care of myself. I'd rather feel things.'

/Unhappy with your distress. Before, too far away to help. Information only. Now you are present – can help./

'But it's *not* helping.' Frustrated at being so manipulated, and reluctant to let go of an instinct which had helped her survive all the years of her life, Jaya sent the fear deep within where it lodged like a seed in her waiting heart. She tried to protect and nurture this fear; it was the only thing that had kept her alive.

On what she estimated to be the third day, she finally found her way back to the viewing port, which obligingly unscrolled before her as if the ship knew that she needed to see her home. She spent the next few hours there, sitting in the lotus position on the warm soft skin of the ship, watching day pass to night and back again while lightning burned high in the storms of the world, flashing against the backdrop of atmosphere. Bharat narrowed down into the sea, lights spread across the nightside like a spider's web over the Ganges plain.

Where was Rakh now? Where was Shiv? And, most important of all, where was Amir Anand? Perhaps closing like a wolf on her men while she sat passive and helpless thousands of feet above the world. She stared at the marbled face of the planet for so long that her eyes watered. Time to go home. She rose lithely to her feet and called, 'Sirru! Where are you? Can you hear me?'

She called again, and then searched for another hour, but there was no reply and no sign of either alien. Angrily she went back to her own chamber, but she was unable to sleep.

Instead, her past ran before her in a kind of waking dream. As she had done in the hospital, she watched the events of her childhood swim by: a set of tiny, distant images. She watched as the ashram burned. She watched her flight with Kamal and Satyajit; the journey to the mountains; the guerrilla encampments. She saw herself walking out on a cold morning, clouds wreathing the peaks and the mist boiling up from the Nandaram valley. She was wearing combat fatigues and there was a M16 slung over her shoulder. She walked with comparative ease, the illness in temporary remission and the voice silent. Jaya watched as her younger self walked down the valley, past the carrion crows that gathered hopefully around the camp, down to the swift-flowing river where she washed her face. It had taken a while to persuade her comrades to treat her as one of them, allowing her to walk where she pleased, but she knew someone was always keeping an eye on her from the fortress. She was their talisman, after all.

Around the bend of the river, crouching by the cold water, she found her husband. Kamal's round face was very serious.

'Jaya,' he said, frowning. 'I've found something strange. Look at this.' He pointed to the river.

Curious, she came to kneel by him and he scooped up a handful of water and flipped it at her. Her hair dripping, she shrieked in mock fury, but before she could retaliate, he was already running up the slope.

'Coward!' She caught up with him at the top of the slope, both of them breathless with laughter.

That had been a good day, but then in her mind's eye she saw the night before the troops moved in. Staring into the alien darkness, she remembered exactly how it felt: the fear tightening her throat, the haunting knowledge that none of them would be there if it were not for her. Responsibility coated her soul like lead. The emotions of that day flooded back, and as they did so, the ship's presence closed around her. Solicitous, oppressive, it began to dampen her feelings like a sponge soaking up spilled blood.

Leave me alone, Jaya willed, *go away.* Resentment surged through her: *You tricked me, all those years ago. You made me believe in something beyond all the lies, you gave me faith.* Yet somehow she felt that she was being unfair. It did not seem probable that the ship had singled her out. If she understood Ir Yth correctly, she was no more than a particular type of person, one whose genetic structure enabled her to act as receiver to the ship's transmitter. She had long since grown tired of the lie that she was special. She was simply the product of long-ago alien tinkering, and now she was cured.

Rising, she made her way back to the viewing port, the walls unpeeling before her until she stood staring down at the circle of the world. She had to get back, to find out what these otherworldly people could do for her, but she was beginning to feel like nothing more than a pawn in an ancient game.

The wall peeled back, and Jaya started. Sirru stepped serenely through the gap, Ir Yth trailing in his wake like a short stout tug.

'I looked all over the place for you. Where were you?' Jaya asked.

The *raksasa* said, apparently on Sirru's behalf, /*The mediator hopes you are well. He apologizes that we have left you alone for so long. We have had much to do. Documentation for a reactivated colony requires much time.*/

Wonderful, Jaya thought. She'd been left alone all this time whilst they got on with the paperwork. Reminding herself to try and remain polite, she said, 'I get tired. Otherwise, I'm well. Thank you.'

She was impatient to find out what their plans were, but held back the question. Ir Yth had proved so evasive in the past that Jaya did not believe a direct interrogation would get anything resembling a straight answer.

/*The mediator wishes to know if you require any-thing,*/ Ir Yth said.

'Thank you both for your concern. Yes, I would like something. I'd like to go back.'

/*Back?*/

Jaya pointed through the viewport. 'To my world. I've been here long enough, and you don't seem to have much need of me. Take me home, please.' Her voice sounded imperious, and too edgy.

Sirru leaned forward to murmur in the *raksasa*'s fluted ear. The mediator's mood had changed. Jaya caught a sense of frustration, annoyance, bewilderment, which moved over her skin like a cold, trailing hand.

/*The mediator asks: What are your impressions of the ship?*/

Jaya thought for a moment. 'It's very strange. I've

never been anywhere like this before. It's like being inside a vast creature . . . half plant, half animal . . . but it's not really either, is it? It's something completely different.' She glanced at Ir Yth for confirmation, but the *raksasa*'s face was bland and blank. 'Look, about going back to Earth—'

Sirru spoke. Ir Yth translated, /*Why such haste? Is it not preferable here? But perhaps you are overwhelmed by such luxury, coming as you do from that primitive, uncouth environment*—/

'I've been in worse places than this,' Jaya snapped. The ship sent an anxious pulse, willing her to calmness, but it slid over her skin like oil and was gone. Jaya did not stop to think. In another second, she was across the floor and had seized Ir Yth by a lower arm. Her fingers sank into the alien flesh like steel wire.

The *raksasa* rocked back on her heels; her lips pulsed in and out. A bolt of raw pain shot through Jaya's hand, throwing her against the wall. Her arm hurt as far as her shoulder, with a sick neural ache. Her stomach churned. Sirru hovered solicitously at her side.

/*That is a small warning only. Never touch me again!*/ the *raksasa* commanded.

Not unless it's from behind, with an iron bar, Jaya thought, numbly. She had wondered what defences the physically peculiar but unimpressive Ir Yth might employ. Well, now she knew. The *raksasa* span to face Sirru, chittering. Sirru looked down at the floor, as if embarrassed. He said something that sounded conciliatory, and touched Jaya on the shoulder. She was flooded with reassurance and puzzlement, but her limbs still felt shaky and hot. She looked mutely at Sirru. After a moment, Ir Yth turned and walked away, and Sirru followed.

Distress settled in Jaya's stomach and for once the ship did nothing to help. The mottled walls of the ship were more like a prison than ever and she thought with longing of the filth and familiarity of Varanasi. *It might not be much of a life any more, but at least it's human. At least it's mine.* She could feel the cold control that the ship was trying to exert over her emotions start to fracture and crack, like a fragile shell.

She stumbled blindly through the cells of the ship, descending through the labyrinth of odours until she reached a small antechamber that opened out onto the nutrient baths. She pushed the walls out of her way so quickly that they did not have time to part, and they folded back on her in waves of queasy, liquid flesh. Her own hoarse breath echoed in her ears. She turned and struck the wall, and the ship yielded like a rubber punchbag. In sudden murderous fury, Jaya lashed out at the wall, raking it with her nails, and a long, slimy strip tore away and fell wetly to the floor.

Appalled, Jaya stood, panting, and stared at it. The scored surface of the wall was seeping, oozing a translucent, reddish fluid. On the floor, the fleshy strip pulsed once, and then was still. In fascinated revulsion she reached out and touched the tip of a finger to the gash, and the wall itself flinched. Awful farcical thoughts raced through her mind, of trying to stick the strip back on. The wall was starting to smell, like something rotten that had lain in the sun. Jaya backed away until she was leaning against the opposite wall. Slowly, the wound flushed a deep, dark crimson, flecked with green. In sudden involuntary motion, Jaya stepped back and the wall parted to let her through. Her own chamber beckoned, and she stumbled towards it, filled with horror and guilt. This time, the ship did nothing to belay her mood.

9.
DEPTH SHIP, ORBIT: EARTH

'What do you think Jaya's so afraid of?' Sirru asked.

Ir Yth evinced bemusement. /I do not know./

'She *is* a Receiver. She spoke to the ship before; she can do it again. Why did she resist my suggestion that she develop a closer connection with the ship? Why did she attack you? You told me you'd explained everything to her, that she seemed amenable.' He frowned. 'Perhaps she doesn't trust us. After all, we've given her no real reason to do so.'

/Why should you wish to go to the trouble of placating her? She is here to serve us, not to be coddled and nursed like a hatchling from a vat./

'It is a *desqusai* matter,' Sirru said, surprising himself with his own temerity. 'It is termed: *consideration*. I would not expect you to understand.' He regretted it instantly.

145

Usually, protected by the scale, this was the kind of thing he might think but would never say. He expected a reprimand for his rudeness to a caste superior, but none was forthcoming. Ir Yth was silent. That was another strange thing, Sirru thought. In front of Jaya, Ir Yth seemed almost deferential towards him, but there was no reason for her to be so. He found that distinctly unsettling.

He curled his feet beneath him and settled back on the mat. Delicately, with as much subtlety as he could muster, Sirru probed the air but could not detect anything emanating from Ir Yth's plump figure. Presumably she was wearing scale of her own, or some *khaithoi* analog; her caste had secrets which were unknown to him, and there was worrying evidence of technology beyond *desqusai* understanding.

Sirru could not read Jaya herself, for he did not understand her personal expressives. It would be easier when he learned her verbal tongue and could use it in the usual way to disambiguate the speech that he felt from her. It was a pity that Ir Yth had had so much longer to study human languages. This was the trouble with pheromonally conveyed information: it did not take semantics into consideration. Meaning was often lost in a morass of emotion. Verbal speech was no better: concepts meant different things in different languages. Thus, on Rasasatra, the two forms of speech had evolved together to bring about a more perfect understanding. At this thought, Sirru smiled ruefully to himself. In a caste-riven, hierarchical society, once understanding had been achieved, the next urgent problem became the matter of learning how to lie.

If, as Ir Yth explained, Jaya spoke without knowing that she spoke, then it could account for the odd discrepancies that he could feel from her. But if someone spoke unconsciously, like a child, then in Sirru's experience they often told the truth. Jaya seemed confused, mistrustful and secretive, but all of these things were to be expected. Apart from that one angry episode, however, he did not get the sense of hostility and resentment that Ir Yth had told him that Jaya felt, or her hatred of the ship. The obvious explanation, therefore, was that Ir Yth was lying to him and, in her *khaithoi* arrogance, not doing a very good job of it. But why?

Sirru took care not to reveal any of this. He hid his feelings behind the scale, and he knew that Ir Yth's abilities extended only so far. She could not tell precisely what Jaya was thinking, and she could not read Sirru's mind as long as he kept the scale at maximum. Soon, he knew, the *raksasa* would rest, and then he would go and see Jaya on his own.

10.
DEPTH SHIP, ORBIT: EARTH

Jaya was asleep when Sirru came through the wall. She woke to the sensation of his long fingers shaking her shoulder. He was kneeling by her side, dressed in his customary pale robes. In the half-light, his skin gleamed like the moon on water.

'Jaya . . .' he murmured.

'*Sirru?*'

Rolling over, she sat up, drawing her knees against her chest in unconscious defence, ready to strike. The alien made no move towards her, but sat back on his curiously jointed ankles to watch her. /*No harm,*/ Sirru conveyed. She felt a warmth in the pit of her stomach. Jaya said, too loudly even though she knew he could not understand, 'What are you doing here, Sirru? What do you want?'

/*No harm./Trust.*/

'How can I trust you if I don't know what you *want*?'

Very carefully, Sirru slid forward so that he was sitting beside her, leaning against the wall. Jaya gave him a wary look that for once needed no interpretation, and Sirru smiled. His arm hovered over her shoulders; the golden eyes were inches from her own. /*No harm.*/ She swallowed against the tightness in her throat.

'All right. Go on, then. Just don't try anything funny.' Though if he had the same talents as Ir Yth, she wouldn't have much of a chance anyway . . .

Reaching up, she took his hand and put it on her shoulder. Slowly, as if reluctant to startle her, Sirru pulled her against him. His left hand slipped beneath her vest to rest against her abdomen. Jaya stiffened, ready to strike, but the touch was impersonal; there was no urgency in it.

148

She tried not to hold her breath. The alien leaned forward so that the side of his throat was touching her own. Jaya squinted, trying to see what he was doing, suddenly realizing that her teeth were clamped tightly together. Out of the corner of her eye, she could see the long curve of his nose; a pensive mouth; a hooded gilt gaze. His skin felt cool and hard, with a flexibility like the surface of horn. His porcupine quills brushed her face. Where his skin touched her own, there was a thin film of moisture. Willing herself into calmness, she relaxed back against him and let his own feelings move through her.

/*Want?*/ Sirru conveyed.

Hell, Jaya thought, panicking. *I was right after all. Men!* She sat up abruptly. The alien drew her carefully back again. There was a prickling of /*need/loss/regret/ hurt/something.*/

'Sirru? What's wrong?'

/*Want?/belonging/place/loss*/

She twisted round to look at him. He blinked down at her patiently. She'd had this feeling before, but not often. After the ashram burned down – though that had been mingled with an odd, guilty sense of relief. And before that had been the countryside: full of rich earth and growing things, heavy spring rain, frogs to play with. Her father's hut, smelling of smoke and spice. Then the mountains, where she and Kamal had been happy for a while, and last of all the city. Varanasi: crowded, stinking of petrol and death and the silty reek of the river.

Her mood met Sirru's, meshed, almost understood.

'You're *homesick*? Or do you want to know if *I* want to go home?'

She thought, carefully and deliberately, of Kamal and the mountains; then of Varanasi, the city of light, which she had come to love in spite of it all. The way the light fell across the roofs at dawn; the familiar smell of food and fire and traffic.

'Yes, I do. I want to go home.' *Thank the gods I've finally managed to get that across.* And then she thought, wondering just how much she and the rest of the world would come to regret it, 'Will you come with me?'

/surprise/pleasure/success/ and then a strange sense of time flickering by. /Soon. Ship?/

She turned her head against his shoulder.

'Ship? What about the ship?'

/link-speak-bond/connection-ship/

She thought of the ship, pointing to the walls around her, and remembered pain and decay.

'Oh, god. I think I hurt it, Sirru. I think I've injured the ship.' Fear and guilt flooded through her. 'Is the ship all right?' But he did not seem to understand, for his grip on her tightened: /comfort/soon home/no harm./ He smelled complex: somehow fresher than the *raksasa*, but the range of odours was unfamiliar to her.

Summoning the courage to ask him the question that had been preoccupying her ever since Ir Yth's arrival, Jaya said, 'Sirru? Can you understand me? My people are dying, from a disease. If you can help them . . .' She tried

150

to picture her hopes in her mind; imagining the little boy in the sewers beneath the hospital, his skin marked with the eerie traces of Selenge. She thought of her release from her illness, and the guilt that she couldn't help but feel that she had been so fortunate, when so many were not. She tried to send the images to Sirru, but he did not seem to understand anything beyond her own pain. His grip tightened; she felt reassurance seeping into her skin.

'Can you help us? Sirru, you've got to understand me!' She grew rigid with frustration, but he shifted so that his arms were linked around her, murmuring to her in his own soft ambiguous language, and he held her until, against her will and still without an answer, unconsciousness took her.

11.
DEPTH SHIP, ORBIT: EARTH

'I believe I have resolved the difficulty with the Receiver,' Sirru informed Ir Yth, not without a trace of smugness. 'She will make the connection with the ship, and then we shall go with her to the planet. I'm sure everything will go smoothly from now on.'

The *raksasa* exuded a small bolt of astonishment, closely followed by chagrin, before smothering it beneath a steely control. Sirru noted this with private amusement.

/Without my help?/

'Naturally, without your expert and valued assistance it

was extremely difficult,' Sirru said, sending soothing expressives right, left and centre. 'But I really felt it would be most inappropriate to disturb your rest for yet another tiresome session. No one could attach any blame to you for that,' he added hastily. 'Shall we say it took one *desqusai* to understand another? I'm sure that in her awe of you, the Receiver became confused, sent out the wrong signals.'

Ir Yth eyed him suspiciously, but Sirru oozed sincerity. He emitted the subtext /*inexperience/excessive enthusiasm/naivety*/ which he had been endeavouring to maintain in the presence of Ir Yth ever since his arrival. A sigh whistled through the *raksasa*'s inverted lips.

/*The Core would be most unhappy if anything were to be –* misunderstood. *Might I remind you of the unfortunate incident on Arakrahali? I understand a temeni contact of yours was the victim – IrEthiverris EsTessekh?*/

'That's correct,' Sirru said warily. Why remind him of Arakrahali at this particular moment? He was certain that Ir Yth was delivering some oblique threat. He must make note of it in the next information upload to his First Body, just in case.

As if she had sensed the thought, Ir Yth said coldly, /*I suggest you mention Arakrahali in your next report – and mention, too, my concern. The Core would not want to see such a disaster take place again. They might even question the viability of* all *the* desqusai *projects, not just this little colony.*/

'Surely not!' Despite the suppressants, which clamped down on this agonizing thought, Sirru managed a level of startled shock that surprised even himself. Perhaps, if he ever got back to Rasasatra, he might consider a career on the shadow-stage. He thought back to his interview in the Marginals with EsRavesh: *And yet, there has been talk that the* desqusai *castes are degenerating, their colonies proving unsuitable for sustained development. It would be a pity, if that were so. Your caste remains a valued part of this society. I'm sure your future success with Tekhei will help to redeem* desqusai *standing in the senses of the higher castes* ... The *khaith*'s words had burned themselves into his brain. And yet another mention of Arakrahali ...

Once more, Sirru edged closer to the idea that this was why he had been sent here: to stop his investigations, to get him out of the way. He noticed, then, that these difficult thoughts were becoming a little easier to sustain. His head seemed clearer. What with all the bureaucracy, and the problems with Jaya, he still hadn't updated his suppressant prescription. It occurred to him that without the rigorous controls of the monitors, this must be the longest he'd ever left it.

He was about to examine the ramifications of this when Ir Yth said, /*It is recommended that you leave me to handle the subtle nuances of communication between yourself and this particular branch of your kindred.*/

Sirru sent: /*apology/humble realization of crassness.*/

The light of suspicion in Ir Yth's filamented eyes did not diminish, but the *raksasa* appeared somewhat mollified.

/*Very well.*/

Sirru said, 'And since it appears that the Receiver has no objection to bonding with the ship after all, I'll see to that now.'

He inclined his head politely in the face of Ir Yth's frosty silence, and stepped through the wall.

12.
DEPTH SHIP, ORBIT: EARTH

Jaya was by no means sure that she had understood what Sirru was trying to convey. After her encounter with him, she was aware of a curious connection between them, a blurring of boundaries. She did not know whether she found this reassuring or disquieting. Probably both. The reality of her situation – that, as far as she knew, she was alone out of all humankind to have direct contact with an alien species – was getting too much to bear. She tried to tell Sirru this.

'It's the responsibility, you see.' Sitting cross-legged in front of him, she reached out and took hold of his thin hard wrists. She tried to send a sense of weight. 'If this all went wrong, it's my fault, isn't it?' The hierarchies of caste, which had dictated the course of her life, now seemed to matter so little. 'How can I speak for everyone?' *I tried that once before, and look what happened.* Her father's body, huddled against the wall; the members of the ashram lying dead; the failed revolution. She must have been radiating guilt and dismay.

'*Desqusai,*' Sirru said, evidently bewildered. She remembered Ir Yth's interpretation.

'The same? How *can* we be the same, Sirru? Oh, I wish you could understand.'

/ship: link-bond/

His hand snaked round to clasp her own.

/come with me/

Reluctantly, Jaya rose and followed. He led her through the maze of corridors and chambers, which more than ever reminded her of the veins of some great plant. As they descended, there was a smell of something green and growing, like walking through cut grass after a rainstorm. It reminded her of the watered lawns of the ashram. Sirru took her through the chamber with the growing-tanks, but the shiny masses of seeds had been reduced to a cluster in a single tank. Jaya bent over to look as they passed and Sirru patiently waited for her. The seeds were bigger; distended with water. Their membranes had become soft and pale, like fluid-logged skin. Sirru said something that Jaya did not understand.

'What?' But he led her on, past the tanks and through the wall of the chamber into a part of the ship that she had never seen before. By the time he stopped, Jaya's calves were aching. She couldn't see anything special about the chamber they were in. It was empty, with a domed ceiling that arched only a foot or so above the top of her head. Veins ribbed the walls, and these were prominent and wet. There was a disturbingly familiar smell, which she could not place. Sirru settled himself on the floor; after a moment, she sat cross-legged before him. His gaze rested on a point just to the left of her shoulder; disconcertingly oblique. She squinted round, trying to see, but there was nothing there. Sirru's golden eyes were distant and abstracted.

'Sirru?'

Something touched the back of her neck, like a quick soft hand. Jaya twisted around, striking out and meeting empty air. Yet, not empty after all ... The air was beginning to curdle around her. Her vision swam, as if she saw the world through tears, and she blinked, but nothing happened. Then, after a moment, everything became start-lingly clear. Sirru was no longer sitting in front of her; he was nowhere to be seen. And the voice that she had heard over the years of her life was murmuring in her mind's ear:

/This is what we must become/we must join, something new must come of us/

She couldn't breathe. The voice was growing thunder-storm-loud and with it came the heat, waves of fever washing across her. She could hear the rattle in her own throat, and a long way beneath the panic her own small voice whispering: *So this is what it's like to die.* She tasted blood in her mouth and her body began to analyse it: old blood, alchemically changed. Distantly, she remembered

156

smearing her menses on the wall of the ship, trying to mark her passage through the maze. She thought of Kamal, face down in icy water turning red, not moving; never moving again.

Her tongue felt cold, like a lump of frozen river water in her mouth. Her vision was gone and she couldn't see the walls of the chamber, only darkness. And then, suddenly, she was looking inside herself. She could see a pattern chasing down her throat, changing as it went, corroding. And then, absorbed into her veins, latching onto smaller and smaller elements of her own body: a virus. It was a moment before she realized what was happening. The ship was infecting her.

For a split second she watched her own mutated lymph system gearing into action, challenging the invader, but it was too late. The virus had locked onto DNA, skeining down genetic pathways, and it brought her down into a tight black heat.

13.
DEPTH SHIP, ORBIT: EARTH

'Link-bonding has commenced,' Sirru informed Ir Yth. 'Soon the seed will be fertilized, and we can send it out to find a world of its own to spore over. A new *desqusai* world, think of that.' He tried to sound eager rather than smug, to allay suspicions, but the look that Ir Yth gave him was a sour one.

/*Excellent news,*/ Ir Yth said.

'Isn't it? And Jaya's link-bonding with the ship proves that the Tekhein *desqusai* are compatible with the rest of their kindred. The Receiver has demonstrated that her people have reached the required level of development for further evolution' – Sirru couldn't resist rubbing it in a little – 'and thus the future of this planet is assured. It'll take time and effort to bring the rest of the population up to this level, to repair the peculiar directions that the sub-species has taken, but at least we know it can be done. I suggest,' he added, cautiously, 'that we communicate the good news to the Core.'

He was expecting Ir Yth to greet this news with relief. After all, if the project succeeded, it would enhance her prestige as well as his own. But in the moment before the *raksasa* turned to face the viewport, she looked far from happy.

Realization struck Sirru like a physical blow. /*She doesn't want the project to succeed. She wants it to fail, like Arakrahali. But why? If the project fails, the* desqusai *are up for termination.*/ Granted, there was a constant jockeying for position among castes, and projects did get sabotaged – but not at the expense of an entire caste. Why would the *khaithoi* do such a thing? Status? To take *desqusai* temeni and colonies for their own, to enhance their standing in the Core marginals, perhaps attain Inner rank?

The idea was like a hot wire, singing down his nerves. It had never occurred to him before that one caste might deliberately connive at another's destruction. The Core occasionally terminated those castes that had passed their sell-by date, that had proved unviable ... but what if they weren't unviable at all? What if such sabotage was a regular occurrence and everyone was just too mentally controlled to notice?

He could feel the surge of the remaining suppressants, trying to clamp down on these disturbing notions, but for the first time in his life, they failed. He wondered if Jaya had felt like this, when they had rescued her from the prison of her own body. He, too, had been a prisoner. His thoughts were racing.

Why had not Ir Yth taken action before? Presumably she'd had to wait for Sirru's arrival, so that any and all blame could be securely placed upon him. The thought made him grow angry and cold. *Well*, Sirru thought, *we'll see about that.*

/Contacting the Core will of course be necessary,/ Ir Yth told him. /However, I recommend that we wait for a little while, until we are sure that the Receiver and the ship have truly link-bonded. We don't want to risk embarrassment by a premature announcement./

'Of course not,' Sirru said, and bowed. 'I will be guided by your wise example.'

Let Ir Yth think that she'd bought some time. He wondered, uneasily, whether he might have underestimated the *raksasa*, but she seemed to relax a little at his words.

/*How* is the Receiver?/ Ir Yth asked.

'She's resting. I suggest we undertake the tests when she wakes.'

And Ir Yth, after a pause, said, /Very well./ She gave him a beady look. /I have been meaning to remind you, now that we are so far from home, that there are obviously full facilities here for suppressant refreshment. You will be wanting to maintain psychological stability in the face of the demands of a primitive culture, and I would recommend that you increase your dose./

Was that a threat? Sirru wondered, alarmed. Had she picked up on any of his thoughts? He wondered if he could find a way to increase the scale's setting beyond its current maximum. If Ir Yth was starting to grow suspicious, then he would need to work quickly to confirm his own deductions. And do something to stop her.

When Ir Yth had gone, Sirru made his way back down to the bonding chamber. He knew that this was foolish, literally like turning back the earth to see if a seed has germinated, but he was anxious and it was difficult to resist. He did not enter the chamber, but touched the wall so that a small slit appeared. The slit was very small and very grudging, which Sirru took to be a good sign. He was unnerved to see that his hand was trembling. He put an eye to the slit and peered through. The chamber had changed. It had shrunk to little more than half its original size. Filaments of viral nexi hung in slender webs from the walls and the floor of the chamber had become slightly ridged. Sirru noted these faint ridges with satisfaction. There were the vestiges of a dark and rusty crust smearing the ridges and Sirru frowned, concerned for Jaya. He stepped back and the slit closed with a moist snap.

Sirru walked swiftly down the veins of the ship, to where Jaya lay. As he went, he noticed that the ship itself seemed to be changing. The atmosphere within it was old and stale, and the walls that surrounded him looked suddenly brittle. He thought of dead leaves in the winter wind, and his skin felt suddenly cold.

He stopped and listened, but the ship told him nothing. He sent questions into the air, but the ship's awareness was turned from him, becoming distant and remote. Swallowing a tight knot of tension, Sirru hurried to find Jaya.

14.
DEPTH SHIP, ORBIT: EARTH

Jaya woke and something was wrong. She ached all over, as if with the aftermath of fever, but her head was clear. Her mouth had a familiar, sour taste of metal and when she put her hand to her face she could trace the dried trails of blood from lips and nose. Her crotch felt bruised. Tense with sudden dismay, she slipped her hand down her trousers, between her legs, and when she brought her fingers back into the light they were wet with blood. It wasn't the dark clots of menstruation, either, but fresh and red.

Nauseated and shaking, she crawled across to the nutrient drip and used the glutinous extract to clean herself as best she could. When her hands were clean, she milked more nutrient into her palm and licked it. The nutrient didn't taste the same. It was sour, like milk on the turn, with a mouldy aftertaste. Jaya hastily spat, thinking: *God, what's the matter with me? What happened? Was I raped? By whom? Or by what?*

She huddled against the wall, arms wrapped defensively around her knees, trying to make herself as small and unobtrusive as possible. She couldn't remember a thing, and it panicked her. She'd rather know the worst; at least then she could get angry. Her ribs ached with the legacy of physical exertion.

Colonists always bring the gifts of sickness. The British gave us cholera . . . But not only colonists; the colonized, too, had weapons at their disposal. *What if I've poisoned the ship? Given it something that will kill it, like thrush or the common cold?* She could not know what she was dealing with, and neither, perhaps, did Sirru and Ir Yth. *We're all in a great experiment; we're all rats in the maze. What the hell has happened to me?*

She found herself suddenly missing Kamal with a raw torrent of sorrow. Somehow, no matter how bad it got, he'd always been able to comfort her. He'd always known the right thing to say, the practical, sensible thing that defeated panic.

The wall was opening. Jaya glanced sharply up and saw Sirru. The mediator's eyes were anxious and she could feel a tension emanating from him, like a taut wire. He crouched by her side and reached out to touch the remnants of blood on her face, making a curious clucking sound, such as one might make to reassure an animal. She scrambled away.

'Don't touch me!' He drew back immediately. 'Sirru? What's going on? What have you done to me?' Her hand brushed the wall and it felt as frail as paper. It crumpled beneath her fingers and tore away in a thin epidermal skin. Sirru reached out and the grip of his hand around her wrist was painful. She tried to break free, snapping back against his thumb, but the long digit just bent and rotated, twisting her arm.

'Let me *go*!'

'Jaya'chantha . . .' His exasperation washed over her, followed by a sense of urgency and panic that left her limp.

/Ship/Ir Yth – danger./ Suddenly, she was filled with his own mistrust and alarm. /And ship is sick./

'The ship's sick?' Jaya stared at him in dismay.

/Ir Yth . . . / followed by a cool rush of certainty flowing from Sirru's skin to her own.

'Are you trying to tell me that Ir Yth has done this?'

A twinge of uncertainty, then again: /Ir Yth/danger./

'I *knew* it.' Jaya hauled herself to her feet, disregarding the pain. She couldn't trust either alien, but from what she'd seen of the *raksasa*, she'd take Sirru's side any day. There seemed a good enough chance that he was the lesser of two evils. She wished she knew more about these people, but until that knowledge could be gained, she'd just have to rely on her instincts. The trouble was, those instincts had to some degree been guided by the voice of the ship, and now the ship was dying. *First Kamal, then this. Now I really have to rely on myself.*

She reached down and pulled Sirru to his feet.

'Come on,' she said, aware that she was effectively talking to herself. 'If there's nothing we can do about the ship, we're at least going to get some answers out of the *raksasa*.'

15.
DEPTH SHIP, ORBIT: EARTH

It would have to be carefully played. Antagonizing the *raksasa* would be a mistake. Sirru hoped he had understood Jaya, but he was by no means certain that they were acting in accord. Jaya stood beside him now, silent, and with arms folded.

'I do not wish to worry you, Ir Yth, but the ship is dying,' he informed her.

/Indeed?/

Sirru said with as much restraint as he could muster, 'Forgive me for my impertinence, but why is it that you do not seem more alarmed?'

Ir Yth gave a fluid four-shouldered shrug. /Desqusai./

'And what is *that* supposed to mean?' So much for restraint.

Ir Yth's petalled mouth fluttered in a simper. /Your caste is not, of course, to be blamed for its inability to control its instabilities. It is primitive, with little appreciation of the aesthetics of modulation. Your conceptual vocabulary is limited. Clearly, the Tekhein project will not, after all, be suitable for ripening. Must I spell it out? Link-bonding has failed. The Receiver's subspecies is not, as I feared, at an appropriate level of development. Her modulations are crude to the point of destructiveness. Link-bonding is an ancient and traditional ritual, which has rarely gone awry over countless millennia. But instead of Jaya's ovum being fertilized by the ship's seed after the gathering process, she has infected it./

'You blame the Receiver?' Sirru said, as the knot of fear that had been contracting within his abdomen snapped and expanded, spreading a chilly weakness throughout his body. Jaya glanced sharply at him, clearly trying to work out what was going on. He motioned her to stay quiet.

/I see no other causal agent. Do you?/

'But the *desqusai* can't afford another failure, not after Arakrahali,' Sirru said, failing for once to guard his words. Silently, he cursed the slip. Ir Yth's serrated shoulder blades rippled beneath the folds of her robe.

/That is a desqusai *problem. Nothing to do with me. I must now go to the translation chamber and apprise the Core of the project's collapse. Then you and I will return to our First Bodies./* She seemed to brighten. /We'll be going home./

'What about Jaya?' He gestured towards her, and felt her question. 'What about the colony?'

Ir Yth's eyes widened in surprise. /The Receiver will remain here, of course. The colony will be taken care of as *the ship's orbit decays. Once I have permission from the Core, I will activate the spread of killer spores. Best that the colony be brought to a tidy end./*

Thinking fast, Sirru inclined his head. 'As always, I will be guided by your actions.' *True enough,* he thought, as Ir Yth swept from the room. He waited for a moment, then checked that the setting of the scale was still at maximum closure. In a way, he reflected, it was a good thing that the ship was so distracted. It was unlikely to betray his presence to Ir Yth. His head started to throb. Jaya touched his arm, made gestures. She pointed towards the wall opening.

'Ir Yth?' she asked. He could feel her mood: a steely coldness.

/Ir Yth,/ he confirmed. Jaya was already heading through the opening. Swiftly and silently, they followed the *raksasa* along the decaying corridors of the ship.

16.

DEPTH SHIP, ORBIT: EARTH

The pungent odour of green decay filled Jaya's nostrils as they hurried through the passageways of the ship. Trailing skeins of skin were peeling from the walls and ceiling, revealing a tarry ooze. Jaya had understood little of the conversation between Sirru and Ir Yth, and she hated not knowing what was going on. But it felt good to take action again, after the aimless, unsettling time on the ship. They hurried through the growing chamber, and with a sick dismay Jaya saw that the seeds had died in their tanks, turning to pondweed and slime. A film of mould covered the surface of the nutrient vats. The place smelled like a stagnant marsh.

Sirru paused, turning from side to side. He reminded Jaya suddenly of a hunting dog; it was as though he was scenting the air. Was he searching for a trace of Ir Yth? Striding off, he led her down a narrow corridor.

'Sirru,' Jaya hissed, though she had little expectation of being understood. 'Where are we going?' She was certain that she had never been this way before. Sirru stopped so abruptly that she cannoned into him. He thrust an arm against her, pinning her against the wall, and she almost cried out. Peering over his shoulder, she could see into a small, glowing chamber. Banks of moving lights were writhing up the curved walls like underwater fireworks. After a moment, Jaya saw Ir Yth, sitting hunched in the middle of the chamber with her back to the door. Her form was indistinct, wavering in the light. All four hands were a swift blur of movement. Jaya plucked at Sirru's sleeve and pointed.

'What's she doing?'

Sirru exuded dismay. /Ir Yth – home/Alone!/Must not!/

Had she understood that correctly? Was Ir Yth running out on them? Sirru looked down at her, and Jaya could see a sudden uncertainty in his face. Alien though he was, she recognized that look. It was the expression of someone who was entertaining second thoughts. Then she remembered the alarm that had poured from him.

/Ir Yth/danger/

It was a terrible risk, but it wasn't the first time she'd had to act on little knowledge for high stakes. She wormed swiftly past Sirru into the chamber. Another stride took her to Ir Yth. Before the preoccupied *raksasa* had time to turn, she struck Ir Yth as hard as she could on the side of the head. The *raksasa* crumpled to the floor without a sound.

An intense humming filled Jaya's head, and she clapped her hands to her ears. She seemed to stand on the edge of a vast gulf. Stars drifted beneath her feet; suns caught in the galactic tides. A red and sparkling world hung above her. She saw a tiny speck, outlined against the shoulder of the planet, and then a face. It swam in the air before her: long and narrow and black, like the face of a horse, with two hot-coal eyes. Jaya reeled backwards. The creature's jointed mouth hinged open, and then everything was gone. She was standing in the little chamber. Gradually, the humming lessened, and the lights faded out. Ir Yth lay motionless at her feet. Sirru was nowhere to be seen. A little trickle of oily blood leaked from Ir Yth's ear.

Jaya knelt beside the *raksasa*. She had no idea where Ir Yth's heart was to be found. The human pulse points of wrist and throat were still. Gingerly, she slid a hand beneath the *raksasa*'s robe and found surprisingly soft, cool skin between serrated ridges. The chest rose and fell;

Ir Yth was still breathing, then. Jaya wasn't sure whether this was a good thing or not. The *raksasa* was scorched down her right side, as though she had been licked with a long fiery tongue. The opposite wall was opening.

Sirru stepped through, carrying something in both hands. It was wet and round, trailing filaments. It was a pale, watery green, traced with scarlet veins. It looked organic, but Jaya had no idea what it might be. At her feet, Ir Yth stirred, and sat up.

/*What happened?*/ Her voice echoed wanly in Jaya's mind. Jaya was half inclined to hit her again, but the memory of that lightning bolt of pain shooting up her arm dissuaded her. They'd have to deal with Ir Yth later. In the meantime, however, it seemed that they had prevented the *raksasa* from doing whatever she had been trying to accomplish.

Ir Yth struggled to her feet. /*I am burned! The communication plate must have malfunctioned.*/

Thinking quickly, Jaya replied, 'I think that must be what happened. We went to find you, then just as we entered the chamber there was a flash, and you were knocked unconscious.' Doing her best to sound concerned, she added, 'Are you all right? Can you walk?'

/*Everything is going wrong! We have to leave.*/

For once, Jaya found herself in agreement with the *raksasa*.

'Come on.' She gestured to Sirru. They made their way back up through the rotting ship, and at last came out onto the high corridor overlooking Earth. Bharat basked in

169

sunlight; clouds swirled in milky patterns above the Himalayas.

Sirru set the thing in his arms down carefully, and ran a hand down the wall. Filaments started to move outwards, creeping down to the floor and exuding a chain of tiny hooks, which locked into the shrivelling flesh of the ship. The wall bulged out. Jaya watched with fascinated revulsion as a pulse travelled the length of one of the filaments. Some kind of parasite, perhaps? It smelled green and ripe. Its surface was covered with a satiny coating of moisture, which glistened in the light. It was growing; expanding as she watched like a water-filled balloon. Sirru touched the pod and it split. Then he picked up the small pod, which was still resting on the floor, and placed it in the folds of his robe.

He motioned to Jaya, who suddenly found herself balking. The thought that the ship might be about to take revenge for its injury came to her. It would stifle her, she thought, extending its fibres down her throat and into her lungs. She flailed Sirru's hand away before she could stop herself. There was the usual rush of reassurance but this time Jaya wasn't buying it; adrenaline was forcing it away. And the ship said inside her head, /I am dying./

It spoke with a small, clear voice like a child's. Ir Yth looked wildly upwards. Sirru grasped her shoulder, but Jaya had ceased to pay any attention to him. She was listening to the ship. It was not its time to die, it told her, but nonetheless it was content. It had lived for a very long time, ever since it was grown from a fractional bundle of cells, millions of years ago, the child of some unknown *desqusai* and another ship. It showed her how it sped out into the darkness of space, until it came to a small blue world and split its pods, releasing the spores that bore carefully engineered skeins of genetic material into the DNA of existing life.

And then it drifted off to watch, dreaming, over its multitude of evolving children. Its sleep had been interrupted only by the sporadic visits of the írRas, keeping an occasional eye on Earth's progress. The ship was Jaya's ancestor, just as it was the ancestor of everyone on Earth; just as she and it would be the ancestors of some other world, if their seed survived. The knowledge, and the realization of a violation that she could not properly understand, was too vast for Jaya to grasp. She was left breathless and disbelieving, and the ship plucked her feelings from her with the last of its strength until she was empty.

In its fading voice it told Jaya that she had done nothing to hurt it; it was not her doing, but that of the *raksasa*. So Sirru was right! At least they knew. The ship was sorry that it had taken genetic material from her, but this was the way of things. The voice inside her head was devoid of malice. It downloaded information into her waiting brain. And it told her where Sirru and Ir Yth had come from: somewhere hot, and incredibly ancient, and unimaginably far away.

The smell of green decay was growing, as though they were in an overheated hothouse. A thick, sticky fluid began to leak from the walls. Sirru's quills rose and rattled;

looking up, Jaya saw that he had understood. He radiated dismay. He placed his palm down flat on the floor. An abstracted expression appeared on his face. He muttered something, then hauled Jaya to her feet, pushing her none too gently in the direction of the pod. Sirru strode across and grabbed hold of the *raksasa*. Ir Yth emitted a sound like a distressed insect. Sirru grasped her firmly by an arm and dragged her after Jaya. He pointed: *In*.

Jaya was flooded with fright and relief, and a sudden overwhelming longing for home. She forced herself to step into the pod. The *raksasa* was crammed in beside her, chittering with distaste. The mesh felt viscous and moved sluggishly. Jaya shuffled backwards as Sirru joined them, so that she was awkwardly sandwiched between two inhuman bodies. She took a deep breath, forcing herself to calmness and suddenly missing the suppressing presence of the ship. The pod popped shut. There was a lurch, then a sickening sensation of acceleration as the pod was, presumably, expelled. If it were not for the mesh that had clamped itself tightly around her lips and tongue, Jaya would have been screaming. Unconsciousness came with merciful speed.

ALLIES AND ENEMIES

1.
KHAIKURRIYË, RASASATRA

There was a storm sweeping in from the north when Anarres finally left the Core Third Marginals. She watched from the high ledge of the wall as the control systems seized the storm, drawing it harmlessly out over the ocean. Lightning flashed along the system's edge; she tasted rain on the wind. Anarres drew the hood of her robe more closely across her face and waited for the barge. It was not long in coming. She stepped quickly over the edge of the ledge, then settled herself as the barge drifted down through the restless air. The pilot, one of the small and insignificant castes, watched her with bright eyes.

'Where to?'

'Khattuyë dock.'

The pilot's many hands fluttered over the controls of the barge, which shuddered as it was touched. Anarres tried to quell the sudden queasiness in her stomach, telling herself that it was no more than the distant storm. This had to be done; she had gone too deep to pull back now. The voice of EsRavesh echoed in her mind: /*Status remapping is not difficult. If one has the right connections, of course. You are very fortunate,* apsara, *in having such connections . . . And all you have to do is a small favour for me./*

Anarres swallowed hard against the thought of EsRavesh's stumpy little hands travelling down her spine. She thought: *I should have kept to my own caste, and ignored EsRavesh's perverted desires,* but it was much too late for that, now. Her clan were depending on her; if her own status rose, theirs would too, and she had already made some dangerous promises. Anarres closed her eyes and willed away regret.

By the time that they reached Khattuyë dock, the skies were clear once more. Anarres left the barge, tipping the already-besotted pilot with a flicker of pheromone-drenched fingertips, and passed swiftly through the gateways without hindrance. The signatures which EsRavesh had supplied made it an easy passage; the gatekeepers were lower caste and no match for one marked by the *khaithoi*. The raft was half empty, with only a few outworkers settled into their mesh. Anarres stripped down to her scale and lay sinuously back. She could feel the virus under her tongue, like a small hot ball. She knew she was imagining it, but it felt so real.

That is the taste of shame, her conscience kindly informed her. Sirru's face swam before her imagination's eye. She had to battle the impulse to snatch up her robes and run back through the gates while there was still time. It was almost a relief when the raft took off.

The journey to the orbital was short. Anarres waited patiently in the queue to disembark, with the result that she was one of the last to exit. As she stepped through the gateway, the *hessirei* of the gate brushed her shoulder with an apologetic finger.

'Please excuse. Purpose of visit?'

Anarres stifled the small quiver of panic and said as she had been instructed to do, 'My visit is a personal one,' followed by a sending of delicate modesty.

The *hessirei* shuddered with embarrassment, but nonetheless insisted, 'A locative must be given.'

Anarres murmured the locative of the orbital's overseer, whom she had never met. 'I'm here to see Uassi SiMethiKhajhat.'

She stumbled a little over the unfamiliar syllables and hoped that the *hessirei* would put this down to maidenly reticence. From the sound of the locative, its owner was a member of one of the weapon castes, and her assumption was borne out by the sudden nervousness of the *hessirei*.

'Excuse, excuse. A pass *must* be produced.'

Anarres gestured assent. 'I have one.'

She pressed her palm against the *hessirei's* own multi-jointed hand, emanating the complex syllables of Core authority. She laced it with an element of personal appreciation and the *hessirei's* thick skin flushed dull crimson.

'Thank you so much for your help,' Anarres murmured, and headed swiftly through the gate and into the bowels of the ship. EsRavesh had supplied her with the location of the translation vaults and she hastened towards them, sending out a complex array of conflicting traces to baffle the sensors. EsRavesh had been very thorough. He had also provided her with an array of code elements for the doors of the translation vaults; as she placed her palms against the screens, she felt her resentment growing that the *khaithoi* had ordered her to do their dirty work for them.

The suppressants muted her anger, but only by a little. She did not know why it was so important to the *khaithoi* that Sirru should be impeded. It was only a small project he'd been assigned to, after all. As for the second piece of information that EsRavesh had given her, she didn't even have a name for the person. Surely it couldn't be that significant. Politics had always bored Anarres to the point of faintness.

After a few abortive attempts, the walls glided open and Anarres found herself in the translation vaults. Thousands of units, each the location of the manifold for a First Body, lined the chambers. She checked her instructions.

First take care of Sirru, and then delete the manifold for a second, un-named person.

Anarres set off down the myriad rows until she reached the locative that signified Sirru's First Body. She paused before the pattern-screen, and ran her fingertips across it. Some sense of Sirru seemed to remain in the outlay, and momentarily it was as though he was standing unseen in front of her, but she was only imagining it. She told herself once more that she wasn't really *killing* Sirru; she was just erasing the pattern for his First Body. He was still alive, far away on that little colony of his, and when he was ready to return, all the translators would have to do was reconstruct his pattern. It would be the same for the second person, whoever that was.

Anyway, Sirru and the other one wouldn't really be lost. The erasure could be attributed to translation degradation, which wasn't all that uncommon, EsRavesh had told her. And by then she'd have her status upgrade, and she and Sirru could be together again. She didn't know why the erasure seemed to be so important to the *khaithoi*, but EsRavesh had been very specific . . .

It's really all for the best, Anarres told herself with uneasy conviction, as she pressed her fingertips against the pattern-screen and introduced the viral overlay that would eradicate Sirru's First Body from the manifold. A light glowed: *Deletion of manifold complete.*

That was one task accomplished. Now, she had to find this second person and do the same for them. EsRavesh had supplied her only with coordinates, not a locative. She called up the manifold listing and searched through it, but she could not make sense of the data. Invoking a help-file, she bent down and whispered, 'I'm looking for element 76,987 issue 360. The manifold was filed about a year ago. I can't seem to find it.'

The help-file hummed. After a moment, it said, 'Locative?'

'I don't have one. Isn't this the right code?'

'The codes have changed. Security precaution.'

'So you can't find it?'

'No.'

How important could it be? Anarres decided to let the

matter lie and get out of here. She could always tell EsRavesh that she'd followed his instructions; he'd probably never know the difference.

She hurried back through the translation vaults and waited for the next raft home to Khaikurriyë. Beyond the view portals, Rasasatra was not visible. All she could see was night, and the endless, unforgiving stars.

2.
VARANASI

Jaya returned to consciousness with a tight band of headache scoring her skull. The pod was rocking to a halt. There was a strong, sweet smell of fermenting watermelon, suddenly pungent, and the pod split to a sight of familiar burning blue sky. Jaya heard herself give a gasp of pure relief. Fighting aside the rotting mesh, she scrambled clear. They had landed, she saw with sudden fright, in the courtyard of the Temple of Durga. She was back in what passed for home.

Behind her, Sirru stepped from the pod in a damp tangle of robes to stand barefoot in the dust of the courtyard. Along the tiers of the red temple the monkeys fell silent, one by one.

'Wait here,' Jaya said to Sirru, and ran to the gate. When she looked inside the gatehouse, she could have wept with relief. Rakh was there. His arms were folded, his Uzi hung by his side. He scowled out across the empty

178

square. She might have been gone only a few hours. What had happened to Anand and his men?

'Rakhi!' she cried, suddenly cross. If she'd known he'd been standing here all along, it would have saved a world of worry. The big man turned, and his eyes widened.

'*Jaya*? Is that you?'

She remembered, then, how much the aliens had changed her. When Rakh last set eyes on her, she might have been ninety years old, but now she was young again. At least on the outside. There had been no mirrors on the ship, but now she could see her own reflection in the office window: a strange, fierce face, hawk-boned.

'Your *hair*. And what happened to your *eyes*?'

'What?' She peered into the glass, and caught a sharp golden gleam. So much for being unobtrusive, now. Her eyes were as yellow as Sirru's own, a tiger's gilded gaze. She'd stick out a mile in anything other than a freak show. Maybe if she wore a veil and sunglasses . . .

'The others saw — that.' Rakh, mustering himself, nodded in the direction of the pod. 'They ran.' His scorn was as palpable as Sirru's emotional speech. Jaya grinned.

A laconic voice came from the back office: 'I didn't.' Shiv Sakai, beaming, poked his head around the door.

Rakh added gruffly, 'I knew you'd come back. But why did you come back *here*?'

'God, Rakh, why did *you*?' She drew him out into the courtyard, where there was less chance of being overheard. She was sure the temple had been bugged. Speaking low into Rakh's ear, she said, 'What happened to Anand?'

179

A small, grim smile appeared on Rakh's austere countenance. 'The government intervened. There have been interesting political developments since you left. Singh has admitted to the presence of an alien; there's been an official statement.'

'And Anand?'

'He's in disgrace. Singh fired him.'

'Why did they send him in here in the first place? To get rid of me, I suppose?'

'Singh says he didn't send him in. That was off the record, though, and I'm sure he's lying. But now Anand's failed, Singh's scapegoated him.'

'*You* had an "off the record" conversation with the Minister?'

'We are terrorists no longer, Jayachanda. We are delegates. I told the Minister that only you knew where the alien was, and the price was Anand. If he got rid of the butcher-prince, then you'd bring the alien back. Which you did.' He spoke as though this had not been mere coincidence. 'However—'

Jaya cut him short.

'Rakhi. We need to keep this place as safe as possible for as long as we can, and work on getting the aliens out of here. Anand might be off the scene officially, but he's not going to rest until I'm dead. A blow to his pride will only make things worse.'

'That's what I'm trying to—'

'So we can't stay here. We're too visible. And something has happened, something unexpected. I don't know what tomorrow will bring.'

'Jaya, listen to me. We've been making enquiries. Anand's working for Naran Tokai.'

Jaya stared at him. 'What?'

'We only found out yesterday. Shiv had him followed, asked around. Tokai's living in Anand's ancestral palace; he's using it as a base. He's hired Anand as a personal security advisor.'

'Tokai's got economic clout, and the power to give Anand anything he wants,' Jaya said bitterly. She leaned back against the wall. 'Being fired from the official military has just freed him up, and with Tokai's backing – no one in the government's going to go against Tokai's wishes. He *is* the pharmaceutical industry here.'

'This only confirms that you are right. We cannot stay here.'

'Start working on it. You know where we can go. And the aliens are coming with us.' Rakh looked at her out of night-dark eyes, not needing to reply. That was the advantage of a shared history. Rakh knew exactly where she was talking about. *Yamunotri: the mountain fortress. The site of our last stand.*

Rakh returned to the office. Jaya strode across the courtyard, fighting the urge to remain against the wall and bask in the heat of the sun. Whatever lay ahead, it was good to be back; away from the dim, green half-world of the ship. The colours of the temple seemed to glow: blood-red walls against the Shiva-blue of the sky. The light lay thick and slow, sending slanted shadows into the shrine, and the hot air spun with dust. Somewhere, she could smell frying samosas, and the oily odour made her stomach contract. She was suddenly ravenous. Maybe Rakh could send the runner to the café across the street. But there was little time to think about that now.

She squinted up into the limitless heavens. *Would the ship crash as its orbit decayed? Or would it simply wither like a plant that had seeded?* Jaya glanced back at the pod, now decomposing in the sun. Ir Yth stood, watching, her four stumpy arms folded uncomfortably about herself; Sirru was exploring the courtyard.

What were they going to do, if they were stranded here? What are we going to do with them? Jaya thought she understood the first lesson of power – *keep it close to your chest* – but now she was not so sure. She only knew that she did not want the aliens to be whisked away to some American laboratory. They belonged to Bharat now. And what was happening in the rest of the world? What were the Americans doing now that Singh had admitted to an alien? That was another thing she had to find out, as soon as possible. Shiv Sakai would surely know.

The thought of power, of a cure for Selenge, kept pounding in her head like the beat of her own heart. So much for her dreams of being ordinary.

Sirru was standing by the wall, whispering to himself. He cocked his head, as if expecting the wall to reply. Jaya gave him a doubtful glance. By now, the pod had decomposed to a tracery of wiry veins. Is this what the ship looked like now, a vast and delicate skeleton drifting on the winds from the sun? What had become of the seed, her own strange child? The thought was deeply troubling. She said abruptly to Ir Yth, 'I need to talk to you.'

/It is hot, here,/ the *raksasa* said, irrelevantly. /I did not think it would be so hot./

Jaya remembered that this was Ir Yth's first actual visit in the flesh. She forbore from asking what the *raksasa* thought it would be like.

'Please come inside.'

The *raksasa* fluted across to Sirru and they followed Jaya up into one of the little rooms on the second tier. Sirru still seemed to be talking to himself, a murmured litany echoing from blood-red walls. Jaya sat on a bench by a window and gazed out over a tumble of roofs, and then the river, molten in the sunlight. It all looked so normal. Sirru peered past her shoulder with interest. A skein of crows flew up into the day and he blinked, momentarily startled.

'Ir Yth,' Jaya said. 'I need to know. What will happen to the ship?'

The *raksasa* began to sway from side to side like a child's spinning top, a disconcertingly uncontrolled gesture.

/It is dying. It will fade to dust and fall./

'And you knew it was dying?' Jaya asked. The answer was obvious, but she wanted to see what Ir Yth would say.

A long, mournful pause, then a jangling discord of

LIZ WILLIAMS

emotions, stronger than any Jaya had yet felt from Ir Yth. A black line of old blood still marked the *raksasa*'s face like a fissure in the earth. At last Ir Yth replied, /No./

Jaya knew that she was lying, but let the matter drop. 'Well, what happens now? Are you stuck here? Will your people send another ship?'

/Eventually./

How long is eventually? Jaya wondered. Aloud, she said, 'I don't know what *my* people will do when they find you're stranded here. They may want to imprison you, experiment upon you—' She was trying to frighten the *raksasa* but Ir Yth merely stared at Jaya with detached interest. 'I think it is better if you and the mediator stay here with me and my – my team, here in my temenos.'

/Very well,/ said the *raksasa* with unexpected compliance. /We will stay here. And you will serve us./

We'll see about that, Jaya thought, but she bowed her head and said, 'Of course.'

3.
KHAIKURRIYË

Anarres sat in her house, looking out over the endless expanse of Khaikurryë, and trying not to cry. She should never have listened to EsRavesh and his promises. Oh, he'd honoured them, all right, revising her status upward to the promised level, and her temenos had benefited as a result. That was the one good thing to come out of all this.

184

But for herself, the increase in status was hollow. Her suppressant levels had been slightly reduced, and with that reduction had come the realization that the increase in status didn't matter anyway, was nothing more than a part of the endless hierarchical shifts within írRas society.

Oh, stop feeling sorry for yourself, Anarres commanded herself, sternly. She got up from the mat and collected a handful of rainwater, splashing it over the vine, which emitted a plangent chord in gratitude. Methodically, Anarres watered all the plants and made sure that the feeding system of the house was correctly timed. Then she went into the sleeping chamber and searched for her plainest, most comfortable robe. She put it on, waxed her face and bound her quills back into their mesh. It was mid afternoon now, and at sunset she was supposed to go down to the Marginals. There was some sort of official function tonight, and EsRavesh wanted her to attend. Afterwards, he told her, she'd be expected to entertain some of the guests.

Maybe it was just her imagination, but his instructions made her uneasy, a premonition of disaster. The deep sunlight suddenly seemed to darken. Anarres blinked, wondering what would happen if she simply ignored Es-Ravesh's request and didn't show up. This was not an option that she normally considered, though it was true enough that in the case of her own caste she enjoyed her work. She had never contemplated disobeying the *khaithoi* before. Perhaps it was to do with the change in suppressant prescription.

The house chimed with a sudden plangent note. Some-one was waiting to come in. Anarres glanced up. /*Who is it, house?*/

The house informed her that the visitor was her clade-sister, Shurris. Her spirits rising, Anarres hastened to the door. Then she stopped. The leaves of the singing vine were bristling in the direction of the door. She sensed nothing from the house, but the vine was alarmed, and normally the vine loved Shurris, who brought it different waters. She stared uncertainly at the vine and brushed a hand along its furred stem. The vine was bristling with static, sending prickles along her skin. The chime sounded again.

/*House?*/

The house replied with a jangling discord of phero-mones. The sense was blurred, as though the message was somehow distorted. Anarres stood dithering in the hall for a moment, then made a decision. Quietly, activating her scale to its fullest extent, Anarres slipped around to the back of the house. From her own terrace, she had access to others, and there was a route down through the ferns that she often took as a short cut on her way to the nearest gardens. Pretending that this was nothing more than a quick jaunt, Anarres slipped between the ferns. She knew that if she thought about what she was doing, she'd lose courage, so she concentrated instead on the thought of seeing Sirru again. That thought hurt, quite a lot. She hadn't expected to miss him so much . . .

Never mind, Anarres told herself with sudden determination. *You made a mistake, and now you're going to put it right. Somehow.*

The question now was who might be after her, and where to go. She had no intention of heading for her family's temenos, or to Sirru's. If someone was pursuing her, then it didn't make any sense to go somewhere that she was known, and besides, she didn't want to place anyone else in danger. The house chimed behind her with an insistent, warning chord. Anarres glanced over her shoulder. She could see nothing through the heavy blanket of ebony ferns, but if the *khaithoi* had sent someone after her, then they might be able to track her by scent. It depended what sort of person it was. The scale would provide some protection, but not much.

Above her, something was moving along the terrace. Through the ferns, Anarres glimpsed a long jointed arm, ending in a bulbous claw. An armoured head, mottled in crimson and mauve, swung slowly from side to side. Its eyes glinted in the shadows of the fronds. One of the enforcer castes. Anarres did not wait to see more. She bolted down through the ferns. And then, with the clarity of panic, Anarres finally had an idea of where to hide. She would go to the Naturals' enclave, and ask for their help. She'd never had a desire to go anywhere near the Naturals before – an unruly, inelegant lot who always seemed to smell a bit strange – but she had heard that they hated the *khaithoi*, and perhaps they might hide her. Anarres fled down through the labyrinth of the city, heading for the enclave.

Under the new laws, the Naturals had been suppressed, herded into the dead temeni at the very edge of the *desqusai* quarter. Before her status update, Anarres had been convinced that this was a good thing, but now an element of doubt entered her mind. She had no conception of what it must be like to be a Natural. The thought of being able to think whatever one pleased was a frightening one, and difficult even to entertain. It violated social order; it was heresy. Anarres was momentarily dizzied by the twinge of pain that snapped through her cerebral cortex as the suppressants kicked into the concept and dispelled it. She shook her head to clear it, wondering what it was she had been thinking about. Then memory returned and the cycle began again.

Anarres hurried on, thinking hard about innocuous matters to dispel her growing migraine. She could hear the enforcer coming down the row of terraces behind her, moving fast and hard through the ferns. Anarres began to run, ignoring the discomfort of earth beneath her bare feet. She came out on the bank of a nearby canal. The dark water gleamed in the afternoon sunlight; it was a place of sudden harsh angles and sharp shadows. There was nowhere to hide.

Frantically, Anarres looked left and right, and saw that there was a barge gliding down the canal. A figure was hunched unmoving in its prow. Standing on the bank, Anarres sent allure out across the water, hoping that the pilot was of a sexually compatible caste. His head snapped up, and she saw the sudden glow of interest in his yellow eyes. He turned the tiller towards the bank, and Anarres sprang over the short distance and onto the deck. Without trying to explain, she bolted for cover beneath the long black roof of the barge. The pilot looked hopefully through the hatch.

Go, go. Anything will be yours! Anarres promised, rashly. The pilot's head disappeared and she felt the vessel shift as he took it out into midstream. Making her way to the stern, she peered out between the cracks. The enforcer was standing bemused on the edge of the wharf, twitching a spiny tail. Anarres sank back into a crouch and took a shaky breath. A shadow fell across the doorway: the pilot, returning. With a sigh, Anarres realized that it was time to honour her promises.

Three hours later, the barge had travelled through a series of locks into the further reaches of the canal network, and Anarres put her head cautiously through the hatch. She could tell that they were approaching the area in which the Naturals were confined. There was a curious smell in the air, like the moments just before a storm. This area of the city was unkempt and untended; no one wanted to get too close to the Naturals in case they picked up some unhealthy clinging notion and had to go to all the trouble of having it eradicated. Thanking the pilot, Anarres stepped out onto an ancient wharf. Its sides were carved with eroded faces of long-abolished castes; she wondered what kind of people had lived here, thousands of years ago.

Reaching out, she touched the wall and felt the material of ancient seeds crumbling beneath her fingers. There was a pungent waft of spice as a cloud of unfamiliar pollen drifted down on a current of air. Anarres watched for a moment as the barge glided away, then started walking swiftly along the edge of the canal.

4.
Varanasi, Temple of Durga

Sirru had been trying to speak to Jaya's temenos, but could not get a word out of it. He cajoled, snapped, and praised, but the temenos remained perfectly and stubbornly mute.

'It doesn't seem to like me,' he mused sadly.

Ir Yth sent: /exasperation/a spike of contempt/ /That is because it is not alive./

His response was immediate: sympathy, loss, a wave of affection for Jaya. 'Her temenos is dead? She should have told me. I would never had intruded. I should not have pressed her so hard—'

Ir Yth said impatiently, /It was never alive in the first place. These of your kindred do not grow their temeni. They build, from earth./

Once again, Sirru was bewildered. He had never met so baffling a *desqusai* caste. They couldn't speak properly, they lived in dead buildings and did not notice the difference. And from what he had found out about their reproductive habits, they were only just beginning to Make. *There is so much to sort out and set right.*

Well, Sirru thought grimly, he'd have plenty of time to learn. Ir Yth informed him that it could be a long time before the next depth ship arrived to find out what had gone wrong. Sirru was trying not to think about Anarres or his home; it was just too depressing. The wider implications of some hideous *khaithoi* plan were vastly worse. Moreover, there was the question of how long he and Ir Yth could survive on this new colony. He was not too concerned about his own physical demise – his First Body rested in translation storage around Rasasatra, after all. He did not, however, want to lose this Second Body. If his Second Body died, the reconstruction team would have to hang around until Sirru 3 or someone else from the temenos got the communication network on-line. And who knew what havoc Ir Yth might wreak here in his absence? Who knew what impact it might have on the *desqusai* caste as a whole? He thought uneasily of Arakrahali.

At least they now knew that Ir Yth was an enemy. *She has been too long from her own kind,* Sirru thought, *and that is lucky for me. She is forgetting how to lie.* No further mention had been made of what had befallen Ir Yth. Sirru had confirmed only that the translation plate had malfunctioned, due to the unstable state of the ship. It was fortunate, he said after a pause, that he and Jaya had been nearby to terminate the attempted connection and rescue Ir Yth from the damaged apparatus before she was too badly hurt.

He was certain that the *raksasa* did not believe him, equally sure that she would pose no immediate challenge to his dubious explanation. Both of them grudgingly recognized that the other's talents might be needed until rescue arrived. It had, Sirru thought now, been extremely fortunate that Jaya had acted as she did. Another few moments, and Ir Yth would have been whisked away to Rasasatra, there to report on the project's failure and secure the doom of the world of Tekhei. They had achieved a reprieve, but for how long?

Sirru could not help but wonder what would happen if he continued to forge ahead with the project. If Ir Yth was desperate enough to sabotage a depth ship in order to discredit *desqusai* development, who knew what she might try here on the ground? He had not yet told Ir Yth about the ship's seed, carefully carried down with them in the pod and now resting in its own armoured shell within his robes. The seed would start presenting serious problems soon; he needed to find somewhere cold, and if this were a typical temperature, then a cold place would be hard to find unless he could somehow gain access to a refrigeration unit.

/*What do you intend to do?*/ Ir Yth asked, after a pause.

'We will consider the viability of the project,' Sirru informed her, stalling for time. 'My first priority will be to examine the current state of communications. Are you conversant with this?'

/*It takes place through electronic media.*/ Ir Yth gave a delicate shudder. /*Unspeakably primitive.*/

192

'I feel,' Sirru said, with something close to sympathy. 'Well, I suppose that's adequate for now, but we'll need to get more sophisticated structures in place as soon as we can. Otherwise contacting the rescue team might be a little complicated.'

/Acquiescence./

'Before we proceed with that, though, I should like to see more of this new world,' Sirru said. 'I need to get a feel for it, for how people conduct themselves. What they eat, and what they drink.' He suppressed a smile at Ir Yth's look of unconcealed revulsion; *khaithoi*, of course, had long since abandoned such indelicate behaviour, at least in the presence of their social inferiors. 'Will you ask Jaya to accompany us?'

/I will ask,/ the *raksasa* said, glumly.

It seemed, however, that Jaya did not think it was a good idea for Sirru to start wandering about the place. It could be dangerous, she said. People didn't know anything about the aliens. Some fanatic might try to kill them. Here she glanced at Ir Yth, who confirmed that a previous attempt had already taken place. It would be necessary, Jaya said, for them to leave the temenos, and soon. She had already decided where to go, and was organizing travel arrangements. But in the meantime, Sirru must stay here.

'I thought you said you'd explained all this in terms of the dominant metaphor?' Sirru asked Ir Yth, who replied, mystified, /I thought I had./

'We are analogous to the entities which correspond to the Primary Makers, I thought.' Sirru's quills rattled briefly. '"Gods", as they call them here. What a strange, brave people, to challenge their Makers.' He was not particularly afraid, confident of his ability to handle this relatively small group of *desqusai*; he had proper speech, for instance, where they did not, and he was fairly well defended. Better that he remain safe. But still, he did want to see the city. If it were inadvisable to go out in plain view, therefore, he would go out unseen.

He waited until Ir Yth had bustled off, then went in search of somewhere quiet and dark. He needed to review his own resources, and he was reluctant to call attention to himself. There was a small, dusty alcove beneath the temple steps, and Sirru slipped into it. He leaned against the grimy wall and closed his eyes, travelling inward. First, he visited the seed, which was now slightly smaller than the palm of his hand, and still quite flat. It had sent thin tendrils around his waist and was now nestling beneath the arch of his ribcage. But it was softer than it should be. The seed was too warm.

Sirru left the alcove and glided along the covered walkway of the temple. He could see two of Jaya's team in a small room, hunched over electronic equipment, but the next room was empty. Sirru stepped inside. Boxes lined the walls, and papers were scattered over a desk. Sirru could make no sense of them. Moving on, he found himself in a third little room, barely more than another alcove. It smelled of food, of grease and spices. The room also contained two white boxes: one on the floor, and one on a ledge.

Sirru opened the door of the first box, and discovered it to be empty. Perhaps it was some kind of heating device? It had dials along the front. But when he opened the door of the second box, he was rewarded with a blast of icy air. The box contained a dish of leaves, some kind of fruit, and a row of brown bottles. Sirru smiled. At the top of the box was another compartment behind a hatch. He had to wrench the hatch open, since the ice had crept around its edges and sealed it shut. Perfect. Carefully, Sirru detached the seed from his person and slid it into the compartment. The seed immediately reacted, sending filaments out into the ice. The box would probably not be cold enough when the seed grew larger, but it would do for now. Sirru closed the box, and slid back to the alcove along the walkway.

Here, he reviewed the bony, flexible cells that lay between his ribs: checking each one for viral decomposition. Everything seemed to be intact. Not being a member of one of the weapon castes, he had not been equipped for destruction, but he checked for mutation in any case. Core knew that there had been enough accidents in the past. After some deliberation, he released a small amount of the relevant substance into his bloodstream. It began to take effect almost immediately, latching onto the yellow corpuscles and spiralling through his veins. He swallowed hard against sudden vertigo.

The virus took swift effect and by the time that Sirru rose and left the little chamber, he felt light-headed. He was anxious to begin the next phase of the project as soon as possible, but caution pulled him back. As he stood indecisively in the courtyard for a moment, something chattered overhead. He looked up to see a snarling face lined with a rim of dusty fur – a *hiroi* of some sort. That, Sirru thought, was serendipitous. The guards clustered at the gate, but otherwise the courtyard was empty. Sirru climbed the steps that led up to the parapet of the temenos.

The *hiroi* were chattering amongst themselves but as he approached, soft-footed, they fell silent and looked at him apprehensively. Sirru sent soothing expressives, not wanting to frighten them away. He crouched down on the warm stone and held out his hand. One of the *hiroi*, bolder than the rest, sidled forward and sniffed at his palm. Fast as thought, Sirru grabbed it by the scruff of the neck. The *hiroi* gave a sharp, yipping howl. It squirmed round and its long yellow teeth met in Sirru's wrist. He gritted his teeth fast against the sudden pain, thinking: *What I do for my job.* He noted with a trace of grim satisfaction, mingled with dismay, that the *hiroi*'s mouth was full of sores.

His wrist was bloody from elbow to palm where the *hiroi* had savaged it. He let go of the *hiroi* and it bounded away, squealing with rage and fright. Jaya's hairy guard squinted up into the twilight, seeking the source of the commotion, and Sirru melted back against the wall. He hissed through his teeth, nursing his bloody wrist and flooding his system with endorphin analogs and biohealers. *This*, he thought through the fading haze of pain, *had better work.*

5.
KHAIKURRIYË, RASASATRA

The enforcer stepped back, clicking open the gate of the pen with a claw. Using its own chemical signatures to control the *írHazh*, it directed the creature through the grounds of the Core Marginals, and out into the city.

Released, the *írHazh* soon picked up the trail. Mandibles whistling through the air, it locked onto the pheromonal traces that its handler had given it, and set off through the underground water systems of the city. The red light glistened from its dark carapace as it surfaced occasionally for air, creeping swiftly through the vents on its numerous jointed legs. The pheromones had been doctored a little, but the *írHazh* didn't know this. It only knew that it was aroused, and at the end of the trail would come mating.

The *írHazh* was not capable of thinking very far ahead, but it had mated before and the memories were still strong within it: the sense of yielding flesh, rubbery beneath its serrated mandibles, steaming gently as the eggs were implanted. Nothing short of death would stop the *írHazh* in its progress, and its very few natural predators had long since been eradicated. It headed through the city, drawn as if by a magnet to the old, dying *temeni* that lined Rhu Jher Canal, and the woman who was to serve as both mate and prey.

6.
VARANASI, TEMPLE OF DURGA

'What do you mean, you'll tell people you aren't there?'
Jaya asked Sirru, via Ir Yth, the next morning. It sounded
an insane thing to say, but at least Sirru had made no
more noises about wandering off into the city. That had
been a distraction that Jaya could have well done without.
She was already working out the final stages of a plan with
Rakh, devising a journey north, to the mountain fastness
that had been their home in the days of revolution. Once
the aliens were safely away from the city and under her
wing, she would breathe more easily. Then all they'd have
to worry about would be the rest of the world.

Shiv had been informative on the subject. Half the US
Navy had been diverted to the Bay of Bengal, though the
government of Bharat had so far resisted giving foreign
jets permission to enter its airspace. That stand-off
wouldn't last long, according to the media. The United
Nations were putting pressure on Bharat to treat the alien
presence as a global issue; there was little doubt that the
UN would have its way in the end.

Ir Yth fluttered her stumpy hands, interrupting Jaya's
train of thought.

/For the hundredth time, the mediator will explain
to people that he is not present and so they will not see
him./

'I may be very stupid,' Jaya said acidly. 'But I still don't understand. And by the way – talking of seeing, what have you done to my eyes?'

The *raksasa* appeared momentarily embarrassed.

/*It was a matter of aesthetics. I decided to make them a more normal colour. I thought this would please you.*/ She hunched her shoulders in a kind of multi-jointed shrug, presumably indicating her indifference as to whether it gratified Jaya or not. /*If you do not comprehend Sirru's abilities, I suppose we'll have to go to the trouble of showing you. Look at the mediator.*/

Jaya did so. Sirru stood with his usual expression of mild bewilderment. His hands were folded in the long sleeves of his robe. As she stared, a strange sensation stole over her. Sirru was ceasing to feel real. She felt that she was looking at a projection, and after a moment, even that no longer impinged upon her. He had impressed her with his total irrelevance.

Abruptly, the sensation stopped. Sirru was back, smiling at her patiently. Unnerved and excited (Could he sustain that over the course of a journey? Could Ir Yth herself?) Jaya said, 'And that will work for everyone, will it? There are troops surrounding this complex. They're supposed to be here for our protection, but I don't want to take risks.' She didn't trust Singh's assurances that Amir Anand was not out there waiting to put a bullet in her, for a start, and doubtless the CIA was working on an infiltration as well. She turned to Ir Yth. 'What about you? Can you still see him?'

The *raksasa* struggled to explain. /*It is a question of*

the nature of speech. Yes, I can still see him. If you turned to another of your kind and said 'I am not here' they would not believe you. But because you do not had a proper understanding of the levels by which meaning is communicated, then you must believe what you are told./

Jaya considered this. She nodded. 'It's a useful trick. Later, we'll think how it might be used.' But she also wondered just what else Sirru might be able to make people do.

7.
MUMBAI

There was a smile on the face of Naran Tokai, but inside the industrialist was filled with a curious mix of elation and rage. He turned to Amir Anand.

'She's back, it seems.'

'I know.' Anand's pale gaze held Tokai's, but eventually even the butcher-prince's confidence wavered in the face of Tokai's iron calm.

'Well, Anand, what do you propose to do about it?'

'Do I have a say in the matter?' Bitterly, Anand threw the newspaper onto the table and gestured. 'I do your bidding and I fall from grace.'

'You fell from grace, Anand, because you failed to do my bidding correctly. Had you captured Nihalani and the alien, we would not have a problem now.'

'I told you. The alien was some kind of projection. It was just a trick.' There was a trace of grim satisfaction on Anand's carved countenance; the thought evidently pleased him. Once again, Tokai noted that his subordinate did not welcome the thought of alien life, and wondered just why this might be. Fear? Or was Anand afraid for his status, as if the carefully racist lies on which he had built his life might be challenged by the presence of something extra-terrestrial? The true aristocrat, Tokai thought smugly, need have no such insecurities. If genetic superiority was innate, how could it be challenged? He said now, 'It was not a trick, Anand. I have made extensive enquiries. And now Nihalani is back – with two aliens.'

'How do you know this?'

'I have a lot of technology at my disposal, Anand. The temple is bugged, for instance.'

'Nihalani will be expecting that,' Anand said, grudgingly.

'Possibly so. But will she be able to do anything about it? We will wait until I judge the time is right, Anand, and then we will simply spirit Nihalani and the aliens away. Nihalani will be killed, and I will convince these people that their best interests lie with me.'

Amir Anand gave a small snort.

'After all,' Tokai said, after a pause, 'that is no more than the truth.'

Anand looked at him. 'So how does it feel, Tokai, to be on the side of right for a change?'

Tokai frowned, puzzled. What weird train of thought

was Anand pursuing now? Patiently, he said, 'But I am always on the side of right, Anand. How could it be otherwise?' He was surprised, and not particularly pleased, to see Anand smile.

8.
VARANASI

Silently, Sirru glided throughout the complex, seeking Jaya. He found her in a lamplit room on the second tier. She was with the tall person named Rakh, closeted over a sheet of paper that Sirru believed to be a map, with a small smouldering stick in her hand. He wished he could ask her what it might be. She was busy making plans for their safety, she had earlier told Ir Yth; they would not be staying long in the temenos. Sirru watched her for a pensive moment from behind the door, then withdrew.

Privately, he shared her fears, though he was not too concerned about other *desqusai*. He was confident about being able to handle assassins, one way or another, but his main worry was over Ir Yth. So far, the *raksasa* had acquiesced to proposed plans. She agreed that it would be dangerous to stay; she had already witnessed one attempt at her own capture, whilst still in her avatar's form, and like most *khaithoi*, Ir Yth disliked personal inconvenience to the point of being a physical coward. It made sense to go elsewhere, Ir Yth had said. It was what she planned to do when she got there that worried Sirru. At present, without effective communications, both of them were stuck, but he was not sure what contingency measures Ir Yth might have up her capacious sleeve. At the moment, therefore, they were circling one another like wary *hiroi*.

Sirru had asked Jaya when they would be leaving. She had told him that they would be unable to move for another forty-eight hours, at most; there were arrangements to be made. Having received this assurance, Sirru decided to take matters into his own hands, and inspect what he could of the colony in the time remaining to him.

He could, of course, simply slip away and leave Jaya to her own devices, but he dismissed this as a possibility. If a second depth ship appeared, it would begin transmissions on the same frequency as the last one, and Jaya had been modified to pick up anything incoming. If they wanted to be rescued, they'd best stick with her. Besides, administrative guidelines were clear that the relationship between colonial staff and local Receivers should be fostered during the early days, and there were dire warnings about departures from protocol.

But a few hours wouldn't hurt, and if Jaya was worried about him wandering about the place on his own, Sirru would spare her the concern and simply omit to tell her. Emitting denials of his presence, he headed for the gate.

As he reached it, a familiar form stepped from the shadows.

/Where are you going?/ Ir Yth enquired, warily.

'Out. I should like a change of scene.'

/Then I am coming with you./

203

'I'm sure you would find it more comfortable to remain here,' Sirru said, more out of a wish to see her insist than because he had any real hope of dissuading her.

/I have seen all too little of this place,/ the raksasa countered. /And much of that was in my avatar's form. Like you, I should like to see something of this colony./ She fell in beside him as he strode through the gate. They progressed down the street, unseen and unspeaking.

The first thing that struck Sirru about Varanasi was its lack of diversity. This was only to be expected in an embryonic *desqusai* colony, but it seemed strange to him nonetheless. He thought sadly of Khaikurriyë: so vast, so multiplicitous. Three thousand castes in the Western Quarter alone: most of them so ancient that only whatever might lie in the heart of the Core knew their origins, some of them less than a million years in the making.

The Core constantly changed and refined, tinkering with the levels of genetic structures in its unending attempt to achieve an optimal aesthetic: observing, pruning and cross-matching in its efforts to maximize the mixture. It was a little strange to be surrounded by this particular form of *desqusai*; everyone looked alike. No one had claws, or multiple arms. He had seen no one resembling the scaled, tailed people who took care of the low-level city tasks.

Whatever lived at the heart of the Core had been producing new phenotypes for so long that the original purpose had probably been lost, Sirru thought, and then realized that yet again he had entertained a forbidden thought. The suppressants were almost gone from his system: heresy brought only the faintest sense of unease. Yet it occurred to him to wonder just how free he really was. The suppressants might be gone, but cultural conditioning, social mores and expectations – all these would remain. He had already made a fool of himself by talking to a dead house. Despite his initial confidence, he wondered just how much he was capable of understanding this new world. Was this what freedom of thought involved? It was starting to seem more like the freedom to doubt.

Walking beside him, Ir Yth glanced absently up, and frowned. Carefully, he steered his reflections back to more conventional channels.

To the Core, this colony of Tekhei was no more than an odd little plant in the corner of a vast, carefully tended garden. Still, Sirru reflected, it was fortunate for Tekhei that it *was* a *desqusai* world, and had the wisdom and experience of an ancient caste, however lowly, to guide it. Some of the more avant-garde projects had proved rather – excessive. To the feelings of the EsMoyshekhal, at any rate. What about that case of the latest *shekei* colony, where half the denizens of the planet had been forced into a mass breeding programme? Or the instance of that little world out on the Fringes, where the atmosphere had been renovated according to *irikhain* standards and the population had been treated to lung transplants? At least Tekhei didn't have *that* to look forward to.

The city also appeared charmingly small; no more than a few large temeni, really. There were many plants, but they were silent. Sirru found this sad. Occasionally he whispered to a wall as he passed, but it seemed that Ir Yth was, annoyingly, right. The city was quite dead.

Sirru began to feel a pleasant, almost nostalgic, melancholy. The temples and towers and houses reminded him of skeletons from which all the flesh had long since fallen away. The sombre, earthy colours reinforced Sirru's dark vision. Yet the city was not silent. On the contrary, it was cacophonous. Sirru was bombarded from all sides by continual scraps and fragments of speech. The place was a turmoil of unconcealed emotion, a bath of pheromonal discourse.

At first, he found this exhilarating. Such naked honesty, unmodulated by any consideration of refinement, courtesy or reticence. How could anyone have any secrets here? And then he remembered that they could not hear one another. It was like being an infant at a party, a perpetual eavesdropper. Among the deaf, he was the only one who could hear.

The lack of inhibition was almost arousing. Beneath the wrap of the robe, his skin flushed and grew warm. *I can say anything!* A child stepped out of a doorway. Filthy, half naked, it stared wonderingly up at the passing alien and Sirru turned, smiled, walked backwards for a step. *You can never lie to the young. They feel too much what you do not want them to feel.*

Ir Yth's rudimentary fingers closed over his arm like a steel trap. /*What are you* doing? *You will endanger us both!*/ she modulated, furiously.

He had let his disguise slip a little. Sirru laughed, and caught the outraged *raksasa* around the waist. *It is a garden, nothing more, with strange paths and stranger fruit.* The suppressants were definitely gone. It was invigorating. Ir Yth gave him a furious glance as he let his disguise fall further. A wrinkled old woman stared, her mouth hanging open in disbelief. With a curious reluctance, Sirru resumed the disguise.

It should not take too long for the communications network to become established. Sirru had decided, upon reflection, that he had been wise not to be too ambitious. He did not want his continued development of the colony to come too quickly to the hostile attention of Ir Yth. Nonetheless, he did not want to rush matters, and it was for this reason that he had placed the first steps of the network on an experimental basis with the *hiroi*. He couldn't afford to let his impatience jeopardize the seed. He did not want to involve Jaya just yet; best to be sure.

Sirru, bringing his attention back to the present, saw that they were heading down through a series of narrow passages towards the glittering band of the river. He was assailed by odours and sounds: hot oil, dung, some kind of pungent smoke that his system recognised as a mild narcotic. Crowds pressed them on every side, giving the Rasasatrans no more than casual glances as their perceptions slipped off the modulation.

Their behaviour was puzzling: the men all seemed to be chewing, and sometimes spat out a stream of what was surely blood. Were they ill? Sirru scraped some up with a finger and discovered it to be a pungent, spicy substance. Small stalls seemed to be selling it, wrapped in a large green leaf. It tasted strong and interesting. He was tempted to filch some from one of the stalls, but reluctantly abandoned the idea. He was not a thief, after all.

Despite its occasionally baffling aspect, Sirru was beginning to feel comfortable in the city; it was not so unlike home after all. He had begun to find the isolation of the ship more than a little oppressive: no siblings to sleep among, wrapped with familiar meshed expressives, each knowing the thoughts of the other ... Only the ship, immense and ancient and sorrowing, and the spiny disdainful presence of Ir Yth. But now he was among *desqusai* once more, even though they were not precisely his own kind. He could come to find that liberating. He saw a woman looking over her shoulder, her face puzzled. To her, at the moment, he was no more than a passing shadow. They stepped through the dead streets and out onto the great curve of the river. Sirru smelled weed and mud and decay. He slowed and stopped, sending a plea to Ir Yth.

The river was made of light. It swallowed the sun, so that the great walls of the city and the sky and the stone beneath his feet all appeared bleached of colour. The river sang to Sirru, the first thing to move him beyond the *desqusai* themselves. It sang of impermanence and the wheel of life and he did not know how it was that it could speak to him, except perhaps through the pain that it had accumulated during its long history.

Sadness settled through him. It was the first thing here that made him feel insignificant, and he welcomed that. But despite the fertile appearance of the river mud, it would not be a good place for the seed. The seed needed somewhere colder. Urgency pressed him. He'd have to do something about that, and soon. The seed was already starting to grow.

Glancing up the steps, he saw that someone was being carried down to the river: a woman on a litter. Small filmy curtains hung from four gilt pillars. At first, he thought she was dead, then saw that she was merely very still. The bearers set the litter carefully down at the bottom of the steps and stood respectfully back as their burden rose. The woman was wearing a simple cream-coloured sari edged with golden embroidery. Jewelled chains formed a complex bondage about her body; from nose to ear, from wrist to elbow. Ruby studs in her ears caught the sunlight like fire and struck sparks from the lapping water. Slowly, and with some ceremony, the woman descended into the waters of the Ganges. Sirru sent questions at Ir Yth.

'Who is that?'

/I believe that the person is an apsara. I have seen them before, when in my avatar's form./

Memories of Anarres snatched at his heart. So, they had such a function here. He said, 'Why is she immersing herself like that?'

/I have no idea. Perhaps it is for purposes of cleansing./

'Really? That water doesn't look very clean . . .'

He was sure that Ir Yth was thinking, *What can one expect, from desqusai?* He added, 'I didn't know they had *apsarai* here.'

/*Apparently it is common. For pleasure, I understand.*/

'And what about the other sexual functions? Status definition, or the conveyance of information? Or interpretation, like Anarr— like someone I know? Perhaps that woman is a courtesan-interpreter.' He tried not to sound too hopeful.

/*There are no other functions, apart from reproduction or pleasure. Sexual intimacy here is limited to one of those two roles.*/ Ir Yth radiated disdain.

'Well!' Sirru said, nonplussed. This colony never ceased to surprise him. But then he wondered if Ir Yth was telling the truth, if she was still trying to prevent him from communicating with anyone else. Undoubtedly, that was the case. And an *apsara* would be the ideal person to initialize the network, if it reached a stage where it could be extended from the *hiroi* . . . He filed away the *apsara*'s pheromonal signature, for future reference.

The *apsara* had finished bathing and resumed her place on her litter. She was carried back through the streets, riding in state ahead of their own little procession as they made their way back. Sirru carefully noted the temenos which the *apsara* entered and marked the path between the *apsara*'s house and the temple, just in case.

It was late afternoon now, and the heat blanketed the city. Sirru relinquished his disguise with a sigh as he stepped through the echoing gate of the temenos. One of the *hiroi* that haunted the tiers of the building had fallen. It lay to one side of the courtyard, twitching a little. Its round, sorrowful eyes were closed and a thin thread of blood trickled from one convoluted animal ear. Sirru gave it a passing glance, and smiled.

9.
KHAIKURRIYË, RASASATRA

Anarres passed old, dead temeni, long abandoned by their clades. The domes of the temeni were blackened and desiccated, as if by fire, and they sagged. Some of them had seeded, and their shattered domes petalled out towards the hot sky. The marks of spores lacerated the nearby buildings and the warm air smelled of a smoky dust. Anarres wondered vaguely whether any of the seeds had been kept, planted elsewhere by clade remnants and lovingly tended into new homes. The temeni must be quite big by now, if so. The ground was barren; Anarres examined her feet fastidiously from time to time.

She was not sure quite what precautions the Core might have made to hinder progress into the temenos of the Naturals. Perhaps it reasoned that their reputation was enough to keep outsiders away, but Anarres's clade used to tell her stories at night of the things that lived deep in the Core, the creatures that glided through its labyrinthine walls, and she gave a sudden shiver.

She had been walking for some time when there was a

ripple in the waters of the canal. Anarres frowned, trying to see down into the oily, sluggish water. At first she thought it was nothing more than a trick of the light, but then she saw that it was a definite shape, moving purposefully towards the wharf and leaving a wake of dark water behind it. Anarres stepped quickly back. She had no idea what forms of *hiroi* might thrive in this deserted part of the city. The Core occasionally set its more experimental projects loose, presumably in order to see how they interacted with the environment. Generally, if *hiroi* couldn't sense you, they left you alone . . .

Anarres touched the scale implant beneath her collarbone in an automatic gesture of protection. The scale flushed cold across her skin. A long, jointed arm slid over the lip of the canal and probed the air. Anarres stood very still. Segmented legs brought the body of the thing onto the bank and with a rush of horror she realized what it was: *írHazh*, a hunter-mater from the deep marginals. EsRavesh kept them for sport, and he had once taken her to a pit fight. Remembrance of the two jointed bodies locked together in mutual destruction returned to haunt Anarres now.

The *írHazh* was huge, at least twice the size of Anarres herself. A cylindrical, plated body terminated in a raised tail. A thick curtain of mandibles, running the length of the creature's body, drifted upwards like waterweed, tasting the air. The scent that emanated from it was rank, like rotten meat, but underneath it Anarres could discern the base notes of a horribly familiar odour: her own.

EMPIRE OF BONES

Her first thought was: *EsRavesh*. He'd sent the thing
after her, to dispose of someone who knew too much.
Anarres took a deep, slow breath and held it, but a shiver
of fear ran down her spine. The scale trapped the fear,
suppressing it. The creature was still tasting the air, searching for her. Then the thing turned swiftly in her direction.
It moved forwards in a rush, but Anarres was already
running, sprinting across the ruined ground and scattering
the dust beneath her flying feet. She could hear the *írHazh*
scuttling after her; the rattling plates and the hissing
bellows of its breath. A wave of sensations flooded over
her, muted by the scale but still discernible: desire, rage, a
lust for death and blood.

And then it was as though she had swallowed a baited
hook and was being reeled in, from the direction of one of
the deserted temeni. A pointed face hung over the wall of
the temenos, seemingly disembodied. Anarres dashed
blindly for the high wall, and just as she thought that she
could not possibly leap up and climb it, the walls split
open. A hand tightened around her arm as her rescuer
dragged her through.

Sprawling on the soft earth inside the temenos wall,
Anarres twisted round and saw that the wall had snapped
neatly shut across the body of the *írHazh*, cutting it in
half. Undeterred, the front end of the creature dragged
itself towards Anarres until the wall extended a soft
pseudopod and closed around it, drawing it inexorably
backwards. The smell of exuded enzymes filled the air as
the pseudopod began to digest the *írHazh*.

Anarres was shaking so badly that she couldn't stand up, so her rescuer sat down beside her and they watched in silence as the house ate the hunter-mater.

'Probably not a bad thing,' her rescuer remarked, quite cheerfully. 'It hasn't fed for a bit, so . . .'

'Your house is carnivorous?' That explained the rank smell, Anarres thought.

'A *erychniss*. One of the very last ones. People don't grow them these days. Fashions change.'

'Aren't you afraid that it might eat you?'

The Natural gave a rueful smile. 'I used to be a city botanist. I modified the pheromonal signatures of the group so that the house wouldn't scent us as food. We'll have to do the same to you. Anyway, the modifications are supposed to make us taste bitter, but the house has never tried to consume anyone. We used to catch *hiroi* for it instead, but it doesn't eat much – I think it's too old. Do you think you can stand up now?' He took Anarres by the arm and led her through the courtyard.

'What's your locative?' Anarres asked, shakily.

'Naturals don't use locatives. I am Nowhere One. And who are you?'

He smiled ruefully at her look of confusion. 'Whoever you are, it seems that someone wants you dead.'

The temenos was in rather better condition than the rest of the neighbourhood, but not by much. Its dome had shattered and lay open to the sky. The rest had been left to grow untended. Fronds of cells skeined from the walls to create a chlorophyll veil, but the air was fresh and damp. Nowhere One led Anarres across the inner garden. The sun was low now, creating a deep light and long shadows. The Naturals, some thirty people, were clustered around a pool of water: the well of the temenos. They looked up, startled, as Anarres stepped into the courtyard. A dishevelled person stood up hastily.

'Who is this?'

'Someone in need of help,' Nowhere One said, firmly.

'She's an *apsara*!'

'I'd noticed,' Nowhere One said, with a reproving rattle of quills.

'You're wearing scale, aren't you?' the second Natural said to Anarres. 'I'm afraid you'll have to deactivate it. We have nothing to hide from one another here.'

'It's best if you do,' Nowhere One said, behind her.

'All right,' Anarres said, after a moment's pause. She turned off the scale. Immediately, she was assaulted by a tumult of unfamiliar emotions and impressions. Ideas which she had never had any thought of entertaining flooded through her mind, disturbing her with their force and novelty. With a gasp, she sat down hard on the nearest mat. The Naturals flocked round her with concern, until Nowhere One waved them back.

'Away, away. She isn't used to us. Not yet.' To Anarres, he said, 'You'd better come with me.'

He took her firmly by the arm and led her into a side chamber. Anarres accompanied him gratefully. Although she had been told that the Naturals had no leader, this individual seemed to possess some sort of authority, despite his uncouth appearance.

'Now,' the Natural said, eyeing Anarres uncertainly. She noticed that he was standing some distance away from her, presumably to mitigate the effect of her carefully engineered pheromones. 'Frankly, this isn't the kind of place that I'd expect an *apsara* to visit. And if someone sent an *írHazh* after you, you must have done something extreme. Want to tell me about it?'

Anarres gazed at him in her most appealing manner and decided to tell the truth. 'I have a problem.' She paused. 'You see, a while ago, I did a little favour for the *khaithoi*, something that maybe wasn't a very good thing to do, and—'

'You must know that it is the *khaithoi* who interpret Core commands where we are concerned. And who execute them. They are the caste whom we hold most directly responsible for our status as outcasts.'

'I'd heard that,' Anarres faltered. 'But—'

'But you think we deserve it, don't you? Do you know why you think that?'

Anarres considered this for a moment. 'I suppose I'm not sure.'

'People become Naturals for various reasons, Anarres. Some are naturally immune to the suppressants that everyone is given, depending on their caste. That usually becomes apparent in adolescence – after all, children are reared in their family pens and it isn't too hard to control

216

them with words. As soon as folk are certified as immune, they are sent to us. Some of us, however, turn into Naturals by default. Perhaps we let our suppressant prescriptions slip. That doesn't happen so often; after all, you know how diligent the Prescriptors are with their seven-month checks.'

'I was late once,' Anarres said, remembering the Prescriptors who had visited her with their clicking, whispering voices and thin, probing fingers. 'They came round to my house and they were so *unpleasant*. They did all sorts of tests and made me pay a status-fine for being late.'

'This society runs on that control, Anarres. People can't be allowed to think what they please. But sometimes folk slip through the net. My own prescription lapsed when I got stuck offworld for a spell – I was a botanist, doing research work on a colony world, and got lost in the backlands. Being in the wilderness gave me time to think about things, and gradually I noticed that thinking was becoming easier. When at last they rescued me, I found myself lying about my prescription – I said I'd taken an emergency dose of suppressants with me. Once I got back here, it didn't take them long to find out the truth.'

'But why does the Core have you cast out? Why doesn't it just have you modified?'

'Anarres, do you think every Natural is a criminal?' Nowhere One gave a small, grim smile. 'The people you see here are gentle, intellectual, elderly and ill. The real troublemakers don't end up here. They're killed – as you so nearly were. But the Core permits us to live, our miserable lives presented as a deterrent and an example. Now, tell me how *you* have come to the attention of the *khaithoi*'s malice?'

Haltingly, Anarres told the Natural the whole sorry story. 'And then an enforcer came to my house . . .'

Nowhere One was staring at her, not unkindly.

'And now you want our help.'

'Yes.'

'I'll have to discuss it with the others. We are a philosophical group based on a mutually difficult biological situation, not a safe house for fugitives – whatever our reputation might be. However, I am intrigued by your story. Why do you think the *khaithoi* wanted you to dispose of this person's First Body?'

'I don't really know. I was frightened of EsRavesh, and he promised that my family would have their status improved – so would I, but that wasn't the main reason. I suppose they wanted to delay my friend's return from this little colony he's had to go to.'

'As we are *desqusai* ourselves, except for a few people from other castes, we are naturally concerned with *khaithoi* machinations. And after the tragedy on Arakrahali . . . Is it possible to contact this friend of yours?'

'I know where he can be reached. He's on a depth ship, orbiting the new colony. Do you have the means to contact him?'

'We have one old communication device. Let me try and trace his current locative and I'll see if there's anything I can do,' Nowhere One said. Anarres assessed him for a moment, trying to detect a lie, but the Natural was giving away nothing. She experienced a moment of envy, for someone who could guard their thoughts in such a way. But it couldn't be too harmful, surely, for him to know Sirru's location; after all, the *khaithoi* themselves already knew perfectly well where Sirru was.

'Now,' Nowhere One added. 'If you are to stay here, you must do so on our terms. And that means no suppressants. When was your last prescription?'

'It's almost due,' Anarres said.

The Natural gave her a narrow look. 'So your suppressants must be wearing a little thin, if it's nearly time for your next dose. Do you think that might have something to do with the fact that you thought to evade the enforcer rather than simply open the door of your house? *Can* you think that?'

'I don't know.' Her head hurt.

'Come with me,' the Natural said, relenting.

Uncertainly, Anarres followed him. She could not quite grasp the concept of being, effectively, a Natural. The thought was frightening and, moreover, painful.

'I don't think I want to do this,' she said. The Natural turned and gripped her by the shoulders. She could tell that she was affecting him, and tried to rein in her pheromonal aura.

Nowhere One said, 'I am taking you in because I am sorry for you, and because I suspect that you might be part of a wider problem that we need to know about. I told you. My caste, originally, is *desqusai* – like your own. As an *apsara*, you obviously possess higher status within that caste, but we still have a caste bond between us.' He sighed. 'Most Naturals seem to be *desqusai*, these days. I have been making enquiries about things that are happening to the caste – but it isn't easy. As I've said, we don't have much technology – we've managed to get hold of equipment from ruined domes, but it's old. You might just be able to help us in some way. I know that becoming like us might be a frightening thought and it may take time for you to adjust, but I don't think you'll regret it in the long run. After all,' he added, 'it's unlikely that you would have come this far if there was not some element of rebellion in your character already. Perhaps you're more of a Natural than you think.'

This was an alarming thought, but she seemed to have little choice in the matter.

'All right,' Anarres said, with considerable reluctance. 'Help me to understand.'

10.
VARANASI, TEMPLE OF DURGA

'We'll leave tomorrow night, as soon as it's dark,' Jaya said. She was leaning on the sill, limed with bird droppings and age, gazing out across the expanse of the town. She lifted a hand and punched the warm marble, idly noting the absence of pain. 'I wanted to go now, tonight. I wish that damn boat hadn't taken so long to arrange. I should never have let my networks slip like this. I hadn't realized how out of touch I was.'

Rakh lifted the rifle so that the sun gleamed down its sights, ensuring that it was polished to his satisfaction. 'It is worth taking time to get things right. The fort in Yamunotri is a good base, even if it is far away.'

Their eyes met in memory; Kamal Rakh had died in Yamunotri. His brother said gruffly, 'I had not asked you this before. I trust you, Jaya. I always have. But there is something I need to ask you now.'

'Ask me,' she said. 'But you should be careful with that trust, Rakhi.' She turned back to the town, a little falcon in the heights. 'I let you down.'

'No, not you. History let us down. It always does. You did what you could.'

She was silent for a moment, then she said, 'What did you want to ask me?'

'These . . . people. Sirru and the *raksasa*. What do they want? Why are we helping them? And what did they do to you? When you left here, you looked old. And now – people have seen you, Jaya. Your pale hair, your golden eyes. The fact that you're young again. People are talking about a miracle. They're saying that these aliens are gods. Shrines are going up all over the countryside, with the most imaginative artwork. Sirru sits by Krishna in a spaceship; Ir Yth and Lakshmi are depicted side by side.'

'How inappropriate. Ir Yth's too much of a prude to hang out with the goddess of love, if you ask me.'

Rakh smiled. 'American fundamentalists are saying that

the aliens are devils, that the last days are here. And Shiv found a Japanese site devoted to alien fashions – people have been dying their hair white and buying golden contact lenses. Everyone sees the aliens as the future, good or bad, but no one knows anything about them. Except you.'

'Everyone's asked me what the aliens want. And I still don't know. They cured me – I don't know how. I think whatever genetic mutation allowed me to talk to the ship also made me prematurely aged, and they fixed my DNA and changed my eyes. But they won't tell me what they want. I searched and searched that ship, Rakhi, and I could find no answers – only more questions. I don't understand what Sirru tries to tell me, and I don't trust Ir Yth. And I keep asking myself: *Why me*? They sought me out because I could hear their ship, but what can I possibly do for them? If Sirru is really some kind of envoy, why are they staying here? They don't seem to be in any hurry to do whatever they're going to do, and their ship is dead. Why aren't they seeking out – I don't know, politicians? Someone in power?'

'Perhaps they came simply to visit,' Rakh said, but he clearly didn't believe it. Jaya gave him a level look.

'Oh, come on. No one does that. They may think they do, like the Westerners who used to come here in their sari petticoats, going out half-dressed and wondering why everyone stared at them, wearing T-shirts with gods whom they'll never worship or understand.' She gave a small snort of genuine amusement. 'No one comes "just to visit",

Rakhi. Everyone comes to take. Everyone comes to *use*.'
She gripped the rough edges of the sill, eyes narrowed.
'We have an opportunity, now, with these people, and we
have to take it, before it's too late. Sooner or later all these
rumours will coalesce and the Americans will send in
troops, or the government here will lose patience. I don't
know what the aliens are doing here, or what they're
capable of, and yes, it worries me. But there's the question
of Selenge. How many people are still dying, Rakh? The
aliens have a cure. They are a weapon that fate has placed
in our hands. I know this. I can feel it. I just need to work
out how that weapon is to be used.' *My father's lies:
Sound as if you know what you're doing and they might
just believe you.* She turned to face him. 'Tell me what's
been happening today.' The old command; they might still
be on the walls of a ruined fortress, looking down over the
northern passes. Rakh gave a small, rare smile.

'We're still monitoring the information channels. Shiv
has extended the hive links into the Web. Do you want to
know what everyone is saying?'

'Tell me.'

'The Americans are becoming desperate; for access, for
information. They are accusing the Bharati government of
withholding information from the UN. They suspect that
something is happening here, but they do not know what.'

'Withholding information from America, they mean.
The USA is the UN.'

'It is not generally known that the mediator is here,

223

though some people saw the little ship, the one you came back in. Those scientists who came here yesterday haven't found any traces from their soil samples.'

Jaya smiled. She couldn't help feeling a bit sorry for the scientists, who had taken so many samples of the place where the ship had landed, and who were so clearly hoping to see an alien. At their insistence, Rakh and herself had showed them around the temple, but Ir Yth and Sirru clearly – and mercifully – had preferred invisibility.

Rakh continued now, 'Maybe we're fortunate that the Americans can't really believe that aliens would land anywhere other than their own country, otherwise who knows what they'd do? Drop a nuke on us, or something. Their ships are already lining the coast, just in case. Bad enough that Tokai and Anand have joined forces against us. Rumours are rife, especially after the government statement. There is widespread talk of Ir Yth, and then of course there is the ship in orbit.'

'Does anyone know what has happened to the ship?'

'There is concern. Its orbit is decaying. NASA has sent a probe, which is apparently trying to gain access to the ship. It has not responded to any attempts at communication.' Rakh sounded as though he was quoting.

'That's because it's dead. There's no one up there.'

'And everyone wants to know why they didn't notice that an enormous spacecraft has been lurking about the solar system.'

'I wondered that, and I don't know the answer. But if Sirru can conceal himself from plain view, maybe the ship could do something similar. What's Minister Singh saying?'

'Singh is counselling caution, but the military are here in force, you know.'

Jaya stared at her old comrade. 'Who else is out there?'

'Many people. *Sadhus, sannyasins,* tourists.' Rakh paused, oddly diffident. 'But that's more because of *you* than because of some rumoured alien.'

Jaya sighed. 'All seeking enlightenment, most of all me. Me and my miracles.'

'Talking of miracles, did you know they're making a movie?'

'About what?'

'You.'

Jaya gaped at him. 'What are you talking about?'

Rakh called down into the courtyard. A few minutes later, Shiv Sakai hastened up the stairs, carrying a magazine. The title on the cover read: *Movie Monthly.*

'Show her,' Rakh said.

'She won't like it.'

'Give me that.' Jaya snatched the magazine from Shiv's hands and scanned the article. There were photographs of a very glamorous woman, evidently clad in Bollywood's idea of camouflage. 'She doesn't look anything like me – then or now. And it says here that she's playing a princess "who sacrifices her position to save India, only to be reunited with the man she loves". God! Who is this Kharishma Kharim? I've never even heard of her.'

'She did a couple of films with P. K. Hawa, and she was

in a rather interesting historical movie a few years ago called—'

'Shiv, I don't care!' Where had Shiv Sakai found the time to develop such an exhaustive knowledge of cinema?

'And she's Amir Anand's girlfriend.'

Irony upon irony! Jaya seized the magazine and hurled it into the waste basket. 'When is this abomination coming out?'

'Next month. If we're still alive, can we go and see it?'

Jaya stared. 'Quite apart from the fact that being played by Anand's girlfriend is a mortal insult, Shiv – aliens have landed, Earth may be about to end for all we know, and you're talking about going to the *cinema*?'

'I want to see who plays me,' Shiv said, unrepentant.

'I hope it's a bit part. Forget about the movies. Just stay on the Web. Hack into wherever you can, find out whatever you can. In the meantime, I'm going to try and talk to Sirru.'

'And then?'

'And then I plan to draw up a list of demands.'

She found Sirru standing on the walls of the temple, looking down on the crowds. He had positioned himself behind a pillar so that they could not see him; he appeared pensive. To her relief, Ir Yth was nowhere to be seen. Jaya touched his arm and he turned and smiled.

'Sirru?' She reached out and encircled his smooth, hard wrist with her own hand. She tried to convey: *I need to talk to you.*

There was a vague sense of encouragement. Jaya

thought, very hard: *I have to know, Sirru. Why are you here? What are your plans?* It occurred to her that she was just like one of those Western tourists she had criticized earlier; if she spoke loudly enough and repeated it sufficiently often, maybe he'd understand.

/*Surprise.*/

Jaya looked at him.

'What?'

He said, aloud, 'Ir Yth.' He mouthed saying-noises, pointed to Jaya.

'No,' Jaya said. 'Ir Yth tells me nothing.' She tried to convey negation, frustration. Sirru stared at her.

/*Nothing?*/

/*Nothing.*/ 'Look,' Jaya said impatiently. *We should have done this in the beginning.* She knelt down in the dust and started to draw. 'Here are you.' She pointed to Sirru. 'Here's Earth.' A circle, one of nine, with a smaller sphere in orbit and a dot for the ship.

'Tekhei,' Sirru said.

'All right. Tekhei. You, to Tekhei. Why?' Feeling a fool, she shrugged, grimaced, mimed incomprehension.

'Ir Yth?' This was spoken with such an air of fading hope that Jaya almost laughed.

/*No.*/

He couldn't believe the *raksasa* hadn't told her; she could see it in his eyes. Sirru pointed to the little stick figure of himself. His long, oddly jointed forefinger trailed through the dust, to Earth. Kneeling back on his heels, he took Jaya by the wrists. She began to feel something that

227

she did not at first understand, but which slowly resolved itself into a sequence of images. Memories. Her own.

She was travelling into the hills, waiting for war, but the countryside through which they passed was peaceful. These were the lowest slopes of the Himalayas, not rich country, but enough for people to live. In other areas Western nanotech had been brought in to collect the crop, but here the women still picked the tea, moving patiently from bush to bush, selecting shoots and dropping them into the wide baskets. Jaya watched them through the binoculars, and the peace and regularity of their lives saddened her. But it was not the sense of a life that could never be hers which seized her now, triggered by whatever Sirru was saying. It was the memory of the tea-pickers, for what Sirru said was both immeasurably complex and extremely simple: /*Harvest.*/

11.
VARANASI, TEMPLE OF DURGA

Sirru sat high on the tower of the Temple of Durga and stared out across the dead city. It was sunset, and the sky had become a deep and beautiful shade of rose-tangerine. It reminded him of Khaikurriyë, and for the first time on this little world, he felt almost at home. Kites wheeled above the river, seeking carrion, and Sirru watched with pleasure as they flocked and swooped. Fragments of emotion whirled up from the shifting throng outside the temple, chemical

228

traces caught on the thermals, rising and falling like the birds. Sirru tapped a bare clawed foot against the dark red stone and tried not to dwell on his annoyance with Ir Yth. He imagined the depth ship's decay, shrivelling up, consuming its own flesh, sacrificing itself so that the deadly spores that it carried could no longer be released. His shoulders sank with relief. At least Jaya's attack on the *raksasa* meant that part of Ir Yth's plan had been postponed.

He had checked the seed that morning. It was still safe in its box, but he needed to keep alert to changes within it until the time for planting was ready. Sirru shivered. He was still not used to thoughts of rebellion. Ideas sneaked up on him, as if from behind, attacking him as he stood unaware, and among them was a growing disobedience of the commands of the Core. This exhilarated him, but he could not help but be afraid. With an effort, he turned his attention to smaller, safer matters.

He was growing to like Jaya. She reminded him of the city in which her temenos lay: complex and strange. Currents of tidal fierceness ran beneath the shell with which she shut out the world; sudden hot flares of temper, depths of sadness which lay like a well within her, limitless and unresolved. He wondered, not for the first time, what had befallen her. She carried her history like a stone upon her back, weighing her down; only on a couple of occasions had he seen her as swift and light as the river. And at that point, Sirru thought with a lightning pang of Anarres.

He seized upon a single bright strand from the emotional melange below, someone's pleasure at the sight

LIZ WILLIAMS

of a loved one, and began to weave it into an expressive
for Anarres. She'd never experience it, of course, but it
made him feel a little better. Complex chains of molecules
shifted and combined to produce a tapestry of impressions:
love and longing and *place*. Above his head, the birds
wheeled on the wind, sensing otherness, and below, the
remaining *hiroi* looked uneasily upwards. The sky darkened to old gold. Ir Yth was asleep in the dim inner
chamber that she had claimed for her own and Jaya was
nowhere to be seen.

Since the moment earlier when he had explained to her
what was planned for Tekhei, it seemed to him that she
had been avoiding his company. Doubtless there was an
explanation for this; perhaps she had misunderstood him.
He decided to seek her out in the morning. Sadly, Sirru let
the expressive drift out across the rooftops of Varanasi and
turned his attention to the courtyard.

Seven of the *hiroi* had now entered coma. He could see
their limp bodies curled on the parapet that surrounded
the courtyard; one lay below. It was impossible to see them
from the courtyard, only from the upper reaches of the
temenos. Jaya had not noticed and Ir Yth, if she had seen,
had said nothing. That last thought made him uneasy; his
project had become too visible. The animals' blood glistened crimson in the last of the light and Sirru felt a
twinge of regret, but the thing had had to be done. If the
hiroi were going to die, they would surely have done so
by now.

230

Sirru reached out, chemically listening to the air, and it seemed to him that he could hear something after all. It was a layered sequence of perspectives, sibilant, murmuring just beneath the edge of sound. It spoke of fear, incomprehension and pain. It was an animal voice. It gave location: the edge of stone, a strip of sky. For a disorientated moment Sirru saw his own narrow face looking down. His toes clenched in brief elation. Things were beginning to move forward.

His thoughts turned to other, more advanced, plans. He wondered whether he should postpone his intentions until the following day, but decided against it. Besides, after his thoughts of Anarres, he had a sudden longing for company.

Swiftly, Sirru descended the tower, climbed over the parapet and down the wall. The stone was crumbling, providing numerous footholds. His unseen defences were in place and as he passed in front of the gates the fierce black-hairy person who guarded the temenos did not give him a second glance. Nor did the soldiers, or the ring of pilgrims beyond them. After a few false starts, he succeeded in remembering the locative of the *apsara* Ir Yth had pointed out to him earlier. Tangible signals of the way reminded him, even in these lifeless streets. He picked up his own lingering pheromonal traces and other scents, too, which functioned as markers: the sudden pungency of dung combined with sweet watermelon, a subtle interface of spices. Sirru slipped through the labyrinth of streets until he found himself in front of the *apsara*'s house. He could smell the strong, artificial odour of her perfume, masking but not hiding her pheromonal signature.

The door was unlocked. Sirru stepped through and found himself in a long, narrow room. It was stuffy and decorated in dark, rich colours. Incense burning before the blue image of a god made his eyes prickle. Sirru prowled around for a moment before finding the staircase. He knew that this was not going to be easy, if his experiences with Jaya were anything to go by. But the woman was an *apsara*, after all, and therefore must surely be versed in basic techniques of communication.

Ir Yth's comments echoed in his mind: *Sexual intimacy here is limited to one of those two roles. Pleasure and reproduction.* He couldn't believe these people were that restricted; Ir Yth was lying, trying to dissuade him from the obvious route to the communications network. Stepping onto a landing, he paused before a door. He could hear sounds within. Sirru dismantled his defences and opened the door.

The *apsara* was lying on the bed, reading a printed paper with pictures on the front. She was surrounded by pillows; all manner of rich materials, encrusted with embroidery. The air was heavy with perfume and the smoke rising from the little stick in the *apsara*'s hand. Fronds of flowers spilled petals across the floor. A fluffy white animal rose to its feet when it saw Sirru, hissed and fled. Slowly, disbelievingly, the *apsara* raised her dark gaze from the pages of her paper and stared at Sirru. Her mouth fell open. She broadcasted simple, total astonishment, uncontaminated by fear. *A good enough start*, thought Sirru. There was a slithering rattle as the paper slid to the floor. The *apsara* whispered something from a dry, constricted throat.

/*Do not be alarmed*/*I intend no harm*/ Sirru radiated, hoping that he really wasn't lying. Then the *apsara*'s mouth opened further and she emitted a long, shrill shriek. Sirru gaped at her, but no one came running. The noise was stopped as abruptly as it started. The *apsara* whimpered.

'Please,' Sirru said aloud, in his own *desqusai* verbal. He modulated it to the Informal Responsive, the kind of soothing language one would use when addressing an infant. She wouldn't understand, but he hoped the tone might convey something. The *apsara*'s eyes were wide and frightened, but at least she wasn't screaming any more. Slowly, making placating gestures, Sirru came over and sat on the end of the bed. He took the *apsara*'s hand and looked down at it. Her rudimentary claws were varnished a pretty shade of peach. It was a soft, plump hand, more *khaithoi* than *desqusai* and quite unlike Jaya's sinewy fingers. Wrist to wrist, Sirru tried to explain. He was not sure if she understood . . .

. . . Rajira Jahan had no idea from which of the numerous hells her unexpected and uninvited guest had come, but after the initial shock she began to speculate furiously. Her

233

visitor was clearly not a human being, which seemed to limit the options to alien, demon or god. Rajira was limitlessly and indulgently superstitious, but she also possessed a strong measure of common sense, and along with everyone else she had been avidly watching the 24-hour newscasts which focused, for a change, on her own beloved city of Varanasi. Moreover, she had not heard of any recent manifestations by deities in the bedrooms of local courtesans, and logic therefore suggested that her visitor was from elsewhere in the galaxy.

And that might mean all sorts of possibilities.

Her ruthless sense of self-preservation kicked in, bisecting fear. Rajira bestowed a gracious smile upon her guest and uttered a single word: '*Chai?*'

Rather to her surprise, her guest appeared to understand this. He smiled. Sliding off the bed, Rajira ran to the door and clapped her hands for the maid. 'Tea! A pot. Quickly!' She waited in the doorway until the maid appeared, snatched the tray out of the girl's hands, and placed it on the table. Then she locked the door behind her. The advisability of doing this crossed her mind, but she dismissed it. Rajira had never yet met a man she couldn't handle . . .

. . . Sirru accepted the tea, a drink that he had learned to appreciate during his brief time on Tekhei, and sipped it cautiously. It was pleasant, but he had not yet grown used to the phenomenon of hot drinks. He pointed to himself and said, 'Sirru.'

'Sirru?' The *apsara* caught on quickly, indicating her own ample chest and saying, 'Rajira.' He thought he could remember her simple locative. He wondered how to explain to this obliging woman the exact nature of his requirements. It was going to be an uphill task, he was sure of that. The problem was that he knew too little about sexuality among this particular branch of the *desqusai*. He thought again of Ir Yth's suggestion that the practice was limited to two basic functions, rather than the wide and varied range that it had come to represent throughout the more advanced temeni. Since reproduction was clearly not what Sirru had in mind, and pleasure was likely to be no more than a side-effect, he needed to clarify matters.

How this woman had become an *apsara* in the first place was open to some question, for she did not seem to possess the attributes of *apsarai* back home. She seemed to have relatively little facility with languages, for a start, communicating purely through verbal modes. But Ir Yth had told him that this woman was an *apsara* and she was certainly behaving in an inviting enough manner. It seemed unpardonable, however, simply to use her services without telling her why. Sirru put down his cup of tea and explained at length about the need to redevelop Tekhei. He explained about engineering, restructuring and the need for a communications network that would serve not only the needs of írRas-*desqusai* but Tekhein-*desqusai* as well.

If she permitted herself to be part of that network, she would be performing a truly invaluable service to the temeni as a whole. Thus Sirru uneasily salved his conscience . . .

. . . *Typical*, thought Rajira Jahan. *Men. They can't wait to get into your bedroom and then all they want to do is talk about their problems.* Her guest was speaking with animation and verve, but she couldn't understand a word of it. Nevertheless, visions of future glories swam through her mind's eye. The aliens must surely be powerful, and if she impressed this odd person enough to become some kind of official consort . . . well. There were many future possibilities that might profitably be explored. Rajira leaned across and placed a finger on the alien's lips.

'Not another word,' she announced with authority. She slipped her arms around his neck. He felt cool and firm, and he smelled pleasant – clean, with a slightly musky undernote that was rather stimulating. He lay beside her, holding her gently, and she nuzzled his throat. She felt suddenly as if she was drowning, bathed in unfamiliar desires . . .

. . . Perhaps this would be easier than anticipated. He allowed the *apsara* to draw him down, and took care to endow her with a meticulous cocktail of pheromones.

Might as well make the transaction as pleasant as possible for the poor woman, he thought . . .

. . . and with professional acumen, Rajira slid her hand beneath the alien's robes. They were folded in a way that took her a minute to locate actual flesh and when she did, she was still not sure. She touched a curved surface, smooth as glass, and then, to her surprise, warm skin. Her hand glided across Sirru's flat belly, caressing and teasing. The alien sighed and shifted slightly beneath her hand. Rajira smiled. Not so different, after all.

Sirru rolled over and kissed her. He tasted of tea, and some more personal taste that she couldn't identify. He was very gentle, taking his time, unlike some of her clients. She wondered, fleetingly, whether there were any more of his kind wandering around, in need of comfort. Then she heard him catch his breath and decided that she'd teased him enough. She ran her hand down the silky skin of his stomach, towards his— Rajira froze. Then she struggled up to lean on one elbow. The alien blinked up at her, murmured something.

'Sirru?'

She forced herself to resume a slower exploration of sudden, uncharted territory.

'Sirru? What is this?' Her fingers delicately probed a yielding ridge. The alien sighed, arching his back like a cat. All right, thought Rajira grimly; you're a professional girl.

So he isn't a human being. Never mind. Get on the right side of him and he might be useful.

Rajira had seen and done many things and the unfamiliar contours of the body beneath her hand did not exactly repel her, but they were certainly very strange. She encountered a triad of ridges, running down into the alien's groin. She settled into his arms and closed her eyes. It was easier if she didn't have to look. The alien said something and his voice took on a recognizable note of urgency. Rajira's tentative touch met something silkily wet, then a hardness. It felt as though she was actually inside him. A ridged wet edge . . .

I can't look, I can't, she thought. Sirru's hands were inside her negligee, arousing her despite herself. With some surprise, a moment later, she realized that she was naked. The ridges were enveloping the fingers of her probing hand, rising up against them, and then something hot and hard and satiny was pushing insistently into her palm. Rajira gripped it as best she could and the alien writhed. It seemed to have – edges, like a spine. Rajira was just about to tell the alien, in whatever language but no uncertain terms, that there was no way on Vishnu's Earth that he was ever going to put *that* inside her when the spines suddenly retracted. The organ drew her hand back with it; there seemed to be a soft socket . . .

Rajira's eyes squeezed tighter shut. With a rustle of robes, Sirru turned so that she was half beneath him. He stroked her, murmuring in her ear and she was suspended in a most ambiguous place between revulsion, fascination and genuine desire.

'Go on then,' she said, through clenched teeth. As soon as he entered her, she could pretend everything was normal. He was shaped differently, but it didn't matter too much and the relief was so great that she relaxed against him and let him take her. He was undulating, pressing against her rather than thrusting, and with a vast, distant sense of surprise she came, on a tide of alien desires. She heard him hiss and there was a slight prickle deep inside as though she'd been touched with a thorn. He kissed her eyelids. Rajira lay shaking.

'Sirru . . .'

'Shhh,' the alien said, human at last. She felt him withdraw, then lift the counterpane up to cover her. She heard the soft snick of the door latch as he left. The reaction to what she had just done, and of what had been done to her, was so overwhelming that it was morning before Rajira realized she had never actually been paid.

12.
KHAIKURRIYË, NATURALS' QUARTER

Anarres woke. It was still dark, but the chill caused by the recent rain was gone. She was staring up at a web of lights: the mesh of space rafts, ships and satellites in orbit above Rasasatra, spinning over the gap of the ruined dome of the

Naturals' temenos. She lay still, listening to the march of her own thoughts, for slowly but surely, she was learning how to think.

It had been several days since she had first met Nowhere One and her prescription was officially overdue. At least the non-names still retained the characteristic chemical traces of their owners, otherwise Anarres would have found it confusing to be surrounded by people who had no locatives. She supposed it was logical enough, living as the Naturals did in a place that had no proper addresses. But there were many other things she found confusing these days. Thoughts that she had never had an inkling of entertaining occupied her mind: thoughts of her own status and what it meant, reflections on what the *khaithoi* and the upper castes seemed to feel they had a right to do to her. It was like being an infant again, lost in a troubling world. Anarres rose abruptly to her feet and went in search of her new companions.

She found Nowhere One busily catching vermin for breakfast and, feeling useless, sat down on the shattered edge of a pod to watch. She had already discovered that she possessed few of the attributes needed for survival. Only a few days before, Anarres reflected sadly, she had been securely established in her own comfortable home eating fresh clear-fish and pickled *intian*, and now she was sitting in the middle of a wasteland while an uncouth near-stranger scurried after house-lice. But better this, Anarres decided, than the stumpy hands and scheming mind of EsRavesh; better this than dead.

Nowhere One returned, triumphant, with a wriggling handful. Sitting next to her, he methodically dispatched the house-lice with a twist of their mandibles until a small pile of corpses was assembled at his feet. A palm-sized solar converter, looted from one of the abandoned temeni, rested nearby, soaking up the last of the light.

'Should have some heat in a minute,' Nowhere One remarked, happily. Anarres regarded him with admiration. Despite his unkempt appearance, and his membership of a most peculiar sect, Nowhere One was a remarkable person. Nothing seemed to faze him; no situation placed him at a loss, and he was surprisingly good-humoured, given the trouble that she'd caused him. If this was what it was like to live without suppressants, Anarres thought, then perhaps she could cope after all. Maybe she would even become a better person for it. And it wasn't even as though Nowhere One was unattractive. She looked at him sidelong as he placed the house-lice in the converter, which sizzled each one to a handful of crisp chitin. His sharp face was kind, even if his quills were untrimmed and his clothes were in tatters. She was in no better shape herself. A few days' exposure to the weather had worn away the last of her face-wax and the remnants of her mesh dress clung to her hips. She thought of Sirru with a sigh, but Sirru was thousands of light years away. She moved a little closer to Nowhere One.

'Have a louse,' the Natural said, shifting uncomfortably. Anarres took the thing with a fastidious shudder, then realized how hungry she was. They split the rest of the lice between them.

'I've been trying to speak to your friend Sirru, but I can't reach the depth ship,' the Natural said. 'Mind you, the equipment we're using is pretty antiquated.' He spoke lightly enough, but Anarres could feel a sharp edge of anxiety. She shivered. Nowhere One leaned across and awkwardly touched her hand. 'Are you all right?'

'I suppose so. I'm confused. I don't know what to think.'

'Perhaps you need some time alone. *We* are confusing you, you know. You're not wearing scale; your suppressants are wearing thin . . . Our ideas are beginning to infect you. Eventually you'll learn to seal the rest of us off, to a degree.' He sighed. 'But I'm afraid we don't have time to let you adjust.'

'Why not?'

'A while ago you told me that you deleted your friend's First Body. Where was it?'

'It was in a storage facility,' Anarres said. 'On a translation orbital.'

'Security on those places is fairly high. How did you get in?'

'EsRavesh gave me the codes.' She held out her arm. 'They were implanted – a set of his own specific pheromonal cues.'

'If they were implanted, do you still have them?'

'I don't know. I suppose so. They don't dissipate once you use them; they're part of my body chemistry now.'

'Unless the implant had an expiry date.'

'I'm sorry,' Anarres said. 'I didn't ask too many questions at the time.'

The Natural's mouth curled in a smile. 'No. I don't suppose you did.'

'Why do you want to know?'

'Because I'm thinking of taking a trip,' Nowhere One said.

'Where to?'

'The orbital. We can go up with a maintenance crew. You'll probably need to borrow some clothes, though. I want you to go as yourself.'

'But you won't find anything on the orbital, surely? I told you. I erased Sirru's First Body.' Anarres felt herself grow hot with guilt.

'That doesn't matter,' Nowhere One said. 'It isn't Sirru we'll be looking for.'

13.
VARANASI, TEMPLE OF DURGA

Jaya paced the inner chamber of the Temple of Durga like a tiger in a cage, memories of her last conversation with Sirru echoing dismally throughout her mind. Spoken so simply, with such devastating innocence, as though no reasonable person could possibly object to such an idea. She was furious with herself, for ever being naïve enough to have hope. The prospect of a cure for Selenge now seemed nothing more than a remote and fanciful dream. /Harvest./ She should have killed him while she had the chance, Jaya thought; there must have been a way. And

243

now Sirru had disappeared, presumably to carry out his sinister plans for humanity.

'Where is he?' She turned on an agitated Ir Yth.

/I do not know./

'Why not? I thought you were his colleague, his comrade. And now the mediator has vanished and you—' The lash of her rage made the *raksasa* take an involuntary step back. 'You have been *lying* to me. Sirrubennin Es-Moyshekhal tells me that we are to be harvested. What does that mean, Ir Yth, goddess of lies? Are we to be some kind of *crop*? Or food for the demons that you clearly are?'

Ir Yth's mouth folded itself away, piece by piece. She turned away from Jaya and slowly, slowly, a remote fury extended from her. The chamber became suddenly cold. A bead of sweat trickled icily down Jaya's spine. Ir Yth's voice in Jaya's mind felt like frost, but there was a fire burning beneath her words, somewhere far away. The pressure inside her mind expanded and grew, and Jaya's knees began to buckle. She remembered a sensation like lightning, streaking down her palm.

/I am not obliged to explain myself. You are a small part of a large organism; a pivot, nothing more. The mediator does as he sees fit; he reports to the Core, as do I. Neither of us need answer to you./ She flicked the pronoun like a whip and Jaya gasped as if she had been struck. The *raksasa* said, in a more conciliatory tone, /We are treating you with consideration; remember that. You are desqusai, after all; you are írRas. You are a person

244

when all is said and done, not one of the hiroi. *And you are not a crop./*

'But the mediator spoke of harvest.'

/The mediator was correct. That is the original aim of the project./

'What does that mean?' Jaya demanded. The *raksasa*'s patience was somehow more terrible than her rage.

/The castes of the desqusai, *like all the írRas, require the guidance of the Core when they reach a certain level. You have reached this point yourselves. You already engineer the* hiroi *to a primitive degree, and now that your genetic structures are deemed capable of bearing proper communication systems, as proved by your sum-moning of the ship, it has been decided to bring you under the aegis of the írRas./*

'You're here to colonize, aren't you? To conquer.' Her deepest instincts had been right all along. Never mind the damned Westerners. An army would come, with weapons beyond imagining.

Ir Yth seemed annoyed. */We do not 'conquer'. We are here to facilitate development./*

'You're here to enslave!'

We have no need to enslave,/ Ir Yth replied. */You are already part of us. How could this not be so? We have made you what you are; we have a duty to bring you into the fold. Can you not see that?/*

'Frankly, no!'

'Jaya? Ir Yth?'

Jaya turned to see Sirru standing in the doorway. His golden eyes flickered from face to face, reading the situation.

'Where have you been?' Jaya snapped. There was a subtle change to the mediator's demeanour, she noted, a certain languidness of movement. He spoke to Ir Yth with a flick of his fingers and walked slowly past them in the direction of his own chamber. Jaya stared after him, resentful and afraid.

'Sirru. Wait!' He did not look back.

/Adjustment to new developments is always hard,/ Ir Yth said magnanimously. /Perhaps you should rest. I intend to./

The note of dismissal was very clear. Jaya went numbly to her own chamber and lay down on the pallet bed. She had planned to get the aliens out of the city on the following night, but what now? Should she tell Rakh to put a bullet in the pair of them? Better yet, assume responsibility and do it herself? But what then? Sirru and Ir Yth were only two people, of an apparently immense empire. Even if she killed them, more would follow . . .

Sleep did not come quickly.

She was awoken by a commotion at the gate. Glancing at her watch, she saw that it was not yet midnight. She could hear a voice raised in wrath: Rakh shouting at someone, and a high imperious voice snapping in reply. There was something curiously familiar about the second voice. Jaya ran down the stairs to find Sirru standing in

246

the courtyard, staring bemused at the gatehouse. Jaya headed for the gate.

'Rakhi? What's going on?'

Rakh turned on her, beard bristling.

'This – this *woman* demands an audience.'

Not another one, Jaya thought. There had already been over a hundred petitioners, claiming they had experienced visions or been sent by the gods. And since the news of her cure had got out, it had been a thousand times worse. Nothing like word of a miracle to bring people flocking to your door.

'Who is it this time?'

Peering past Rakh's camouflaged shoulder, she saw a girl standing in the entrance to the temple, head thrown back. Jaya froze.

Farmed orchids adorned the length of glossy hair that fell to the girl's feet. A ruby bhindi glittered between her frowning brows, but if it were not for the scowl, she would be remarkably beautiful. And she was also horribly familiar, for Jaya had only recently set eyes on her photograph, splashed across a double-page spread in *Movie Monthly*. Kharishma Kharim.

Behind the actress was strung a motley array of followers, one of them was leading the elephant on which Kharishma had apparently arrived. Why had the militia allowed her through their ranks? Weren't they supposed to be protecting the temple? One look at the besotted face of an army major, however, hovering in the midst of the followers, explained that mystery. Taking a deep breath, Jaya said, 'Well.'

Kharishma tried to push past Satyajit Rakh, who thrust out an arm and pinned her against the wall of the gatehouse. There was an angry surge forward from the followers, but then everyone became very still. Turning, Jaya saw that Sirru was standing at her shoulder. He looked at Kharishma rather as one might look upon an angry, pretty child, with a kind of tolerant indulgence. Ir Yth peered around his shoulder.

/Who is this?/ Ir Yth asked.

'This is a woman who is portraying me in a film,' Jaya said, through gritted teeth. There was a brief pause whilst Ir Yth translated, then the *raksasa* said, /The mediator wishes to know if this is a Second Body? Did you resemble one another before your sickness?/

'A Second Body? No, I've only ever had the one body, Ir Yth.' What was the *raksasa* talking about now? 'Shrimati Kharim is playing me in – a piece of entertainment. In the movie, she is apparently an aristocrat. I'd surmise that Shrimati Kharim likes the idea of being a warrior heroine.' Merely because you allow a certain myth to be cultivated around your name does not mean you have to believe in it, and Jaya knew exactly what she was and was not. Unlike some people, apparently.

Kharishma had been staring at Sirru and Ir Yth with a most peculiar expression. Jaya was reminded that the two aliens had really had very little exposure to people since they had arrived, and that Sirru had not, to the best of her knowledge, been seen at all. Kharishma murmured something and fell to her knees in the dust. *Typical affected theatricality*, Jaya thought. She had seen the sudden glint of calculation in Kharishma's beautiful, kohl-lined eyes just before her obeisance.

The movie star's followers swayed like a field of reeds. Slowly and gracefully, Kharishma rose to her feet and raised her arms so that they were curved above her head. Her knees remained bent beneath the magnificent sari. Her jewelled fingers fluttered against her brow as she began to dance: *bharat natyam*, the great and ancient dance of the south, which depicted the course of the god Krishna's life. Jaya too could dance, but never so gracefully or well, and she watched with a sick sense of irritation as Kharishma undulated in the dust. Sirru was watching closely, with an intensity of interest that verged on the predatory. But after a very few minutes, everyone's attention was wrested elsewhere.

The scream came from the parapet of the temple. Looking up, Jaya saw a figure balanced on the battlements. The man must have climbed up the outside wall of the temple, since Rakh and the army had been so assiduous in not letting anyone through the gates. The man was holding a box or a can; she could not see clearly from this distance. He shook it over his head and after a moment the stench of petrol drifted down. He paused, raised his arms high above his head in a parody of the dancer below, and wailed a blessing aloud. It was a blessing on Jaya herself, on her supporters, on the aliens; it prophesied glory to all Bharat.

It was a lengthy and exhaustive blessing, and everyone stood paralysed apart from Rakh, who was already racing through the temple courtyard and up the stairs.

After an electric moment, Jaya followed him, but she was only halfway across the courtyard when the figure on the battlements lit a match. He went up like a bomb. There was a unanimous gasp from the crowd, which gave the brief and illusory effect of a vacuum, for the figure on the battlements seemed momentarily to burn more brightly. Jaya watched in horror, which was all that anyone could do right now. From the corner of her eyes, through the open gate, she saw a surge through the front rows of the crowd as they realized the human torch was about to fall. He plunged from the battlements like a meteor, and he made no sound at all. Perhaps he was already dead. She did not even hear him land.

Kharishma crouched in the dust, her hands pressed to her mouth in a silent scream. Jaya had to admit that immolating oneself in front of a gathering of hundreds of people was a fairly effective way to steal someone else's limelight, but she could take no pleasure in the fact, however much she might have despised Kharishma. Sirru was staring at the place where the immolator had stood with an expression that suggested this was just another part of the show. Ir Yth appeared merely baffled, with a trace of disgust. Not the only one, Jaya thought, and shouted to Rakh, 'What are you waiting for? Close the gate. *Close the gate.*' And he did as she told him.

14.
KHAIKURRIYË

Nervously, Anarres stood at the edge of the ledge, looking out across the city. Far below, a barge floated like a leaf in the wind. A glittering band of light defined the coast and she could see Rasasatra's ancient sun sinking down towards the sea. The great wing of the raft rippled above the landing ledge, casting shadows over the faces of the crowd.

'What if someone notices us?' she hissed to Nowhere One.

The Natural shifted uneasily. 'Just keep yourself concealed from anyone who's a lower caste, until you have to speak to the gatekeeper. I'll do the same. This is a service raft – most of these people are low-level personnel. If we come across anyone of a higher level who might see through the concealment, we'll just have to keep the scale turned up and hope they don't take an interest in us. If anyone asks, you're going to see a client and I'm a maintenance worker.'

'Could they tell you're a Natural?'

'Eventually, yes. We'll just have to hope for the best.'

The gates leading onto the ramp of the raft slid open. Anarres stepped forwards, trying to merge with the throng of people. If the implant didn't work, or if EsRavesh had broadcast her description . . . But there was no reason for him to suspect that she would want to go back to the translation orbital. Anarres hoped that Nowhere One could be trusted. She had never heard of the person whose first body he sought in the vaults, and the Natural had told her nothing more than the name.

Anxiously she scanned the crowd, and saw no one who resembled a *khaith*. *But then, I wouldn't necessarily see them. They can make themselves invisible to me.* The thought of being followed by some slinking, unperceived nightmare made her quills hackle. The Natural squeezed her hand.

'Are you all right?' he whispered.

'Nearly.' She had escaped the *khaithoi* once. She could do it again, if she just kept her wits about her and remembered to be brave. As she drew near to the gate-keeper, she dropped the concealment and exuded as much allure as she could. The gatekeeper gave an audible gasp. So did Nowhere One, who slipped through the gate in the aura of Anarres's magnetic sexuality.

Several people looked round, but Anarres was already through the gate and onto the raft, drawing her conceal-ment about her once more. From the corner of her eye, she saw Nowhere One sliding into a corner behind a hanging veil of mesh. She followed him and sat down.

Nowhere One seemed rather breathless; Anarres hoped he wasn't claustrophobic, or had a fear of flying.

'Do you think anyone noticed us?' she asked, to take his mind off his surroundings.

Nowhere One turned to her rather desperately and said, 'Quite frankly, all I can think about at the moment is sex. How do you *do* that?'

'It's my job,' Anarres told him, bewildered. 'I don't think we can do anything about it now. I'm sorry. Someone might see.'

'I'm not suggesting we— Let's talk about it later, Anarres.' He took a deep breath. 'If there *is* a later.'

There was a faint jolt as the raft lifted. Anarres shut her eyes, trying not to think about their destination. But then she opened them again. She had to start thinking ahead; she was long since past the point where she could pretend that things weren't happening. She had to take responsibility for her actions. She stared out into the darkness as the raft surged upwards. It was not long before it docked.

Anarres and Nowhere One waited impatiently in line as the maintenance workers moved off. As Anarres stepped in front of the *hessirei* at the gate, it looked up sharply.

'Madam! I have seen you before.'

'That is correct,' Anarres told him with dignity, trying to overcome a flutter of panic. 'You remember me from my last visit, when I came to see the orbital's overseer, Uassi SiMethiKhajhat.'

'Must see your pass once more,' the *hessirei* mumbled, lowering its head. Anarres reached out an imperious hand and stiffened her fingers to activate the implant. There was an electric pause.

'Most acceptable,' the *hessirei* said. Anarres leaned across, murmuring into the whorl of its ear and sending out the aura of her allure. When she straightened up, Nowhere One was not to be seen.

Gliding swiftly past the bemused *hessirei*, Anarres found herself once more in the corridor that led to the translation vaults. Nowhere One stepped from behind an arching, chitinous pillar.

'Where are the vaults?' he whispered.

'Through here.'

Anarres and the Natural hastened along the corridor, ducking out of view whenever a maintenance person appeared.

'SiMethiKhajhat must have quite a reputation,' Nowhere One murmured. 'The *hessirei*'s terrified of him.'

Anarres agreed. She hoped she would never meet the overseer. EsRavesh's implant would baffle the sensors to some degree, but there was no point in taking chances. They reached the vaults, and Nowhere One halted.

'There must be thousands of them,' Anarres said. 'Last time, I had Sirru's coordinates, but now . . .'

'There are a lot of administrative personnel offworld, that's why. The storage units of their First Bodies should be logged according to sector.'

'And which sector are we looking for?'

'It's called EsIttikh.'

'Where's that?'

'It's one of the more recently charted areas of space, out on the galactic edge. There's not a lot in it – a few suns, a few dead systems. And a little world called Arakrahali.'

15.
VARANASI

Rajira Jahan, courtesan of Varanasi, was glued to her imported Mitsubishi DVD, seeking news of her departed alien lover. The previous night seemed an eternity away and she found herself wondering whether the whole event had been nothing more than a dream. It was, indeed, similar to some of the visions that Rajira had experienced in her brief and cautious flirtations with opium. But as soon as she saw the fleeting glimpse of Sirru, standing in the courtyard of the Temple of Durga behind the shoulder of Jaya Nihalani, she knew that it was real.

Rajira, adept at noting opportunities for power, had no intention of letting this one slip by. Summoning her latest maid, who also acted as her secretary, she ran a finger down the list of the day's bookings.

'Shri Matondkar – the elderly gentleman, you remember? He's been a client for years, you can reschedule him for next week, he won't mind. Usually just wants a chat these days, anyway. Shri Khan – better keep him on the list; he's wealthy. A banker. Shri Sharma – definitely keep him. A politician, from the Punjab. He comes here for conferences.' She reflected for a moment. 'Not precisely blessed with the looks of Krishna, that one, but stamina: my God! They say he's got a positive *harem* back home.' She reached the end of the list and frowned. 'Who is this? He's down as a question mark.'

'He wouldn't give his name,' the maid said. 'He phoned.'

Rajira felt a small shiver of anticipation. Was there any chance that this could be the alien? With the prospect of the day's activities before her, she found herself dwelling on stranger flesh with a sensation that was close to nostalgia. The alien might have been anatomically challenging, but at least he knew how to treat a girl. 'Mr X, eh? Did he sound local?'

'He spoke excellent Hindi. And he says he knows you. He said: *Remember the hibiscus tree.*' Puzzled, the maid frowned, but Rajira was immediately transported fifteen years into the past.

Then, she had surely rivalled Lakshmi for loveliness, even if it might be heresy to think so. That's what they'd called her in those days, only partly joking: *the Goddess of Love.* People had compared her to her most famous predecessor, Sushma the Beautiful, heroine of a hundred stories. Just as Sushma had done three hundred years before, Rajira had gone one day to the market and met a prince. Unlike Sushma, however, she had been shopping not for rare silks, but for the latest Western videos. And it was while she was standing in the shade of a hibiscus tree, clutching a copy of *Dreamville II* and fanning herself against the heat, that her prince had appeared. True, he'd been driving an army jeep rather than riding the white horse that had been the mount of the prince in the legend, but otherwise it was exactly the same. They had been lovers for a year, until the prince's mother had found out that her son was seeing a courtesan.

Now, Rajira could smile at the memory. That had been a scene and a half and no mistake. Her prince had been abruptly recalled to an army base in the north, but had sworn to return one day. For a while, Rajira really believed it, but then she had realized the truth and concentrated instead on investing the large sum that her beloved's mother had given her to ensure a dignified retreat. She had followed his career, of course, and read the rumours of military brutality with some dismay. He hadn't been like that with her, but then who knew what men were capable of?

And now here he was making an appointment, only fifteen years too late. She sat down at her dressing table, and began to apply her makeup with more than usual care.

Towards the end of the afternoon, Rajira ushered the Punjabi politician firmly out of her boudoir and waited nervously for the arrival of the visitor. The door opened, and a man stepped through.

'Rajira! You haven't changed a bit.'

Apart from an additional twenty pounds, Rajira thought. Still it was nice of him to say so.

'Neither have you, Amir.' She stepped forwards and took his hands, stood looking up into the cold blue gaze that had made her weak at the knees fifteen years before. But too much time had gone by, and she knew it. She said, 'Well, I didn't expect to see you ever again. I thought you were getting married?'

Amir Anand gave her a rather hangdog look in response. Rajira knew that look: it was guilt. She had seen it a hundred times; men loved to exert control over someone, if they felt their own relationship might be slipping away from them. All her clients that day had been married men, though she knew for a fact that the banker's wife was cheating on him. And she'd heard rumours about what the politician's lady got up to when he was out of town, too. But that was just the way of the world. At least no one had to worry about AIDS any more; though as soon as they found an inoculation for one disease, another seemed to erupt in its place.

'How is the dear girl?' Rajira asked, just to rub it in. Anand let go of her hands and sat heavily down on the bed.

'I don't want to talk about it,' he said.

'Then let me bring you some tea,' Rajira replied. 'Or would you prefer whisky?'

'Whisky,' said Anand, gloomily. After that, it didn't take long to get the whole story out of him: how Kharishma was becoming more and more obsessed with power, how she was trying to wangle her way into politics, how she'd changed. Rajira noted that he studiously avoided using the term "unbalanced", but it was clear that this was the root of it.

'But do you love her, Amir?' she said at last. She was surprised to find that her voice was so steady, and even more amazed when the image of the alien slid into her mind, eclipsing the older pain. She even managed to look

Anand in the eye when he said miserably, 'Yes. Yes, I do.'
Then he groped for her hand and added, 'Rajira? You know
that you – you were—'

'Hush,' she said. 'Don't say anything more.'

16.
VARANASI, TEMPLE OF DURGA

'*Moksha*,' Satyajit Rakh said, gloomily.

'What?' Jaya looked up from the Web reports and the
headset that connected her to the Net. Her head was
beginning to pound. She blinked in the dimmer light, the
memory of the screen still scrolling across her retinas.
Rakh's face was filled with a sour sadness. He repeated,
'*Moksha*, if you die in Varanasi by the sacred river.
Liberation from the wheel of life. That's why that man
killed himself last night – there are rumours that the aliens
are gods, that they've come to take us all to heaven.
Apparently the suicide decided he couldn't wait. They've
already put up a shrine to him across the square. People
have been visiting it all morning – Shiv says it's got your
photo in it, as well. You could be becoming the centre of
another cult, Jaya.'

'I'm starting to get used to that.' Jaya sighed. 'What
happened to Kharishma?'

'She's set up camp across the square. With a pavilion.
I've issued a complaint to the Minister, as you instructed,
but the troops all adore her. You saw the elephant?'

Jaya gave a sardonic nod. 'Almost as difficult to miss as Kharishma herself. Was it an elephant, though?' She had a memory of something bigger, with huge sweeping tusks and a white mane, and an even vaguer memory of an ex-lover of Kharishma's being the director of a wildlife park in northern Uttar Pradesh. 'Looked like one of those purported cloned mammoths to me.'

Rakh shook his head, unsure. 'What do you think Kharishma wants?'

'She wants to be famous,' Jaya snapped. 'What else?'

She pointed to the computer screen, where Shiv was downloading a clip from the forthcoming movie. In the absence of more concrete information, the film was causing a great deal of attention throughout the media. Jaya, Shiv and Rakh watched it in silence, and some bewilderment. In the clip, Jaya was portrayed as aristocratic, victorious, vengeful, and magnificent. It seemed to be a typical time-honoured Bollywood production, complete with songs.

'Not going for realism, are they?' Shiv remarked.

Jaya snorted. 'I don't see too many allusions to mud and dysentery, no. Look at that' – as Kharishma battled her way across a crocodile-infested river. 'She's still got her lipstick on!'

'I know,' Shiv said, artlessly. 'And you were such a mess most of the time.'

Jaya gave him a chilly look. 'I'd like you to keep your eye on Kharishma, as long as we're here.'

'All right. Are we still planning to leave tonight?'

Jaya sighed. 'Yes. I think so. If we kill the aliens, more

will come, and besides, they're the last bargaining chip we have left. But if they're planning genocide . . . Oh, I don't know, Rakh. I don't know what to do. We'll keep to the original plan and go north. I'm going to get some rest.' She slapped Rakh on the shoulder with an old affection on her way through the door. 'Guard us well, Rakhi. As you always have.'

Later, however, she was deep in some uneasy dream when Rakh shook her awake. The sun slanted in through the windows, suggested that it was already past noon.

'Commander? Excuse me. You have a visitor.'

'What, another one? Goddess . . . Who is it this time?'

Rakh's teeth flashed white in a grin.

'Someone you might be pleased to see. For a change.'

Jaya sat up. There was a small figure at Rakh's elbow, who stepped awkwardly forwards. The Selenge had taken so great a hold that it was hard to recognize him at first.

'Halil?'

The last time she had seen the boy was in the sewers beneath Varanasi General, on the day of her escape from the hospital. She reached out and hugged the boy. Halil felt slight and frail in her arms, bird-boned. He gave a wide, shy grin.

'I wanted to come before, but I couldn't. I was ill,' he explained, unnecessarily.

'We found him inside the courtyard,' Rakh said, with an unmistakable note of warning in his voice.

'Halil?' She drew the boy beside her. 'Sit down. Tell me. How did you get in?'

The child readily replied, 'Through the passages underneath the temple. They lead into the sewers, end up out on the river.'

'Rakhi, I thought you had people posted down there.'

'Who do you think caught him?'

'Halil, why did you come here? To see me, or—?'

'I heard there are some people here. From another world. I wanted to see them. And you, too,' he added, loyally. 'No one sent me, if that's what you're thinking. I'm not a spy.'

Jaya was not sure that she believed this, but whatever the truth of the matter, she did not think that Halil had very long left to live. And maybe he was not the only one. All the hopes she had that the aliens might be able to heal her people settled in a knot in her stomach. A tight anger constricted her throat and she took the child by the hand.

'Come on. You want to see the aliens, do you? Well, let's go and see them, then. Rakh, go back to the gate.'

She found Sirru crouching by the main entrance of the great hall. He was running his fingertips across the stone step, his hands twisting in a complex pattern. She had no idea what he was doing, but it seemed to her that there was a trace of furtiveness in the golden eyes. He glanced indifferently at the child.

'Sirru? I want you to meet someone. This is Halil.'

She gave the child a little push between his thin shoulder blades, propelling him forwards. Halil dug his feet in for a moment, then stepped towards Sirru. He was almost eye to eye with the crouching alien. They

262

regarded each other gravely for a moment, then Sirru reached out and turned the child's face to the lamplight. He moved the boy's jaw this way and that, considering the striations of Selenge, like snail tracks across the skin. Soon, when the disease entered its last leprotic stages, Jaya knew that the flesh along those striations would be eaten away, and then would come liver failure. Halil's joints had stiffened, too.

An unmistakable look of speculation entered Sirru's gaze: relating to what? Suddenly uneasy, Jaya took a step forward, ready to snatch the child away, but Halil stood as if entranced. Sirru's long hands cupped the boy's face for a moment, and the alien's eyes narrowed. Then, with a movement so swift that Jaya did not even see it, Sirru's sharp nails opened up the child's wrist. There was blood from palm to elbow. Halil gave a sharp, startled cry and sank to the floor, mouth working in shock. Jaya sprang forwards, but the alien was no longer there. He had dragged the child into the corner, backed up against the wall.

'Sirru!' she cried. 'Let him go. Let him go *now*!'

A wave of fear, so strong it was almost palpable, made Jaya stumble to her knees. And though she struggled against it, she could not rise. It was not her own fear, but something imposed from without, goading her adrenaline into override action. Neutralized by Sirru, she could only watch helplessly. His own wrist had been injured, she saw as he pulled back the sleeve of his robe. She watched with horrified fascination as the skin of his arm began to pull back, crawling up his arm like someone rolling back a sock. Layers of muscle exposed themselves and then the slow seep of blood from a vein. It might be arterial blood, but it looked too dark. He pressed his own bleeding flesh against the child's injured wrist, so that the blood mingled. Halil's eyes were wide, his mouth open in a silent rictus shout.

'Sirru,' she croaked. Her throat felt as though a hand had closed around it. *'What are you doing?'* A stray memory snapped at her of the room on the ship; the walls closing in on her, and pain.

Sirru was murmuring to the boy, and Jaya caught the soft drift of reassurance. 'Sirru?' she whispered again, and the alien looked up. His face was filled with pity. He sent:

/*frustration*/*anger*/*sorrow*/*wrongness*/

'What?'

/*wrongness*/*incorrectness*/*failure*/

The child's head was drooping. Sirru raised the boy's bloodstained wrist, which already seemed to have closed, and fastidiously licked it clean. Jaya stared, appalled and still unable to move, but then Sirru's grip was abruptly released. Her calf muscles shook like jelly. She crawled as quickly as she could across the floor and reached out a trembling hand to the boy's throat.

'Halil! Are you all right? I won't let him touch you again.'

The pulse was strong; Halil was unconscious. Sirru's free arm, cleansed of blood, snaked around her waist and pulled her close.

'Don't touch me!' She tried to pull away, but his grip was too strong.

He gave her a reassuring pat on her forearm.

/good girl/finished now/better/order restored/

'What in the name of hell have you *done*?'

He squinted round so that he could look her in the face.

/why, healed/

He seemed surprised. She looked down at the child. Perhaps it was just her imagination, but the silvery striations of the disease appeared to be fading. Sirru drew a gentle finger down the child's cheek.

'Jaya?'

'Yes?'

/Many?/

'What do you mean?'

He tapped the child's face.

/Many?/

'Yes,' she said, trying to gather her confused and angry thoughts and project the right emotion. 'Many of them, Sirru. A lot of sick people.'

The hope of a cure for Selenge, the whole reason for her need to keep the aliens close, returned with full force. Warring with it, however, was that later echo . . . *Healing and harvest.* How did those two fit together? If indeed they did. After what Sirru had just done to the boy, she was more confused than ever. Worrying over understanding like a jackal with a bone, Jaya shrank from the alien's grasp and sagged back against the wall with the child's head in her lap, so that they were sitting in a row: a family from nightmare.

17.
ORBITAL, RASASATRA

'Hurry up,' Anarres hissed. 'Someone's bound to notice what we're doing.' She shifted from foot to foot in agitation as Nowhere One scrolled through the list of translation logs.

'I'm nearly there. EsItta . . . EsIttgi . . . EsIttikh! And here's the file for Arakrahali.' He pointed to a vault in triumph.

'Only one person?'

'There was only one administrator on Arakrahali,' the Natural informed her. 'A *desqusai* named IrEthiverris. And a *khaith*.'

'But I recognize this vault,' Anarres said. She looked around her, certain now that she had come here once before. 'I'm sure this is the person that EsRavesh told me to erase.'

'Interesting,' Nowhere One said, softly. He slid the storage container out of the vault. It was roughly the size of the palm of his hand, and fitted easily into the sleeve of his robe.

'You're stealing that?' Anarres said, wide-eyed.

'That was the whole point of the trip.' Nowhere One closed the vault. 'Let's go.'

266

'But who is it?'

Nowhere One smiled at her. 'IrEthiverris' First Body. I want some answers about Arakrahali and there's only one person who can give them to me.'

Together, they hastened out of the chamber containing the vaults and back along the corridor. But as they reached the docking bay, someone stepped out in front of them, towering over Anarres and the Natural. Beneath a robe encrusted with ornamental wire, the being's skin was a deep black, like a bruise, and his eyes were a startling light lavender. A spiny crest rose along the crown of his head and he had long, attenuated fingers. He spoke, in a high whistling voice.

'Madam! I am overseer of this facility. I am Uassi SiMethiKhajhat. I have been looking for you. My *hessirei* gatekeeper told me that you were seeking me. I fear you have become lost.'

His lavender gaze flickered over Nowhere One. The Natural, with an anxious glance at Anarres, sidled back into the shadows.

'Come with me,' the overseer said. He turned, flicking a hand towards the Natural as he passed. Anarres caught the tail end of a stinging hail of pheromones. Nowhere One gave a brief hiss of pain.

'Maintenance people! Always getting in my way,' the overseer snapped. He led her through a maze of corridors, to what was evidently his private chambers. 'Sit down. Now. I did not summon an *apsara*. Why have you come to see me?'

Anarres, thinking fast, noted the encrusted wire of the overseer's robes, and the waxed sheen of his face. She saw that the spines of his crest were inlaid with metal grooves, and that the long claws were polished to an obsidian shine. Anarres cast her eyes modestly towards the floor and murmured, 'We *apsarai* gossip among ourselves. Word has got around about the weapons caste.' Taking a risk, she whispered, 'You see, normally I am affiliated to the *khaithoi*, but . . .'

'*Khaithoi!*' the overseer snapped. 'A vile people. I will not permit them on this facility, higher caste though they are. They are constantly requesting access, but I baffle them with bureaucracy, divert them with security checks.' His crest rose at this evidence of his own cleverness.

That explained why EsRavesh had initially sent her here, then. 'So I'm sure you understand why I might seek the company of someone more . . .' Anarres reached out and drew a finger down the overseer's arm. '*Enticing.*' She caught her lip between her teeth and gazed up into Si-MethiKhajhat's lavender eyes.

The overseer's spines prickled with pride. 'You are a connoisseur, then! What a delight. We understand one another, I can see. Let us dispense with the formalities and begin. I prefer to initiate my first sexual act with Fourth Position, moving on to Sixth as we become more familiar with one another.' He indicated a set of bonds attached to the floor. 'I am also fond of the use of artificial restraints. How about you?'

Anarres sighed. But rather this than capture. She hoped

Nowhere One had found somewhere to hide. She turned to the overseer and smiled. 'That sounds wonderful.'

Some considerable time later, Anarres rose from the couch and re-tied the laces of her dress. She glanced down at the slumbering form of the overseer and wondered whether her lie about gossiping *apsarai* might actually be true. SiMethiKhajhat certainly had some interesting hobbies. A year or so ago, Anarres might have been shocked, but after EsRavesh, anyone seemed acceptable. She had to find Nowhere One, but first, it seemed worthwhile to take a look around the overseer's private chamber. If he kept files, they did not seem to be here. Quickly, she searched through the racks of robes. SiMethiKhajhat's wardrobe was even more extensive than her own had been, and Anarres entertained a pang of regret for all her lost clothes. She'd probably never see her house again. But if that meant being free of the *khaithoi*, it was worth it.

In an annexe, she found an equipment deck. A communication harness hung on the wall and, after a moment of indecision, Anarres slipped it off its hook and rolled it up into a thin coil of mesh. Hadn't Nowhere One said that the Naturals' own pilfered technology was antiquated? This was a translation orbital; presumably its communications array would be powerful enough to reach other worlds? She was not sure, but she folded the mesh into her sleeve and crept stealthily out of the chamber.

To her immense relief, Nowhere One was loitering by

269

the entrance to the docking bay with a service-brush. His quills flared up when he saw her.

'What happened to you? I've been worried out of my mind!'

'I'll explain later. We have to go.'

They had an uneasy wait for the next raft, but boarding was not a problem. Anarres, now known to be the consort of the overseer, did not have to show her pass again. Within the space of an hour, they were once more standing on the landing ledge, in the hot, soft darkness of Khaikur-riyë. Anarres leaned back against the wall and closed her eyes.

There was a sudden confusion behind her. An alarm began to shrill, but it was a moment before she realized that it was actually silent. It throbbed through her, reverberating up and down her bones.

'Anarres!'

She turned.

'Come with me.' Nowhere One grasped her hand and dragged her along the ledge. She tried not to look down. The alarm sent weakness through her body, causing her to stagger.

'What's happening?' she cried.

'I don't know. Maybe your recent client's found his mesh missing.' He motioned towards the far end of the ledge and Anarres stiffened. The beings moving towards them were immense. Indigo carapaces glittered in the lamplight; pincers twitched.

The Natural hissed, and Anarres stumbled as they raced

270

around a corner. She caught a brief, vertiginous glimpse of the ground, a very long way below.

'I've got you.' The Natural's hand was clamped around her arm. '*Now.*' Grasping her around the waist, he stepped off the ledge into thin air. Anarres cried out, then found that they were not falling. They had stepped into an airwell, and were now proceeding swiftly but steadily downwards. The glistening shaft of a building towered up alongside the well; spines arched from its sides. Squinting up into the night, she could see their pursuers slide forth into nothingness. They resembled a pair of long-legged crustaceans, tossed from a high building.

'Can't we go any faster?'

'No. But neither can they.' The Natural gestured downwards. 'Look. See that barge?'

She could feel his pointed chin resting on the top of her head. They were nearly level with the gliding air-barge; its navigation lights sent a beacon through the darkness. The Natural was pulling at her dress, tugging it outwards.

'What are you *doing*?'

'Moving us.'

Slowly but surely, they were drifting to the edge of the airwell. Nowhere One gave a tug at his own ballooning robes and then there was a blast of air like a punch in the face. Finally, they were falling. The barge seemed to rush up from below, piloted by a very startled face. The air was knocked from Anarres's lungs as they hit the arch of air that sealed the barge, and then the deck. Nowhere One was already crawling to the front of the barge, knocking the pilot aside. The pilot's hiss of wrath was abruptly silenced as the Natural elbowed him in the throat. The pilot sprawled across the deck. The barge veered and turned and Anarres, who had only just gained her feet, was knocked backwards by the sudden acceleration.

Peering over the side of the barge, she saw that the landing ledge had receded to a tiny slit in the distance, with the great wing of the raft hovering above it. The barge veered between towers and domes, beneath the immense span of bridges. The whole hot world smelled of growth and growing, the air saturated with the green fragrance of night-plants. Nowhere One steered the barge higher. Tides of information drifted by; pheromonal eddies snatched by the wind and carried upwards on the wells of the world. Anarres looked back for signs of pursuit but the backdrop of the city was simply too huge for anything to show. By degrees Nowhere One took the barge lower, until they were sailing over the temeni below. This part of the city was grim: bleak, barren land interspersed with ruined domes and abandoned towers. It smelled of dust. With a rush of hope, Anarres recognized the Naturals' Quarter.

The barge dropped sharply and wobbled to a halt several feet above the ground. Nowhere One deactivated the air shield and leaped to the bald earth below.

'Quickly. We don't know who might be watching.'

Anarres raced after him towards the shadowy shelter of a ruined pod. When they reached its sanctuary, Nowhere One leaned against the curving wall, his chest heaving. Suddenly Anarres, too, was breathless. She sank down until she was crouching on the ground and Nowhere One collapsed beside her, reaching out to take her hands. She could feel the weight of the capsule in his sleeve: the First Body of IrEthiverris, last and only administrator of Arakrahali.

And then four stilted figures moved out of the shadows.

18.
VARANASI, TEMPLE OF DURGA

/*What is your opinion of Jaya's Second Body?*/ asked Ir Yth. Sirru was sitting cross-legged on a mat, holding a bowl of tea. It was one of the few substances here that he found straightforward to digest; most other things seemed to require an inordinate level of processing in order for no waste to be produced. Ir Yth would eat only ground rice, and appeared to be living off her own inner resources; already, her plump face was beginning to look a little drawn. Sirru glanced at the *raksasa* with interest and considered her question.

'I did not think she entirely resembled Jaya,' he said doubtfully. 'But I could have been mistaken. After all, we were responsible for some extensive modifications when Jaya visited the ship. I must say, I didn't know there was that level of advance here.'

/*There has been some success with cloning over the last twenty years or so. I confess, I have studied the progress reports closely and my understanding was that*/

273

Making was still in its infancy. But I fear,/ Ir Yth remarked with some embarrassment, */that all the desqusai look alike to me./*

'I suppose that's natural,' Sirru said, swallowing his irritation. 'But why then are both bodies activated at the same time?'

Ir Yth said loftily, */It is clear that you have not understood that Tekhei has different laws from our own enlightened society. One frequently sees primitive violations of common practice in such projects. Clearly it is permitted for both bodies to be extant simultaneously./* She paused, then said with studied indifference, */Do you intend to visit the Second Body?/*

'Why not? We should go soon; there are plans to leave the city tonight, to ensure our safety. It will be helpful to have two Receivers. I wonder why they were not both activated at once . . . Maybe something retarded the other one's development.'

/Perhaps she might assist when the rescue ship arrives,/ Ir Yth suggested, helpfully.

'Perhaps so,' Sirru said. He had taken to activating the scale armour whenever he was with Ir Yth, tuning it to a low setting so as not to betray its presence. He did not think the *raksasa* had noticed. It was fortunate that he had already taken steps to ensure that the communication system should be well underway, although the incident with the child had only increased his anxiety.

Something had gone deeply wrong with the Tekhein project over the course of its history. He thought with dismay of the viral indices eating away at the child's body; this should never have happened. Something must had gone dreadfully amiss with the regeneratives, far back in the Tekhein past, for such mutations to occur now. And why hadn't the Core been informed long before this? Then they could have quietly shut down the project and spared its unfortunate inhabitants generations of suffering. If there were two things that Sirru could not abide, they were misery and waste.

/When should we visit the Second Body?/ Ir Yth persisted. The *raksasa* was up to something, Sirru was sure.

'Later this afternoon, perhaps?' he suggested, innocently. The *raksasa* agreed, with what Sirru perceived to be a faint trace of relief. Surreptitiously, and under the guise of scratching, he turned the scale to a higher setting.

'Well,' he added, pointedly. 'I wish to rest. Shall we meet in the courtyard, in a couple of hours or so, and visit her together?'

Sirru returned to his small chamber, which overlooked the courtyard, and waited. A half-hour or so later, as predicted, he saw a short bundled figure heading hastily across the courtyard. He slid over the sill and down the wall of the temple, sensitive fingers easily finding handholds. The guard at the gate was not fierce-black-beard, but a younger man barely more than a boy. He was alert over the gun in his lap, but Sirru slipped easily past him. The shadowy shape of Ir Yth was heading across the square to where the white pavilion stood. Sirru followed, skirting the rows of army vehicles and picking his unseen way through the makeshift tents and huddled bodies that filled the square.

The *raksasa* hurried to the entrance of the pavilion, which was illuminated from within like a great glowing sail, and relinquished her disguise. There was a flurry of movement from within; Ir Yth disappeared. Sirru hastened to the side of the pavilion. Its walls were secured by ropes, and there were plenty of cracks through which one might watch suspicious goings-on.

Jaya's Second Body was sitting on a long couch arranged with cushions. She was wearing a length of golden material, edged with red, and the light flashed and melted from the jewels at her throat. A small group of acolytes sat before the couch, talking in low voices. At Ir Yth's entrance, Jaya's Second Body gasped. One hand went to her throat, clutching the necklaces as one might when faced with a robber. Ir Yth bowed with frosty politeness, as befitted the greeting of goddess to mortal. The Second Body opened her mouth and stammered something. Then, recovering herself, she motioned to a place on the couch beside her. Tea and fruit and sweets were brought, which Ir Yth ignored. The Second Body radiated surprise, excitement and alarm. Softly, looking nowhere but the woman's dark eyes, Ir Yth began to talk.

Sirru could not understand what she was saying, since it was directed purely at the Second Body, but the expressives that were emanating from Ir Yth to lend weight to her words were very clear. She was warning the Second

Body. She was talking about terrible things, frightening things, and over and over again he heard his own name. Gradually an expressive coalesced and took shape. The project could not be allowed to succeed. Failure must be engineered, otherwise destruction of the Tekhein *desqusai* would result, but the administrator – Sirru himself – must not know. Ir Yth could not go to the authorities directly, because the administrator might find out and exact a terrible revenge.

Sirru, alarmed, listened intently. Even after the events on the ship, he could not control his outrage at Ir Yth's treachery. It was unheard of for a member of a project to undermine it in this manner; a violation of all manner of codes. The Core itself had ordered the project, stating explicitly that the Tekhein *desqusai* should be brought into line with the rest of their kin, to all the advantages and advances of the rest of the írRas worlds. Sirru thought, with sorrow, of everything he had seen so far on this world: the dreadful poverty, the primitive forms of speech which seemed to lead to so much confusion and strife, the wars and revolts mentioned by Jaya. The child's illness: so horrible and unnecessary. Once the planet was brought under Rasasatran control, none of these things would be a problem any more.

Yet here was Ir Yth telling the Second Body that Sirru was on Tekhei to cull and enslave the population, neither of which was true. Once full redevelopment had occurred, Tekhei would be left largely in peace, perhaps with a small administrative presence to maintain the superstructure, but otherwise under its own jurisdiction. Sirru had no intention of murdering anyone. Why would he?

But the conversation which he was now overhearing was final corroboration that Ir Yth, smug *khaith* that she was, had been placed here not as facilitator but as saboteur, to guarantee the crash of another project. Just like Arakrahali. Yet another failure might convince the Core back home that the *desqusai* should be phased out. If that happened, then not only this small world of Tekhei, but *desqusai* temeni and írTemeni everywhere would be integrated; their castes discontinued and their genes thrown back into the webs of the Core.

Genetic meltdown, thought Sirru, and his cool skin flushed colder. He couldn't let the project collapse. The future of his own caste was at stake, and he also had a duty to finish what he was assigned here to do. Tekhei might be a project gone awry, but he was damned if he was going to let it be eradicated in this way, not now that there was a chance of mending things.

Across the courtyard, the tethered beast raised its great head and cried, as if mourning what was to come. Within, Ir Yth was still whispering poison into the Second Body's ears, but Sirru had heard enough. Slipping from the wall of the pavilion, he went back across the square to the temple, making plans with every step.

19.
VARANASI

Kneeling before a little statue of Durga, Kharishma Kharim bowed her head with as much humility as she could manage and prayed. She thanked the goddess for her guidance, for her wisdom, and most of all for her beneficence in granting the mandate of heaven, albeit in the rather improbable form of Ir Yth, to Kharishma herself.

There was a movement at the door. Kharishma glanced up and saw the face of Amir Anand reflected in the gilt of the statue and her heart leaped. She felt a sudden rush of gratitude to the goddess. After all, Jaya Nihalani had no prince to worship her; just some mountain boy, some peasant-turned-terrorist who was in any case dead. Unbidden, the image of Jaya as she had last seen her swam into Kharishma's mind: lean and lithe, silver-haired and golden-eyed. Why, she'd looked almost younger than Kharishma herself – ruthlessly, the actress suppressed this unwelcome thought. Forcing a smile, she rose gracefully to greet Amir. His face was an odd chalky grey. He said in a whisper, 'What the hell is that thing?'

'Darling? What—?'

'That – that creature. Out there in the main tent. The *alien.*'

Kharishma realized, with a heady rush of power, that Amir was actually afraid. Ir Yth was lending her authority

279

in more areas than one, she thought. Graciously, reassuringly, she took Amir by the arm.

'Don't worry, darling," she said. 'Everything's all right. The alien – Ir Yth – has explained everything to me. I'm going to save the world.'

20.
VARANASI, TEMPLE OF DURGA

Twilight had just fallen, and Shiv was spanning down the walls of the Web, seeking secrets. Jaya, still shaky with shock, leaned over his shoulder and stared grimly at plans as they hatched. She had put the boy Halil to bed in the most comfortable chamber; he seemed numb and drowsy, but she doubted he would sleep well.

'Where does this come from?' she murmured.

She pointed to the shifting uncertainties of the screen. Words stabbed out at her: *Enslavement. A cull. What have I done?* Jaya wondered with a cold flush of dread. *What demon have I conjured up now?* Whatever it was, she was responsible. She had to finish what she'd started. Shiv murmured, 'This has just come in through Reuters. Through a via-channel based in Singapore.'

'Do you know where it originates?'

'It's very recent. The report mentions a source in Varanasi.' Shiv shifted uncomfortably in his seat and would not meet her eyes.

'Does it give a name?' Jaya asked, in a voice that could have reached all the way to hell.

'Yes. Yours.'

There was a long, electric silence. As if he had not spoken, Jaya said, 'This claim that the aliens have come to enslave us. Do *you* think it's true?' She turned to Rakh, who gave an unhappy shrug.

'Who can say? It's as likely as anything else.' He met her gaze without expression, trusting her, as always, to do what was right. *But then again, I never was a real oracle, was I?*

'If it's true, then the worst fears are the right fears. And yet—' And yet Sirru *had* healed the child. The dichotomy still obsessed Jaya: *Healing and harvest.* If Sirru had come to murder and enslave, then why cure Halil?

'No surprise there,' Rakh said, in response to her last words. 'You said it yourself. Everyone comes to take. But to take what?'

As if on cue, Sirru appeared in the doorway. His usual insouciance was gone; the pointed face looked drawn and tired. If he could hear emotions, Jaya thought, then he must feel as if he was being shouted at right now. His arms were wrapped around himself; she wondered whether he was cold.

'Sirru?' she said, quietly.

The alien murmured something that she could neither hear nor understand. Then he said a word that was entirely intelligible.

'Ir Yth.'

Dipping a long finger in Shiv's tea and disregarding the latter's protest, the alien drew a line along the table top, then a square with four circles at the corner. He gestured around him; after a moment, Jaya realized that this signified the temple. Sirru drew the square, then another circle, and a line that connected the two. He repeated the *raksasa*'s name.

'Ir Yth went to Kharishma today?' Jaya's eyes met Rakh's dark gaze. 'And told her something?'

'Kharishma must be ripe for the plucking,' Rakh mused. 'The *raksasa* doesn't seem to have had much luck in influencing *you*.'

'It makes a certain sense,' Jaya said. 'That's what that bitch wants to be, after all – Jaya Devi, out to save the world. But is she wrong?' Stepping across, she placed her hands on Sirru's shoulders. They felt hard and bony beneath her hands. He gazed down at her, his expression unreadable. Jaya turned to Rakh and Shiv Sakai.

'Go now. We've got things to discuss.'

'But, Commander—' Rakh must be upset, she thought, to resurrect that old title.

'Don't argue with me, Rakhi. Please. Just go.'

Reluctantly, they left and closed the door behind them. Jaya rested her forehead against the alien's breastbone. The skin at the back of her neck prickled; she did not like being so close to him, after the episode with the child.

'Sirru. I need the truth from you. Why are you here?'

She thought it with all the force she could manage,

mentally shouting, projecting out. And Sirru dutifully replied,

/duty/tired/miss-complexity-home-other selves/afraid/ no harm/ A pause. /Harvest/

If she was to trust him, it would be a decision and not an instinct, for the latter could deceive. She sensed bewilderment and even affection: how easily could he lie, she wondered? And he had cured Halil.

/Danger/you/your people—/ 'Ir Yth.' /Distress/betrayal/ fear/

'Ir Yth?'

'Ir Yth.'

'All right,' Jaya said wearily. She thought of the voice of the ship, living in her mind for so many years and now silent, and then of Ir Yth, whom she neither liked nor trusted. And then, again, of the child: healed, but at what cost to his psyche? *At least you seem the lesser of many evils, Sirru, whatever your methods.*

She could, of course, wash her hands of the whole lot of them, but that would mean trading the gamble of power back down to outlaw status. Once again, she had responsibilities, and she had to live up to them. Besides, there was a cure for Selenge, and it rested with Sirru, not Ir Yth. *How much do I have to lose? And there might be a world to gain.*

'Come with me,' she said to Sirru. Taking his arm, she led him out into the courtyard where her men were waiting. With a deep, unsteady breath she said, 'We're leaving. Tonight, as planned. Things are getting too hot here – Anand, Tokai, Kharishma's people, the military. There are too many jackals circling. And we're taking Sirru with us.'

She could see the doubt in Rakh's face, but he wouldn't publicly challenge her word. He said, practical as ever, 'What's to be done?'

'We need to find a safe haven, somewhere we can plan.' She knew, as well as he, that there was only one place that could be described as safe: Yamunotri, the fort in the mountains. Sirru was looking from face to face, trying to understand.

'Very well, then,' Jaya said. 'Start packing up. We're moving out.'

But that was easier said than done.

An hour later, Jaya went up onto the battlements. Across the square, in the hazy lamplight, she could see movement. Raising her night-sight binoculars to her eyes, Jaya saw that the perimeter of the square, packed to bursting point the day before, was already half empty. People were being led away. Men in a uniform that Jaya did not recognize were clearing the throng; silently and – for Bharat – without fuss. Light glinted off the butt of a gun. As she watched, Jaya saw a familiar stumpy figure bustling out of the pavilion, four arms folded in a complex insectoid huddle. The lithe form of Kharishma Kharim strode after Ir Yth.

Jaya shifted position to see where they were going, but they vanished out of sight behind the billowing pale wall of the pavilion. She did not need the activity in the square to tell her that something was happening. Change rode the air, reminding her of the days of her ill-fated revolution. She noticed for the first time that the temple monkeys had all disappeared. Jaya headed back down into the courtyard.

At the gate, she found Rakh arguing with someone in an uncharacteristic whisper. His back was turned, but there was an equally unfamiliar air of helplessness in the set of his shoulders. He appeared to be pleading. Jaya went to find out what all the fuss was about and saw that a woman had appeared at the gate. At first, Jaya thought she was young, but then she saw that the woman's face had the betraying sheen of nanofilm, a flexible mask that moved as she spoke. From a distance, the effect was convincing; from close to, it was eerie. Carefully dressed hair fell to her waist and she was clad in a plain sari with a patterned hem that Jaya only belatedly realized was made up of the interlocking Chanel logo. A drift of swooningly opulent perfume greeted Jaya as she stepped into the gatehouse.

'Shrimati Jahan,' Jaya said, recognizing her at last. Rajira was, after all, the most infamous courtesan in Varanasi. 'What are *you* doing here?'

First movie stars, now whores. Rajira Jahan's presence was baffling: an overblown rose in a field full of thistles. Rajira stepped forward and clutched Jaya's hands in a startlingly powerful grip.

'Please . . . You have to help me. Where is he?'

'Where is who?' Jaya asked, though she had the unsettled feeling that she already knew.

'The – the visitor. The alien.' Rajira's eyes met Jaya's,

285

and the courtesan flinched as she encountered a golden glare.

'He's inside. Why?' The last thing Jaya wanted now was further complications. She motioned to Rakh. 'Make sure everything's going as planned.' With a palpable air of relief, Rakh vanished in the direction of the cellars. Rajira whispered, 'He came to see me. Last night. We – that is, he—'

This may have been a becoming display of modesty, but Jaya was losing patience; also belief. '*What?* Sirru's one of your *clients?*' She found that she was more astounded than anything else, but beneath it all a swift jealous pang contracted her heart. She felt utterly and unreasonably betrayed. *Men! God, it doesn't matter* where *they come from . . .*

The suddenness of the feeling made her catch her breath, but the prospect of squabbling over the alien with Varanasi's most legendary prostitute was too undignified to be borne. Besides, the look in Rajira's eyes told her that the woman's claim was not only true, but deserving of pity.

'Well – I mean – what happened?' Jaya said, faintly. For once, she felt completely at a loss. Hesitantly, Rajira told her. Either the woman was a complete fantasist or she was telling a story that approximated to the truth. And to Jaya's own surprise, she found herself inclined to believe the courtesan.

'All right,' Jaya said. She leaned back against the wall. 'But what are you doing here?'

Rajira was still gripping her wrist in a steely clasp. 'I have to see him. I think I'm ill.'

Jaya gaped at the courtesan.

'Ill? What do you mean?'

'I don't know what it is. I feel feverish, and I keep hearing – well, *voices*.'

Where have I come across that particular set of symptoms before? Jaya thought, with a further stab of shock.

'And I'm afraid that, well, if I've given the illness to – to anyone, maybe to one of my clients, and then if they associate me with – with the alien . . .'

'But why would anyone associate you with Sirru?' Jaya asked, then realized her own naivety. 'Oh.'

'I told a few people.' Rajira had the grace to look downcast.

'"A few people" being a few newspapers, I suppose.' Jaya rubbed a weary hand across her eyes. 'Look, I'm really sorry, but this isn't a good time. Sirru can't see anyone at the moment.' *But what are we going to do with her, then? If she's already talked to the media . . . And what if she's a spy?* The decision was a quick one to make, but it was the kind of damage limitation that Jaya had grown to hate. She said, 'Go in there and tell Rakh that you're coming with us. But any trouble, any scenes, and I'm leaving you behind, do you understand?'

'I understand.'

'Well, all right, then.'

Jaya followed her latest recruit hastily back into the

LIZ WILLIAMS

courtyard. Rakh was crouched by the opposite wall, staring up into the glistening sky.

'We're ready to go.'

'Good. What are you looking at?'

'Helicopter. I don't recognize the insignia.'

Jaya could hear a distant pounding as the helicopter turned. A flock of sparrows fluttered up from the towers of the temple, alarmed by the intruder.

'Where are the others?'

'Waiting in the cellars. Including the alien.' Rakh frowned. 'I found him in the kitchen – he was rummaging in the fridge. Maybe he was hungry. I've contacted the boatman, too. He's ready.'

'Then we're going,' Jaya said, but as she turned the helicopter rose up over the parapet of the temple, a dragon-fly in the lamplight, and wheeled between the towers. Jaya seized the courtesan by the arm and pulled her towards the inner temple. Rakh was already running, keeping close to the temple wall. Jaya veered away, pulling Rajira with her, and sprinted back towards the doors of the temple. The helicopter was wheeling around. Pushing the courtesan ahead of her, Jaya ducked beneath the arch and ran for the cellars.

The faces of her little troop and their guest were pale in the darkness. The sudden flare of torchlight brought other faces out of the walls: carvings of *raksasas* and *apsaras*, demons and gods. For a moment, all of them seemed real to Jaya, multiplied into a thousandfold life. Then, with a jolt of alarm, she saw that some of the faces

288

were alive, after all. They were small and pinched, and each black eye caught the light of the torch and returned it in a point like a bright, hot coal. One of the faces chattered at Jaya, revealing long yellow teeth. They were the monkeys of the Temple of Durga, who had so recently disappeared, and now were found.

'Go, *go*,' Rakh said, and each one – Shiv, Rajira, little Halil and last of all, with a long unfathomable look at Jaya, Sirru himself – filed down into the tunnel. Jaya took a quick look behind her. It seemed to her that she could already taste the acridity of nerve gas drifting down into the cellar, but the monkeys leaped down from the ledges and slipped past her, creeping up towards the light in a curiously concerted movement. She had no time to wonder, but followed her companions down into the dark.

She did not know how old these cellar passages might be. The Temple of Durga was not itself ancient, dating back only as far as the eighteenth century. But – so they said – Varanasi was the oldest city of all Bharat, and what lay beneath its coil of streets could only be imagined. Jaya put out a hand to steady herself over rough footing, and her fingers touched things that felt disturbingly human: the curves of a hip, the line of a face. Carvings, no doubt, a relic of older worship on the site, but the stone felt unnervingly alive, cool and moist beneath her hand. Her fingers brushed against a smile. She thought she heard noises behind her, and every footstep was magnified into the sound of pursuit.

Sirru hurried just ahead of her, bending occasionally

when the ceiling became low. The narrow quills quivered and twitched, perhaps sensing information from the air. Jaya thought wonderingly of Rajira. Jaya had never been a voyeur, but she would have given a lot to be a mosquito on the wall during *that* particular confrontation. She couldn't understand Sirru's behaviour: at once so normal, and so strange. And he had managed to slip out with no trouble at all – that was the most worrying thing. What else might he have been getting up to?

She fought down that unfamiliar pang of jealousy. He wasn't her lover, after all, and she'd never even considered him physically except as a possible threat. She hadn't considered anyone after Kamal, and it suddenly struck her that maybe it was time she did. But the thought felt disloyal and she pushed it away. Still, if Sirru wasn't her lover, he *was* her alien . . .

Perhaps Ir Yth was right and Sirru's caste were no different from humans after all. How depressing. She had no wish to end up as one of Krishna's dancing girls, or the modern equivalent. Sighing, Jaya picked her way through the passages, longing for air and light and sense.

21.
KHAIKURRIYË

The four enforcers strode forward, their robes rustling. Even through the darkness, Anarres could see the membranes quivering along each side of their long necks, sending terror into the air with methodical ease. Behind the enforcers, the walls of the ruined pod began to shrivel. The wall shredded into filaments like a dead leaf, and a fifth enforcer stalked through the gap. Something was drifting in from the courtyard: a soft, sparkling cloud. Beside Anarres, Nowhere One gave a sudden rasping gasp. A moment later, she could feel it seeping in through the slits of her skin, numbing the passages of her nose and mouth. The world flickered on and off, darkness and blinding light, wheeling crazily upside down as Anarres fell.

Only a moment later, or so it seemed, she blinked awake. She was lying on her back, encased in a wet web. The binding was not particularly tight, but it was sticky, and struggling against it only enmeshed her further. There was an old, sour taste in her mouth. The wall of an unfamiliar chamber curved above her, pulsing slowly in and out. Unknowable impressions glittered through the air, and with a slow horror Anarres knew where she must be: inside the Marginals, a prisoner. Slowly, so as not to disturb the bonds any more than necessary, she turned her head.

Nowhere One lay only a short distance away. His eyes were closed. Anarres could see a long thin foot, the toes curled defensively against the sole. Her skin prickled.

Reaching down with her chin, she managed to activate her scale implant; it would do little good, but she needed at least the illusion of a defence.

There was a soft sucking sound as the walls opened and someone stepped through. It was EsRavesh. The *khaith*'s plump face was pursed with distaste. He stood for a moment, staring down at Anarres with an air of disapproving satisfaction. He reached down and deactivated her scale. Anarres's first thought was for the manifold. He must not find out about IrEthiverris. As forcefully as she could, Anarres began to emanate allure.

/*I don't know what good you think that will do,*/ EsRavesh said, with contempt. /*Do you fancy yourself irresistible?*/

'There was a time when you seemed to want exclusivity,' Anarres managed to purr.

/*I have become bored with the notion. Besides, you are a troublemaker. Consorting with this—*/ He gestured towards Nowhere One's prone form and Anarres caught the sting of pheromones. /*Wilfully flouting the natural order. Why did you visit that orbital?*/

'I won't tell you.'

EsRavesh said nothing. Gradually, she felt a pressure growing inside her head, until it felt ready to explode. 'Stop it!' she cried. With a great show of reluctance she said, 'We wanted to find out if there was a way of restoring Sirru's First Body.'

/*If you followed my instructions correctly, you would have had no such opportunity.*/ The *khaith* was smug.

292

Anarres looked away. /*Ah, it seems that you did. What a pity that you were so diligent in carrying out my orders.*/ The beady yellow gaze sharpened. /*You are concealing something! I can sense it.*/

'No, there's nothing,' Anarres cried. The *khaith* swooped, the thick, rudimentary digits working their way through the sticky folds of the mesh, pinching and probing across her breast ridge and between her legs.

/*What is this?*/ Triumphantly, the *khaith* snatched up the skein of the communications mesh. /*I see. You hoped to contact your* desqusai *lover; warn him perhaps? I fear I must disappoint you.*/ He tucked the mesh into his sleeve. /*And now, I have things to attend to. I will not return. We have reflected on this matter, and it has been our judicious decision that your use is at an end. But for the sake of our past relationship, I am prepared to make one concession.*/

'What?' Anarres whispered.

/*I have a great interest in experimental gardening, and I have long been of the opinion that the carnivorous domes are a vital part of any healthy ecosystem. We have managed to grow such a dome from spores found in the Naturals' Quarter, mingled with genes from the Core's own seed banks. The results have been most interesting. You are sitting in one of them now. It will eat anything that remains in it, and it was last fed yesterday. So I'm afraid I shall not be staying long, but rest assured, your corpse will not be wasted. It will provide valuable nutrients for our latest project. I'm sure that you won't begrudge your body – after all, we írRas do love our gardens, don't we?/*

With a flurry of robes, he was gone through the wall. Her head pounding, her mouth dry with fright, Anarres lay back on the floor and tried to think of a plan.

22.
VARANASI

Perched precariously on the edge of an elephant that was, in fact, a mammoth-resurrect, Ir Yth stared down at the scene below with carefully disguised trepidation. The *raksasa* had never been so close to so large a creature before, unless one counted certain of the inhabitants of the inner Core Marginals, and she did not like it. She did not like the smell of old hide and meat, and neither did she care for the hairy, dirty texture of the wool that was clutched in all four of her plump hands. The mammoth swayed and jolted as it made its laborious progress across the square.

Ir Yth's latest ally was balanced on its neck, just in front of the canopy in which Ir Yth herself sat. Kharishma's head was thrown back, her jasmine-scented hair partly concealed by a helmet of antique design. She seemed to be talking to herself, murmuring soothingly beneath her breath, and Ir Yth was starting to have serious doubts about her chosen course of action. It was becoming evident even to an outworlder that Kharishma's behaviour went a little further than eccentricity warranted.

Ir Yth had asked that Kharishma take her immediately to the authorities, so that she could make it plain to the government that Sirru represented a threat and must be neutralized. Kharishma had been reassuring. Certainly they'd go to the government, in the morning, and tell them everything. It had taken Ir Yth no more than an hour to realize that Kharishma had lied to her, and she was furious with herself for not detecting the lie. Perhaps Kharishma herself had believed it.

But Kharishma, mad though she might be, also had power of a kind: money and connections and people who, it appeared, were willing to go into battle for her. It had dawned on Ir Yth only moments ago that Kharishma's troops were nothing to do with the regular military. She asked Kharishma where they came from, and the woman said with a strange smile, 'They're just extras.'

Ir Yth did not know what this meant. Kharishma continued, 'Not the helicopter, though. That's for real. Media. Channel Nine.' She gave Ir Yth a coquettish glance from beneath her long lashes. 'Aren't I clever?' Ir Yth could not bring herself to agree. She had definitely chosen the wrong ally, Second Body or not. All this Jaya-stock seemed to be either contrary, argumentative, or downright mad.

Ir Yth comforted herself with the thought that at least this bizarre attack upon Jaya's temenos was likely to accomplish its object in the long run: that of generating confusion and mess, discrediting *desqusai* involvement in interplanetary affairs, and providing the justification for the *khaithoi* to put forward evidence that the *desqusai* caste as a whole should be terminated. Once that was done, *desqusai* holdings would become *khaithoi* holdings, assimilated by the next caste up, and *khaithoi* prestige would correspondingly increase. She allowed herself a moment of admiration for EsRavesh who had, after all, been the person responsible for developing the radical new meme that allowed *khaithoi* to start questioning the commands of the Core for the first time in their history, permitting them – literally – to begin thinking the unthinkable.

Cheered by these happy heresies, Ir Yth gripped more tightly as the mammoth lurched forward. Troops were pouring in through the gate, scattering briefly as an aircraft with unfamiliar markings shot low across the square. Kharishma glanced up, grimacing.

'Oh, fuck. *That's* the military.'

She nudged the mammoth behind one large ear with a cattle-prod and the beast rumbled forwards through the temple gate. There was very little to show for the onslaught. Kharishma's followers milled about, occasionally firing stolen machine guns into the sky, but the courtyard was almost deserted. Almost, but not quite, for along the outer parapet of the temple gathered a group of twenty or so monkeys. They sat in silence, in a long row, and stared down at the intruders with bright, animated eyes. Slowly, their heads turned, as though they were a single creature. With a sudden burst of rage, Ir Yth realized what Sirru had done. She plucked at Kharishma's sari. Irritated, the would-be liberator of Earth turned.

'What?' Then, evidently realizing that she was addressing a goddess, she added perfunctorily, 'Forgive me.'

/*The* hiroi. *See?*/

'I don't understand—'

Ir Yth pointed to the monkeys. /*Those creatures. They
carry a – a plague. They must be exterminated.*/

Kharishma looked doubtfully at her new mentor. She
said, 'Are you sure? They're sacred animals; they've
always lived here in the temple. Besides, they look healthy
enough to me.'

Ir Yth sent a pheromonal warning; just a small one but
sufficient to cause a quiver to run through Kharishma's
slender frame, like a stone cast into a pond. She was easier
to influence than the original Jaya, that was certain. Maybe
Jaya had grown used to pain.

/*Plague. They must be killed. Or everything is lost.*/
Had Sirru managed to infect anything else? The *hiroi*
were bad enough, but even though they might be closely
related to humans (presumably why Sirru had selected
them for his accursed experiments) they were not sufficiently sentient to relay a message. The human *desqusai*,
on the other hand, were another matter entirely. If a
communication virus should enter human beings . . . But
surely they would still not be powerful enough to contact
a depth ship, relay information about Ir Yth's betrayal
and ask for help and rescue. Or would they? Jaya was a
Receiver and had spoken to a ship, but the ship had been
in close orbit. To contact a depth ship over a greater
distance, any message would have to be amplified by

a relay station, and Sirru did not have access to such a thing.

And then Ir Yth was struck by a terrible thought, which caused her to sway dangerously on the back of the mammoth. Jaya had link-bonded with the ship; their genes had merged to create a being that would, under the proper conditions, become a ship itself one day. And Sirru had told her that the bonding had been successful; indeed, it had been this catalytic piece of information that had precipitated her own act of sabotage. She had assumed that the seed had died with the ship, but what if she was wrong? What if Sirru had brought it to Tekhei, in its early, dormant state? If the seed was allowed to grow, in a suitably cold place, then it could act as the amplifier Ir Yth feared.

Darkness filled the air, and for a brief moment the sun became a black circle of eclipse, fractured by stars. Ir Yth's expressives occasionally verged on the poetic. But then the *raksasa* turned to find that someone was staring at her.

The newcomer was a tall man, who was standing in the back of one of the military vehicles. There was a calculated insolence in his stare, but beneath it she could sense a strong current of fear. Ir Yth sent the same reproving expressive that she had most recently deployed against Kharishma, and had the satisfaction of seeing the pale eyes widen.

Kharishma leaned down from the back of the mammoth and cried excitedly, 'Amir! Over *here*, darling!' as if she were not already the most visible thing in the vicinity. A spark appeared in the man's cold gaze.

'Kharishma! What do you think you're *doing*? I've just had the commandant on my mobile, asking what the fuck's going on. Didn't I tell you I have no authority any more?' His voice was seared with a bitterness that Ir Yth could palpably feel. 'Stop this play-acting immediately! Who *are* these people?'

Kharishma sagged back against Ir Yth, radiating frustration and astonishment.

'Well, you couldn't seem do anything about *her*,' she said, in a small, injured voice, 'And that other one, the other alien, you don't know what he's planning to do . . .' She drew herself upright. 'I just want what's best for humanity!'

'Oh, for gods' sake. You can't tell reality from fantasy, Kharishma. Get down off that thing and tell these people to go home before you get arrested.'

Ir Yth was suddenly overtaken by a wave of fury. A hatred of this hot, dusty, primitive little world, of its peculiar and arrogant inhabitants – and of all the mad *desqusai* – rose up to choke her. She longed for the stifling silences of the Core Marginals, for the peace and the darkness and the comforting presence of others like herself. She wanted to go home, stay with her clade in the Marginals and never set sense on *desqusai* again.

'You don't understand!' Kharishma cried plaintively, and spurred the mammoth forwards into a lumbering trot.

They had reached the main door of the temple. This was barred against them, but Kharishma (with a glance at the media helicopter circling above), smoothed back her hair and raised a decisive arm. One of her men hefted a rocket launcher to his shoulder.

'Kharishma!' Amir Anand shouted. 'Where did you get that thing?' There was a deafeningly soft crunch and the door was blasted off its hinges. Victoriously, Kharishma prodded the mammoth on into the temple.

/Wait! What if it is a trap? This is foolish!/ Ir Yth made her feelings plain, but her new ally was riding on a wave of adrenaline and vengeance for old, imagined slights, and for once Ir Yth's wishes were no more than the dust.

The temple monkeys, terrified by the rocket, broke rank and ran. Their flight was curiously choreographed, they poured down from the parapet and bolted to every direction of the compass, over the walls and through the gate. Soon, they were gone. Ir Yth gave a hiss of annoyance. Sirrubennin EsMoyshekhal had been cleverer, and swifter to act, than she had imagined. If *desqusai* could deceive *khaithoi*, their elders and betters, then it was high time for the caste to be terminated.

Kharishma slid down from the mammoth's back and ran into the temple, leaving Ir Yth perched miserably in the saddle. Ir Yth glanced down. The ground seemed a very long way away. It had been a long time since the *raksasa* had felt fear, but she felt it now. She did not like heights, nor unpredictable alien *hiroi*. What if the beast took it into its head to run off?

'Goddess?' a voice said, from the other side of the mammoth. Ir Yth turned to see the tall, pale-eyed stranger. He had spoken the word with the faintest, subtlest trace of irony, but then he bowed. She could still sense a raw fear in him, but he had conquered it enough to address her, and Ir Yth allowed herself a moment of admiration. Reaching up, he held out his arms and said reassuringly, 'Come on. Slide down. I won't let you fall.'

Ir Yth did not want to show weakness in front of this *desqusai* stranger, and she hated the undignified manner in which she was compelled to turn in the saddle, hitching her robe up over her bare ankles. Such immodesty . . . But she was desperate to get away from the huge creature, so she obeyed the stranger's instructions. He caught her easily, then stepped back and allowed her to rearrange her robes and her dignity. She could still feel his fright: a fear of difference, a fear of inferiority . . .

/Thank you./

'You're welcome. I am Prince Amir Anand.'

/I have heard of you. Where is Kharishma?/

'Enjoying the fruits of her display, I would imagine.' The stranger stared at Ir Yth. 'You've made a curious choice of ally.'

/I believed the woman to be something she is not,/ Ir Yth said, rather stiffly.

'That's not uncommon with Kharishma,' the stranger said, unhappily. *He's in love with the woman*, Ir Yth realized. She could feel it burning inside him. He went on, 'You want contacts, don't you? People of power.'

301

/That is correct. My Receiver has proved ineffective./

'Your—? Well, never mind. I believe I might know someone who can assist you,' Amir Anand said soothingly. 'A man named Naran Tokai.'

23.
VARANASI

Sirru's eyes, adapted to the lower light levels of Rasasatra, did not have too much difficulty in picking out the details of his path. He observed the carvings along the wall with interest, noting familiarity of form: some of the oldest variations of írRas castes. Many phenotypes had sprung from the original Hundred Castes of ancient legend and there must now be several thousand different forms, scattered across an equal number of worlds. Only the Core knew for sure just how many types there were; everyone else had long ago lost count.

Perhaps these carvings were a legacy of earlier visits from Rasasatra. Though infrequent, an impression would undoubtedly have been made upon the locals. Some castes, like the *khaithoi*, were still extant; others (serpent-limbed; *hiroi*-headed) had long since been discontinued. Under the present circumstances, that was an uncomfortable thought.

The packed earth of the passage felt moist beneath the pads of Sirru's bare feet, cool and not unpleasant, but he was looking forward to getting back out into the air. He could see the sky through the eyes of the *hiroi*, a starry indigo bowl vaster than anything else they knew, but the information was scattered and fragmented. He had a sudden, disconcerting image of Ir Yth, looking utterly monstrous, and for a brief jarring instant, he felt the *hiroi*'s terror. Then they were gone, in all directions at once, and the connection became meaningless.

Sirru tried to sustain it, but it was hard. Once the proper network was established, he could detach himself from the *hiroi*'s visions, but for now, he needed to act as nexus. And not only for the *hiroi*.

It was starting to work. He was beginning to receive fragments of */information/impressions/emotions/* passed down the viral line that Rajira Jahan had so obligingly facilitated for him only a little while before. The network must be growing by the day, as Rajira's lovers passed on the virus to their own sexual contacts. He glanced down at a hand that was not his own, fractionally reflected on a history of which he had had no experience, and felt fleetingly cold. The growth of the network made him even more anxious to reach a place of safety for the seed, which he could feel occasionally stirring against his side. Sirru was so lost in speculation that he hardly noticed when the little procession came to a halt.

Jaya pushed her way to the front. Ahead, Sirru could see a door. Jaya wrenched at the door, muttering beneath her breath, then stood back and looked ruefully at her bleeding hands. Sirru stepped forward, intending to help, but the black-hairy person managed to open it after a brief struggle. There was a familiar smell of weed and river

303

mud, which after the dankness of the passage was almost sweet. They had reached the river.

Sirru waited patiently for the others to file outside, and then he followed them. Without proper /sense of place/ it was difficult for him to locate himself, but after a moment he recognized the curve of the river. Their little group had come east of the temple and were now standing on one of the huge stone landing stages that jutted out into the water. No one was about. Only a *hiroi* of some kind – large, horned – splashed about in the shallows. The air was warm, and singing with insects. Above the landing stage, Sirru could see a representation of one of the *desqusai* Makers; following his gaze, Rakh smiled with a fierce glitter of teeth and spoke. There was a moment before the sense translated: /Sitala/maker of plague/ Sirru hissed with pleased surprise. At last. It was becoming easier to understand the verbal speech of his new associates, as his embryonic network fed information back to him.

Jaya spoke to Rakh, urgently, and Rakh pointed down-river. A barge was coming: a long, black craft covered with canvas. Baskets of some kind of fruit rested on its decks. Sirru watched the current rippling the water as it nudged the landing stage. Grimly and in silence, Jaya motioned her companions on board. As he passed her, Sirru was aware of a strange constraint emanating from her, and it took him a minute to realize that she was trying to hide what she was feeling from him. She was not doing very well – chords of anxiety, distrust and weariness flowed from her, with an ambiguous note of tension – but she was trying nonetheless. He couldn't blame her. He wondered uneasily how difficult it would be to convey his needs in verbal speech, and learn her own.

The barge rocked as Jaya leaped down off the landing stage. She and Rakh hustled the passengers beneath the tarpaulin. It was sticky and hot, and smelled of rotting fruit. Sirru was preparing to remain on deck, disguised, but Jaya's head went up with a jerk and she motioned to the tarpaulins.

'And you.'

He understood that. Deeming it best not to argue, and pleased with his sudden comprehension, Sirru did as he was told. He ducked into the cargo hold. Jaya followed him. She was talking to Rakh, quickly and low, and Sirru could not grasp the complex drift of their conversation. He surveyed his companions, one by one. Jaya's troops were settling themselves as comfortably as they could in the cramped space, but the *apsara* Rajira was sitting bolt upright on a box and staring at him. Her mouth was set and the dark eyes were anxious.

Sirru was still surprised by her sudden arrival back at the temple. He did not understand why she should wish to see him, being under the impression that they had completed a commercial transaction. It occurred to him, not for the first time, that he had seriously underestimated the extent of his ignorance about this branch of his caste. He thought with unease of IrEthiverris, and of Arakrahali.

24.
KHAIKURRIYË

The dark red walls of the cell were glistening. Already, Anarres could smell the thick odour of digestive enzymes, seeping through the chamber. It was growing hotter.

'Nowhere One!' Anarres cried. 'Wake up!'

The Natural stirred, and groaned.

'Anarres?' He blinked up at the pulsing ceiling. 'Where are we?'

'We're going to be eaten!' She added hastily, 'Don't struggle, it'll make your bonds tighter.'

'It's an *erychniss*,' the Natural said, twitching. 'Like the house.'

Finally, Anarres remembered. 'Your house wouldn't eat you, you said, because you'd altered your pheromonal signatures. That means we're safe!' But then she recalled something else. 'And you said it might not work with other houses.'

'It seems we're about to find out,' Nowhere One remarked. His voice sounded as matter-of-fact as ever, but she could sense his fear. She swallowed, trying to overcome alarm. The smell grew stronger in the fierce, green heat. Something was bubbling up from the surface of the cell and Anarres could taste acid in her mouth.

'Lie still,' the Natural whispered. 'Moving around will encourage it.'

Anarres forced herself not to move. A thick, slimy seep was creeping under her calf. It burned.

'Nowhere One,' she cried, and the Natural said, 'Lie *still.*'

The side of her shin felt as though it was on fire. She tried to glance down, to see what was happening. The sheen of enzymes covered the floor, gleaming like molten metal. As Anarres watched, the cell floor split from end to end, revealing a mass of sharp spines, and the enzymatic gloss began to carry her towards it.

25.
THE RIVER

Jaya crouched in the prow of the barge and stared back in the direction of Varanasi. The city had been long swallowed by the haze, for they had left the Ganges now and were some miles up the Gomati river, heading towards Lucknow. Beyond lay the upper reaches of the Gomati and from there Jaya had organized transport north to the mountains. She'd always had the time-honoured instincts of the revolutionary: when trouble comes, head for the hills. They would journey up into the high barren country and the ruined fort, up in the passes that led to the lake of Saptarishi Kund. Amir Anand knew some of this terrain, but not all, and not as well as Jaya. Even if Anand was reinstated and they were discovered, the military would find it difficult to send troops into such country. She was hoping that Kharishma had managed to divert attention for the moment; an unlikely and involuntary ally.

Shiv, hunched over his satellite-linked laptop, had managed to tap into military communications. It seemed that the actress had been acting on her own initiative, without support from elsewhere, and the Bharati military had now swarmed in and taken over the temple complex. Jaya wondered uneasily what had happened to Ir Yth.

Jaya sent a brief prayer to the goddess of vengeance: *Lady, be with me now.* The barge went along so slowly that it made Jaya tired. Even on the river, the night heat beat down on her, drawing beads of sweat. She had plaited her new pale hair and bound it into a knot at the back of her neck, but she still couldn't quite get used to her healed skin. It looked too young, as though she was no more than a child, but it also seemed curiously resilient. Earlier, she had caught her hand on the door and torn it, but now the skin merely showed a faint white line like an old scar. This, more than anything else that had happened in the last week, frightened Jaya. If it hadn't been for her mother's ring, she might have wondered whether it was her own hand at all.

She leaned her arms on the prow of the barge and stared ahead, squinting into the darkness. At the edges of the river, buffalo were snorting and splashing. A flock of cranes wheeled out across the water. It was good to get out of the city, and back to a place where she could hear herself think. She remembered the ashram, not as it was on the terrible night of the attack, but in the early years: a green place filled with peace.

The prow of the barge struck a cross-stream current and light was flung dazzling into Jaya's eyes. She seemed to see from a multiplicity of perspectives: all directions at once, dizzying and meaningless. It was as though she was back in those early days – not that long ago now – when she had escaped from the hospital and experienced her visions of the ship. But there was not the same hint of strangeness about this sensation; this was familiar. Something was happening, Jaya thought, and as she did so the connection was abruptly severed, with a suddenness that made her gasp. The boatman, a man for whom Jaya had done many favours, turned in alarm.

'Jaya Devi? Are you all right?'

'I'm not sure.' She felt as though she had raised her hand and drawn a bolt of lightning. It was strangely like the touch of Ir Yth. 'I think so.'

'It is the heat,' the boatman said, as if Jaya was royalty. 'Perhaps you should go beneath cover. Rest for a while.'

'Maybe that's a good idea.' Suddenly, she wanted nothing more than silence. Shaken, she crawled beneath the tarpaulin. Her men were asleep. Rajira Jahan's perfumed head lolled back against the tarpaulin wall, but she was still awake. Jaya could see the glitter of an eye as she stared at Sirru. The alien himself appeared to be meditating. He sat in the lotus position on the boards of the deck, his hands curled decorously around one another. The golden eyes were open, but he did not blink as Jaya came in. Reassurance emanated from him like a glow; she wondered whether he was comforting the others or himself. Jaya settled herself on a mat on the floor and curled up. She intended to stay awake, but heat, fatigue and stress melted the barriers away and she allowed the alien emotions to move through her, as gentle as cool water. Soon, she was asleep, and did not dream.

When she woke, it was early in the morning, and they had reached Lucknow. The alien was nowhere to be seen. Jaya scrambled to her feet, dazed with sleep, and pushed the tarpaulin to one side. Lucknow stretched along the banks of the river: a mess of apartment blocks and machine shops and old-tech industry, its improbable Victorian clock tower rising like a finger to the heavens. Pollution hung like a veil above the city. At first, Jaya did not see Sirru sitting in the prow of the boat, but then he moved and she recognized him. He was silhouetted against the growing light in a series of monochrome images: black quills, pale skin, dark robes. He turned his head to greet her, his long neck extending further than the human norm. He reminded Jaya suddenly of an owl. She went to stand by his side. Grimly, she pointed beneath the tarpaulins.

'Why can't you stay where you're put?'

/Too hot./

He peered up into the light. He seemed utterly unconcerned by all that had befallen him, Jaya noted – not without a degree of irritation.

'I'm trying to help you, for gods' sake,' she said aloud.

310

Then, belatedly, she realized he had understood what she said.

'Sirru? Do you know what I'm saying to you?'

Sirru did not reply. Rajira Jahan's tousled head appeared around the edge of the door.

'What are you doing out there?'

Jaya extended a hand to the courtesan, helping her through the doorway. Rajira's face glistened with sweat and she looked plumper and older; she must have deactivated the nanomask.

'What are we going to do now?' Rajira asked, coming to sit heavily on the bench.

'We head on, upriver. I have to find someone. Someone with transport. They should be waiting for us. Then we go north, to the mountains.'

Rajira said disconsolately, 'And what are we going to do after?'

'We'll let *after* take care of itself,' Jaya said, unwilling to tell Rajira more than she had to. She had not given up the possibility that the woman might be a spy. She added, 'Don't worry. I'm good at making plans.'

Rather to her surprise, the courtesan smiled. 'I know. I saw a bit of that movie they're bringing out. There was a clip on the TV the other night. Very thrilling.'

'That isn't me, you know,' Jaya said, annoyed all over again.

Rajira grimaced, then glanced at her curiously. 'Was it really like that? Did all those things really happen to you?'

'Yes, they did, and no, it wasn't. It wasn't glamorous

or exciting. It was just— We did what we did, that's all. We did what we thought we had to do.'

'You know, my people are outcasts too,' Rajira said after a pause. 'And I believe some things will never change.' She spoke with calm assurance, as if the world was set in stone. 'I had a lover who was of a higher caste – besides my clients, I mean. It didn't work out. I believe now that such things are karma. I believe in the laws of the world. But I admire you for trying.'

'Thank you,' Jaya said, with sudden embarrassment. There seemed little else to say. Spice and smoke drifted out across the water. The barge veered north, taking them past the city.

26.
KHOKANDRA PALACE, UTTAR PRADESH

Kharishma sat sulkily at the edge of the veranda, staring out across the gardens. Tokai watched her for a moment, smiling, then turned to Amir Anand.

'Prince, you have excelled yourself.' He bowed. Anand tried, unsuccessfully, not to look smug. 'At last. Where is the alien now?'

'Waiting to see you.'

'Take me to her.'

It had been a very long time since Naran Tokai had experienced excitement. Usually, his emotions ran a subtle gauntlet from satisfaction to displeasure, but now he found that he was actually intrigued at the thought of meeting this Ir Yth. Who would have thought that incompetent Anand and mad Kharishma would, between them, have managed to snare such a prize? He followed Anand up into the decaying, airy heights of the palace. The alien was standing by the windows, her stocky figure draped in a pale and intricate sequence of folds.

'Madam?' Tokai murmured. The alien turned. Tokai raised his head fractionally, taking note of the smooth ivory carapace, the round eyes and fleshy convoluted mouth. The cane transmitted a complex series of emotions and impressions emanating from Ir Yth. Some were familiar, some so strange that Tokai could not place them in any kind of context.

/You are a Sequencer?/

'Pardon me?'

/One who is an expert on pharmaceuticals./

'Yes, that is correct. I am Naran Tokai.'

/Anand has told me a great deal about your valuable work./ Turning, the alien directed an expression at Anand that might almost resemble a simper, but her evident gratitude was belied by the weird impressions coming to Tokai through the cane. It was the first indication he'd had that Ir Yth's words, heard inside the head, had little relationship to what she was actually feeling. There was no sign that Anand had detected anything amiss. It must be the cane.

Tokai said smoothly, 'The work that we do here must seem very primitive to you.'

/*Primitive, yes, but not without interest. You make medicines, is that not so?*/

'We do,' Tokai confirmed, adding diffidently, 'Kharishma and Anand tell me that you might require some – support?'

Ir Yth visibly swelled, like a toad. She said, /*I was sent here to bring humanity into the fold of a great galactic empire, so that it might benefit from such a benign alliance, but there are tensions between my caste and others. Another was sent, with a very different purpose. To destroy.*/

'Destroy?' Tokai echoed, sceptically. How ironic it would be, he thought, if he ended up as humanity's saviour.

/*It may sound excessively dramatic,*/ Ir Yth said, evidently put out, /*but it is the case. My adversary seeks to facilitate the spread of a lethal disease, and blame it on me.*/

'Indeed.' Irony after irony was being unravelled here. Tokai could detect layers of lies through the betraying sensors of the cane. 'Well, obviously, since the very survival of my species is at stake, you must have all the support that you need. How may we assist?'

/*The disease has already spread to certain animals. The hiroi – the monkeys in the Temple of Durga. They must be found. Tests must be conducted upon them and an antidote developed. This should then be released, in some controlled way, so that it protects as much of the population as possible. I believe that I can cure the disease, but we must work swiftly.*/

'Perhaps it might be a good idea if you were to talk with my research personnel,' Tokai said, after a pause. 'They have the expertise which you seek, and you may also be able to give them valuable instruction as to other diseases that we might encounter.'

/*A wise suggestion,*/ Ir Yth communicated.

'I shall arrange for transport this afternoon. Are you comfortable here for the present? Is there anything I might obtain for you?'

/*Water.*/

Tokai bowed again, and rang the bell for a servant. Accompanied by Amir Anand, he made his way back down to the terrace.

'Well?' Anand demanded.

Tokai paused. 'She is lying to us, Amir. I can feel it. *This* tells me.' He raised the cane. 'Pheromonal discord lies beneath everything she said.'

Anand stared at him in horror. 'That's – that's a problem.'

'No, Amir. It is an opportunity.'

Tokai resumed his progress through the palace, swinging the cane in an almost exuberant manner as he did so. As they came out onto the veranda, Kharishma sprang out of her chair, her expression demanding answers, but Tokai walked past her without a glance.

27.
KHAIKURRIYË

The sharp spines of the cell caught Anarres's bonds and they tore, leaving rags of her passage behind her.

'Nowhere One! Where are you?'

'Behind you.' The Natural's voice was high with an unfamiliar panic.

But then Anarres saw that the spines were growing smaller and sparser, until they were sliding down a smooth, narrow tunnel. Dim light was diffusing through the cell walls, revealing the thick tracery of leaf veins. Below, the tunnel tapered to a narrow point and stopped. Anarres could think only of being trapped at the end of that tunnel, and slowly digested. But as she opened her mouth to scream, she was carried into the tunnel's end. A tight hole opened. Anarres, compressed and buffeted, was squeezed through like an egg. A muffled cry from behind suggested that the same thing was happening to Nowhere One.

Then she was lying face down in a mass of rotten pulp, which smelled like the mulch with which she had nourished her house-vines. Nowhere One's pheromonal modifications had worked. The cell had found them bitter, and spat them out. Her bonds had been left behind on the spines of its maw. They were underneath the Marginals, and free. She raised her head, and gave way to a fit of sneezing.

'Anarres?'

'Nowhere One? Are you all right? Where are we?'

'Reach out with your hand.'

Anarres did so, and encountered something hard and damp extending above her head. 'What is it?'

'We're in the root system.'

Anarres felt around her. The roots grew in a great tangled mass, but there was enough space to move between them. It was as though they rested in the branches of some great underground tree.

'How do we get out?'

'We'll just have to make our way through it,' Nowhere One whispered.

'Why are you murmuring?'

'Because I heard something moving about up there. I don't know what it is.'

Anarres thought of the *írHazh* and shuddered. 'So where can we go? Does this system even lead anywhere?'

'I think it might. The temeni are connected, you know; their root systems allow them to pass nutrients and information back and forth. I'm sure this house talks to others, and it can only do that through the root system or pollination.' There was a pause. 'Before it was killed, that is.'

'But what if there are other carnivorous plants in this area? Would the modifications work for those, too?'

'We'll just have to find out.'

There was a short, heavy silence.

'We'd better start moving, then,' said Anarres.

28.
THE RIVER

They had passed Lucknow, and were far upriver. It was Jaya's turn to take watch. She sat in the prow of the barge, huddled close against the side of the boat and shielded by canisters. The rifle was balanced across her knees and she smoked a cigarette covertly, sentry-style, so that its light was concealed in the hollow of her hand. Her time on the ship did not seem to have cured her nicotine cravings, after all.

The river lapped gently against the side of the barge and the rising moon was scattered across its waters. Jaya stared up at the moon and thought: *I've sailed across those seas. I've watched the lightning of the world.* It seemed strange that someone who had never before left Bharat should have seen so much, all at once, like devouring a sweetmeat. She still couldn't quite believe it. Whatever might have befallen her there, the time on the ship seemed dreamlike and long ago; a vision conjured in childhood. *I suppose it was. Perhaps it's better that way.*

Unwillingly she remembered Amir Anand and the day of her husband's death; herself lying in the dust and the mud, out of sight, while the butcher-prince put bullet after bullet into Kamal's spine. Yet even this worst memory seemed rendered distant by time and the things that had happened to her: raw wound changing to old ache. It felt disloyal, as though she was starting to forget Kamal, but then all the memories of him flooded back and she knew she never would. Pain might pass; memory would always be there. She wondered, once more, what had happened to her in that strange, closed room on the ship. As soon as there was time, and language enough, she would talk to Sirru and get some answers.

Sitting back, she tried to imagine Sirru's world, thinking hazily of lightning among the spires of some vast city; juggernauts cruising through the heavens like Shiva's chariot. *Does he miss his home? What kind of life does he have there? Is it really a* devaloka, *a realm of the gods? Or is it more like hell?* She reached down and crushed the cigarette against the damp boards of the barge. Time to go.

By dawn, they had left the barge and the river far behind and were headed up into the hills in two ATVs driven by hastily summoned former supporters. Bareilly lay behind them; soon they would be at Dehra Dun and Mussoorie. They had not forgotten Jaya Devi in these northern wastes, and the reason was still evident. The villages that they passed through were poor, no more than hovels clinging to the dusty roadside.

Jaya's oddly assorted entourage elicited no more than passing interest, but Sirru kept out of sight, concealing himself by his usual mysterious means. Jaya was eager to get going, out into what might pass for freedom. Once they were in a place where she could count upon a degree of support, she would leave Rajira and Halil behind. The boy had been very quiet, perhaps still in shock from his traumatic cure, but the erosion of Selenge had faded from his skin and he was able to walk without pain.

Rajira kept close to him, some maternal instinct aroused by the child's evident unhappiness. Whenever Halil had something to say, he whispered it to the courtesan and she relayed it to the others. The child would no longer speak directly to Jaya, and when he looked at her, she could see the spark of accusation in his eyes. Another failed follower. Sirru said nothing, and Jaya couldn't tell what, if anything, he was feeling.

By the following noon they were already climbing into the foothills. There was a mass of cloud rearing up over the mountains and the sky was grey with rain. It was beginning to be familiar territory. Jaya remembered a time when every rebel in Bharat had flocked here, ready to join the alliance and hungry to become part of a movement which would sweep the country clean of caste and corruption. Now, no more than a handful of years later, their naivety seemed incredible. Sirru, she realized with a flash of insight, would change more by his presence than a thousand troops ever could. Her own myth had been swept up and captured by others: Kharishma's beauty might take her further than Jaya could ever have gone. But they were not going to take this myth away from her, she thought as she gazed at Sirru; this story was all her own. The ATV skidded to a halt, wheels spinning in the mud. Jaya leaned out and spoke to the cursing driver.

'How far are we from the pass? Ten kilometres?'

'Maybe twelve.'

'Then we'll walk the rest of the way. Is the road still blocked beyond Drumai?'

'I think so.'

'All right, then. We couldn't get the vehicles up there anyway. If anyone should come after us, tell them that we were headed for Shurat. And act as though you're frightened.'

The driver gave a grim grin. 'If it's Amir Anand who's coming after you, that shouldn't be so hard.'

Jaya slapped him on the shoulder. 'I don't know who it will be. Anand's fallen out of favour. But if you should see him, if you get a chance at a shot at him, you'll take it, won't you?'

The driver's gaze was opaque with memory as he turned his head. 'Anand has no welcome here. Not after what he's done. If I get a clear shot, I'll take it.'

Jaya nodded. 'We'll leave you now.'

She stepped down from the vehicle, stretching, and made her way across the muddy track to the shelter of the neem trees to light a cigarette. Hunger gnawed at her stomach; she'd been forgetting to eat again. Sirru came to stand by her side, picking his way through the mud. When he reached the soft grass at the side of the road, he raised each foot and shook it fastidiously, like a cat. He gazed at her solemnly. A shaft of light shot through the rain clouds, falling down through the leaves, and for a moment he was nothing more than a tiger pattern of shadows. Yet his ivory skin seemed duller this morning and his eyes did not appear quite so bright. When he glanced at her, he did not seem to see her. It was as though he was looking inward to some distant horizon.

'Are you all right?' She tried to send a sense of concern but he was shutting her out. She could not get even the slightest indication of what he might be feeling. The fear of sickness, never far from Jaya's mind, returned to haunt her. Stupidly, it had not occurred to her that Sirru could fall ill. He seemed so much beyond the usual mortal world that she sometimes forgot he was as much flesh and blood as herself, just cast in a different form. And he had cured her. He had cured the child. He was a healer, despite the weird, anomalous savagery of his methods. A healer and a harvester: like the gods themselves, who kill and cure at their own strange whim.

She had been so wrapped up in her own reactions that she had not really given time to thinking of how the alien might be responding to the loss of the ship, a different gravity and atmosphere, alien food. If Sirru died . . . And then she told herself not to be a fool. He wasn't going to die. But what if he did? Everyone else who had ever been close to her had died, after all, except Rakh and the remnants of her army. Easy to become superstitious . . .

She glanced uneasily at Sirru but he was staring at the rain, which dripped from the pointed ends of the leaves and caught the growing light into diamond droplets. It was easing off now and they were losing time.

'All right,' Jaya said, and extinguished her cigarette. 'Let's start walking.'

The little procession headed up the mountainside: Rakh and Shiv, Rajira and Halil, and then last of all Sirru. Jaya turned once to give a last wave to the drivers, who stood with their antiquated rifles cocked across their shoulders, guarding her again from what might come.

29.
SOUTHERN HIMALAYAS

Sirru had no idea where Jaya was leading him. His geographical knowledge was, to say the least, hazy, and he had never been so far from a city. On his own world, Khaikurriyë extended across Rasasatra's single vast continent: any spare ground had been annexed millennia ago, during the Remodelling. Even the mountains lay in what was now parkland. Sirru was confused by the heights that now lay before him, at first assuming that they had strayed into the territory of some higher caste, but though there were plants, there seemed to be very few temeni. However, it was pleasant to be surrounded by living things once more, and Sirru could concentrate on the progress of the communications network without distractions.

It was beginning to impinge upon him now that he was in the company of three of his nexi: all infected in different ways. Jaya, as a genetic Receiver, would probably prove to be the most stable, and this pleased Sirru, who felt that he needed to explain things to her in rather more detail than he had already. She did not trust him, and this was upsetting. Sometimes, now, he saw through the eyes of Rajira, Halil and Jaya almost as well as he saw through his own. Their thoughts, fragmented though they were, lent meaning to his own vision.

To his private delight, he was beginning to learn the words for things, the layers of the world. He learned their senses of self, their places within their culture. He was startled to find that Rajira was one of its humblest members rather than a respected citizen, and wondered uneasily what reception Anarres might meet if she should ever visit this world. He learned that the child was still suffering from the lethargy left by the disease, but that the boy was planning to run when he recovered his strength.

Sirru sighed. He supposed that it had been a mistake to seize the child in such a savage way, but he had needed to demonstrate to Jaya that the disease which so preoccupied her was relatively simple to cure and he had feared that she might not have let him near the infant. Next time, gentler methods could be employed, but now one member of the party, at least, hated and feared him. That would have to be rectified. If he had time, he would try to win the child over. Halil was a nexus, after all, and therefore precious. Besides, it was a matter of common decency.

And then there was Jaya, into whose head he saw most deeply. Sirru felt that he was really getting to know his Receiver, and as the viral link between them grew, so did his affection for her. Rajira reminded him a little too much of a *khaith*, with her soft plumpness, but Jaya – small, lithe, and bony – was more recognizably *desqusai*. Ironically it was Rajira who remained attracted to him, in what was evidently a rather baffled way. The link effected by their congress was still extant; he had, in effect, hard-wired himself into her hormonal array. Sirru suspected that he would have to do something about that before much longer.

He thought wistfully of a return to his First Body and his normal life. Who knew when, if ever, this would be; Core alone knew what havoc Ir Yth had already managed to wreak. Sirru experienced a moment of pure fury, an emotion so foreign to his usual state of equanimity that it took him aback.

His mood and concept suppressants were long gone now, broken down into harmless cells and faded from his bloodstream. Forbidden thoughts came to him now with increasing frequency: rage at the cavalier way in which the Core moulded the castes to suit its own dark purposes; the manner in which Making was so carefully controlled; the way in which groups such as the Naturals were promoted as examples of the Core's tolerance and were in reality suppressed by being forced to live on the fringes of society. The oldest legends related how the beings of the Core were the most ancient in all the galaxy, how every intelligent form of life stemmed from them and how they were therefore entitled to absolute dominion over the thousands of worlds beneath their sway.

Was it even true? *What are they, our Makers? What manner of thing?* No one had been allowed into the heart of the Core for thousands of years, its demands were

interpreted and filtered down the castes through the mul-
titudinous arrays of the Marginals. *Perhaps there isn't
even anything there. Perhaps they're all long dead, and it
is the Marginal castes themselves who run the universe.
Perhaps there are no suppressants, and we are so controlled that we police our own thoughts.*

This last thought frightened Sirru more than any other,
and his skin flushed cold. The three nexi halted, and turned
to look at him, moving eerily as one. Sirru distributed
hasty reassurance as unobtrusively as possible; the last
thing he wanted was to alarm them. He tried to turn his
mind from new and disturbing thoughts, and concentrate
instead upon learning from the nexi.

Gradually, he gleaned the words for sky and sun and
rain, and for the feathered *hiroi* which flashed through the
branches of the trees. He was intrigued to find that a few
of the oldest root-words still persisted: words that were
honoured among his people for the length of their lineage.
Without their customary layering of emotional tone, they
were flat and bland, but they were nonetheless recognizable. Phrases darted through his mind like the creatures in
the trees and slowly, slowly, they began to make sense.
The thought of being able to communicate effectively with
Jaya, and find out what she was really thinking, filled him
with anticipation. That night, while her dark figure sat
hunched over the gun and the golden moon floated up
above the mountains, Sirru sent out a tentative message.

*

Cradled beneath a tree, Rajira Jahan stirred in her sleep, but did not wake. Halil mumbled, afraid, and Jaya raised her head and gave Sirru a long, uncomprehending glance. In far and troubled Varanasi, a woman lying on a bed tossed and turned. Her skin was already hot with fever; she had succumbed more quickly than the others. In the Punjab, a man sat by a window with a jug of ice water, for he could not sleep, but the dreams came to him nonetheless: regular pulses of coded information. He did not understand, Sirru saw, but this did not matter. After all, a radio does not comprehend the information it transmits and receives.

30.
RESEARCH LABORATORY, TOKAI
PHARMACEUTICALS, VARANASI

They had found one of the monkeys. Younger than the rest, and with a withered leg, it proved easier to capture than the rest. Tokai's hirelings reported that the monkeys moved with an eerie, concerted effort, flitting like spirits through the labyrinths beneath the temple, but the little one was slower and had been left behind. Now, the monkey sat with listless indifference in the corner of its cage. Tokai had not yet permitted any of the research technicians to touch it, and ordered it to be placed in Level Four isolation. He now stood at the airlock to the isolation ward with Ir Yth, watching the little figure.

/This place is your laboratory?/

'One of them, yes. I have others, throughout Chile and Japan. South East Asia, too.'

/An extensive network./

Tokai gave a small smile. 'I should like it to be larger.'

/That is a distinct possibility./

Deprecatingly, Tokai said, 'This world must seem very small and limited to one from such a vast empire.'

/Very small, yes. The Empire consists of many thousands of worlds, many billions of souls. It is not only the oldest civilization; it is the only one./

Imperceptibly, Tokai sighed. Despite his distrust of Ir Yth, he found himself moving in and out of sympathy with her. Her modesty, her reserve and her apparent need to maintain honour were surprisingly Asian, but the arrogance and the condescension with which she treated her new allies was surely not. Tokai was not used to being dealt with in this manner, and it infuriated him. He took care not to show this, and had dosed himself with a cocktail of pheromonal suppressants in order not to betray himself. He suspected that Ir Yth gained a great deal of unwitting information by such a method, as indeed he did himself.

/I will investigate the animal,/ Ir Yth informed him now.

'We have an extensive range of precautions—' Tokai began, gesturing to the blue suits that hung on the wall, and to the airlock itself. Ir Yth gave him a scornful glance.

/There is no need for unnecessary encumberment. I do not require protection./

'But there are a great many lethal viruses contained within this chamber. Do you see the containment racks? If you were to accidentally release something—'

/I am not that clumsy. Open the door./

'Very well. But I'm going in with you. Give me a few minutes to suit up and—'

/I will go alone./

'No.'

Tokai and Ir Yth glared at one another for a moment, and then the *raksasa* conceded.

/Very well. I am here to assist, not cause further problems./

She waited with evident impatience while Tokai methodically went through the rituals of suiting up. Together, they stepped through the door of the airlock, which hissed shut behind them. Tokai released the second door, and Ir Yth strode through into the isolation chamber as though she owned the place.

Ir Yth went straight to the cage in which the monkey was kept. Releasing the catch, she reached in and grasped the monkey by the scruff of the neck. It hung, squirming, from her stumpy fingers.

'Wait!' Tokai cried. 'What are you doing?'

Hauling it out of the cage, the *raksasa* studied it for a moment. Tokai watched in paralysed revulsion as a long, thin, red blade extended from between the *raksasa*'s furled lips and stabbed at the base of the animal's throat. The monkey gave a single small squeak and went limp.

'Wait—' Tokai whispered, appalled at this vampiric

329

display. Memories of the stories of demons told to him in childhood returned with alarming clarity. Ir Yth ignored him. The red tongue was straight and stiff, but occasionally it quivered. And then it retracted with the speed of a lizard's, its curled end flickering briefly over Ir Yth's lips.

/*Interesting,*/ Ir Yth said, as if to herself.

'I'm sure,' Tokai remarked, weakly.

/*It will take a little time to analyse.*/

Something was moving beneath Ir Yth's robe. Tokai could see the material above her ridged breastbone fluttering, as if stirred by an invisible breeze. Ir Yth's golden gaze was bland and blank.

/*I see . . . It is indeed a virulent plague.*/

Without his cane, and sealed off from Ir Yth's betraying pheromones, Tokai could only assume that she might be lying.

'How terrible,' he said, sincerely.

/*But it can be treated. An antidote can be manufactured.*/

'That's wonderful news.'

/*But it will not be easy. I require assistance. I also require – certain considerations.*/

'Perhaps you would be good enough to instruct me.'

/*I require knowledge of your operations. What is this?*/ The *raksasa* held up a glistening phial.

'Please put that back!'

/*You seem agitated,*/ Ir Yth said.

'That is a sample of the virus that causes a disease called Selenge, an illness of which you may have heard.

There is no way of knowing what it might do to you – you are not human, after all, and—'

But once again he was too late. With a deft twist, Ir Yth removed the stopper of the flask and tested the contents with her tongue.

'Madam! Ir Yth!'

The raksasa turned a gilded eye upon Naran Tokai.

/This is manufactured./

'What are you talking about? It's a retrovirus; it—'

/I have had some experience of the diseases of this world. They are naturally occurring, harmful mutations of the original communication mechanisms with which the írRas supplied this biosphere. This is not natural. This has been made. I congratulate you, Tokai. This branch of the desqusai is more advanced than I had believed. What is it for?/

'What do you mean?' Tokai asked, trying to recover his shattered composure. The prospect of being blackmailed by Ir Yth was not an appealing one.

/Its function. Such things are not manufactured for personal amusement. Permit me to speculate. I know that certain societies here are divided by caste, just as my own society is. Jaya has told me that her own caste is extremely lowly, but that they used to have a more equal position. That equality was eroded with the advent of a new political order, and subsequently sealed by the advent of the disease called Selenge, which affected primarily the lower castes and therefore caused them to be mistrusted and shunned, and confined to the filthier jobs. It must

*have been a very good excuse for the authorities to
continue to revoke their privileges. You have a virtual
monopoly on the pharmaceutical industry in this part of
the world. I wonder what you have done to earn such a
position./*

'Very well,' Tokai said, warily. 'You seem to have an
admirable grasp on political realities.'

*/I am not here to challenge your actions. Local politics
hold little interest for me as long as they do not interfere
with Core plans. Indeed, the use of such mechanisms to
control the stability of a society is a method that the Core
itself has employed. It is the sign of a developed order. But
your manufactured viruses might serve as a carrier for
the antidote. And now, I should like to make further
investigations./*

The fragile body of the monkey lay unmoving in its
cage. Tokai felt equally drained as he watched Ir Yth
bustling about the laboratory, tasting and testing his fatal
creations with all the enthusiasm of a child in a sweet
shop, feasting on poisonous candies.

YAMUNOTRI

1.
SOUTHERN HIMALAYAS

They had now been travelling for over a day, heading up into the high passes. Rajira and the child were clearly finding it difficult, and Jaya planned to leave them at the first place that seemed reasonably secure. Unfortunately, this was not proving easy to find. Once, these lower slopes had been covered with smallholdings and summer pastures, but Amir Anand's scorched earth policy had taught this part of the north a hard lesson. Now, the hills were silent and bare, with only the thin grass growing sparsely on the heights. The ruins of houses by the side of the road, bullet holes still stitching the faded white plaster of their walls, were another legacy.

It was not only the past that preoccupied Jaya. She was becoming increasingly certain that Sirru might be ill. He had grown silent and withdrawn; his narrow face seemed pinched and paler. When dawn once more broke over the mountains, she stepped stealthily across the ranks of sleeping bodies and stared down at him. They had taken shelter in one of the ruined compounds, in the mouldy hay of a cattle shed. Sirru was asleep, too. He lay flat on his back with his hands crossed over his chest like a fallen statue, his face peaceful and remote. But his skin was ashen, and his breathing was quick and shallow. Rajira Jahan whimpered in her sleep and Jaya turned. She could see a film of sweat glistening upon Rajira's brow. Halil, too, muttered and mumbled, locked in dreams.

For a brief, unnerving moment, Jaya could see the content of those nightmares. Halil was dreaming of the alien: a tall pale presence, with a demon's teeth. Jaya sat back on her heels and looked inwards, searching for signs of illness, but there were none. She felt alert and alive, her awareness heightened to almost animal sensitivity. The glimpse of another mind that she had just received was nothing like the speech of the ship. It was close and low and human; familiar. It seemed ironic to Jaya that all about her should be falling sick whilst she was the one who was well. Gently, she crouched by the child's side and brushed a hand across his forehead. Halil's skin was cold as mountain snow. Wondering, Jaya tucked his blanket about him and left him in peace.

As she stood back, she saw that Rakh was awake and watching her. There were questions in his gaze and Jaya nodded.

'Something's wrong.'

Rakh struggled sleepily to his feet and accompanied her out into the compound. This high in the hills, it was chilly, and there was the glaze of ice on one of the water tanks. No wonder the child's temperature was so low; she hoped that was all it was. She wrapped her arms about herself in reflex action, yet she herself could not feel the cold. She said, 'I think they're ill. Rajira and Halil, and the alien.'

Rakh said, without surprise, 'It's always the way.'

'What do you mean?'

'You said it yourself. Colonizers. They bring sickness with them. Sometimes they die.'

'But he healed Halil.'

'Did he? By attacking him? You just said that the boy's sickening again.'

'Yes, but I don't think it's with Selenge. That doesn't start like this, it begins with a rash and vomiting.'

'Who knew what diseases they carry with them? Perhaps that's the plan. Maybe Sirru is a carrier. A sacrifice.'

'Maybe,' Jaya said doubtfully.

'If it wasn't for the fact that Sirru healed the boy,' Rakh said, 'even in such a manner, would you let him live?'

Jaya looked at him. 'I don't know. But even if I didn't, I don't think others would be far behind him. We ought to wake them,' she added, briskly. 'Find better shelter, if we've got wounded on our hands.'

But Rajira could not be woken with the others. Jaya came back from a hasty wash in the water tank to find Rakh kneeling by her prone body.

'Rakh? What's wrong?' Jaya asked.

'I don't know. I can't wake her.'

'Wonderful,' Jaya said bitterly. 'First everything else, and now this . . .' She glanced across at Sirru. For a moment, she thought he was still asleep, too, but then the golden eyes snapped open. The warmth of unexpected relief spread in a rush through Jaya's stomach. At her side, Rajira murmured something and woke. She blinked up at the worried faces around her.

'Rajira?' Jaya said. 'Are you all right?'

'Yes . . . I think so. Except I had dreams . . .'

'What sort of dreams?'

'I could hear other people. I was in their heads.' Rajira sat up and clutched her shawl more tightly about her plump form. She looked down at her own ringed hand as though she'd never seen it before. 'Where are we?'

'Not far from a place where you'll be safe,' Jaya said, with a confidence that she did not feel. Rajira glanced uncertainly towards Sirru. The alien was now sitting cross-legged beneath the cross pole of the cowshed, his robes folded neatly about him. He was wearing an absent smile, which lent him an unsettling resemblance to a skinny Buddha. Jaya scrambled across and felt for his pulse. Sirru looked down at her without surprise. His skin still retained its coolness; she wondered how sickness would manifest itself in one so strange.

Are you all right? she tried to convey, but she got the impression that he wasn't even listening to her, as though she was nothing more to him than one of the flies which hummed through the undergrowth. 'Very well,' Jaya said, wearily. 'Let's get going.'

As they progressed up the slopes, the landscape became increasingly familiar to her. There was the cluster of rocks

336

behind which they had hidden when Anand's militia stormed the valley. That boulder over there was where her lieutenant Hakri had died. With a chill Jaya remembered turning to speak to him and seeing him sitting peacefully by her side, quite dead, his mouth slightly open as though on the verge of a reply. There was the spring that had tasted of snow melt and freedom. All these memories of place returned to Jaya as they travelled, and she knew that Rakh felt the same. They did not speak, but he moved to walk beside her, as he had done for so many years now, to lend her strength.

Towards the head of the valley, the first peaks were visible. They towered up like clouds, tinged with the light of the sun, floating and unreal. It had been a long time since Jaya had been in these mountains, and these were only the foothills of the Himalayas. Remembered awe caught her throat and she thought: *We should not be here. This is somewhere sacred, somewhere only the gods should live.* She noticed that Sirru was staring straight ahead, purposefully putting one bare foot in front of another as if drawn by the magnet of the mountains.

They met only a herd boy with a straggly flock of goats. The child sat silently on a boulder as they passed and gazed at them with wide, frightened eyes. Along the valley, Jaya could see a building; another cottage abandoned in the wake of revolt. It seemed derelict, and no one came out to watch them go by. Jaya was thinking ahead, wondering whether the fort at Yamunotri would be the same, how it might have changed. The past was compressing, folding back upon itself; it seemed only a few days since she had last walked these passes.

She gazed ahead to the distant peaks, falling now into their familiar configurations: Swargarohini's spires hidden in cloud; the summit of Bandarpunch arching against the backdrop of the sky. Her husband Kamal had known these mountains from childhood, raised here among the changing light and the glacial air, and it was her belief that he had come back, his spirit renouncing the wheel and rebirth and fleeing into the snows like the Christian ghosts were said to do. Yet she did not think he would know her if he should glimpse her again. She felt, somewhere deep in her heart, that he had become another kind of being altogether, something as ancient and strange as Sirru who now walked by her side. And she thought to herself: *What are we becoming, for surely change is not so far away?*

Her senses still retained their unnatural alertness. She could see a hawk coasting on the air, far down the valley, and though it was no more than a speck in the distance she could hear its thin sharp cry. Voices floated past her on the wind like the spirits of the dead, and she could hear the thoughts of those around her in fragmented cacophony. Accustomed as she had become to speaking with the ship, this did not seem so strange and gradually she learned to filter them out. Rajira was weary; Halil afraid. She placed a comforting hand on the child's shoulder but he shook it away; she could feel his resentment like a burning coal clasped in the palm of his hand. He still blamed her, and there seemed little enough that she could do about it. She had tried talking to him, but he wouldn't listen.

It was very quiet. They had come up onto the path now, and Jaya was concerned that they might meet a pilgrim heading up towards the little shrine that lay at the gate of the fort, but there was no one. The land was empty as far as the high peaks. Far away down the valley, she could hear the bells of the goats. A bird rocketed up out of the thin grass and was gone. Jaya stepped around the curved wall of rock and the ruin of the fortress was there before them, unchanged. The Yamuna river, no more than a torrent slicing through the rocks, boiled down towards the valley. The fortress stood on its left bank. Veils of steam from the hot springs drifted across the stones.

The place where Kamal had died was still there: a rocky ledge jutting out across the river. The old story said that if you bathed in the waters of the Yamuna, you were spared a painful death. So much for that. Jaya had to force herself to look, but of course there was nothing there. Before her surrender, she and two of Kamal's lieutenants had carried the body up into the glacier, to the lake of Saptarishi Kund. She tore her gaze away from the rock and strode grimly on.

The fortress was deserted. Traces of the revolution's last stand still remained: a rotting rucksack tossed carelessly into a corner. Empty cartridge cases littered the stone floor. It even seemed to her for a moment that she could see footprints in the dust and blood on the walls, but then she looked more closely and there was nothing there. With Rakh, she allotted rooms for the night: herself, Halil and Rajira in one of the abandoned antechambers, the men in another. Sirru had found his own place, out in what had once been a garden but which was now little more than a tangle of weeds around a pond whose water was as dark and still as the bottom of a well.

When all the necessary tasks were done, she went down to the shattered shrine. The silver image of Yamuna was still there: serene lunar daughter of consciousness and the sun. Perhaps the goddess of the moon would look favourably upon visitors from another world. Jaya breathed a prayer, but had no garlands to offer. The shrine was cold and damp, and she did not stay long.

Tomorrow, they would head up towards the lake and the passes. There were too many memories here, and besides, Jaya did not like retracing her steps into a place that Amir Anand knew so well. She turned over possibilities in her mind. He would surmise that she had headed up here, but would he think it was too obvious a place for her to be, or would he suspect that she was attempting a double bluff? Now that Ir Yth had remained behind in Varanasi, would he even care? Jaya believed that he would, and that being demoted would only have fuelled his fury.

She had expected to die here, during those days of revolution, and now she could feel change coming in like a storm over the horizon's edge. She sat on the window sill, perched high above the stones of the hillside, and listened to the wind. Rajira, wearing a petticoat and holding a sodden sari in her hand, stifled a gasp.

'You shouldn't sit there like that. What if you fell?'

I've already fallen, she felt like saying, but she smiled at the courtesan and shifted to a more secure position. Turning her head, she watched the kites wheel high above the valley, no more than motes in the clear air. Thunderheads were massing over the peaks and she took a deep, anticipatory breath. Far below, she could see Sirru. He walked slowly, picking his way across the stones, and paused to stare out at the mountains. She saw his arms slide about his own waist and she wondered whether he shivered. Then he turned and walked slowly back towards the fort. He moved like someone old. *Like I used to move, before they cured me.*

Threads of understanding were beginning to pull and weave within Jaya's mind. *Colonization and disease.* Sirru had suggested that something had gone badly wrong with this little world, but what, exactly? To people who could speak without words, who spoke with a language of the body, what would sickness mean? Would it mean the same thing as it did to a human? She had lain close to illness all her life: listening to her father talk about the medicine markets, how everything was sewn up by the multinationals and how illness was the only legacy that the poor had to give. *'When the British came, they brought cholera. They brought syphilis. They brought influenza. Disease accompanies colonization like flies accompany shit.'* And the conjuror's daughter thought now: *But what if disease was the purpose of colonization? What if it was not originally intended to harm? Can illness have functions other than destruction? What does "harvest" really mean?*

There were too many questions ... She turned to Rajira, who was shaking the sari out of an adjoining window. Waterdrops sparkled in the sun.

'Rajira? This morning ... I thought you might be sick. Are you all right?'

The courtesan gathered up the sari and frowned.

'I don't know. I keep hearing voices; I told you that. And it's like a fever – it comes and goes. Sometimes I feel hot.' She gave a rueful smile. 'But I haven't had so much exercise in years. Maybe that's it.' But a lost look crossed her face for a moment, as though she sensed that something might be very wrong. Her mouth tightened and she turned back to her laundry. She barely seemed to notice when Jaya slipped away.

2.
VARANASI

Kharishma had done her best to take Jaya's place, but she came a poor second. Tokai's people reported that many of the acolytes who flocked around the Temple of Durga had drifted away, in search of new dreams and diversions, and Kharishma was enraged to find that far from being the centre of attention, she had managed to quieten the whole affair down. The military had come and sniffed around the temple, accompanied by UN teams, and despite exhaustive tests had apparently found little to occupy them. American soldiers had finally been allowed in, under Pentagon command. Kharishma had gained some satisfaction from their obvious approval of her, but their general had been a cold-eyed man who seemed to regard her as an unwelcome distraction. Eventually she had been forced to withdraw.

Kharishma did not know how Tokai had gained access to his information, but he seemed to have been granted a remarkably free rein by the government of Bharat. Scientists had taken soil samples from the temple courtyard, but apart from the little animal that had been captured, the monkeys that had once haunted the precincts had vanished. Kharishma did her best to find out what was going on, but Anand wouldn't tell her a thing, and she rarely set eyes on Tokai. Perhaps that was just as well, because Tokai frightened her, with his old turtle's face and lipless grin, and the cane always seemed to be sniffing around her sari skirts.

A few moments of excitement came when Kharishma was interviewed by both Bharati and UN authorities. But though she tried to explain that she was the important one, and Jaya Nihalani no more than an upstart *dalit*, they didn't seem to be listening. In her saner moments, during the restless darkness just before dawn, she remembered the look that had appeared in a German journalist's eyes after a few minutes of talking to her: a kind of wary, watchful amusement, the sort of expression that one might indeed assume when conversing with the mad. When

Kharishma remembered this look, she flung herself from her bed and began to pace the echoing precincts of the Khokandra Palace.

The *raksasa* had chosen not to be seen by anyone except Tokai, Anand, and Kharishma herself. Ir Yth seemed able to flicker in and out of view; annoyingly but predictably at the least convenient moments. During the interviews, Kharishma had intended Ir Yth to be her *pièce de résistance*, given the infuriating absence of the second alien, but Ir Yth had suddenly assumed an unbecoming modesty.

She was weary of dealing with the *desqusai*, the humans, she told Kharishma. Tokai was different. He understood her; he was sympathetic. When in Varanasi, Ir Yth went into seclusion in the isolation lab; here, in Khokandra Palace, she kept to the little shrine. She seemed to require neither food nor water, and Kharishma's attempts to gain access to her had proved unsuccessful. Indeed, entering the shrine in a rage a few nights ago, Kharishma had found it quite empty. She remembered looking around her, baffled, for the *raksasa* had not been seen to leave. Then, in a corner of the room, she saw a pair of cold golden eyes staring unblinkingly at her, and nothing else.

Kharishma, unnerved, had fled the shrine and had not been back since, but she was determined to face the *raksasa* again. After all, she told herself self-righteously, it had been Ir Yth who had first sought her out and whispered promises of glory in her ear. Wasn't she supposed to be the saviour of the world? She had risked everything and nothing had happened: no plaudits, no congratulations, no alien villain served up to the authorities. Kharishma smacked her fist against the warm stone of the garden wall in frustration. She couldn't help feeling that the action was going on elsewhere, without her, and that she could not bear. It was centre stage or nothing.

Wait, a voice whispered, inside her mind. It wasn't like the silent voice with which Ir Yth communicated; it felt as though someone had lodged deep in her bone and blood and was whispering to her.

'What?' Kharishma murmured, startled.

/ Came back from the market this morning and I said – / – what is happening to me? My head hurts – / – I want a glass of water – /

The voices were all different: male and female, young and old. Kharishma did not recognize any of them. She looked wildly around, suspecting a trick, but the garden was sunlit and empty. She sank down the garden wall among the overblown roses, her arms wound tightly about her knees, and began cautiously to listen.

3.
KHAIKURRIYË

Anarres and Nowhere One travelled slowly, relying on smell and touch to make their way through the tangled root system. It seemed to go on forever, but Anarres had no idea where they were heading, or even if they would ever be able to make their way up and out. Every time she faltered, she remembered the *írHazh* and the touch of EsRavesh and the memory was enough to spur her on. She clambered grimly over roots, beneath trailing lines of fungus, and the earth was thick and clammy beneath her feet. Anything, she thought, would be better than death at the claws of an írHazh, even a stifling end below ground. And almost anything would be better than the punishments EsRavesh might devise, if he ever caught up with her.

'Have you noticed,' Nowhere One said cheerfully, somewhere off to her left, 'that there's enough air down here to breathe? So it must be coming from somewhere.'

'But where?' Anarres froze as something skittered along the root below her. 'What was that?'

'I don't know,' Nowhere One hissed. 'Stay still.'

Anarres complied, then yelped as something ran across her hand. She felt a prickling of myriad legs.

'There's some kind of creature down here!'

'Probably lots of them,' the Natural said, which did not reassure Anarres at all. Then, to her immediate right, something started to rustle. Anarres's hands shook on the hard, curved surface of the root.

'Nowhere One?' Abruptly, the Natural was at her side. He clasped her as the mulch beneath their feet came alive with a thousand writhing forms. Anarres shrieked, and buried her face in his shoulder. A carpet of moving life swarmed up her spine, wriggling amongst her quills. A moment later, they were gone. There was a sharp, decisive crunch.

'I know what these are,' Nowhere One said indistinctly, through a mouthful of something. 'House-lice. Want some?'

'No!'

'Suit yourself.'

The house lice had disappeared, for which Anarres remained profoundly grateful, but climbing over the slippery roots was a nightmare task. The roots were wet, and coated with some kind of film that Nowhere One said was a protective measure against decay.

Anarres, standing high above Nowhere One's head, called down, 'I can't feel where it ends. It goes higher than I can reach.'

'Can you climb any further?' The Natural's voice floated up from far below.

'I don't think so. The roots seem to curve back on themselves.'

She thought she heard him curse.

'It's the end wall of the Marginals. Its own root system is sealed off from the rest of the city, in case anyone tries to infiltrate it.'

'What can we do?'

'Stay here for the rest of our lives and grow pale on house-lice, or think of a plan.'

'I'm coming down.' It felt suddenly lonely, up here in

the stuffy darkness by the end wall. Anarres slithered along the roots to the floor.

'The trouble is, I've no idea how to break the barrier. You'd need a heavy-duty meme to get through this. Or a large axe.'

'Could we convince it to spit us out?' Anarres asked.

'That would be hard. This is the wall of the Marginals, not a carnivore.'

'I wonder what parameters they've set?' Anarres wondered aloud. Something was tugging at her memory. Her own house had gone through that peculiar period, when it didn't want to let anyone else in. Now, she was sure that EsRavesh had done something to it. But Sirru had managed to get in, by lying to the house. She told this to Nowhere One.

He reached out in the darkness and grasped her arm.

'How did he lie? Did he tell you?'

'Yes,' Anarres answered. 'Later that night. A friend of his had modified the scale so that when you gave it the right instructions, it broadcast an emergency code. And the house opened up.'

'Scale modification needs a lot of work, and we don't have the tools,' Nowhere One said. 'But we might still be able to lie . . . You still have EsRavesh's implant, that you used to get into the translation storage area; you have *khaith* codes.'

'But they were keyed into the orbital itself. Surely they wouldn't work here?'

'The codes will retain an impression of EsRavesh. If

you can activate the implant, and enhance it so that the wall thinks a *khaith* is standing before it, trapped in the root system, it might open up.'

'Enhance it? How?'

'Anarres, you do it all the time. You are constantly manipulating your own presence – your own pheromonal signature. This time, you'll have to do it with someone else's. I don't think you realize how powerful you can be.'

'I'll try,' Anarres said, doubtfully. 'But I've never done this kind of thing before.' But even as she spoke, she thought, *But maybe that is what an apsara does. Reflecting a lover back upon themselves, enhancing them in their own eyes. I am like a mirror. They look at me, and they see their own prowess and allure.*

She touched the implant, and thought about EsRavesh. She conjured up the image of his stumpy hands and thick petalled mouth. She recalled the musty odour, and wove it expertly into her own pheromonal array. She overcame her revulsion, feeding sexual arousal back upon itself to generate a fantasy of the *khaith*, conjuring the impression that it was he who was standing before the wall of the Marginals. She could sense Nowhere One, off to the side, and, slowly, the presence of another. Gradually, with a corner of her mind, she became aware that it was the dome to which the end wall belonged. She could feel the sunlight on its arch, high above ground; the wet depths of the earth beneath her feet. Chlorophyll seeped through its veins. It was like her house, but larger and more complex.

It sent, inside her mind, /*What are you doing down here?* /Astonishment/alarm/ *I must alert someone!*/

/*That will not be necessary*,/ Anarres sent hastily, her modulations laced with overtones of EsRavesh. /*I was undertaking an inspection, and became trapped. I require access.*/

/*There is another with you. It feels wrong; it is not a clade member. I will alert clade.*/

/*Do not be concerned*,/ Anarres sent, as forcefully as she could. /*Please let me through*,/ She took a risk. /*You know I dislike disobedience!*/

The dome cringed. She had never felt a dome experience fear before, but this was deep and flinching with remembered pain. The part of Anarres's mind that was not preoccupied with simulating EsRavesh gave way to outrage, that the *khaith* should so mistreat a dwelling. But then a small crack opened in the wall, and there was no time to waste on pity. Anarres pushed Nowhere One swiftly through, and dived into the sanctuary of the root system beyond the Marginals.

She had felt sunlight on the dome of the Marginals, but when they eventually resurfaced, it was dark. It took some time to get their bearings, and when they did so, Anarres realized that they were nowhere near the Naturals' Quarter. They had come up through a seed pod in a park. It had spored in the night, and the air was filled with flying pollen. Choking, Anarres and Nowhere One stumbled down to a nearby pool where the air was clearer.

'It doesn't really matter,' the Natural said, batting away a night-bee. 'We'd have to come out sooner or later. We don't have the technology to reanimate IrEthiverris.'

'What are we going to do?' Anarres asked. 'Could we steal something?'

'We're going to have to be very careful where we go and who we speak to,' Nowhere One said. 'I'm hoping that EsRavesh will assume we've been devoured by his plant, but if he finds out that we've escaped ... He'll already have put a watch on your family.'

Anarres sat up straighter. 'But I know who *will* help us. They're probably under surveillance too, but if we can get a message to them and arrange to meet—'

'Who?' Nowhere One asked, but she could see the realization in his eyes.

'The EsMoyshekhali. Sirru's family.'

4.
YAMUNOTRI, HIMALAYAS

The network was starting to function. Sirru sat cross-legged by the small black pool and listened to what it had to tell him. He was lost in other people's lives: images, sensations, thoughts. Occasionally he tested the taste of a word on his tongue. Much of what he learned surprised him, and much of it saddened. Pain lanced down the viral lines like lightning down a kite string: he re-routed it into his own nerves, learning what it was to hurt in the manner of these new kindred. It was too soon for the embryonic network to summon a depth ship; he did not want to impose too great a strain upon his new communications system. He sent his single message of instruction: *Wait. Listen to what I tell you. The time is nearly here.*

A mosquito hummed in from the bushes and settled on his hand, but he did not notice. It penetrated the thin skin on the inside of his wrist, sipped alien blood for a moment before realizing its mistake, then whirred away. Part of Sirru went with it. Distinctions which separated him from the world ceased to be meaningful. There was no *inside/outside* any more, only the network of virally transformed consciousness which was slowly beginning to grow.

He reviewed his nexi. There were now over four hundred: the virus spreading fast, finding willing recipients and donors every hour. By and large, the nexi were all adult. The very young and the very old, being largely if not entirely free from sexual activity, remained untouched. And this was just as well, for Sirru did not yet know how fragile these new *desqusai* would prove. Generally, the infants of his own people bore such communication best when they were very young: babies who had not yet had the interference of language to stand in their way and whose needs and desires might be easily met.

From the symptoms he had observed of those around him, it would not be too long before the first infected nexi passed into the initial stages of coma, and then it would be down to himself and Jaya – also a nexus, but sufficiently revised during her sojourn on the ship – to coordinate the network. At some point, Sirru supposed, he was going to have to explain this to her. He told himself that it would be better to do this when he had a greater linguistic grasp, but he knew, deep down in the wells of his conscience, that he was afraid of what Jaya might say at being so used.

The thought that it might not be acceptable to employ people involuntarily in this manner was also a new concept to Sirru. He had been created for certain tasks, he reminded himself uncomfortably, like all the *desqusai*, but he had been accustomed to the idea from his Making, whereas these people had not. Only the thought that he might, ultimately, be able to save their lives and his own prevented the voice of his conscience from being overwhelming.

He blinked. A new voice had entered the fray, cutting through the melange of sounds and impressions like ice water.

/*What are you?*/ Sirru asked, surprised.

And the voice replied, /*I am the seed.*/

5.
VARANASI

'You see, Amir, the situation is really very simple,' Tokai remarked. Amir Anand turned to stare at him and Tokai reflected once again that the man did not look well. The handsome face was haggard, stripped down to the lean blades of cheekbone and the fierce arch of brow. His eyes seemed paler than ever, the colour of a too-hot sky. It would be inconvenient if Anand fell sick, Tokai thought. Aloud, he said, 'By the way, are you all right? It seems to me that you are not quite well.'

'I'm perfectly all right,' Anand snapped, and Tokai saw that he had once again wounded the man's pride. 'Merely the heat. I hate this stinking city.' He prowled across to the window and stared out across the wasteland of Varanasi's industrial estate to where the tower of the Temple of Durga punctuated the horizon like a needle pointing to heaven. 'I'll be glad when we return to Khokandra.'

'Which will be very soon,' Tokai reminded him, soothingly. 'We head back tonight, once Ir Yth has finished her various preparations. She claims to be feeling the heat, too.'

'Those preparations,' Anand said, eyes narrowing. 'What is she doing, exactly?'

'I am not entirely sure. Whatever it is, we may be sure that it is not what she *says* she is doing. That is what I meant when I said that the situation was simple. Ir Yth informs us, and every time she does so, she lies. That removes one more option from the equation.'

Anand stared at him in obvious dismay. He shook his head, like a dog bothered by flies. Tokai watched him, wondering. He had seen Anand make this gesture several times over the last few days, as if he was trying to clear his head. Anand said with cold politeness, 'That's a big risk to take, Shri Tokai.'

'I don't think so. Remember, Ir Yth has come to us for help. This suggests that she does not possess extensive resources of her own. And indeed, I have seen no evidence that there are any resources other than Ir Yth's own person. No landing craft, no weapons, no communications equipment . . . And some very reliable sources inform me that the great vessel that was orbiting the Earth has now decayed like a fallen leaf and blown away on the winds from the sun. I do not think, Anand, that it is Ir Yth who has the advantage here.'

He could see that Anand was dying to ask him what his plans were, but he merely waved a hand in a dismissal that the butcher-prince had no option but to accept. 'Go now. Prepare for our return to my palace.' He pretended not to see the sour glance that Anand gave him on his way out of the door, but simply sat and smiled, waiting for Ir Yth's latest news.

6.
KHAIKURRIYË

Anarres hovered at the edges of the chamber, watching nervously as Sirru's siblings fiddled with the manifold mesh.

'I'm still amazed,' Sirru's sister Issari said, looking askance at Anarres. 'You persuaded our own house to give us your message? From a pod in the park? I didn't even know domes could talk to each other.' She glanced across at the neat hole in the floor, through which Anarres and Nowhere One had so recently appeared. 'I hope you haven't disturbed the house roots.' Her tone was disapproving. 'And you say that my brother's in some kind of trouble? I mean, when that colony of IrEthiverris' started to go wrong, of course everyone was horrified, but I never thought—'

'Did you know IrEthiverris?' Anarres asked, curiously.

'Yes, of course I knew Verris. He was one of Sirru's greatest friends. I never thought I'd see the day when we'd be illegally reviving him in the living area. How did your' – she frowned at the shabby figure of Nowhere One – 'friend come to know him?'

Nowhere One hastened to explain. 'When I became a Natural, I started thinking about the desqusai – why so many of the caste became Naturals. Was it some inherent tendency, I wondered? Or could it be that someone wants us to break the rules – so that we can be cast out and scapegoated? Once I'd started thinking along those lines, I began to look more closely into desqusai affairs. And then I found out about the tragedy of Arakrahali. I want to talk to IrEthiverris – find out how much information was downloaded into his First Body.'

He stepped back from the mesh, which was beginning to glow.

'Well, this is the moment of truth. Let's see if Ir-Ethiverris can speak for himself.'

The glow deepened. Anarres and the EsMoyshekhali held their breath. Lights flickered over the surface of the manifold container. The manifold peeled back and a nano-filament grid began to form in the air above it. Anarres watched as muscle and sinew and bone began to be reconstructed along the grid. In a few moments, it was complete. A spindly form stood wild-eyed before them, quills bristling.

'Where am I?' asked IrEthiverris EsTessekh.

7.
YAMUNOTRI, HIMALAYAS

Sirru was sitting so still that at first Jaya did not see him. He gradually resolved out of the background, the shadows of the bamboo striping his skin. She breathed a sigh of relief at his emergence. She had not been able to find him all day, and was beginning to fear that he might have upped and left altogether. But no, it seemed that he had merely chosen to make himself invisible. This was not reassuring; if he chose to go, she was not only unlikely to be able to prevent him, but might not even notice. His eyes were open but there was no sign that he was aware of her presence. Stifling the urge to speak, Jaya sat down opposite him and waited.

At last, Sirru turned to her and said, 'Jaya? Change is coming.'

The words were so unexpected that for a moment she

didn't understand him. He had spoken in Hindustani, a little slurred, but perfectly intelligible.

'Sirru! Can you understand me?'

'Little.' That was in English, which Jaya read and understood, but could not speak well.

'Please – the first language you used. How? I mean, how are you learning my language?'

'Through illness. Not through pain.'

'I don't understand.' Then she thought uneasily of Rajira and Halil. *Did you teach them, Sirru, through pain?*

'Illness connects. Everything wrong here. Here, on this world, illness brings pain, ending. This is not purpose. I have to make things right.' His speech was peculiar: the words were the right ones, and his pronunciation was adequate, but the rhythm of the speech was strange. He ran words together, or left pauses where none should be. Jaya remembered the voice of the ship, speaking in her head throughout her life, and the worsening sicknesses which no one could understand or cure. *Illness connects.*

'Have you brought an illness here?'

'Many. When project first began, írRas started usual virus lines. But wrong mutations. Tekhein *desqusai* have not developed correctly; error in gene programme, perhaps. Don't know. This must be corrected.'

'You said – you told me in Varanasi, at the temple – that we are to be harvested.'

'Yes.'

'What does that mean?'

'Abilities must be harvested. Viral lines must be reformed if development is to continue.'

'I don't understand. Do you mean people will have to die?'

'No, not die. *Harvested.* Redeveloped.'

Jaya couldn't help feeling that this sounded worse.

'In this world, to harvest means to – to reap. To *kill*.'

'But you have fruit?'

'Yes.'

'Harvesting fruit does not kill tree.'

'No, but—'

'I did not come here to kill,' Sirru said patiently. 'Only to gather in the ones who could be made ready. Others will not be harmed.'

'Sirru, what have you done? What's happening to Rajira? And Halil?'

'Rajira is a nexus.'

'A nexus?'

'A node for communication web. I began this, through sexual transmission with her. By blood, with the child. Perhaps wrong method.' He frowned, a startlingly human gesture.

'Almost certainly the wrong method!'

'With you – ' and here he gave her a long, elliptical look, as if he was unsure as to how the words might be received ' – with you, your genetic mutation was redeveloped by ship. Ship made you what you are now. A nexus, but the first. The strongest. The one who will not go under the sleep when network comes on-line.'

Jaya stared at him. 'What have you turned me into, Sirru? Some kind of transmitter?'

She could hear something cold running beneath the steely calmness in her voice. Sirru said, with resignation, 'This is what I came here to do. Blame me if you must. Since we are stranded, I have had new ideas. New concepts, understanding through the viral lines. I know you think what I do is not right. But it is what I have been created to do. I know about free will. But all will starts from concepts that are *given*. I do not have free will as you would like to think it, and neither do you. You could not teach me to be human-*desqusai*, Tekhein. I am not.' He stared at her gravely, letting his words sink in. 'This thing I have done, this network, is common means of communication. Restructuring must begin with this. With *desqusai*, different castes. Hierarchies. Some are suited for communication. Some for other tasks, like you. You are a Receiver, a ship-speaker, foremost. The first, here, but there will be others.'

Wryly Jaya said, 'That's just as well. I don't like being special.'

'You are not special,' Sirru replied. 'Others with same genes. You are merely first.'

'You mentioned a caste system.' *Whatever it is*, Jaya thought, *somehow you've always heard it all before*. 'Based on what? On – on abilities?'

'On the – the diseases that are best for the person,' Sirru said. Jaya sat back on her heels and looked at him. *No harm. And like all colonizers, he really does think he's here to help. Maybe I should just kill him now, but it's too late, isn't it? Whatever he's done has taken root and taken hold. Sexual transmission – how many people has Rajira infected? How long did it take for AIDS to take hold?*

'I do not know if I have done the right thing,' Sirru said, and she looked up sharply at the bewilderment in his voice. It was so familiar. 'I only did what seemed right at the time. And if I don't do it, then I think we might all end now, Jaya.' In a few words, he explained exactly what Ir Yth had been plotting. Jaya stared at him in horror.

'We have to find her. I'm wondering now whether we should ever have left Varanasi.'

'Ir Yth needs help. She cannot act alone. I know, now,' Sirru said, and his expression became curiously abstracted. 'I know what is happening.'

'How?'

'Your Second Body – I can hear her thoughts. She is now a nexus. And so is the man called Amir Anand.'

8.
KHOKANDRA PALACE

Throughout the short journey back to Khokandra, Kharishma complained. She did not like the dust, or the heat, or the flies, and she was increasingly worried about Anand. He was as attentive as ever, but she got the feeling that he'd only agreed to take her along to keep her quiet. She sat sulkily in the back of the ATV with a scarf wrapped over her face.

'One would think you'd never grown up in Bharat, young lady. Why don't you move to Los Angeles, if you don't like it?' Tokai said over his shoulder. It was the only thing he'd said to her all morning.

'This is my home,' Kharishma said, with as much dignity as she could muster. Beside her, Ir Yth gave her a glance that might almost be one of sympathy. The *raksasa*'s plump face was pale and moist, and her gilded eyes were hollowed. Her arms were folded protectively around herself in a complex, jointed mass, like a dead spider.

/*When will we reach the destination?*/ Ir Yth's voice echoed unhappily in Kharishma's mind and the actress had to stifle a giggle. *How much further, Daddy? Are we nearly there yet?* Aloud she said, 'Not long. That's right, isn't it, darling? We'll soon be there.'

'Another hour.' Anand swerved to avoid a pothole in the road, bouncing the occupants of the ATV into the air. Ir Yth's face seemed to close in upon itself like a sour fruit and Kharishma stifled a sigh. The long journey had taken its toll; she felt flushed and feverish, and her head was beginning to ache with a slow, dull pound that echoed the beat of her heart.

To take her mind off the jolting vehicle, Kharishma closed her eyes and rested her head against the seat, imagining the demise of Jaya Nihalani. It had to be quick, she told herself. She'd been in too many films where the villain – not that that was the case here, of course – took a leisurely few minutes to explain to the hero exactly why he was about to die, and how. Kharishma wanted no such chance of escape given to Jaya. A bullet in the back of the head, and a swift, merciful death. She wasn't a sadist, after all. But it was increasingly becoming clear to Kharishma that if Jaya lived, then she could not. They were like two forces which couldn't occupy the same space without mutual destruction.

Kharishma's imagination spun away, travelling down long, strange roads, but she slowly became aware that Ir Yth was watching her with an unwavering, unreadable gaze.

/*What are you doing?*/ the *raksasa* asked, suspiciously.

'I'm thinking.'

/*There are echoes in your head!*/

Kharishma turned on Ir Yth with such sudden fury that the *raksasa*'s eyes widened in alarm.

'What are you saying?'

/*Your neural pathways are filled with echoes. Of other traces. Look at me,*/ Ir Yth said, and ignoring the bouncing of the vehicle she put her hands to either side of Kharishma's face. Her palms were soft, and unpleasantly moist. Kharishma struggled to escape, but the *raksasa* held her fast.

'Amir! Stop the car!' Kharishma squeaked, but as she opened her mouth even wider in protest the *raksasa*'s long red tongue whipped between her lips. There was a sharp sting in the roof of her mouth and the tongue was abruptly withdrawn. Ir Yth sat meditatively back. Kharishma's mouth was flooded with the hot iron taste of blood.

'Amir,' she cried, indistinctly. The ATV swerved off the road and stopped with a jerk. Tokai peered nervously over his shoulder.

'What's going on?'

Anand leaned over the back of the seat and grabbed the *raksasa* by the collar of her robe, hauling her forward. The vehicle filled with the icy emanations of the *raksasa*'s fury, but to Kharishma's considerable, if pain-filled, admiration, Anand hung on.

'What are you doing to her?'

/Let me go!/

'Let her go, Anand. At once!' Tokai's voice carried the whip-crack of command. Reluctantly, Anand released Ir Yth and she settled into the corner of the seat, grumbling inaudibly.

/The next time you lay hands on me, you will die./

'It will be worth it,' Anand informed her, coldly. He spun the wheel, taking them back onto the road to Khokandra.

9.
KHAIKURRIYË

To Nowhere One's manifest relief, IrEthiverris remembered a great deal about Arakrahali.

'Uploads to my First Body were frequent,' he told them,

sitting disconsolately at the edge of the living area. 'I intended to make even more regular updates, but my *khaith* administrator kept coming to me with this, that and the other. She also seemed to have become very friendly with her Receiver. He was quite a young man, and I suppose he found my administrator exotic – the people of Arakrahali were quite short, so maybe he saw her as tall and slender. I don't know. Anyway, I'm sure they were lovers. I kept finding them whispering together, and after a couple of months I noticed that people would vanish whenever I came near them. It was as though they didn't trust me. And by the time I did my last information upload the atmosphere in the place had totally changed – they'd never seemed particularly delighted that we were colonizing them, but they were resigned to it. But then they seemed to grow more and more hostile. And finally I discovered the truth – the *khaith* had sabotaged the communications network, and turned it against them. That's when they started to die. It was the last upload I made. I've no idea what happened to my Second Body.' He blinked into the sunlight. 'A dreadful situation. Those poor people. I must say, though, it's nice to be home. Even under these conditions. And Arakrahali cuisine was awful. I'd rather eat house-lice.'

Anarres slid down beside IrEthiverris, and explained about Sirru. He stared at her in horror.

'Does anyone know what's happening on Tekhei?'

'Unfortunately, no.'

'But if anything happens to Sirru's Second Body, then

that's it. He'll be dead. And why wasn't my First Body erased?'

'I rather suspect that's the plan,' Nowhere One remarked.

'You've only got your First Body because I couldn't find it,' Anarres said.

'What?'

'When I first went to the orbital, to erase Sirru's manifold, EsRavesh gave me another set of coordinates, and told me to erase that manifold as well. But I couldn't find it without the locative. We're sure it was *your* manifold.'

IrEthiverris gaped at her. 'You tried to erase my First Body? What have I ever done to you?'

'I'm truly sorry,' Anarres faltered. 'I was a different person then. I did what the *khaithoi* told me.'

'I think I want a bit more of an apology than that, young lady!'

'This can surely wait,' Nowhere One soothed. 'We have an urgent matter on our hands. We have to contact Sirru and tell him to be very careful. Otherwise, he'll be dead.'

10.
Yamunotri, Himalayas

Next day, Rajira and Halil could not be woken. They lay against the wall, with Rajira's arm curled protectively around the child's slight frame. Rakh stood over them, scowling with worry.

'We can't leave them here.'

'No, we can't. But we can't take the risk of Anand finding us, now it seems likely that he knows where we are.' Frustrated, she leaned her cheek against the cool stone lintel. 'How to avoid him, though? And we don't know who else might be on our trail, either. The militia, foreign spies . . .'

'We don't know what's wrong with Rajira and the boy. They might die. Can't the alien do something?'

'Sirru,' said Jaya grimly, 'already has.' She explained about the communications network. Rakh's eyes narrowed as he tried to understand.

'So all these people – you, and these two, and others – are now linked. By a kind of virus. Why are *you* not in a coma, then?'

'Because I think my system was modified on the ship.' She took a deep breath, not wanting to acknowledge her next words. 'I might be more like Sirru now than I am like a human.'

'You are still my brother's wife. My sister,' Rakh said gently, at the loss in her words.

'Thank you, Rakhi.'

'How does it work, this net of disease? And you say Amir Anand is part of it?'

'Anand must have become infected through one of Rajira's line.' She grimaced. 'I can see how Kharishma

367

might drive a man to seek out prostitutes . . . Sirru tried to explain about the network. He said that what we think of as diseases are mutations of systems that the írRas left when they first came to this planet, millions of years ago. They are our creators, Rakh. They started us off, linking our genes with a symbiotic set of diseases. But something went wrong on this world. Sirru's people don't get sick. They don't live forever; they wear out eventually, or suffer heart failure, or simply choose not to continue. But they don't suffer from the range of viral and bacterial infections that we do. They use diseases as mechanisms for all sorts of things: communication, information storage, learning. But those "diseases' are benign. Sirru wants to set the world right again. Or so he says. And I'm not sure what "right" might mean.'

'And do you believe him?'

'I don't know. I think I'm beginning to. But you see, Rakh, he can influence people to think things, and I don't know how much of it is me and how much of it is Sirru making me have ideas.'

'If you can think that,' Rakh said, 'then it is possible that he is *not* influencing you. It seems to me that he is powerful enough to make you unquestioning. Your uncertainty has always been your strength.'

Jaya stared at him. 'And here was I thinking you all followed me because of my wonderful sense of conviction.'

'No. We followed you because you questioned yourself, all the time. You were never a blind leader, wrapped up in your own sense of surety. And that is why I am following you now. Do what you think is best,' Rakh said. 'I will support you.'

'Then stay here,' Jaya said. 'Stay here with Shiv Sakai and guard Rajira and Halil. If they wake, then try to get them somewhere safer. I will go on with Sirru.'

For a moment, she thought Rakh was going to baulk at that, but then he gave her a wintry, rueful smile. 'After all my fine words . . . Very well. I have talked myself into the trap, haven't I?'

'We don't have very many choices. I don't want to leave them here, but if we can't wake them . . . There are no settlements anywhere nearby; vehicles can't get up here. And I have to get Sirru to a place where no one can find him. I'll explain things to him.'

But when she attempted to do this, she discovered to her dismay that the alien had other plans.

'It is too late. I told you. Ir Yth already knows where we are, and so do her new allies,' Sirru explained.

'How?'

'Haven't you heard them?'

'I'm hearing things all the time but I can close it off. I have to. It's just voices whispering in my head like a damned echo chamber. I'd go mad if I couldn't tune it out.'

'Then you have not learned who it is who is whispering. Anand is now a part of the network – you know this – and so is his consort, your Second Body.'

'Please stop calling her that.'

'Kharishma, then.' He stumbled over the name. 'We are all linked, now, by only a few degrees of separation. I can see through their eyes – flashes, glimpses, fragments, but enough. And they can see through ours. They do not yet understand what is happening, but I believe that Ir Yth does. I saw her, out of the eyes of your Second— via Kharishma. Anand knows this country, Jaya. He knows where we are, and he can come for us whenever he wants. At least before the network gains critical mass and comes on-line.'

'When will that be?'

'It is not far off now. But Ir Yth has other plans. I learn from Anand that she is concocting an antidote to the virus that facilitates the network. This is what Anand has been told, anyway. I doubt very much that Ir Yth will stop there. I believe she has a more widescale termination in mind.' He was speaking fluently now, Jaya noticed, and the accent was flattening out to resemble her own speech.

Jaya said, 'Then how can we stop her?'

'We need to use her allies to our own advantage. The truth,' Sirru said 'needs to be spread. But I will need your help, and that of Rajira and the child.'

'What are you planning to do?'

'Come here,' Sirru whispered.

She took a step back. 'Not before you tell me what you're going to do.'

'I am going to send the truth down the lines of the network, to Kharishma.'

'Why to her?' His gaze met her own and she could see the calm ruthlessness in his eyes. She wondered whether he even realized that it was there.

'Because she is already half-mad, and she might be easier to convince than others. I do not know if this is possible yet. But I need you, now.' He held out his hands, palms upturned. Warily, Jaya edged forward and took his hands.

'Jaya,' he said, almost fondly, and pulled her forwards so that her head was resting against his breastbone. She could hear the slow beat of his heart, far within. And then it was as though the wall of his chest was opening up, so that there was no flesh and bone and blood between them, but only limitless space. She wondered, for an unnerved moment, what sex with him must be like. It felt strange, to be both invader and invaded.

She could sense Sirru, the outer walls of personality, emotions ebbing and flowing like a tide, carefully regulated and controlled for the most part but with sudden eddies and currents that, Jaya suspected, were taking Sirru himself by surprise. Across what seemed like a great gulf, she could sense constraints, the duties and compulsions and functions that formed the core of his being. For a disconnected moment, she experienced herself as Sirru did: similar in structure, but far less ordered and cohesive, as though she was nothing more than a rind encasing a mass of undifferentiated impulses. The impression was not a pleasant one.

But then both of them swept by the other and into the embryonic reaches of the viral net. Jaya was suddenly aware of the sleeping forms of Rajira and Halil, and the mesh that was forming itself inside their minds: an array, ready to receive and transmit. Beyond them, at what seemed like no greater distance, were others.

/*Ready?*/ Sirru's speech reverberated through her body.

/*Ready. I think.*/

/*Now.*/

11.

KHOKANDRA PALACE

Kharishma lay very still, hoping that the voice would go away. She had been hearing it off and on throughout the night. She tried to ignore it, but the voice was lodged in her head like an insect in amber. It was soft and insidious; it poured poison into her ear, but it was also seductive. It spoke to her sense of honour and necessity, flattering her vanity and her need for power. It told her that she and she alone could set matters right. It told her that Ir Yth had lied. It told her that Ir Yth must be disposed of, and how this might be done. The thought of killing the *raksasa* was an appealing one. Kharishma had come to fear Ir Yth: the terrible assault in the car, the way that the *raksasa* could turn her knees to water with a single glance, the manner in which she could make Kharishma feel emotions that she had no desire to experience. Kharishma huddled against the pillows, thinking that it would be good to do the bidding of the voice and get rid of Ir Yth. But then the door opened and the *raksasa* herself appeared.

It took only a single glance for Kharishma to see that

Ir Yth was perfectly well aware of what had just happened. She tried to leap from the bed and run, but she was paralysed. A chilly languor spread through her veins and her head was suddenly too heavy to support. It lolled grotesquely back against the pillows as though she was nothing more than a broken doll. She could feel a thin thread of saliva trickle from the corner of her mouth.

'Don't,' she whispered, through locked lips.

The *raksasa* glided closer, to stand over Kharishma. */You have been listening to lies. I know. I can hear them in your head. But since you have become a nexus, you might as well be made use of./*

Methodically, the *raksasa* began to fold back her sleeve, baring a pale, soft forearm.

/Do you know what you have become?/

Kharishma tried to gesture "no", but she couldn't move her head. She tried to think of nothing, fixing her gaze on the cracks in the plaster and concentrating with all her might. Slowly, her body arched back until her heels were dragged along the sheets and she was bent in a strychnine curve above the bed.

/Let me into your head,/ the *raksasa* commanded, */or I will snap your spine./*

Kharishma, bent like a bow, was abruptly unstrung. She collapsed back onto the bed and the *raksasa*'s presence surged through her mind.

/You will be the first weak link,/ Ir Yth said, with grim satisfaction. The skin of Ir Yth's forearm peeled back, layer by layer, until it oozed droplets of dark and oily blood. The

373

raksasa held her wrist above Kharishma's gaping mouth until a single drop of blood coalesced and dropped. It seemed to the stricken woman that it took an eternity to fall, as though the world had slowed and stopped. Then the blood splashed across her tongue, stinging as it went. Kharishma began to shake, a tremor that began at the tip of her tongue and passed down her body like lightning, leaving a trail of neural fire in its wake. Her mouth gaped open, but her throat was sealed, the muscles refusing to respond, and she could not scream. The virus was racing through her cells, searching for the initial infection. Distantly she understood what Ir Yth had done. The virus would itself infect the communications network, sending instructions of mutation down the viral lines until each nexus convulsed into death.

Amir! Kharishma shouted, inside her head, but he was already awake and aware. She snatched a glimpse of the stairwell that led from the main hall of the palace to her bedroom as he raced up the stairs. She tried to shut herself down, but she couldn't fight the invader within. The enormity of what Ir Yth was prepared to do suddenly crashed in upon her consciousness; it was as though all Kharishma's inflated self-importance and paranoia and sense of destiny had contributed to this moment and her realization of what she had to undertake. Anand was coming through the door, the gun raised; Ir Yth turned but he was already poised to fire.

/No!/ Kharishma cried, inside his mind. /Me, Amir!

374

She's infected the network. You have to kill me! Before it's too late!/

And to her horror and triumph and surprise, he turned the gun on her and fired. The bullet hit her square in the chest and she was flung back against the wall with the force of the impact. There was no pain and the virus held her fleeing awareness together for a split second, enough to see Anand drop to his knees beneath the weight of the *raksasa*'s fury, and his own grief.

/*You next, then,*/ Ir Yth hissed, but for Kharishma there was nothing but darkness and stars.

12.
YAMUNOTRI, HIMALAYAS

When Jaya recovered consciousness, it was dawn. She raised her head and discovered that she had been lying in Sirru's lap. Her cheek was marked with the pattern of the folds of his robe. She was very stiff and very cold, but the life moved swiftly back into her aching limbs. She recovered faster these days; she could have done with this ten years ago. Above her, Sirru's grave face looked down.

'Are you all right?'

'I think so. What happened?'

'Ir Yth fed something back into the network – instructions for the virus to change, become lethal. But the termination of the nexus prevented further infection.'

375

Jaya sat back on her heels, rubbing her neck.

'You mean Kharishma Kharim *died*, Sirru. I might have despised her for making a mockery of my life, but that isn't the point. When you live with death, you learn what it means. She may have been mad, she may have done the right thing for the wrong reasons, but she saved us. Doesn't that mean anything to you?'

Sirru said, very gently, 'Yes, it does. But death to us is not the same tragedy that it is to you. When you are developed, you will understand this.'

'God, Sirru. That's development?'

'We don't identify ourselves as you do. We can remake her, if you wish.'

The golden gaze was bewildered. Jaya looked at him and sighed.

'Just before she died, I saw Anand ... If he's infected too, why didn't Ir Yth get at him? What *happened*, Sirru?'

But the alien shook his head.

'I do not know. Anand is like a light that has gone out. I cannot sense him.' He added, diffidently, 'If you wish to be away from me for a while, I will understand.'

Jaya nodded. 'I think that's a good idea. I'll talk to you later.' She felt as fragile as a moth emerged from its cocoon, a legacy not only of the time on the network but also of the renewed realization of difference between Sirru and herself. He was the colonizer, someone to whom the natives were no more than resources to be utilized. *And like all colonizers, he thinks he's doing us a favour.* Despite the gulf between them, she felt closer to Sirru than to anyone except Rakh. And that, she thought now, was a bad way to be. She wondered, not entirely irrelevantly, whether Amir Anand might have British blood.

She wandered slowly out of the compound and onto the hillside. The dawn light above the rim of the mountains was as cold and clear as water. An owl sailed down the valley on great silent wings, heading into the shadows after hunting, and the air smelled fresh and scented with herbs. Jaya sat down on a nearby stone and knotted her hands in her lap, and for the first time in many years she prayed, not to Durga of vengeance, but to Sarasvati: goddess of knowledge, and understanding, and good judgement. Qualities which, Jaya felt, she sadly lacked.

13.
KHOKANDRA PALACE

'It is a good thing that I am a light sleeper,' Naran Tokai said, icily. He gazed down at Ir Yth as she crouched over the prone form of Amir Anand. 'Although the racket that has been going on in here would wake the dead. I should like an explanation.'

/I owe you nothing. I need give no account of myself to you./

'Indeed? I beg to disagree. I am quite well aware, madam, that you have lied to me from the moment we first met. I have played along because I hoped for some personal advantage to come from all this. But regrettably, I am by no means now sure that this will be forthcoming.'

He took a step forward. The cane informed him that Ir Yth was attempting pheromonal interference. Tokai smiled.

'I'm afraid that won't work with me. I'm not like poor Anand, you know, governed by my hormones. In fact, I have very few left. So you may very well be shouting commands, but I fear I am deaf. Now. I require an explanation.' He took another step, making sure that he was well out of Ir Yth's reach.

/Get away from me./

'We're not a very well matched fighting pair, are we? An old man, and a – something.' He stroked a finger down the pommel of the cane and a razor-edged ridge glided out. 'On the other hand, I'm armed and I don't think you are. At least not with weapons that will harm me. Wake him up.'

/I cannot./

'Wake him.' The pointed tip of the cane hovered in the direction of Ir Yth's midriff. Muttering to herself, the *raksasa* looked at Anand. Some kind of interference was taking place, revealed by the distorted messages that were reaching Tokai through the cane. Anand stirred and groaned.

'Anand? Get up, please.'

The butcher-prince crawled to the bed and hauled himself upright, staring fixedly away from the ruined corpse of Kharishma Kharim.

'Why did you kill her, Anand? A lover's quarrel, or something more serious?'

In a hoarse, strained voice that sounded nothing like his usual cultured tones, Anand explained. 'We're linked. To the other alien. It told Kharishma that Ir Yth plans to destroy humanity. Kharishma believed it.'

'I see. Well. Destruction of the world's population. Ambitious, but I'd like to know why—' Tokai began to say, and something snapped deep within the *raksasa*'s golden gaze. He could feel panic boiling off her, even without the aid of the cane. Ir Yth rushed at him, crouching low like an insect, with a curious scuttling motion. Anand leaped for the gun.

'No! Don't shoot her!' Tokai cried. He dodged away, but the *raksasa*'s tongue flickered out, lancing across his forearm and leaving a bloody trail in its wake. Cursing, Tokai, with a neat and economical motion of the cane, whirled around and spiked the razor point through Ir Yth's throat. The *raksasa* crumpled to the floor without a sound. There was suprisingly little blood, though Tokai noticed absently that Ir Yth's throat seemed to be trying to seal itself. He held the cane at the ready, but the fluttering flesh subsided and the *raksasa* lay as still and stiff as a dried spider.

'Well, Amir,' Tokai said, in a voice that was not as steady as he would have liked. 'It's entirely possible that we've just saved the world. Perhaps you and I are destined to be heroes, after all.'

But Anand was kneeling beside Kharishma's body, his face stricken. 'And perhaps not.'

Tokai found it hard to grieve for a woman whom he barely knew and in any case disliked, but the exigencies of face impelled him to honour Anand's mourning. Anand wanted to bury Kharishma in the rose garden, but Tokai wouldn't let him. Kharishma's body must be taken to the lab, along with the desiccated corpse of Ir Yth, for tests. This unleashed an outburst of cold fury from Anand, which Tokai placidly withstood, dwelling all the while on how best to get rid of Anand when the time came. At last, Tokai grew tired of the tirade and pointed out the realities of Anand's position, or lack of it, yet again.

'Might I remind you that you have nothing? Your ancestral lands are now mine. You are the last of your line. I have sufficient influence with the authorities to have you put away for life or simply killed, and I do not think there are many who would mourn your passing. You will do, Anand, precisely as I say or face the consequences.'

'You forget,' Anand said, through gritted teeth. 'I am your one last game piece. I know where the second alien is, and Jaya with him. Without me, it is *you* who have nothing.'

They stared at each other, locked in stalemate, then Anand spun on his heel in disgust and left the room. Later, he returned, to deliver a strained, white-lipped apology that was mirrored by Tokai's own. They needed each other, it seemed, and neither liked it.

Prudently, during Anand's brief absence, the old man had already had Kharishma's ruined body removed and sent to the lab, so Anand was forced to compromise with a ceremony in the garden. Tokai declined to attend, and so the only mourner was Anand himself. Tokai watched him as he knelt, head bowed, among the falling petals of the roses, drifting down on the evening wind. He watched for a moment, feeling nothing, and then he turned away and reached for the phone, to contact the lab in Varanasi.

It seemed that the results of the *raksasa*'s autopsy had already proved exciting, and promised to be profitable. Ir Yth was a walking factory of disease; the complex ridges of her torso were a honeycomb of hived cells, each containing neat layers of viruses. Tokai's researchers did not yet know what any of these might be capable of; they were proceeding, naturally, with the utmost caution. Tokai only remained behind to keep an eye on Anand. If matters had progressed ideally, he'd have had the butcher-prince in cold storage, too, but he needed Anand in order to track down the other alien. Having lost Ir Yth, useful though her death might yet prove, he was eager to retrieve his second game piece. But as soon as the results were fully analysed, Tokai thought, he would see if he could gain access to this curious and alien network himself, and remove the need for Anand.

14.
YAMUNOTRI, HIMALAYAS

Jaya lifted the field glasses from her eyes and squinted into the glare. Amir Anand's convoy was not yet visible, but she knew they were coming. Sirru had taught her how to filter the mass of the network, concentrating only on certain minds. Ir Yth was dead. When she learned this, Jaya felt herself grow weak with relief, and she lost no time in telling the others. The knowledge warmed her, but she couldn't help remembering that Ir Yth was only one of many. There were probably millions of *khaithoi*, and what if all of them were the enemy?

She kept getting fractured glimpses through Anand's eyes: the mountains at dusk, enveloped in mist; a hawk rising high over the pass. Something of Anand's helpless rage against a world that he felt had betrayed him was also communicated down the network and for the first time Jaya began to feel that she understood him. A family that had sided with the British whose blood they shared; a legacy of separation from the people whom the Anands governed; then the loss of fortune and place had all contributed to make the butcher-prince what he was today.

But Jaya did not want to understand Anand. He really did believe that caste made him superior to anyone who wasn't Brahmin or Westerner, and it was the unquestioning racist arrogance of that belief which made her so angry. And yet she couldn't help feeling a reluctant pity, that he was just as much a victim of the system which produced him as she herself. And yet, and yet . . . *I decided long ago that I was tired of being a victim. How about you, Amir?* She tried to send the question to him, but he wasn't listening and she doubted it would make a difference.

They had left the fortress at Yamunotri behind. Rajira and the child were deep in coma and could not be moved, so Jaya had returned to her original plan. Years ago, she remembered standing on the slopes of these very hills and watching a plover lure a hawk away from her nest, flopping across the scrub with a trailing wing. But once the plover was sure that the hawk was led from the nest and confused, she had taken off like a rocket into the trees where the predator could not follow. Jaya and Sirru had become plovers, heading into the heights to draw Anand away. Jaya planned to take Sirru into the glacial fastness beyond the lake of Saptarishi Kund, and it would not matter if Anand knew where they had gone. If he followed, he would be as easy to pick off as a fledgling in the nest.

The sun hovered low, for it was almost evening now and there were thunderheads over the peaks, tinged orange with the light of the sun. There was the smell of rain on the wind and a cloud shadow sailed across the slopes, darkening Jaya's sight. She wondered what was happening back at the fort. The last glimpse she had had was of Rakh waiting at the foot of the fortress as they left, holding two of the automatic M16 rifles.

'One for you and one for him,' Rakh said gruffly.

For some reason, Jaya had expected the alien to protest, but he looked at the rifle thoughtfully for a moment, then slung it over his shoulder.

'Don't do anything with that unless I tell you to,' Jaya said, hastily.

Sirru's gaze was bland. 'Naturally not.'

Rakh reached out and clasped Jaya's hands. 'Commander?' She stared at him, numbly. 'I believe that my brother is watching over us both. He will show you the paths. If we do not see one another again— Well, I wish you luck.'

'God go with you, Rakh,' Jaya whispered. '*Bhagwan tumhara raksha karey.*'

He smiled. '*Ayushmaanbhav*, Commander.'

Live long. 'I'll try.' It sounded too much like a last farewell. She could not bring herself to smile in return. She turned abruptly and headed up the path, Sirru by her side. She did not look back.

She carried no supplies with her, only the gun and a small bladder of blood from a goat slain the day before, a sacrifice to Durga. She hoped the goddess was listening. Now, as they made their way into the mountains, Jaya shouldered the gun. It felt as though she had regained a lost limb, as if she had been snatched back in time to the person whom she used to be. It was hard going, but she was used to this terrain. Kamal had taught her how to use it to her advantage and she followed the goat tracks up into the high rocks. She turned to Sirru, saying brusquely, 'All right so far?'

'All right.'

He seemed to have had no problem keeping up with her. She glanced down as they climbed, and saw his clawed, jointed toes curling over the edge of the rocks. There was a smear of blood along the side of one foot, and she fought back pity. When they reached the crest of the ridge that ran like a blade above the valley, she stopped and looked back. An outcrop hid the convoy from view, but she could see the round tower of the fortress, no larger than a pebble against the vastness of the mountains.

'Come on,' Sirru said, encouragingly. 'It is not very much longer.'

She squinted up at him. 'How do you know? Are you reading my mind?'

He smiled. 'No. I have been here before.'

Jaya stared at him. 'You've—? *When?*'

'I walked, like this. On the day when you could not find me.'

'Why?'

He was gazing towards the lake. 'I had a task to do. We should continue.'

Ignoring her questions, he led her, slipping and sliding, down the slope to where a narrow stream bisected the thin valley. They followed the watercourse, running fast and cold down from the glacial lake, and after what seemed like an eternity of scrambling over the sharp and ancient rocks, they reached the lip of the valley. The lake stretched below, glittering in the falling sunlight. Sirru gazed at it pensively.

'There?' he asked, and Jaya could tell from the tone of his voice that he was hoping the answer would be no. She smiled.

'Not quite. You didn't get this far, then? We're going round, not over.'

She took him down the path that an ancient glacier itself had cut, trying to remember the exact path down to the lake. After an hour, she estimated, they would cut through the cliff to where the lake rested like a dark eye in the cradle of the mountains. She had not been back here since their last flight down from the heights, after they had sent Kamal to his rest beneath the cold waters of the lake. Reborn, Jaya wondered, or resting with the dead? She didn't know what she believed any more, and perhaps she never had.

'Jaya? What's wrong?' The alien paused and reached out, touching her arm. She must radiate sadness, she thought, spreading loss into the desolate landscape. She said, 'My husband is buried here.'

'Not long ago, I think.'

'No, not long. Three years. It seems like forever.' She stared at Sirru in the gathering darkness, but she couldn't tell what he was thinking. He took her hand in his long fingers and began once more to walk, up towards the lake and the dead.

15.
YAMUNOTRI, HIMALAYAS

Anand crouched panting on the floor in the shadows as his men continued the search. The sickness, if that was what it was, raged through him. He felt as though he had been splintered into a myriad sharp shards and scattered across the length and breadth of the country. He saw out of many eyes at the same time, and he shook his head again and again, trying to focus on the two most important voices:

Nihalani and the alien, like a magnet to the north. He knew where they had gone, up into the glaciers that swept down from the southern wall of the Himalayas. They were hoping that he would not or could not follow them, but Anand had gone too far to draw back now. It wasn't merely Tokai's threats and insidious promises that spurred him on; it was simply a question of honour. Now that Kharishma was gone, honour, Anand felt, was all he really had left.

He no longer believed that Tokai had any intention of restoring the slightest measure of his family's lost fortune, and he had been vain and a fool ever to think it. When Tokai no longer had a use for him, Anand would be killed. The prospect did not seem to matter any more. It seemed to him that he could still hear Kharishma's voice echoing in his head, as though she hadn't really gone all that far. But nothing mattered now more than Bharat. Kharishma had helped him to see that; her sacrifice was part of his own. Ir Yth was dead but the other one remained, and Anand knew that the alien must be killed. He could hear it now, spreading its lies. Perhaps more would come, but change must be stopped, just as it had before when he fought so hard against those who threatened the caste system. The world must be preserved. Honour demanded it.

The fortress was filled with Nihalani's presence. He could sense her in every corner. Something brushed his face and he sprang to his feet, but it was nothing more than a cobweb, disturbed from the rafters by gunfire. He felt as though her hand had reached out and, mockingly, touched his cheek. *Witchcraft* . . . He could feel it, enchantment pounding through his head like a storm on the point of breaking. Nihalani's hated voice reverberated in his mind. He stumbled across to the window and looked down at the slope of the hillside. Halfway down lay the body of Satyajit Rakh, sprawled in death. Beyond he could see the little square of the ATV in which Naran Tokai patiently waited for results, well away from danger.

There was a shout from high in the fortress. Anand made for the stairs and found himself on a small landing, high in the fortress roof. His second-in-command stepped out, covered in dust and dirt.

'There's someone in there. A woman. I think she's dead."

Anand brushed past him. The woman was lying on a pallet of straw. Her face was pale as wax and she didn't seem to be breathing. Then he detected a faint pulse in her jaw. He slapped her across the face, but she didn't respond. The soldier shone a torch into her eyes and then, to his astonishment, Amir recognized her. It was Rajira Jahan. With Kharishma dead, the memory of that visit made him grow hot with shame. Rajira's eyes snapped open and suddenly he was staring up at his own startled face. It was the same countenance he saw in the mirror every day: the winged brows and pale eyes, but the expression on his face was not one that he recognized. It was the lost face of a child. Rajira spoke, but her lips did not move. There were others, like points of light across the darkness of an inner plain, but Anand's attention was drawn by the presence of someone: a lodestone of the north. He was seeing through Sirru's eyes, gazing out at a familiar landscape past Nihalani's shoulder. Nihalani and the alien were at the lake.

16.
YAMUNOTRI, HIMALAYAS

Jaya scrambled down a slope of shale towards the shore. Sirru had already reached the bottom of the slope and now stood gazing out across the water. The light had almost gone now, and only a last ray of sun touched the peaks of the mountains with a line of rose, as though the snow had caught fire. There was a cold breath of wind from the lake and the water ruffled against it, lapping across the stones. Jaya stumbled to a halt beside the alien. Somewhere behind them, in this wilderness of stone and ice, Anand was stalking them.

'It's cold,' Sirru said.

'Yes, it is.' She glanced uneasily behind her, somehow expecting to see the figure of Amir Anand step over the ridge with a gun in his hand, but the land was silent and nothing moved.

'Where now?' Sirru spoke in a thin, distant voice, as if his attention lay elsewhere entirely.

Jaya shouldered the gun to a more comfortable position and Sirru did the same, mirroring her with unnerving precision.

389

'There's a pass leading up through the Yamara. Comes out into Shiringri valley.' She was speaking more to herself than to Sirru, reminding herself of the way, but the alien turned and began to stroll along the shore. She felt like shouting at him: *Don't you realize the danger we're in? Don't you care?* but she had a feeling that Sirru was following a wholly different agenda. Frustrated, she headed after him.

She could see a single star, glowing above the faraway peaks of Nanda Devi. It was too bright for an ordinary star; it must be a planet. The dusk that surrounded her seemed suddenly immense, as though she stood above the universe itself. The lake that lay so short a distance away was as vast as an ocean, and she could almost hear the dead as they whispered beneath its waters. *Imagination*, she told herself impatiently, *it's running away with you* – but Kamal seemed suddenly very close. She could feel him walking by her side, and though she knew it was nothing more than weariness and grieving, she did not dare turn her head.

Sirru stopped and faced her, and his eyes were yellow in the twilight. She didn't know what to think any more. She strode past him, leaving the ghosts behind, and stopped in dismay. The narrow pass that led up into the Yamara was no longer there. The narrow fissure between the rocks was blocked by a fall of boulders and shale: a landslide from high on the cliff, too steep to climb. Cursing, Jaya started up the slope, but the alien pulled her back.

EMPIRE OF BONES

'You should not. Not safe.'

'Hell, Sirru . . .' Her voice was no more than a whisper
as she realized that she had trapped them both. The only
way out was back, or across the cold dark waters of the
lake. But it was too far to swim, and they'd freeze in
minutes.

'We'll have to go back.' *Make for the path into the
valley, and wait. I'll shoot whoever comes over the ridge.
When morning comes . . .* She shivered, thinking of the
cold night ahead. Patiently, Sirru said, 'Then we will go
back.'

Coming back down the shore path, Jaya stumbled and
the alien took her arm. She leaned against him. Thoughts
spiralled through her tired mind: *Is this the right thing to
do, should I turn him over to Anand now?* Then there was
a pincer grip around her arm and she was thrown back
against the rocks. She gave a small, startled cry and a long
hand closed over her mouth. Sirru whispered, '*Be quiet.
Up there, on the ridge.*'

'Where? I can't see, Sirru, it's too dark . . .' Her suspicions about his night vision were finally confirmed. 'Can
you see who it is?'

'Not *see*. Too far away, and only for a moment. But it
is Anand.'

Jaya thought so, too. She was halfway in his head, after
all, and the sudden glitter before her sight was the starlight
on the waters of the lake, seen from above. She could feel
the past closing around her and cutting her off. *Anand, we*

391

*helped to make one another what we are. And you and I
are not finished with each other yet.* Her fingers closed
around the gun, tucking it tightly against her side.

'Nihalani!' Amir Anand's voice echoed back from the
mountain wall, and inside her mind. *What does he expect
me to do, shout back?* 'Listen to me. Your people are dead.
You've nowhere left to go. You're protecting something
that will be the ruin of us all. If you give the alien up, I'll
let you go free.' Jaya said nothing. The hard edge of Sirru's
body was pressed against her own between the protection
offered by the rocks.

'What will you do?' the alien said, with soft and careful
neutrality.

She took a deep breath. 'I've made my decision. I'm
staying with you.'

She could hear Anand slithering down the shale bank
and risked a shot. It ricocheted away into silence. Then a
bullet whined away from the rock beside her, splintering
the granite into sharp shards. She threw herself back,
wriggled along the stones to the doubtful safety of the
escarpment edge. For all his threats, she thought, he was
in the same position that she was. He couldn't see her, any
more than she could see him, yet they were both halfway
inside one another's minds. Then Anand's voice said within
her head, /*Do as I tell you. Surrender the alien. Before he
destroys everything we know.*/

And Jaya replied with silent anger, /*But is that even
worth preserving?*/

/He has lied to you. I am sure of this. Just as the other one did./

Jaya said, /Maybe he has. But I do not think that he intended to lie, and Ir Yth did. That is the difference./

She turned to Sirru, but the alien had gone.

Then, /The network's coming on-line,/ Sirru's voice said clearly, and she understood with the rush of his thoughts that the death of one of them could now throw the entire network off track, shatter the minds of the nexi, like crashing a computer program. Sirru was bending, reaching for the automatic rifle just as Anand swung round. She could hear the alien's thought: /If I kill Anand, the network could be damaged/death at the point of activation/a failed nexus/everything will be ruined/but if not, Jaya will die./

She doubted whether Sirru had fired a gun in his life. She reached inside her pocket. She had first formed the plan some time ago, on realizing that she and Anand shared thoughts, but she had hoped not to use it. There was too much of a risk that it might not work, but then, conjuring was all about risks and illusion.

The trick would be to shut enough of herself off that Anand could not hear her thoughts. The tranquillizers that she had palmed in the hospital, all those weeks ago, nested in a plastic wrap in her pocket. Swiftly, deliberately focusing on the scene before her, she swallowed three. The pills worked fast. A moment later, her vision blurred. She caught Anand's confusion as her consciousness started to slow down and her thoughts become muzzy. She slid the gun down by her side, her finger on the trigger. The rocks were sharp beneath her. She took the bag of goat's blood from her jacket and punctured it, her hand trembling under the drug. *Have I overdone the damn pills?* She could no longer feel Anand: the tranquillizers were working, shutting him off. The blood seeped down her face, wet and thick. She lay still, her eyes half-closed, her face and side as bloody as Durga's own. She willed her mind into stillness.

'Nihalani!' Anand's voice was thick, the cultured accent stripped away. He shook his head as though trying to clear it. She could just see him, standing amongst the rocks above her. She did not yet have a clear shot. Torchlight glinted from the barrel of his AK-47. She heard the intake of his breath as he saw her below him: crumpled, bloody, unmoving. The shock of seeing her below him, wounded or dead, was enough; all the conjuror needed was a second or two, to make the illusion complete. He leaned around the corner of the rock to get a better look. She saw his shoulders slump a little, relaxing. She heard the click as he shot the bolt down on the gun, but she was already bringing up her weapon. The tranquillizers made it hard, but she was used to fighting her body. Her finger squeezed the trigger.

The shot was the loudest thing in the world. Amir was still standing over her, high on the rock, and her first stupid thought was: *Why, he's got married.* There was a crimson tear between his eyes. His mouth was open slightly with surprise, and then he fell and the world changed. Then for no more than a fraction of a second, Jaya was ripped apart. The network had come on-line. She was everywhere at once again: watching from Sirru's eyes down the barrel of the rifle. She was Rajira and Halil, relaying instructions down the complex network of an alien virus. Jaya followed the viral line down through a hundred minds; if it hadn't been for the tranquillizers, she realized with horror, she might go mad. She sensed Anand's consciousness as it fled away, snapped by death but still somehow present, receding fast and with a terrifying sense of exhilarated freedom.

The linked network was reaching out, sending messages across a relay so vast and alien that Jaya could not comprehend it. She could see her own sprawled form: Sirru's viewpoint. He had reached the rim of rock where Anand's body lay. And then another perspective: seeing a frozen tableau of Sirru's small figure above the shore. *Who's that?* Whoever it was, they must be standing in the middle of the lake. Startled, she scrambled to the rim and looked out over the dark surface. Something was coming across the water, gliding like a huge, unfurling sail.

An unfamiliar voice, directly overhead, said startlingly loud inside her mind /*Receiving/Communication network now on-line/Please respond.*/

But something was already replying. A depth ship, out near somewhere named Zhei Eren. A torrent of information flooded through Jaya's head and it was too much to bear, but the curling *thing* above her picked it up and redistributed it calmly throughout the network.

/*First Stage is confirmed/preparing to enter system orbit/ship's Receiver prepare.*/

Jaya was flung back into the confines of her own head, but not out of the link. She could still hear the others, but information was relayed around her, sidelining her so that she could concentrate on the ship. She knelt in the dust, shaking, covered with drying blood. Sirru dropped the rifle and crouched by her side.

'Jaya? Are you hurt?'

She shook her head.

'The network is on-line. A ship is coming. And your child is safe.'

'What?' She gazed at him wonderingly and he reached out and gathered her against the cold folds of his robe. Something flickered over her shoulders; she could see light from the corner of her eye. Into her ear, Sirru murmured, 'Jaya? Speak to your child, and it will speak to the depth ship.'

'Speak to it? What *is* it?'

'It is the seed, what else? The child of the ship, and your own self. It has grown in the cold. Listen, and speak. That is what you have been designed to do, Jaya.' His voice was gentle, as always, but beneath it she heard the unmistakable note of warning. *You have no choice any more. The world is a different place from now on. For both of us. For everyone.*

'I'll try.' Jaya shut her eyes and listened. It was as though a door opened in her mind. The well of the stars lay beneath and a god's voice said, /*Maintaining orbit.*/

It was not the voice from her childhood, the first and oldest ship of the Tekhein system. This ship was young by comparison and its voice was green and glowing.

'What shall I say?' Jaya whispered.

And Sirru said, 'Tell it that everything is well. Project development is proceeding normally, as planned.'

TEKHEI

1.
DEPTH SHIP, TEKHEI

The warm walls of the ship pulsed with life beneath Jaya's hands. It was in low orbit now, and Earth filled the viewing screen, Bharat on nightside, starred with veins of lights. She had been here for almost a month. *Oracle, magician, goddess, terrorist, and now envoy to the stars. We are many things, we* dalit. She had passed through so many transformations that surely one more wouldn't hurt.

For now, like everyone else on Earth, she was *desqusai*. The visitors, themselves a caste of the írRasi *desqusai*, seemed pleased. *It's becoming a Tekhein ship now,* they said of her improbable daughter, the seed, bonding to Jaya and to Earth before sailing out into who knew where to found a new colony. *Welcome to the fold.* Negotiations were opening up with the major pharmaceutical corporations. The visitors were sidelining governments with airy insouciance. Jaya increasingly heard the name of Naran Tokai. Everyone was waiting for the *desqusai* overseer, one EsMirhei.

Yet she was not only an envoy, now. She was a mother, parent to a – *what*, exactly? She placed her hands flat on the viewing screen and leaned her head against its invisible

398

surface, feeling once more as though she stood with nothing between her and empty space. At the very corner of the screen, she could see a fold of sail, where the seed floated serenely in the darkness. She had seen the seed's face only once. After the gun battle at the lake, she had gazed wonderingly up to see it hovering above her. The seed's arms were crossed over her breast; fierceness was fading from a face that was the image of Jaya's own. Pale hair streamed down the seed's back, but her skin was a wan, luminous green and her torso terminated in a series of complex folds, extending out from hips and shoulder blades to form an undulating mass of material, sails rather than wings.

/Parent! Are you safe? Are you harmed?/ the seed had demanded, back there on the shore of the lake. Jaya had quickly replied that all was well: the emotions emanating from the seed were flayed and raw and needy, the only way in which she resembled a child.

/Is it time to go? Please?/Atmosphere—I cannot—/

Sirru had stepped in at that point, directing the pod down from the depth ship. He had gently, but firmly, pushed aside Jaya's pleas that they go back down to the fort first, at least give Rakh and any other of the dead a decent burial. And see to Rajira and Halil.

'We don't have time. The seed needs to get above atmosphere, and I don't think she'll go unless you go with her.' With the unseen network now on-line, his spoken speech had at last become wholly fluent.

'I can't just leave them, Sirru. What about Rajira?

What about Halil?' she asked, frantically, but the alien said soothingly, 'They will be all right; don't worry. Everything is under control, now.'

She did not find that reassuring. She was going to argue further, but then she looked up to where the seed's sails were fluttering in distress.

'All right. I'll go up with her. But then, let me come back, see that the people we've left are all right.' She emphasized the "we", but she did not think Sirru was listening. And she wondered how much any of them would really matter to him now that they had served his purposes.

Sirru had agreed, but once they were in space and on the newly arrived depth ship, Jaya had been sucked into a seemingly endless bustle of conferences and tests and meetings with her strange new kindred. The only spare time she had was spent sleeping, or standing for a few minutes by the viewport while the seed drifted alongside, her own hands pressed against the invisibility of the screen like a young seal alongside a boat. They spoke, mind to mind, Jaya teaching the seed everything she knew about the world below. *When it is time for you to begin a new world, remember this. You may need this knowledge.* And the seed had agreed, drinking in information with all the eagerness of the young. But the seed's face was growing less human by the day, as though it were an effort to sustain it in the face of the immense genetic changes taking place within, and what Jaya felt for her was responsibility and concern, not the love that she should have felt for her daughter. Or even the affection that she had, come to that, felt for Halil.

At that thought, she felt a measure of relief: she had spoken to both Halil and Rajira, now part of the new network. They were excited, and scared, and being well looked after as a crucial part of a new society. But would that society really be an improvement on the last? Jaya wondered. The *desqusai* seemed benign enough, but her relationship with Ir Yth hadn't exactly given her a high opinion of the *khaithoi*. She recalled Sirru's explanation of what was in store for Earth.

'Tekhei is in such a *mess*, Jaya. All these conflicts, these wars based on nothing more than aggression and territorialism—'

'You're a fine one to talk! What about the *khaithoi's* attempt at genocide?'

'Don't worry, Jaya. Everything's going to be sorted out. No more wars, no more damaging diseases. The caste system will be dismantled. And we'll make sure the problems with the environment are put to rights.'

'Sounds wonderful,' Jaya said, sceptically.

'Don't you believe me?' He looked a little hurt.

'Oh, I believe you, Sirru.' She reached out and touched his arm. 'It's just— Will you make the trains run on time, as well?'

He frowned. 'Transport should be the least of your worries.'

There were some metaphors that emotional speech left untouched. Jaya smiled. 'I just mean that there will be a price, Sirru. Very few things come free. You know, there is a belief in my country that there are four ages of human existence, or *yuga*s. And people say that these are the *kali-yuga*, the last and darkest days. It does not make me very hopeful.'

'Neither you nor I can say if that belief is true, Jaya. But I can tell you this. There will be a price.'

'Do you think this is the right thing to do, Sirru? To come to another world, take them over without so much as a by-your-leave? I know you say we are your kindred, but that doesn't mean a lot to us, you know. A lot of folk are going to think that you're here to exploit the planet.'

'I know. But colonization is what we *do*. The drive behind our society is to expand always, to increase our cultural order. It is not economic. It is an overpowering sense of social duty. It is *dharma*.'

The familiar word was startling, coming from alien lips. It seemed Sirru had learned something of her culture, at least. After that conversation, she did not feel quite so misunderstood. Not all the old guard were gone, either: she had spoken also with Shiv Sakai, himself now a part of the network. She didn't dare ask how he'd managed that, but he seemed to be in his element. And Rakh, he had told her, now lay beside his brother on the shores of the lake, in peace at last. Jaya still grieved, but at least Rakh hadn't been left to lie on the stony hillside for the vultures and kites. The dead are always forgotten, in the midst of the making of history; Jaya was determined that this should not happen to Rakh.

'Jaya?' Someone placed a bony hand on her shoulder, calling her back to the present. She came across to join the írRas: her own kind, or so they kept telling her. Everyone was very friendly, evidently anxious to make the Tekhein kindred feel less like poor relations. The visitors conversed in whispering, sibilant voices, their quills rattling like the wind in bamboo, sending careful modulations of emotion across the air. The scale nano-armour that they had given her felt cool against Jaya's skin, and it sealed her off from their emotions. Unfortunately, she thought, it did not protect her from her own. Among the *desqusai*, it was difficult to pick out Sirru. They all looked alike, to Jaya's eyes: tall, thin, pale, golden-eyed. This inability to recognize him made her sad, and somehow guilty.

Suddenly lonely, she went in search of Sirru. She finally found him down by the growing tanks, peering in at the dense mass of foliage. Or maybe it wasn't foliage at all, but something else: skeins of virus, written large, or some kind of embryonic life. She was coming to realize that she couldn't describe the world according to the old categories any longer, but she didn't know how to replace them. The air in the growing chambers was fresh and green, like a garden after rain. Sirru smiled at her as she came in.

'What's been happening today?'

'Many things.' Sirru sighed. 'None of them very interesting. I had reports to complete.'

'How boring, to be an interplanetary colonist,' Jaya teased. Sirru blinked.

'That depends on the planet. And you? How are you?'

'Me? I'm confused.'

'Why?'

'I don't know what I'm supposed to do here. The seed is changing, I don't know how I'm supposed to help her, or how— Oh, a hundred things confuse me, Sirru.'

Sirru glanced at her with sympathy.

'There is always a transitional period. At present, you are being very helpful. And when the network on Earth is fully operational, then you will have your own work to do. Relaying information between here and Rasasatra. Interpreting the instructions of the Core, along with the ship.'

'And if I refuse?' she said, with careful indifference. Sirru gave her a long, measured look. Then he said, 'We can find another Receiver. Your genetic structures are not unique; you were merely the first to come on-line. But I would rather have you here.'

'And I don't have anything to go back for, do I?' Jaya mused aloud. Sirru did not reply, but busied himself with the growing tank.

After a moment, he said, 'You may be interested to learn that I have filed a formal complaint against Ir Yth and the *khaithoi*. It is not done to question the practices of one's betters, but this is an exceptional case and Ir Yth, at least, must answer for her actions.'

'But Sirru, she's dead.'

He glanced up, surprised. 'No, no. Both of us were here in Second Body, after all. Ir Yth's Second Body only has been terminated, the form in which you knew her, and with its termination, Ir Yth's First Body has been permitted animation once more back on Rasasatra.'

Jaya digested this for a moment. 'So what about *your* First Body?'

'It's in a translation chamber, orbiting Rasasatra.'

'So if you go back – what will happen?'

'"I" will not be going back. This Second Body' – he gestured – 'will be stored as data in a manifold here, and my First Body will be reanimated. Whenever that is. Whenever the Core allows.' His tone was uncharacteristically acid and Jaya winced. It had not really sunk in before that Sirru might not have been all that thrilled to receive this posting. Earth was such a little world, in comparison to what she had now heard about other places. She couldn't help smiling at the thought of the alien invasions she'd seen in the cinema: beings of great and evil power, sent to dominate the world. *Instead we get a couple of minor civil servants, embroiled in petty office politics.*

And talking of politics, there was something she still had to do. After Anand's death, Jaya found that she possessed new knowledge, as though he had downloaded secrets into her head in the moment of his demise. She did not think that this knowledge had been disseminated beyond Sirru and herself; Anand's death had been too disruptive. But she should not wait too long before using this newly gained information. She headed down into the ship, to the place where rafts were grown.

2.
TOKYO

Naran Tokai sat behind his desk and let imagination take him where he wanted to go. The harvest yielded from Ir Yth's body had been a bountiful one, and Earth's new friends had proved generous in sharing their knowledge. So many new sicknesses; all benign. At least physically, Tokai thought, wondering what the social symptoms would be. In conjunction with the írRas, Tokai Pharmaceuticals had already been busy manufacturing the drugs that would enable humanity to utilize this new and alien technology to its maximum effect. Drugs to facilitate viral communication; to enhance learning; to shape and change the genetic frameworks of humankind within the limits prescribed by the *desqusai* írRas. It had been a little galling to discover that the *desqusai* were no more than one of the lower írRas castes, but Tokai was learning to live with the loss of face. He could, at any rate, be a big carp in a little pond.

The sunlight spilling through his window was momentarily darkened. An immense shadow passed across the wall. Frowning, Tokai crossed cautiously to the window and looked down. A rippling membrane covered the ornamental courtyard; he could see his koi fish flickering golden through its translucent surface. Before he had time to contact his security team and order an immediate investigation, the door to his office slid open and Jaya Nihalani stepped through.

Alarmed, Tokai nonetheless regarded her with curiosity. She looked nothing like the woman he had seen in countless security videos during her life as a revolutionary. She was dark and small and graceful, and her eyes were fierce. Fleetingly, Tokai wondered whether alien technology might be harnessed for lucrative cosmetic purposes also. Through the cane, he got an impression of spices, and an underlying musk.

'Good afternoon,' he said, sidling the cane towards the alarm system. 'Might I ask what you're doing here?'

'I think vengeance is in order,' Jaya said.

'I see. Well, I understand that's the goddess Durga's speciality. You've come to kill me, then? How regrettable.' He would retain his dignity, at any rate. Tokai had no wish for a dishonourable death.

'How predictable.' Jaya's lip curled. 'Durga's jackal I may be, but I have no intention of killing you.'

Tokai paused. The tip of the cane quivered into stillness.

'I intend to use you, Shri Tokai.'

'For what?' Tokai asked warily.

'My alien colleagues are anxious to harness your resources. Since colonization seems inevitable, they might as well do so. However, I intend to make sure that you are answering to me as much as possible.'

Tokai's eyebrows rose. 'I think I'm capable of persuading your alien colleagues to deal with me directly.'

'It isn't my alien colleagues you have to worry about. It's the bullet an Indian assassin is likely to put in your spine when the world learns that you're responsible for Selenge.'

Tokai became very still.

'Anand knew, Tokai. I don't know if he found out or if you told him, but he knew. And without meaning to, he told me, in the minute before he died. My friend Shiv Sakai has hacked into some very old lab records. We have quite a lot of evidence. I don't think the news would make you very popular. The UN might even see fit to have you up on the Geneva convention. I don't think the West approves of biological warfare on civilian populations – not when it's perpetrated by foreign businessmen, at any rate.'

'What do you intend to do about this?' Tokai asked.

'Actually, nothing – not to you, anyway. I think you're too useful. You see, I am learning to be subtle. Do what I tell you, and your secret will be kept. If anything happens to me, Sirru will inform the world.'

'Very well.' *Acquiesce now*, Tokai thought, *and solve the problem later.*

Jaya bowed, keeping a close eye on him, and backed out of the door. As she reached it, she said, 'One last thing. I find that I'm not entirely willing to relinquish my allegiance to Durga. As a test of your loyalty, and for all the people who have suffered from Selenge, I would like to see a web headline in the next few days. Announcing the terminal illness that has been so regrettably contracted by Minister Singh.'

And then she was gone.

3.
DEPTH SHIP, ORBIT: EARTH

Sirru sat expectantly by the translation pad, awaiting news. It had now been several days since he had issued his complaint against Ir Yth, and although he was well aware that the wheels of the Core ground exceedingly slowly, he had hoped for a slightly less leisurely response than this. Attempted genocide was a serious matter, after all, even if it was just *desqusai*. At length, the translator signified an incoming transmission. Sirru hastily ran his fingers across the pad, outlining his personal codes.

The face of a Core representative, flanked by official symbols, manifested in the air before him. The face had a long lantern jaw and slanted eyes beneath a crest of bone; it was not a caste that Sirru recognized. Presumably this was a member of a caste from deep within the Marginals.

'What is it?' the representative demanded.

'Recently I issued a complaint,' Sirru said, transferring the number of his report as he spoke. The representative's eyes shut tightly for a moment as it processed the information.

'I don't seem to have— Ah, yes. Here we are. I have it now.'

'Might I ask whether my report has been transferred to the Core, to the attention of someone who might usefully consider it?'

'Your charges against Ir Yth írRas EsTekhei/current

locative: Ir Yth EsShekhanjin SiSamakh/ are currently on the waiting list for consideration.'

Sirru was aware of a hollow sensation growing in the pit of his stomach.

'And how long is the waiting list?'

'There are currently nine thousand, three hundred and ten cases awaiting appraisal by the relevant personnel.'

'What!'

'This is standard practice.'

'But we are talking about a question of attempted genocide by one caste against another, not some minor infraction of regulations.'

'It is standard practice.' The being briefly shut its eyes, as though pained by having to explain basic protocols to this unruly, wild-eyed *desqusai*. Sirru wondered whether the concept of inter-caste genocide even made any sense to it, whether the being might be subject to epistemic suppressants of its own. The *khaithoi* must have influenced it, somehow; he was certain that this was not 'standard practice'.

'Feel this, I have temenos privileges, accrued over several generations,' Sirru said. 'Might it be possible to trade some of those in and get a quicker hearing?'

The representative consulted some inner protocol.

'Such privileges are granted by law to First Bodies only.'

'Why? Oh, never mind. I suppose I'll have to come back to Rasasatra and sort it out in First Body, then.'

With a distant and supercilious sense of satisfaction, the representative said, 'That will not be possible.'

'And why not?'

'Because you no longer possess a First Body.'

Sirru rocked back on his heels, astonished. 'Excuse *me*, but I suggest you check your records. You'll find it in translation archive 495, 671 (b).' He waited impatiently whilst the representative translated these figures into the appropriate chemical formula, mumbling inaudibly as it did so.

'The archive in question has been deleted.'

'What? How? When?' He was aware of the indignity of babbling.

'Unknown. Perhaps there has been some archive malfunction in the translation storage manifold. It has been known to happen. Deletion occurred a short time after your departure from Rasasatra.'

Ir Yth's khaithoi accomplices, thought Sirru, with fury. He persisted, 'So what you're telling me is that you have no record of my original corporeal form? We'll just have to re-translate this body, then.'

'I am afraid that will not be a simple matter. The *khaithoi* have invoked a penalty as a result of delays experienced by the project. They wish you to serve a contractual term covering the initial phase of colonization.'

'But that could take a year or more!'

'That is correct.'

'It is little short of a disaster. Will my complaint be

411

upheld if I'm now permanently instantiated in my Second Body?'

'Your complaint is now pending until your legal status is confirmed. And now, if you'll excuse me, I have another transmission waiting.'

Without waiting for a reply, the representative's long face began to fade.

'Wait!' Sirru cried, but it was too late. The transmission ended. Sirru sat down on the floor and wrapped his arms around his knees. The fact that he had been blithely wandering about through all sorts of dangers in one fragile body was forcibly brought home to him. What if something had happened to his Second Body? His *only* body? Presumably this was one of the possibilities that Ir Yth had had in mind. The thought also occurred to him, however, that this *khaithoi* manipulation might prove to be a blessing in disguise. Without the epistemic suppressants, he had changed. If he were merely re-instantiated in his First Body, with its suppressant levels intact, then he would presumably be unable to think the things that he was thinking now. If his current form were copied back on Rasasatra, he would be as conceptually free as he was at present.

A day after that, the call that they had all been waiting for came through: Earth's overseer was here. EsMirhei was tall, languid and wan, like a plant that had not had enough sun. He was from a rather higher *desqusai* caste level than

Sirru. His quills were bound in an elegant fall down his back, his skin was ornamented with inset gold wire. He greeted the assembled *desqusai* with a remote charm and turned his attention instantly to Sirru.

'The team appear to have made some sterling efforts prior to my arrival. Good work!' he said, with a warmth that sounded rather simulated to Sirru's sceptical ears.

'Thank you,' said Sirru. 'I think you'll find the ground-work is in place.'

'Excellent news. I shall make a personal inspection. A tour, don't you think? Get the lie of the land and see how our kindred comport themselves. I trust there's been no trouble?'

'Minimal public disorder. You know how these things are . . .' Sirru murmured soothingly, dismissing the month of riots and tumult produced by the announcement that Earth had new masters.

'Must have been terribly trying for you.' EsMirhei's quills gave a shuddering rattle. 'Still, necessary period of adjustment, I suppose. And this is our little Receiver?'

He bestowed a lipless beam upon Jaya.

'This is EsAyachantha IrNihalani IrBhara'th.'

EsMirhei blinked. 'What a wonderfully *exotic* locative.'

'But you can call me Jaya,' said Jaya, through gritted teeth. 'It might be easier.'

'"Jaya",' EsMirhei remarked, meditatively. 'Charming. And are you ready to assume your duties?'

'What duties?'

'Jaya has been fully briefed on the nature of her links

413

with the communications network, and will serve as the principal nexus between Tekhei and this ship,' Sirru said hastily.

'Splendid! Well, I'm sure you're all dying to get on with things, so let's not stand on ceremony, shall we? No need to be formal with me. I look forward to becoming one of the team,' EsMirhei informed them. Taking a clearly infuriated Jaya by the arm, he swept her out of the chamber in a flutter of robes and a pleasant, if discernible, waft of perfume.

Despite his languid and frivolous manner, EsMirhei proved to be a conscientious and energetic envoy, to Sirru's private dismay. He insisted on a thorough debriefing of all aspects of life in Tekhei, and gradually an extensive if idiosyncratic picture was built up from Ir Yth's preliminary studies, Jaya's recollections, and the network itself. EsMirhei spent a great deal of time linked with Jaya, holding her hands and humming to himself as information was channelled through the network and into his enthusiastic brain. He was clearly keen to throw himself into the development of the colony, and was insistent that Sirru should accompany him to the surface. He had prepared a tour of suitable places: Varanasi was first, in tribute to Jaya, and then Tokyo.

'The Americans want to see him, of course,' Jaya informed Sirru.

'But does EsMirhei want to see the Americans? Their government can be of little interest to him. Industries, perhaps. But I understand that most of those are located to the south, in – where is that place?'

'Mexico? The industries are only there because it's cheaper. I can see you have quite a bit to learn about where power lies on this planet. You must understand, Sirru, this sidelining of government is presenting all sorts of problems.'

Sirru said, 'In turn, you retain some curious delusions about the way in which your world is run. National governments have little or no relevance to the running of the global economy, or the political systems. It is the multinational corporations and the groups of individuals who run them who pull the strings. Like the – what are they called? Oh, yes – the Bilderburg group. And these are the people with whom we must deal. Naran Tokai, for instance. Governments understand this; it's only a few politicians whose egotism makes them blind to the true state of affairs. And anyway, by the time that restructuring is complete, those governments will be largely ineffectual. Tekhei will primarily be a communications centre, a relay station between Zhei Eren and the Khiamak systems. Don't worry. EsMirhei knows what he's doing.'

'I know,' Jaya said, in a thin voice. 'That's the problem.'

'Once we've sorted out minor issues, such as over-population and territorial disputes, we'll have a modern and efficient system.'

'Complete with those suppressants you told me about.'

'Some social control is necessary, even on a world as old and enlightened as ours.' He smiled as he said it, so that Jaya would not take offence, but she was frowning.

'Sirru, that's dreadful. That's nothing more than brainwashing.'

He sighed. The trouble was, he was starting to agree with her. 'I told you. None of us is entirely free. Even now, I can't think as I please. I am a product of certain processes, a child of my place and time. And your own branch of the *desqusai* are the products of your neuro-chemistry, too. You have your own fixed beliefs, without the help of artificial memes that burrow into your mind. Where do your people draw the boundaries? I do not regret what I am. How can I? But there are aspects of my society that I am starting to question. As to what will ultimately happen to your world – that depends on the Core.'

'Sirru, what lives in the Core?'

'Many castes. At the heart of it live the Makers, the ones who created us all.'

'Will I ever meet them?'

Sirru, rather shocked, said, 'No, of course not. It is not for us to see them.'

'They must be like gods.'

'They are what they are.'

'I've had enough of gods,' said Jaya, but Sirru peered into the growing tanks, and pretended not to have heard her.

She added, with a narrow-eyed gaze that he was start-

416

ing to find familiar, 'And these suppressants you're all given. We've got access to all Tokai's resources now, and a hold over him. What if we could find an antidote – before your project gets fully under way and we're all meme-washed?'

'I am beginning to discover what is meant by an infectious idea.'

'Once a revolutionary, always a revolutionary, Sirru. I'm not built to be part of the establishment. It's strange. You are one of the most powerful people I have ever met. You come to take over worlds. And yet you and I are in such similar positions.'

Sirru considered this. 'On my world, I suppose the Naturals are closest to your caste.'

'In that case,' Jaya said thoughtfully, 'perhaps I should be talking to the Naturals.'

Three days later, Sirru and EsMirhei reached Tokyo. Sirru was concerned that Naran Tokai might let something slip about their earlier interactions, but the industrialist was as slippery as a *khaithoi* manipulatrix, and said nothing. He did, however, appear tired; he had been obliged to visit India, he explained, for the funeral of an old friend.

EsMirhei expressed genuine delight at the progress Tokai Pharmaceuticals had made in developing the viral ranges for Tekhein use.

'And breeding suppressants? You've made progress with those?'

EsMirhei, it seemed, was most concerned that the Tekhein themselves should not suffer the burden of their history any longer than necessary. 'Once the population is down to manageable levels – shouldn't take more than a couple of generations – we can start restructuring the genetic bases, but for now our priority must be to make sure that our new colony is healthy, happy and fed.' Tokai merely bowed.

Later, EsMirhei confided, 'You know, EsMoyshekhal, your little Receiver didn't come on-line a moment too soon. I'll have to release extensive epistemological constructs into the population at large just to calm things down and pave the way for rational thought. Some of the *ideas* these people have! Where they got them from, I have no idea. The whole colony's been allowed to get way out of hand. I don't know what the administrator was thinking of.'

'I think Ir Yth had her own agenda.'

'*Khaithoi*,' sighed EsMirhei, with an ironic flutter of delicate fingers. 'One simply can't expect them to take the wider view. A few judicious adjustments, and I'm sure that half of the problems facing this planet today could have been solved generations ago. The hormonal imbalances, for example. Dreadful state of affairs. Worse than Naturals.'

'At least the Naturals have the advantage of some sort of status. Originally, at least.'

'Well, precisely. The juvenile males of Tekhei are particularly distressing . . . Still, we'll sort all that out, I feel sure. Your man Tokai seems to have matters well in hand. Now. Where should we eat, do you think?'

When Sirru got back to the depth ship, it was already late. Jaya was asleep. Sirru went wearily back to his own chamber, feeling weighted by worry. He was stuck here, helpless. Who knew what the *khaithoi* might be getting up to back home? He sank down on the mat and put his head on his knees. The communications mesh chimed.

Sirru looked up. The image of the seed was floating before him.

/*I have a message for you,*/ the seed informed him. /*This person is unwilling to contact you via another channel; she says she carries secrets.*/

Anarres's image was manifesting at the far end of the chamber. Sirru nearly ran to embrace her before he realized that she wasn't really there.

'Sirru!' she cried. 'Finally!'

'Anarres?' His beloved was wearing a most disreputable dress, he thought. And she appeared to be smudged with something. Dust? Soot? 'Where are you?'

'It's a long story, and I don't have much time. I'm at your family's temenos. Sirru, are you all right?'

'Yes, but I very nearly wasn't. What a mess. They've lost my First Body, and I have to get back to Rasasatra. I have to press charges against the *khaithoi*, and they've taken out some kind of injunction to delay me getting home. I—'

'Don't worry about the *khaithoi*,' Anarres said, grimly. 'You won't be the only one pressing charges. And if the Core courts call you as a witness, you'll have to come home, regardless of whether the *khaithoi* try to stop you.'

'What do you mean, I'm not the only one pressing charges?'

Anarres gestured towards the shadows behind her shoulder, and someone bent down to peer through the gleam of the communication mesh.

'Hello, Sirru,' said IrEthiverris, with a smile.

4.
KHAIKURRIYË, RASASATRAN SYSTEM

EsRavesh's stumpy hand travelled up and down Ir Yth's spine, pinching and probing. Ir Yth stood bristling with offended modesty, but could do nothing. EsRavesh was her superior, and moreover, she was in no position to protest about anything. She was fortunate, EsRavesh hissed into her mind, that her First Body had been permitted re-activation, and had not simply been flushed from the manifold.

/Might I remind you,/ Ir Yth quavered, /that it was not I who failed at Tekhei, but my Second Body?/

/And might I remind you,/ EsRavesh said, /that you are still legally accountable given that you were undertaking regular uploads of information, including your sabotage of a depth ship? If anyone finds out . . ./

/But my Second Body was apparently slain!/ Ir Yth
shuddered.

/Your Second Body failed,/ EsRavesh said. /That's all
either of us need to know!/

/Where is Sirru EsMoyshekhal now?/ Ir Yth asked,
hoping to distract him.

/On a depth ship, orbiting Tekhei, along with a growing
seed that will soon head out to found another world of its
own. The Tekhein project is proceeding as planned. People
are saying that the desqusai must have something to them
after all, if one of their administrators can survive the loss
of a depth ship and the threat of death from hostile natives,
and still manage to deliver a project to deadline. And the
ex-administrator of Arakrahali – whom I thought I'd managed to delete – is filing a suit against us for attempted
genocide. It seems he has evidence. The situation is entirely
lost, due to your own ineptitude. Now,/ EsRavesh ordered,
/come here. I have recently lost a valuable apsara. And I
have needs that are not being met./

5.
DEPTH SHIP, ORBIT: EARTH

When Sirru went in search of Jaya next morning, he found
her in communion with the ship. She floated in the
cradling embrace of one of the nutrient tanks, her pale hair
drifting about her like waterweed. She looked very small.
Her face was still and remote, and her hands were crossed

421

over her breasts as though defending herself against the world. But as Sirru watched, her grip gradually relaxed until her hands were floating free. He sighed, thinking of what else the *khaithoi* might do to bring destruction to his people before his complaint got a hearing in the Core. He pictured Ir Yth's First Body bustling about on Rasasatra, plotting and scheming. Bureaucracy might succeed where Amir Anand had failed; paperwork and office politics might yet prove the death of them all. It was a pity, really, that world-changing was such a tedious process.

Jaya looked so serene, but Sirru doubted that her dreams were peaceful. *Once a revolutionary, always a revolutionary, Sirru.* Would it really be possible to manufacture a suppressant antidote? Together, could they change the fabric of his society, as they had altered hers: rising up against that vast and ancient empire of bones and genes and blood and flesh? Reaching out, he grasped the cold anchor of Jaya's hand, feeling the thin band of metal which ringed her finger, and watching the red stone glitter in the watery light. He hoped it would not be too long a wait.

END